FADED SKIES SERIES

HEIR

ASCENDANT

MATTHEW S. COX

CURIOSITY QUILLS PRESS

A Division of **Whampa, LLC**

P.O. Box 2160

Reston, VA 20195

Tel/Fax: 800-998-2509

http://curiosityquills.com

© 2017 **Matthew S. Cox**

www.matthewcoxbooks.com

Cover Art by Eugene Teplitsky

http://eugeneteplitsky.deviantart.com

ISBN 978-1-948099-14-1 (ebook)

ISBN 978-1-948099-15-8 (paperback)

If we go on the way we have, the fault is our greed and if we are not willing to change, we will disappear from the face of the globe, to be replaced by the insect. - Jacques Yves Cousteau

PART I
INNOCENT DECEPTION

ONE
DREAM LIFE

iscarded wrappers littered the slate-grey countertop, rustling as small hands added one more to the pile. Maya couldn't remember the last time a housekeeper prepared her meal—not that it took a lot of skill to unpack a thin, octagonal plastic tray and toss it in the Hydra. A minute later, four unidentifiable blobs in separate compartments had absorbed enough moisture to expand into a substance similar to the stringy meat-in-gravy she recalled giving her dog, plus a portion of green beans and mashed potatoes.

The only difference was how it smelled—the dog food was better.

A brown horror rested at the center of the tray in its own little chamber. It was supposed to be a dessert, but if she saved it for last, it would be rock hard. If she ate it first, it would scald the inside of her mouth. Maya stood up on tiptoe to reach into the Hydra, sucking air through her teeth as she tugged at the hot plastic tray, then scurried to the table and dropped it fast, rubbing her hands on her oversized beige sweater to cool them. With a sigh, she fell into the chair, staring at the comm terminal while picking at her dinner and letting one dangling foot sway. Endless weeks and months of the same three choices for dinner left her uninterested in tasting it.

Whatever meat sat under the heavy, brown gravy, its scent reminded her of having a dog. Tiny and white, he had regarded the pedestrian offering of rehydrated food as though it came from on high. Like Maya, he'd gotten the same unidentifiable substance every night, but the little guy had been excited as if each time was the first he'd had such a treat. A frown formed around the fist mushing her cheek to one side. She couldn't recall the dog's name or what had happened to him, catching only brief glimpses of having had a pet at some point in the past.

She left the empty tray on the table and plodded down the long corridor across the penthouse apartment and the four wooden stairs descending to the living room, a vast expanse of dimly lit sparsity. At a pair of sliding glass panels, she sat cross-legged on the tan carpet and gazed out over a glittering city of steel, glass, and neon light. Gusting wind pushed the scent of rain in around the closed doors.

Whirring, a little louder than the machine that cleaned and dried her hair, grew in strength to the right. Maya leapt to her feet, standing stiff at attention as a hovering drone skimmed along outside. Gleaming white shrouds, twelve inches around and emblazoned with the word *Ascendant* in silver, covered a ducted fan at each tip of the triangular machine. A large gun on its undercarriage swiveled at her, seconds before a grid of green laser light covered her body. After a momentary pause, a happy chirp accompanied its weapon returning to a neutral orientation, and the drone tilted forward, flying off. She lowered herself to sit once more, glaring at the slogan 'Building a better you!' below the name of her mother's company until the machine drifted out of sight to the left.

She couldn't hear the people far below in the street, but they seemed sad like her. Everyone kept their heads down and shuffled along, a river of grey-clad bodies indistinguishable from each other save for subtle variations in height. Most wore the same drab poncho and filter mask; everyone feared breathing in Fade. No one made eye contact with anyone. Several larger drones hovered over the crowd, patches of radiant light adding color to the blank world. Their frames as big as motorcycles, the four-fanned Authority bots on the hunt for criminals and non-conformers were double the size of the corporation-owned ones circling her building.

No one ever smiled; at least, not unless they happened to be selling something.

Overcast sky darkened, fast enough for her to perceive the change to night. Today had been a remarkable day; Mother had shown up at the penthouse apartment to check on her. Elation at gaining her attention, even for one solitary hour, had long ago turned to resentment. Mother hadn't been as much concerned with *her* as she'd been with getting some good photos for use in the latest ad campaign.

Being the daughter of the CEO of Ascendant Pharmaceutical Corporation sucked.

An hour past dark, she gave up on waiting for the telltale glow of Mother's helicopter coming in for a roof landing and trudged to her bedroom. Maya changed into a shin-length nightdress and started to crawl into bed, but stopped with one knee up on the mattress. She got down, went to the door and, as if sneaking up on a sleeping monster, crept to the comm terminal in the hallway. At the center of an eight-by-ten panel of dark metal, a round steel eye as big as her fist greeted her with a slow-blinking red light.

"Maya," she said.

"Voiceprint recognized. Good evening, Maya Oman. It is past your bedtime."

She sighed. "I know. Outbound call please, Vanessa Oman."

The terminal remained silent for thirty seconds before the regal face of a woman in her middle thirties appeared, a midair hologram. Long, black hair cascaded around high cheekbones and perfect ebony skin. Every time Maya saw her, she felt self-conscious at her lighter tone. She wanted to be dark like Mother, not the medium brown she'd been stuck with. Always, Maya wondered if her appearance had something to do with her mother's distance.

The cadence of a recording in a stern woman's voice filled the corridor. "This is the private vid-mail inbox for Vanessa Oman, CEO of Ascendant Pharmaceuticals. If you have the necessary clearance to contact this number, leave a message. Otherwise, please disconnect this call and await the arrival of Authority Officers."

"Begin message," said a digital tone.

"Mother. It's Maya. You didn't come home... again. I guess you've gone to one of the other apartments. Good night." Maya turned her back on the console. "Terminal, end call."

The walls flickered and went dark as the holo-projector cut out. Maya spent a moment admiring moonlight glinting off the silver glitter in her raspberry toenail polish before emitting a soft sigh and heading to bed.

TWO
BODY COUNT

Pressure on her face dragged Maya out of sleep. Two bright green spots hovered over her; an enormous metal hand covered her mouth and pinched her cheeks. The scent of a sweating man mixed with industrial chemicals flooded her nostrils. She let off a pitiful, muffled scream and kicked through her blankets at a chest rigid enough to hurt her toes.

A gun slid out of the darkness; its icy barrel against her forehead pushed her skull into the pillow as the green eye spots shrank with a faint electronic whirr.

"Be still. One sound, you die." His breath smelled like rotting meat.

Maya attempted to nod, but couldn't move her head.

"Blink twice if you understand."

She did. The man removed his giant hand from her face. He leaned up and away, keeping his weapon aimed at her. Room lights came on; his eyes shifted color, becoming yellow. His great dark-blue arms, bigger around than her chest, appeared metal, as if hundreds of small interlocking ingots had flown together in a devouring plaque that advanced well over his shoulders and shrouded the sides of his head. The interface between steel and skin resembled the teeth of a gear. More guns peeked from the folds of a long military-style coat. At her stare, mechanical lens-eyes jutting an inch out from his head clicked and narrowed further. His broad face and wide nose were similar in hue to her skin: creamed coffee. Not a trace of humanity remained in his glare.

Maya had no doubt this man could kill her.

A woman, younger than Mother but not by much, slipped past him. His bulk made her seem like a child. Black fatigue pants swooshed as she cleared the end of the bed in two strides. Thick dreadlocks hung down to her belt, studded with trinkets, beads, and wooden rings. She wore a nylon harness with a pair of handguns, several cases, and two silver grenades over an olive-drab tank top. A long-sleeved camouflage shirt draped loose and unbuttoned over everything, sleeves rolled up to the forearm. The woman scowled at Maya with contempt, a look dire enough to make her raise an arm to protect her face.

"Don't give me that shit," grumbled the woman. She bent forward to yank the blankets away from Maya. "You're a Citizen; I ain't gonna feel no sorry for you."

"How we lookin'?" the huge man asked no one. Seconds later, he grinned. "Sounds good."

The woman's loose outer shirt sagged open as she leaned forward, grabbed a handful of Maya's hair, and held her still for a brief but disdainful stare. "Roll over, hands behind you."

Maya did as instructed, and didn't move despite the creak of unwinding tape. She winced but kept quiet while the woman crushed her wrists together and cinched them with the sticky plasticized ribbon. A painful grip about the ribs swung her perpendicular to the bed. Maya whimpered as the angry woman gathered her legs together and wound more tape about her ankles.

A harsh slap to the back of the head silenced her.

"Quiet. Damn Citizen brat. You and your kind don't know the first thing about suffering up in this palace. Don't you dare give me that. The more pathetic you act, the more I ain't gonna regret this."

She lay like a loaf, offering no protest. Once the woman bit off the tape and squeezed it in place, she pulled Maya over onto her back by a fistful of fabric. She tilted her head, peering up past heaving breasts at the sweat-covered face hovering over her with an expression that asked the woman why she was being so mean. The silent plea seemed only to enrage her abductor more.

"Step it up, Genna. We're made," said the big man.

Genna's oversized camouflage shirt shrouded the girl like a tent when she leaned her hands on the bed, on either side of Maya's head, trying to peer out the bedroom door. Dog tags slipped out of the woman's tank top and hit her in the face. She flinched, glaring at the dark brown arm inches from her face. The point of a black crescent moon tattoo peeked around her right shoulder. Maya cringed away from a drop of sweat landing near her eye. Genna slid backwards to her feet and shrugged a large, empty bag off her shoulder.

"Are you kidnapping me?" Maya whispered.

"*Maldita niña*," muttered the huge man. He poked the top of her head with his pistol. "Shut up!"

"If you're taking me for ransom, you're wasting your—"

Genna pressed a line of tape over Maya's mouth.

Widening yellow machine-eyes gave away a strong desire to inflict pain. "Dammit, kid, you don't listen."

The woman added a second length of tape, making an X over Maya's mouth. "Calm down, Moth. You kill her now, and we just wasted a bunch of time and effort for nothing. Took Head weeks to find this princess."

"*Loco hombre de rata*," Moth grumbled.

A skinny Asian man in black pants, jacket, and gloves raced into the bedroom and stumbled to his knees when he tried to stop. He had a gun out, but it seemed like a little toy compared to the one pointed at her face. "Shit! Authority's here."

The metal-armed man whirled about, aiming at him, eyes wild with panic.

"Shit, Moth," the man gasped, holding his hands up. "I'm not a damn Korean. Come back to now."

"That was fast," said Genna, as calm as if the sons of Jeva had come bearing religious literature. "Guess Headcrash is slipping."

Moth scowled at the window. "He must've missed a sensor."

"Yeah, yeah... you got the drones," Genna muttered to no one. "But they found us somehow."

"So? No big deal." Moth smiled and aimed at the door. "All that means is this op just got a body count."

THREE
EXODUS

aya's calm faltered to impotent squirming. She'd seen enough entertainment vids to believe a civilian belonged on the floor in a gunfight. An Authority Officer, head to toe in blue armor and black, full-face helmet, rushed in. Moth lurched forward in a single stomp, driving his fist into the man's chest. Splinters of hardened resin flaked around steel knuckles on impact with a sharp, crackling *crunch*. The armored figure vanished out the door in the blink of an eye. His flight ended with a heavy crash in the corridor outside. Moth leveled his pistol off and fired twice, rattling the windows.

He laughed.

Genna grabbed the tape around Maya's ankles and yanked her off the bed like a slab of meat. She hit the floor on her back and lay still, staring at the ceiling while Genna used the bed for cover, aiming a smaller handgun at the doorway. Moth rushed into the hall with frightening speed for a man of his size.

"By order of the Authority, you are to surr—"

Boom.

A splattering crunch followed the rapport of Moth's gun. "Minimal contact. Only a few blueberries. Pack it up, we're moving."

An Ascendant drone whizzed past the window; the flickering orange light of muzzle flare filled the room as it fired on people outside.

The Asian man jumped over the bed and landed on his knees at Maya's side. He glanced at her with a hollow smile. "That's a cute kid. Nice choice. Didn't you have a boy, though?"

Genna punched him in the side of the head, knocking him through a disintegrating nightstand. Maya kept herself as calm as she could manage given the continuous thunder of a gunfight in her home.

"Don't you dare bring him up! He's got nothing to do with this," shouted Genna.

"Ouch." The Asian man rubbed his jaw. "It's got everything to do with Sam, doesn't it? That's why you want the Xenodril. You got some kinda righteous avenger thing going on."

"Fuck you, Icarus. You're high, as usual. Remember what happens to wax wings." Genna dug her fingers into Maya's arm and stuffed her headfirst into the bag like an object. "Make one noise, kid, and you're never going to see your mother again. You don't gotta be alive to get ransom; they just gotta think it."

Maya went limp as the woman forced her into a fetal position and zipped the duffel closed. Her world became dark, save for a little speck of light from a pinhole in the bag on the peach-hued silk over her knees.

"Hey, that's kind of messed up," said Icarus.

Nylon tightened into a cocoon as the bag rose into the air.

"What is?" asked Genna.

"I was gonna say we should grab her favorite doll, you know, to maybe keep her calm or some shit. But look... there ain't a single damn one in the room."

"Maybe she doesn't like dolls," said Genna, her tone flat. "I didn't."

"Anything I say to that will get me punched again."

Genna laughed. "You're a wise man, for a doser."

"Yeah but..." Icarus paused. "Still kinda messed. Ain't even one *toy*."

The bag swayed side to side, matching the motion of the woman's brisk walk, continually bumping Maya against her back. She squirmed in a series of tiny movements, testing the painful tightness binding her hands and feet. Coupled with the confining enclosure, she didn't have any room to move. She doubted she possessed the strength to break free and would need to cut the tape. With nothing to do at the moment but wait, she gave up struggling.

Maya's head struck a hard surface, presumably her bedroom's doorjamb or the one at the end of the corridor outside it. The next several gunshots she assumed came from Genna, closer and quieter than Moth's hand cannon. Sliding glass doors hissed, and the patter of rain on the bag told her they ran across the deck where Mother's helicopter sometimes landed. The alien whine of a drone circled far to the left.

"No, please!" a distant woman screamed.

Maya tried to yell through the tape as the weight of a body hit Genna from the left, crushing her into the woman.

"Gen, the pilot's unarmed!" yelled Icarus. "We don't need to kill her."

"Outta my way! They're all guilty." Genna growled and grunted, struggling to get away from him.

Maya twitched at the heavy *thud* of a body striking the deck nearby. A distant female scream accompanied the scuff of boots and gunshots. The bag jostled with a run for a few strides, then someone grabbed the other side and jerked them to a halt, Maya bouncing up and down. She stilled with a shift in weight. Genna seemed to be dangling from the bag rather than carrying it.

"We ain't got time for that bitch," said Moth. "Killing one Authority tool ain't gonna bring Sam back."

A meaty thump came from somewhere close.

"Cute." Moth chuckled. "Was that supposed to hurt?"

"Fuck you, Moth. Fuck you." Genna thrust her body forward, yelling, "You're lucky, bitch!" Two gunshots went off. "You keep running. Fuckin' murderin' cowards!"

A short period of silence followed, punctuated by the clatter of boots on the deck. The bag swung around and fell hard on a metal plate. Maya made no sound.

"Can you fly this thing?" Icarus asked.

"Yes," said Genna and Moth in unison.

"Only to the ground," Moth muttered. "Fuckers'll track it. Still faster than the elevator."

"Swarming with Authority." A new voice, tinged with static, came from overhead.

"Head's right." Genna's voice moved away. "No. I'll take us to the edge of the Sanc."

Someone climbed past the bag, and the *whump* of an ass hitting a seat above and behind followed. Whining turbines gathered strength, drowning out the noise of two doors sliding closed as the beating of rotors emerged. Gravity increased for several seconds before it fell off. Turns caused the unattended duffel to slide back and forth within what Maya assumed to be a small Authority helicopter. Her body suffered the mercy of whatever metal she bumped into. Every wriggle seemed to make the tape tighten, and the cocoon-like bag squished her legs into her chest.

The uncomfortable flight ended in a few minutes. Before Maya even realized they'd landed, Genna's muttered cursing drew close and the nylon prison sailed into the air with a harsh yank. Maya braced for impact, but hit only the woman's back. She kept quiet and waited, bag swaying as they ran for several minutes. A handful of hard turns and sudden stops caused short periods of floating followed by crashing into the woman carrying her. Muttering surrounded her, indistinct save for Moth's deep timbre talking to someone over a comm about which tunnel to choose.

With only sound to go by, she had no idea where she'd been taken; it felt like she'd spent hours trapped inside a bag. Sudden weightlessness lasted barely a second before her body slapped into a hard surface; she couldn't suppress a whimper.

"Hey, you just dropped a child, not a sack of gear," said Icarus. "Didn't you used to be a mother?"

The toe of a boot pressed lightly against Maya's back, stepping close to the bag. The Asian man gurgled and gasped for breath.

Genna's voice came from right above her, in a low, threatening tone. "Look, you drugged-out piece of shit. She's not a child. She's a Citizen—privileged, pampered, rich, comfortable, ain't got no damn clue what the *real* world is like."

Icarus wheezed and coughed. "Is that her fault? What would Sam say if he saw you hittin' on a little girl?"

A body thudded into the ground close by; labored breathing rasped inches from Maya's face.

"Bitch," whispered a male voice.

The tape over her mouth prevented her from smiling

A scrape of heavy metal slid on paving in the distance. The bag went airborne again, soon squeezed against Genna by the narrow vertical shaft they descended. Echoes of boots on steel rungs, a thick, moldy smell, and total darkness, suggested a sewer. Maya hated feeling helpless. She couldn't escape—yet—so she listened. Mother had always prided herself on her ability to find the advantage in any situation. Maya wondered how much of the trait she'd inherited.

Echoes of dripping water, squeaking rats, and boots sloshing in muck continued for quite a while with little conversation or hesitance. These people seemed to know where they were going now, without the constant need for guidance from the man on the other end of the radio.

Genna's rhythmic gait stumbled with a blurted, "Fuck!"

The bag slipped off her shoulder and swung; Maya's shins absorbed the brunt of impact with a hard post that rang out with a bell-like *bong*. The tape kept her scream inside.

"Keep a hand on my shoulder," said Icarus. "You're in my element now, sweet cheeks."

"You call me that one more time, and I'll make a necktie out of your guts."

"You wanna hit of Vesper? Open your eyes to the dark, too."

Genna lurched as though she shoved him. "Keep that shit to yourself. I'd sooner get implants." She grumbled. "Why'd I get stuck carrying the brat?"

The clap of a hand on leather echoed into the distance.

Icarus chuckled. "Must be your nurturing motherly instinct."

Swoosh.

"Missed me," he said. "Remember, I can see down here."

Click.

"Gah!" he screamed. "Bitch. Great, now I'm fucking blind!"

"And I have a flashlight," said Genna, a hint of smile in her voice.

Icarus's muttered curses grew distant with an irregular sloshing gait. Maya pictured him staggering along, unable to see, with a hand on the wall. Light glinted in from pinholes in the nylon; too small to offer any view of the outside, they reminded her of stars.

"That sack is hangin' like dead weight," said Moth in a deadpan voice. "Make sure you didn't kill her yet."

Maya decided she did not like Moth in particular.

The bag dropped again, but this time settled gently on the ground. The zipper opened a few inches. Maya squinted at Genna's blinding flashlight until the stink of mildew and rot caused an involuntary convulsion.

"You still alive?"

Maya nodded.

Zip.

Darkness.

FOUR
SEEDS OF DISCORD

Maya listened to the scuff of boots on dirt and paving for many long minutes, fidgeting at her bindings despite knowing it futile. Constant swinging motion during the journey might've rocked her to sleep had she been comfortable, but not in the middle of a kidnapping. Eventually, they jogged up a long set of switchback stairs, around and around. Soon after exiting the stairwell, the echoing scrape of a door conjured the image of a cavernous space filled with the stench of garbage, urine, and decaying meat. A few steps in, the bag landed on the floor—not quite dropped.

She lay still, curled on her side, as people moved and shuffled about for about ten minutes. Eventually, someone approached and the zipper opened. Genna knelt close with an unreadable expression. Maya squirmed enough to peer up at her, and they stared at each other for a few seconds. With a smirk, Genna pulled the bag out from under her, dumping her face down onto a large, red, moth-eaten throw rug rife with the stink of old socks. Whatever pattern the maker had woven into it had long since faded to irregular blotches accented by rat turds, one of which lay inches from her eye. Maya wriggled around and sat up, bracing her hands on the coarse fabric behind her back.

Most of the wall to her left was gone. The enormous gap revealed miles of blackened, scrapped city stretching toward a distant glittering jewel of civilization. Flames lit the dark here and there, small cook fires or things still burning from endless civil unrest. Old high-rises, bent and broken, leaned at dangerous angles. Small figures scampered among the exposed steel girders of the closest building on the left, playing in the snowy static glow of a faltering electronic billboard. The children all wore rags and dirt; few had shoes. Their small bodies climbed with practiced ease across the steel jungle, laughing and calling to each other.

A warm summer wind kept the stink of wet mold at bay and tossed Maya's long, straight hair out of her face. Unsure how to process the sight, Maya lay there on the rug, bound and gagged with tape, watching other children play. She fidgeted with a halfhearted attempt to break free while wondering how children on the verge of starvation could be happy. A distant woman's voice called, and the feral children effortlessly glided around the exposed steel beams, scrambling one after the next into a shadowed doorway.

To the right of the breach, a glass desk nestled between the wall and a pile of junk, topped with several computers and holo-displays. Rats crept about, sniffing at wires and exploring crumb-laden plates made of old lids. Most of the systems were naked; bare wires and circuit boards lay exposed to the air, components patched and spliced into each other in ways their manufacturers had never intended.

A man in a battered rolling chair swiveled around and stared at her; wild, curly hair twitched in the breeze, his paunch barely reined in by a grimy tank top. Vitiligo splotches of beige and pink mottled his dark brown face and hands. Blue-grey eyes widened at the sight of her. He seemed terrified of a bound nine-year-old. The chair creaked, threatening to crack as he leaned away. One of the intangible holographic panels behind him looked like a nose-cam view out of an Ascendant drone flying around her penthouse home.

She thought him an enormous rat, building a nest of trash to hide in.

"Put her in the back!" he wailed, pointing at her. "She's watching me."

One of the rats stood on its hind legs and put a paw on the blotchy man's arm. He picked it up like a beloved pet and stroked its fur.

Click.

Maya looked toward the noise behind her. The black-painted blade of a combat knife scraped out of a metal sheath on Genna's harness. A small gust rattled the wood and metal bits in her dreadlocks. The woman knelt beside her, staring down at her with a worrisome neutral expression. Maya gazed again into Genna's eyes. Hatred had receded, though she sensed little compassion. The woman bent forward and put the knife to the tape between her ankles.

"No!" screamed the pudgy man, still petting the rat. "She'll kill us in our sleep. I told you not to bring her here. We needed a safe house. We could've set up a shipping container out in the Spread. Stashed her in that. Keep the heat away from us."

"Stow it, Crash." Icarus flung himself into an old reclining chair on the near side of the rat nest. "You're a paranoid bastard. She's just a kid."

Genna ignored the hacker's continuing protests and cut the tape. Maya didn't flinch as the sticky substance peeled away from her legs. She remained docile as Genna pulled her around to repeat the process and free her hands. A practiced flip of the wrist inverted the blade, and Genna slid it back in the scabbard without looking before taking her by the hand, pulling her upright, and leading her a few steps to a metal-framed bed against the interior wall, opposite the rat-nest computer desk.

Maya sat on the side, hands in her lap, wearing a sad face as though she'd been grounded. Genna held up a pair of electronic handcuffs, took one look at Maya's tiny wrists, and pointed at the footboard. Without a word, Maya slid back and turned to put her legs closer to the frame. Genna locked one end around her left ankle and the other to the bed. The girl stared at the cold metal. A five-digit code display above a row of tiny rubber buttons smeared a red glow across her skin.

More comfortable than the tape, but equally inescapable.

She looked up at Genna and mumbled through the X.

"Yeah, sure, kid. Pull it off if you want. It'll hurt." Genna wandered off to the left and went past a disaster of a once-green sofa, heading into a hallway leading deeper into the apartment. "I need a damn shower. Scream and cry all you want. No one out here is gonna give a shit."

"Put her in the bathroom," Headcrash said. "Or the closet. Or somewhere she can't see us. If she can see our eyes, she's gonna infect our minds." Spittle foamed around his teeth as he rasped, "You've already killed us by cutting her loose."

The woman gave him a sour look and vanished behind a door, slamming it a second later.

Maya pulled her nightdress down over her knees and set to the task of peeling the tape away from her cheeks. Moth distracted the splotchy man from his ramblings about a child slitting their throats in the night by yelling at him in regards to the Authority showing up.

After wadding the removed gag into a ball, she tossed it to the floor and curled on her side. The mattress stank like wet dog, likely due to the missing wall and steady breeze of humid air. At least it was summer so she wouldn't freeze in her nightie. She passed a few minutes flicking rat droppings off the bed while listening to the hiss of water from pipes in the walls. How long would it take Mother to realize she'd been taken and send help? Five more minutes? Ten?

"You sure you got the right kid? *Cierto?*" Moth's best attempt at whispering sounded like normal speech.

"Y-yes." Headcrash gestured at his terminals. "I checked it eighteen times. Every site, every decoy."

"*La niña* don't look much like Oman," Moth said. "Skin's too light, almond-shaped eyes, slight build."

"The bitch is pretty damn skinny too," said Icarus.

"Skin's too light?" Headcrash reached out to pet a rat.

Moth snarled. "No, *chiflado*, her mama's dark like Genna."

Icarus laughed. "She's the same color you are, Ramirez. Maybe you her daddy."

The doser's grin died under Moth's glare. He broke eye contact with the giant and focused on repacking his infiltration gear.

The hissing of water pipes in the walls ended with a distant squeak. Headcrash muttered about checking numerous residences and security schedules, confident the one with fourteen guards was a fake.

Genna walked in, trailing the scent of a recent shower.

"I don't have a father." Maya's tiny voice silenced the room. "Mother ordered a custom genetic profile. A little American with select features from Southeast Asian, Sudanese, and Egyptian was combined with her egg. Mother wanted the perfect pretty face for commercials to sell medicine." She picked at the mattress for a moment before looking Genna in the eye. "It's the only time I see her... when we are recording an ad. She doesn't even call to say good night."

For several seconds, only the distant moan of the wind through the shattered buildings broke the quiet.

"Oh, my heart fucking bleeds," Moth muttered.

Genna ignored Maya's glance, looking away and a bit downcast. The woman emitted a soft grumble a few seconds later and trudged over to the ancient couch on the left side of the room, in what had been the corner before the outside wall fell off. Moth walked out, heading down the hallway past the bathroom to the kitchenette. He took a seat at the table, barely visible around a corner of exposed cinder blocks. Sporadic clumps of drywall clung to nails wherever rotting studs remained. His shadow illustrated the procedure for disassembling and cleaning a handgun. Soon, a new chemical stink slithered over the mildewed air.

Headcrash stared at Maya for several minutes before he attempted to turn his back on her. After a series of half spins and sudden reversals, he managed to focus on his terminals again. Maya grasped the top of the foot rail with both hands and pulled herself closer, listening while fidgeting with the thin silk spaghetti strap over her right shoulder. She frowned at a small gold-colored tag. What Vanessa had paid for her nightie could feed these people for a month.

"Persephone," Headcrash whispered, gathering a rat from the computer and letting it go on the desk. "Resend last message."

Muted beeps simulated the clicking of keystrokes as 'Enter Password' appeared on the screen.

Headcrash looked at his compatriots, as if weighing their ability to overhear his whispering. Maya leaned closer, tilting her head to listen to the man a few feet away.

"Quantum Reach." The words leaked from his throat, air without voice.

Maya smiled and scooted back.

"Message transmit success," chimed the computer.

She lay flat and reached over her head, but the chain kept the pillow away from her. Once more, Maya curled on her side and closed her eyes. It wouldn't be long before the Authority showed up to rescue her.

"Something's not right." From the sound of his voice, Headcrash had moved away from his desk, trying to be quiet. "Look at her. She's going to sleep, calm as a cat. Children don't fucking do that when you kidnap them in the middle of the night!"

"She's a Citizen," Genna muttered. "Citizen's don't live in the real world. They have no goddamned clue about pain or suffering. They don't know shit doesn't always have a happy ending. In her little mind, she's convinced Mommy will make good on the ransom and she'll be home in a few hours."

Headcrash sucked air past his teeth. "Then why did Ascendant Pharma ignore our first message?"

Maya rolled over to face them, watching them with narrowed eyes. She tugged at her leg, more annoyed by the unwanted anklet than trying to get it off.

"She has no concept of what's happening to her or how much danger she's really in," Genna whispered. "It's... almost kinder."

The hacker made an odd warbling noise.

"Is that pity I hear?" Icarus asked.

Genna gave him a close-up look at her middle finger.

Headcrash ambled across the room and curled up under his desk, behind the shifting pile of junk, clutching a rat like a stuffed animal. Genna tried to relax on the couch, but couldn't stay in the same position for more than a minute. Maya gazed into the fabric pattern of the mattress before her eyes, almost comfortable in the sporadic bursts of warm air from the large swath of missing wall. After several long minutes, the dull clicking of interlocking metal plates sliding over each other invaded the silence. Moth trudged across the room, headed for another hallway on the right.

"Do your arms hurt?" Maya sat up, looking at the giant without fear.

He stopped in mid-stride, bringing a disbelieving glare around on her as though he wanted to hurt her for daring to speak to him.

"I'm sorry if they hurt."

Moth exhaled through a clenched jaw. "You tryin' to grate yourself to me so I won't kill you when we're done?"

"Ingratiate," Headcrash said, pointing a rat at him. "The word is ingratiate."

Moth grabbed his crotch at the hacker. "*Aquí tengo su clase de inglés.*"

"It won't work, will it?" Maya tilted her head.

The coldness in his voice left her no doubt. "No."

"Then it won't matter if you tell me. How did you lose your arms?" She scooted closer. "If you're going to kill me anyway, then you can be nice to me for a little while first."

Moth flexed his right arm; metal ingots scraped as his fist clenched. "Songnim City. Some dink bastard with a MPRS-18 got inside our perimeter in the middle of the night." He glared at Icarus.

"Son of a bitch!" roared the skinny guy. "I'm not a goddamn Korean, you fuckin' cretin. Go eat some burritos or something."

"Go eat some burritos?" Headcrash's barely-awake voice wafted up from the floor. "That's the best you can come up with?"

"Screw you, too." Icarus leaned back as if to go to sleep.

"You fought in World War Three?" Maya twisted her leg, appraising the cuff like an expensive bit of jewelry. "Maya Oman wasn't even born then. You must have seen bad things. So much fighting and killing. I'm sorry if you lost friends. Did you have to watch people die a lot? You must've killed a lot of enemies."

Moth's electronic eyes widened with a whirr; yellow light glowed in the faint sheen of sweat upon grimy cheeks.

"Do you always talk about yourself in third person, kid?" Headcrash asked.

Maya gave him a blank stare before tilting her head back to peer up at Moth. His right hand twitched, sporadic rattling gestures that made him look ready to go for a gun any second. Yellow pupils had narrowed, staring at something existent only in his mind. "Your name is ironic, isn't it?"

He shook off the mental cloud and snarled at her. A drop of sweat fell from his nose.

"I mean, moths are small and you are not. So, it's ironic." Maya glanced down at the mattress, idly brushing her fingers over the top of her right foot.

"It's short for Behemoth," said Icarus. "Grunts can't handle words more than one syllable."

Blood vessels swelled out of Moth's face; he glared. "If you die, the money's only gotta go three ways."

"Knock it off," Genna said. "No one is killing anyone. Not until we get paid."

Moth whirled, pointing at her. "We'd be rich and on our way already if you didn't demand so much Xeno."

"Yeah, what the hell do you want it for, anyway?" asked Headcrash. "You got the military vac shot. Fade can't touch you."

"Ascendant sells Xenodril for two hundred bucks a dose even though it costs them under a dollar to make. I can sell it for fifty a shot and get six times what you're asking for in cash. To them, it's cheaper to ransom the brat in meds."

"It's a bit late for Xenodril. Sam's dead." Moth stared a challenge at her.

"Horseshit." Icarus sat up, looking annoyed by the delay of sleep. "This is about your son. We all know you're gonna give the shit away."

Genna flew from the sofa and advanced on Icarus, but Moth held her by the shoulders. She settled for punching him in the chest, not that he felt much. The big man whirled, throwing Genna like a rag doll over the couch

"Hey, get off her!" Icarus sprang to his feet, leaping at Moth.

Without looking, Moth caught Icarus by the throat and held him off the ground one handed. Sweat beads on the giant's forehead slid down his face in rivulets. Amber metal irises narrowed to pinpoints. Icarus bumped the bed as Moth squeezed. Maya leapt backward, her flight cut short by the handcuff around her left ankle. She sat motionless, left leg pulled taut, while the men grappled, until a stripe of silver caught her eye.

A panel of thin plastic stuck out of Icarus's back pocket, covered with a pattern of thumbnail-sized black derms. Moth throttled the skinny Asian, banging him repeatedly against the bedframe. Maya struggled to crawl forward over the bucking mattress while the men wrestled. She seized the drug sheet with two fingers and tugged it away when Moth added a second hand to Icarus's neck.

"God damned dink, trying to sneak me from behind!" Moth roared. "I'll fucking kill your entire kimchee-swilling family."

"Moth!" Genna screamed and jumped on his back, catching him in a headlock. "It's Icarus. You're not in Korea. You're hallucinating again. He's fucking *Chinese!*"

Maya scooted as far back as she could and sat on the drugs.

No amount of straining on the part of Genna and Icarus combined seemed capable of overpowering the monster with a body more metal than flesh. Headcrash peered over the pile of stacked crates and junk he'd used to build a 'fort' around his workstation. When it appeared murder would not happen, he looked at Maya, shivering at the sight of her placid calm.

"You're not in goddamned Korea!" Genna screamed, punching Moth in the back of the head. "This is Baltimore!"

Moth's rapid breathing slowed, his snarl faded, and he released his grip on Icarus's throat, dropping him from eye level to a foot and a half shorter. Gagging, Icarus collapsed to all fours and wheezed while the giant stormed off into the back hallway. Genna returned to the sofa, sitting with her face in her hands.

Making sure to keep the drugs out of sight beneath her, Maya lay back and closed her eyes.

FIVE

SO FAR AWAY

aya stirred at the sense of motion near the bed. Genna looked down at her with an expression at an unreadable point between pity and disgust. A plastic bowl with dry cereal nuggets rattled as she dropped it on the mattress.

"You as bony as the Frags... for all that money you have, don't you eat?"

"Frags are thin because they don't have much food out here, and there is sickness." Maya sat up, careful to keep her butt on top of the derms. "I'm thin because I was made that way. Vanessa thinks it looks better in the ads." She stared at the bland pellet cereal. "I think Xenodril should be cheaper. Sam didn't deserve to die."

Genna stormed away. Maya disregarded the offering, leaning forward to fuss with the metal tethering her to the bed. She looked up moments later when Moth loomed over her.

"Why are you wasting food on a dead girl?" He swiped the bowl and wandered off while munching.

"I..." Genna stood at the edge of the room by the swath of missing wall, staring off at the broken landscape while the trinkets in her hair clattered in the wind. "Look, when the time comes, I don't want to watch."

Moth crunched another mouthful; crumbs sprayed when he said, "It was your idea. She's a Citizen, remember? Represents everything you want to destroy. The heir to the Ascendant Empire killed on a live netcast. If that doesn't wake society up, nothing will. Oh, you're gonna watch. Them Brigade pussies don't have the balls for an op like this. We're going to change the world."

Maya looked down at a rat making off with a spilled nugget of cereal.

"Is it really necessary?" asked Headcrash. "What if it backfires? The Authority would hunt us down if we kill her, maybe as bad as they go after the Brigade. They have eyes everywhere."

"If we let her go, she'll be able to describe us," said Icarus.

"Do you think I care if you steal money from that woman's company?" asked Maya. "I'll tell them you kept me blindfolded and tied the whole time."

"You're a Citizen." Genna's voice lost energy, sounding resigned. "You'll do it just to spite us Nons. Just because you can. Just to feel better than us."

"What do you think, Genna?" asked Moth. "Shoot her, or throw her out the wall?"

Genna flinched. Maya glared at the electronic restraint.

Icarus burst out laughing.

Even Moth gave him a surprised look. "Cold…"

The Asian man muttered and babbled at someone who wasn't there.

"He ain't laughing at how to kill the girl," Headcrash said. "He's seein' shit. Been mumbling for the past two hours in his sleep. He thinks the aliens that sent the Fade are here, psychically manifesting to him."

"That's a stack of shit," barked Moth. "Ascendant made it so they could sell the cure."

Genna raised an eyebrow, almost smiling. "You sound as paranoid as Headcrash."

"I've heard all the rumors," Head muttered. "Some alien microbe trapped in asteroid ore. Ascendant scheme, Authority, old US military or Korean weapon… God being done with humanity. Maybe it's the Earth wanting to start over." He cradled the rats. "My little friends don't get Fade because they haven't pissed off the planet."

Moth shook his head. "Shit, man, if you don't do drugs, you need to start."

Icarus jumped up, pawing at his clothing. "I'm fuckin' out of Vesper. I n-need to go." He jogged for the door. "Be right back."

Moth caught him with a palm to the chest. "Oh, de ninguna manera, amigo. Your ass is stayin' right here. No one leaves until this is done."

"Someone who leaves could be going to turn in a reward to the Authority," Maya said. "Betraying everyone else for money."

Headcrash almost exploded. "Y-yeah… s-she's right." He shrank into his seat, shaking and whispering to himself. "W-why the hell is she helping us?"

"That's bullshit, man!" Icarus shuddered. "I'm fuckin' rattling, bad. I need Vesp."

Moth shoved him off his feet with a casual thrust of his arm. Icarus caught air, hit the wall, and slid to a seat on the floor in a rain of crumbling plaster. His attempt to get back up stalled as Moth pulled his gun.

"Sit your ass down. No one leaves."

Icarus cried, arms twitching out of control. "Come on, Moth. Y-you know what happens to me without it."

"Night blindness. I hear Vesper causes paranoid hallucinations, too." Genna waved her hand in a spooky gesture. "The darkness comes alive, and you see stuff what ain't there. This why I ain't touchin' the shit. Stop askin'. I didn't take that shit when Uncle Sam asked me to, and I sure as hell ain't gonna do it on yo' say so."

"It renders the optic nerve hypersensitive." Maya swished her feet side to side. "When the dose wears off, the dendrites remain excited and random neuro-electrical impulses cause optical illusions. What the brain does with the images varies on an individual basis, but it's often unpleasant."

Genna gawked at her.

Icarus gnawed on his hands.

"That sounds like paranoia." Moth chuckled. "Maybe you should give some to Crash."

"Oh, you're funny." Headcrash snorted, wiping his nose. He tried to check his terminal, but seemed unable to bear having his back to the room long enough to pay any attention to the screen.

Moth dragged one of the battered kitchen chairs into the exit hall and took a seat near the only way out of the apartment that didn't involve some fifty odd stories of free fall. Icarus collapsed in a heap next to the recliner he always wound up in.

Maya curled forward, arms around her legs, chin resting on her knees, and stared at the distant flickering lights of the Sanctuary Zone, an island of silver far away upon on a black field of ruin.

Her home seemed so far away, as if she'd never been there at all.

SIX
HEAD GAMES

eadcrash watched her without blinking for almost fifteen minutes before he left his nest and approached. Maya looked up at him, face blank. He covered his mouth with a splotchy hand that reminded her of a coloring book where a child didn't fill in the outline. He seemed to sense her curiosity and concealed his fingers in his clothes, though the same effect patterned his face as well.

He crept closer. Maya scooted toward the metal footboard, concealing the Vesper sheet while shifting sideways and tucking her tethered leg under herself. Her free foot dangled off the side. Headcrash sidled nearer, frowned at Moth, and paused as if to calculate the limit of her reach before taking a seat on edge of the mattress near the pillow.

A long stare did nothing to change the curious look on Maya's face. She showed no fear of the bedraggled, pudgy man. It took a while for him to find the nerve to extract his hand from his pocket and hold out a candy bar. Maya glanced at it, making no effort to reach for it. He started to lean it closer to her, then second-guessed himself and tossed the offering, terrified to cross some imagined dotted line delineating where she could not get him.

Maya picked up and opened the treat, the crinkle of plastic making him flinch. She tapped a finger behind her ear. "Why don't you have a plug? You're a hacker, right?"

"Don't trust them. I use old tech. S'why they call me Headcrash."

"Thought it was 'cause you're fucked in the head," muttered Genna from the sofa.

He flashed a sarcastic, tongue-protruding face at her. "Sixty or seventy years ago, computers used long-term memory storage in the form of hard drives. Magnetic heads floated microns away from rotating physical platters. Sometimes when they failed, these heads would touch the spinning disk and scratch the substrate from the surface, ruining it—a head crash. Alfonse started calling me that because I like to use the old tech. A wire in the brain lets the Authority into my thoughts. All the new systems have backdoors they can use to watch you. Old stuff isn't compatible with their sniffers."

"Alfonse called you that because you're fucked in the head," said Genna.

He ignored her, kneading his fingers in his lap and mumbling. "Moth shouldn't have taken your food."

"You're nice," Maya whispered, nibbling on the chocolate while aiming a smile at Head. A tickle upon her toes made her glance to the right at a two-inch roach crawling over her left foot. She flicked it casually toward the desk where it landed on its back, legs scrambling at the air. "You're not like the others."

Four rats swarmed on the insect and devoured it.

Headcrash edged a little closer, whispering, "I can't hear you."

"Do you think it's strange how little security was at my home?" she whispered, quieter than the last time. He slid closer. "For who I am, there were only two officers."

"I killed the four outside with the drone," mumbled Headcrash while kneading his hands in his lap like a small boy confessing.

"Two came by helicopter," said Maya, even softer. "Only two were guarding me."

"What are you saying?" Headcrash hopped close enough to put an arm around her, but recoiled from physical contact. He looked up; Icarus muttered to himself, English and Chinese twining back and forth, equally incoherent in the throes of a comedown phase. Moth sat by the door, far enough away not to hear them. Genna snored. "What are they planning?"

Maya leaned against him, holding the candy bar in both hands while nibbling. "The Authority let you take me because one of your friends is either an undercover or an informant." Headcrash covered his mouth to stall a shriek. "One of them is probably Brigade." She bit off a hunk of candy and chewed it at an agonizing slow pace. When Headcrash seemed about to burst, she snuggled against him. "I think it's Genna, since she wants so much Xenodril. It has to be for the revolutionaries." Maya tapped herself on the right shoulder, whispering, "She's got their tattoo."

He stared at the sleeping woman, his constant faint tremble growing into visible shakes.

"It could be Moth, too, since he's ex-military. I learned in class that most of the Brigade terrorists are disillusioned veterans. They want to overthrow the Authority because they feel they were lied to about the war. That's why they just execute them on sight." Maya looked him dead in the eye. "As well as anyone with them."

Sweat oozed from every pore on his face. "N-no... You don't think? I-if they think w-we're Brigade, they'll kill us."

Maya wobbled her head in gesture of maybe. "It might even be Icarus since he's good at breaking into places. Don't you think he would have had to learn how to disarm security systems and electronic locks from either the Authority or the Brigade? He's a doser. Dosers make mistakes. If he was a simple street criminal on his own, he'd be dead or in jail by now. Someone's helping him, but who?"

Headcrash looked his friends over, gaze stalling at each one in turn. He slid an arm across Maya's back, pulling her tight like a teddy bear that would protect him from the enemies surrounding him. While he stared at Moth, paralyzed in fear, she reached under her backside and pulled the derm sheet out. Candy bar held in her teeth, she hugged him in defiance of the stink of a months-delayed bath and tucked the chems into a pocket inside his jacket.

"Thank you for being nice," she whispered after gripping the candy bar again. "I'm sorry you have to live out here."

He whimpered as he stood, wild glare shifting from one person to the next while ambling back into his nest, staring at Genna as if trying to see her arm through her shirt. As soon as he vanished behind the pile of trash separating his desk from the room, the terminal chirped a loud tone. Headcrash screamed and put a hand on his sidearm. He stared at Maya and babbled, spittle flying. She gave him an innocent face while gnawing on the candy, figuring he'd finally realized she'd been close enough to grab his gun but hadn't. His lips twitched; he stood paralyzed by pure dread. Maya frowned at the handcuffs, twisting her foot to study the code panel.

Five little numbers stood between her and freedom.

SEVEN
LIGHTS OUT

Headcrash seemed to summon up a great effort to break eye contact with her, and faced the terminal. "Sniffer soft found a hit on a keyword."

The rolling chair creaked as he let his weight drop; the deflating cushion launched a cloud of dirt and two rats into the air. He muttered to the terminal, which responded by creating a holo-screen, an amber pane of light filled with shimmering dust particles. Moth and Genna moved to the desk, both folding their arms. The image of Vanessa Oman filled in the center, standing behind a clear podium with little Maya at her side in a shimmery, metallic aqua dress and high heels. 'AONN-Bulletin' scrolled along the bottom of the screen.

'Live' blinked at the top corner of the Authority Official News Network feed.

"...yet another attempt by unknown criminal elements to undermine the confidence of our Citizens. I assure you, rumors concerning the abduction of my daughter Maya, the face of Ascendant Pharmaceuticals, are just that—rumors. As you can see, she is right here, healthy and happy."

The little girl waved to the cameras, aqua lipstick stretched into a million-dollar smile.

Headcrash typed with fury, bouncing several bits of trash—and one rat—off the desk.

"Miss Oman," asked an unseen woman, "can you comment on possible Brigade involvement?"

"Shadow pattern checks," Headcrash said. "The kid's really in the shot; it's not digital manip."

"Has to be one of the android fakes," Genna muttered. "They're putting on a show for the sheep."

"Mmm." Moth grunted.

"Ordinarily, as you know, we cannot divulge information of this nature. However, given that nothing actually happened... I can say that we do, at this time, believe the Brigade is attempting to initiate a propaganda campaign intended to embolden the desperate criminals who dwell outside the Sanctuary Zone. If they can convince people that *my* daughter was kidnapped, it makes the Authority seem weak, vulnerable." Vanessa narrowed her eyes; ice formed on her next words. "I assure you, we are neither weak nor vulnerable."

"I don't buy it," said Moth. "Brigade don't have the balls to pull this off."

"Brigade doesn't wanna involve kids in a war," rasped Icarus.

Genna pursed her lips. Headcrash whipped around to glare at Icarus, worry in his eyes.

Except for the twitching Asian, her kidnappers all shifted to look at her after the video feed cut to a local weather report warning of increased risk of bacteria parasailing on a southeasterly wind. A faint female voice reminded everyone to update vaccinations and ensure they had a ready supply of Xenodril on hand.

Maya looked down at her painted toenails. After a moment of silent staring, she spoke without emotion. "The woman is lying. There will be drones. You should turn off the lights so they can't see me from outside."

"Drones have night vision," Moth said.

"Yes." Maya glanced up at him. "But a dark hole in the wall will attract less attention. If the whole building is dark except for one space, where would *you* search?"

"What?" Icarus snapped out of his haze. "No way. You can't turn off the lights! It's dark!"

"It's always dark." Genna walked past the bed, swiping her hand at the wall and killing the lights.

Moonlight from the missing wall painted the room in blue-tinted shadows, enough to see people by shape provided one's optic nerves hadn't been scorched by Vesper.

Icarus jumped from his chair and chased her, only to be once more caught in a one-handed chokehold by Moth. Maya crawled as far back on the bed as she could, covering her ears from the shouting match between the two men. The yelling fizzled out in a few seconds, their argument ending with the exclamation point of Moth throwing the smaller man back into his recliner.

The ex-soldier stepped closer, pointing. "Sit your ass down. We're too close to fuck it up now."

Genna crossed the room to stand again at the opening, inches from free fall. One stress crack or shift in balance would send her fifty stories down. Nothing about her demeanor suggested she cared one way or the other if that happened. Maya finished the candy bar and lay back on her side, watching the dancing, serpent shadows of the woman's hair lofting in the breeze. Castoff light from the distant city glowed along her front while her back remained in silhouette.

"Genna? What are you looking for?" Maya asked.

The woman ignored the question, but a glistening tear formed at the corner of her eye.

Headcrash almost fainted when the terminal emitted the loud bell-ringing noise of an ancient telephone.

Icarus twitched, gazing into the back hallway as if looking at something... hungry. He pointed at nothingness and whispered, "They're watching me," in a continuous repeating stream.

Vanessa Oman's face appeared on the holographic monitor. Her skin gleamed; dark chocolate turned to milk where her angular cheekbones caught strong overhead lights. She sat at the head end of an onyx conference table. Maya remembered walking back and forth along that same table, modeling outfits for marketing people to decide on.

"So, you're the Frags that keep bothering me." Vanessa held up an arm. Maya walked into the frame, and her mother's embrace. "You don't even look competent enough to be Brigade."

"We ain't fuckin' Brigade," Moth barked.

"Or Frags," whispered Headcrash to one of his rats. "Frags are wild."

"Who are they, Mother?" the child on the screen asked. "Who's that girl that looks like me?"

"No one important." Vanessa erupted in haughty laughter. "A bunch of simpletons looking to find money where there isn't any to be had."

The call dropped.

EIGHT
RAMPING UP

eadcrash stared aghast at dead air. Genna looked equally capable of killing someone or bursting into tears. Moth showed little reaction. Icarus continued pointed at nothing, whimpering and asking empty air not to take over the Earth.

"Now what?" Headcrash tapped one finger on the glass-top desk.

"It's a trick," Genna said, her voice icy. "It's got to be a trick. Holographic kid, a fake."

"I checked it again." Headcrash launched into a muttering explanation about the technical details of discerning digital manipulation.

Moth swatted him across the back of the head and pulled a knife. "We need to convince that bitch we're serious."

"Oh, man." Headcrash cringed and gave Maya an apologetic look.

"What?" Moth shrugged, blade glinting. "Citizen hospitals can reattach fingers."

"Wait." Genna held up a hand. "That might bite us in the ass. Try something less bloody first."

Moth scowled. "You *are* going soft on us."

Genna stared at him without blinking, adding a slight aggressive lean forward.

Eight seconds later, the behemoth stomped over to the desk and slammed the knife down.

"Fine." Moth grabbed a rat that had crawled onto a small device, and hurled the furry creature out the missing wall.

Headcrash leapt from his chair, shaking and screaming, "What did you do that for? Why did you kill him!?" Tears rolled down his face.

Moth shoved the smaller man back into his seat. "It's a damn rat, *chiflado*. If you don't wanna join it, shut your hole."

Leaving the hacker to weep over a rodent, Moth swiped the holo-recorder, jammed it into Genna's chest, and stomped over to the bed after she clutched it. Maya kept eye contact as he approached, until he grabbed a fistful of her hair and pressed his gun into the side of her head.

"Beg your mother to save you," he said in a near growl.

"I usually have makeup on for filming."

Genna seemed unsettled by the blasé expression on Maya's face, but started the recorder.

Maya raised her hands in surrender as Moth lifted her butt an inch off the mattress by her hair.

"Mother, please help," she droned. "I've been kidnapped, and they are going to kill me if you don't pay them. I am very scared. Please save me."

Everyone stood speechless for a moment.

"Yo, this kid's got some damage." Icarus broke into a fit of nervous tittering, pointing at Maya.

"Do it again." Moth shoved the child sideways into the mattress with the tip of the pistol. "Cry this time, or I'll cut off something you'll miss."

Maya sat up, fixing her hair. "You're wasting your time. I tried to tell you before, that woman will never pay a ransom. Crying and pleading won't work. All that'll do is make her happy she's causing me to suffer. I have to act like she's unimportant. The only way to get a reaction out of her is to make her feel insignificant. That makes her angry."

"Bullshit," said Genna. "S-she's your mother. She can't value money more than her own child."

"Citizen, remember? You said we're not real people." Maya offered a blank stare during a long silence. "I'm not supposed to say this, but you seem like you've got a legitimate gripe. I'm not Maya Oman. I'm an android made to look like her."

"Nice try, kid," Moth muttered. "We know all about the decoys. Head found you."

Maya shrugged. "Didn't you think it was strange how little protection they had around my penthouse? You're amateurs, barely holding together. Far from a professional military squad." She pointed at Genna. "You're angry and suicidal. You deserve some revenge, but you want it so badly you'll take stupid chances." She pointed at Moth. "He's a head case, probably kicked out of the military for stress disorder, and that guy in the chair is drugged out of his mind. Your electronics guy's afraid of his own shadow and isn't even using modern gear. You think you could have just walked in and abducted the daughter of Ascendant Pharmaceuticals? Vanessa Oman has seventeen homes, only nine of which are unclassified, and all have fake Mayas."

Headcrash sputtered, looking back and forth between her and the terminal. "I'm sure. I spent days hunting for the kid. Everything I found pointed to that location being genuine. I'm sure... and I'm *never* sure about anything. They made the security light to look like a red herring on purpose, thinking we'd skip it."

"Not sure enough," Moth grumbled.

Icarus seemed to shake off the craving and wobbled to his feet. He staggered over, swimming around Moth's huge arm, and grabbed Maya by her head, thumbing her eyes wide before forcing her mouth open and examining her teeth.

"Looks real." He glanced over his shoulder. "Yo, Head, you gotta PMRI over there?"

"In this shithole?" Headcrash held three rats, petting them as if to comfort the oblivious creatures for their loss. "We're lucky I got the splice up and running."

Moth clutched her hair and yanked it aside to expose the back of her neck. Maya kept a disinterested expression. "No interface jack. She's lying." He gestured at Genna. Once she started the holo-recorder running again, he jammed the pistol in the top of Maya's head. "Look here, *Miss* Oman. We have your brat and we don't care about emboldening shit. Fuck politics. Fuck the Xenodril. We want money. Forty million or we'll start sending back pieces of your little drug princess." He shoved her face first in the mattress and pointed at Genna. "Send that."

Maya didn't move for a few minutes, waiting for Moth to walk away before pushing herself upright. Icarus paced in an expanding figure eight. Every so often, he'd flinch from an unseen shadow moving in his mind. Moth resumed guarding the hallway out, anticipating the doser would attempt a sprint for the door again.

An electronic whirring noise passed by the gap.

Headcrash dove for cover under the desk. "Drones! They've found us."

"Calm your shit." Genna walked up to the edge of the hole. "It's a bioassay unit, probably testing the air for Fade."

"Need Vesper," Icarus wheezed. "Come on, Moth. You can come with me. I only need to see Missy Hong. She's at the treatment plant; it'll take ten minutes."

Moth flung him across the room. "Sit down, shut up."

The drone came back around the other way. This one had two fans at the end of a thin wing-like strut, and a long, trailing tailfin. Maya thought it resembled a paralyzed dragonfly.

Headcrash whined. When the noise passed, he leapt up, pointing at Genna. "You're Brigade, aren't you?"

She looked away and gazed over the city for a quiet few seconds. "What the fuck are you talking about? Where do you come up with this shit?"

Head's entire body shuddered as he shook his finger at her. "The Xenodril. You wanted the drugs for the Brigade to distribute to the people. No wonder Alfonse said be careful!"

She scowled. "You're paranoid."

Moth glanced at her. "You don't sound very convincing, Genna. For once, the *chiflado* makes a little sense." He leaned in her direction. "Why else would you want all that Xeno?"

Genna looked at him, eyes vibrating with rage. "Relax, Moth. This ain't Songnim. No one's gonna blindside you here. Trust me."

"Need... dose." Icarus ran at the door. "I can't... they're biting at me!"

Moth palmed the Chinese man's chest, lifting him with little effort and tossing him into the recliner, which collapsed over backward in an explosion of dust and foam bits.

The terminal chirped. Headcrash swiped at the keyboard. Letters faded in on the holographic panel: "Ransom request denied."

"Fuck!" roared Moth. "Dammit!" He seized a broken coffee table with one hand and hurled it out the hole, roaring incoherently.

Seconds later, distant children's screams of fright preceded a hollow, echoing *crack*. The innocent voices burst into a cavalcade of obscenities at whoever threw what almost hit them.

Moth tore his hand cannon out from under his arm and pointed it at Maya. For a second, the metal around her ankle seemed to constrict. She raised her chin and stared defiantly at him.

"Fuck it, this is over." Moth growled. "Getting rid of this bitch now, and we go our separate ways like none of this happened."

"No!" Genna leapt to her feet; a cloud of dust swirled out of the couch behind her.

"Shut it, bitch!" Moth rounded on her. "You fucked us all askin' for

Xenodril. That went and made 'em think it's political. This is still my operation, and I say it's pooched."

"Since when is it *your* op?" Headcrash started loud, but ended on a whimper.

Maya stared down the barrel when he aimed back at her. "You shouldn't do that."

"Sorry, kid. I left my conscience in the streets of North Korea."

"Go ahead, shoot me," she said in a near whisper. "But you should know that I am equipped with a one kiloton nuclear warhead that will go off if this body sustains injuries sufficient to cause the death of a human being."

Moth twitched; sweat exuded from his head like a gentle squeeze on a wet sponge. Headcrash gathered as many rats as he could grab in a hug, as if that would help. Icarus stared at the giant, sizing him up for an attempt to get past. Yellow cybernetic eyes whirred wider.

"Remember the rad orphans?" Maya asked in an eerie, calm tone. "The little androids begging for help in the warzone? No one could tell them apart from real children. Soldiers would take them in because they felt sorry for them. Once they detected sufficient people around them, they'd detonate. If you saw their eyes glow, it was too late to escape."

Moth's arm shook.

"I see you remember them. I wonder how many innocents were shot, mistaken for walking bombs? Is that why you're able to kill me? Did you mistake a real child for a walking bomb? I have the same explosive in me, but I can't set it off on purpose. It will only go off if I"—she made air quotes—"die." Maya looked at Genna. "There are a lot of squatters in this building. Many real children. They sound happy here, even in squalor. I think they are happier than Maya. They're not Citizens like she is, and they get to stay up past bedtime. Do you want them to die too? I can hear them outside. They have no clue they're about to die to a nuclear bomb."

Genna leapt on Moth's arm and pulled his gun away from Maya. "Don't."

"Bullshit." Headcrash stopped smooching the heads of rats. "She's not an android; she ate a candy bar!"

Maya flicked her gaze to Headcrash, her movements precise, mechanical. "What good a decoy would I be if I couldn't act like a real girl? I can eat. I can go to the bathroom. I can cry. I can make noises like I'm hurt. Nanobots break down any food I consume, reassembling it on a molecular level to use for internal repairs. Whatever I don't need comes out in the form of fake waste." She looked at Icarus. "That's why I don't have any dolls in my room. I *am* one."

Genna pushed at Moth until he walked away from the bed. "Put the gun away. We have to think of something else. These people"—she waved at the ceiling and floor—"don't deserve to die."

Moth glared at Maya, who didn't flinch.

"I-it does explain how she's s-so calm." Headcrash shivered.

Icarus fixed his chair upright. "We can sell it to this guy I know in the Spread. He buys old androids. High-tech model like her would sell big. What kind of power core you usin'?"

Maya stared at the red glow on her ankle from the electronic handcuff's screen. "Anders-Owen Model Six. Fifty thousand year plutonium-based fusion cell. Estimated useful life remaining: forty-nine thousand, nine hundred ninety-one years."

"That's gotta be at least a half mil," Icarus said. "My guy will pay NuCoin for that. Physical money. Untraceable."

"So, who is it?" Headcrash twitched. "Which one of you is the Authority spy?"

"Probably you, motherfucker." Genna growled. "You're the only one to even suggest it. Tryin' to get it out there before anyone wonders if it's you."

"Maybe you're fuckin' Brigade." Icarus pointed at Genna. "You ain't military, or you'd be half toaster like Moth."

Genna squinted at Icarus. "I learned how to duck."

The big man snarled.

Maya ignored the building argument and name calling. Angry shouts and physical confrontations blurred into the background of her attention as she leaned forward. A little finger with silver-flecked raspberry nail polish poked at the rubber buttons on the cuff around her ankle.

00001

00002

NINE

PROBABILITY

hile the argument raged on, Maya kept keying one number after the next as fast as she could work the tiny rubber buttons.

"Enough!" Genna shouted. "We all need to calm the fuck down before we kill each other. The mission ain't over; we just have to figure out something the bitch wants."

"She ain't gonna ransom a damn decoy robot." Headcrash whimpered as he flopped in his chair. "We're well and truly fucked."

Beeping became noticeable over a short silence.

00144

"What the hell are you doing?" Genna walked over to the bed and grabbed Maya's wrist.

"Escaping while you argue. This is a five-digit code. One hundred thousand permutations. Factoring that you are not complete idiots, I've eliminated combinations where all five digits are the same or using patterns of ascending or descending sequential numbers. That leaves 99,970 possibilities. At the rate of attempting one combination per second, I will be free in at most 1,666 minutes or twenty-seven point six five hours. If everyone is going to sit around with no idea what to do, I'm leaving before someone gets stupid and murders a thousand people."

Genna stared, jaw open.

"Ballsy," Moth said.

Icarus scoffed. "It's a damn robot."

"Sit tight. Even if we can't ransom you, you're worth NuCoin to a 'bot dealer." Genna turned to leave, but stopped at a small hand on her arm.

Maya tugged until Genna sat next to her.

"I'm sorry you lost your son. It is wrong that you had a child you cared for and Fade took him, while Vanessa has Maya and does not even like her."

Genna's eyes bulged. She sucked in a breath as an old emotional scar seemed to peel loose. "They did a fine job on you, whatever you are. I've seen humans with less convincing empathy. Ain't that always the way." She chuckled, wiping her tears. "Only machines seem to care. Guess it's hard to program greed." The woman sat there in silence for a while, gazing out the hole over the broken civilization. "He was only a little older than you when he died. I watched the Fade take him, and I couldn't do a damn thing." She turned away, one hand to her cheek, shuddering as rage weakened to sadness. "His fingers turned grey within hours. Day by day, it crept, sucking the life out of him. At night when it's quiet, sometimes I think I still hear his hollow moaning."

"I am sorry for making you sad. You were a good mother to him. It isn't your fault. I understand why you tried to kidnap Maya. I don't think she would blame you."

"She's manipulating you," Headcrash yelled. "It's a damn machine; it wants you to feel sorry for it."

"What for?" Moth asked. "You know we'd be out of here and rich if she didn't ask for Xenodril. Damn corporation doesn't want to give up its golden egg."

"It would have been cheaper for them to give you the drug." Maya looked at Moth. "It costs forty seven cents per dose to manufacture. It is wrong that woman's company sells it for over two hundred dollars. You wanted forty million? Assuming you sell the Xenodril for fifty dollars a dose, a quarter of the price, an equivalent amount of medicine would have only cost Ascendant four hundred forty-one thousand and change. You should've asked for *all* drugs. That woman might've agreed to that just to be rid of the nuisance of having to deal with this situation."

"Stop staring at me!" Headcrash ducked behind the rat's nest, shaking. "The Authority is watching and listening to us through her."

Moth pulled his gun.

Genna jumped up and grabbed it. "Moron! Do you want to nuke us all?" Her voice wavered with a trace of sadness.

Maya tilted her head back, gazing into the ceiling with her arms dangling limp at her sides. After a moment, she made eye contact with Moth. "I am unable to establish a wireless connection to the AuthNet. There is no signal here. We are too far away from the Sanctuary Zone."

"She's lying!" Headcrash wailed.

"You tapped a hardline, correct?" Maya gestured at the pile of junk. "We are two miles beyond the range of the signal dampers. You should know the AuthNet is unreachable far outside the walls to prevent hacking. Your connection is a splice on an old backbone line running from Baltimore to DC. The Authority is as blind as Icarus in the dark."

The shaking Asian man held up a middle finger—aimed the wrong way.

Moth looked between the hacker and the girl. "Well, Crash? Is there wireless here?"

"No," he whimpered.

"Paranoid fuck," Genna muttered.

Maya keyed in the next code, but it failed to open the cuff. "If the Authority is watching us, it would be with Moth's electronic eyes. High-density PCM microwave transmission arrays were standard issue for augmented infantry in the Third World War, correct?"

"Stop that," Genna whispered, resting a hand on the girl's shoulder. "Don't make me break out the tape again."

Maya pouted and draped her hands in her lap. "She's not going to give you anything. You should let me go and get out of here before the Authority drones find you."

"What if—" Headcrash peeked over his barrier, gun pointed at Moth.

"I'm gonna break that off in your ass, fat man." Moth reached for him. "Then I'm going to throw your stinking rats overboard one at a time and make you watch."

"No!" Head wailed and crawled under the desk. "Don't hurt them."

A fluttering beep emanated from the terminal in time with a flashing orange light. Everyone froze in silence.

Moth leaned toward Headcrash, arms wide, gun held out. "Well... answer it!"

TEN
GHOSTS OF WAR

The hacker reached up, his hesitant gesture hovering long enough for a rat to scurry over his arm to the desk. Once his finger breached the hanging wall of light, piercing the button, the perturbed face of Vanessa Oman tinted the room with shades of gold and brown. Rustling and uncomfortable breathing surrounded her, perhaps a crisis team or one of her famous midnight board meetings.

"I'm not going to say this again. You cretins will not get anything. In what world did you think abducting my daughter would allow you to extort even one dollar from Ascendant Pharmaceuticals?" The woman scowled. "Go ahead, kill her. I'll make another one. I've got plenty of eggs in the freezer."

Little fingers dug into the mattress.

"I can see her behind you. Go ahead, shoot. I'll even watch if it will get you Frags to stop pestering me." Talon-like fingernails, lilac streaked with arcs of silver, clicked on the table. The impatient drumming echoed off the walls.

Maya stared at her lap, her voice lifeless. "She has dozens of androids just like me. She's trying to make you set off the bomb. It will make her laugh to watch you kill yourselves."

Headcrash hung up the call. Icarus screamed at the sudden dimming and dove for cover behind his recliner. Moth stomped around in the exit hallway, kicking the wall and swearing. Maya leaned forward, feet together, and rested her chin on the peak of her knees. After a moment of no one speaking, she looked up at Genna. The woman had been staring at her, statue still since the video feed. Twin lines of wet streaked over dark cheeks.

"Sorry about Sam," Maya whispered. "It's Vanessa's fault. Xenodril should be free."

Genna ran a hand over Maya's hair, pity in her eyes. Giggles of children outside, up far past their bedtime, echoed on a momentary breeze. The woman exhaled and trudged to the couch, beads and trinkets in her hair clattering.

Moth settled down ten minutes later and fell into his sentinel chair, chin braced against his fist in *The Thinker's* pose. Genna held her head in both hands, rubbing her temples while studying the floor. Headcrash whispered soft, comforting things to his rats and fed them cereal beads. Maya eyed the tiny rubber buttons on the cuff, doubting the veracity of Genna's threat to retie her. She slid a hand down her leg, fingertips inching closer to the restraint.

Icarus screamed and ran up on Moth. "The shadows are coming! Dammit, Moth, I need a score. I'm out, man... I coulda sworn... Fuck the Authority, you paranoid bastard."

Genna bounded to her feet, grasping the pistol under her arm.

Moth launched him across the apartment with a one-armed shove, landing him square in his recliner. "Head's the paranoid one. I'm a realist."

"You're getting good at that," said Genna. "Hitting the chair."

Icarus roared, clawing stuffing from the armrests as he leapt upright, gun drawn. He started to charge at Moth, but Genna slide tackled him, lacing her legs with his before she torqued his wiry body to the floor with a hard twist of her hips. Two shots went out the gap in the wall. An explosion of pigeons filled the air outside. Genna rolled up on him, grabbing and pounding his arm into the floor until he lost his grip on the gun. He kicked at her head, broke away, and got to his feet. She caught his ankle as he ran, dragging him back to the ground. He raked at the carpet, but it peeled up in his hands as she pounced on him. Icarus gurgled as she applied a headlock with a knee in his back.

"You!" Headcrash pointed at Genna. "That tattoo... you *are* Brigade! Y-you set us all up!" He swiped the pistol off his desk and aimed at her.

Genna glanced at her torn shirt and exposed arm. With a grunt, she rolled to use Icarus as a body shield. "Head, you paranoid motherfucker, calm down."

Moth grabbed her in one hand, Icarus in the other, and lifted the pair off their feet.

"Looks like a Brigade crest." Moth squeezed the back of Genna's neck. "Now why would anyone in an illegal, secret organization get a tattoo like that?"

The pistol rattled in Headcrash's trembling hand.

Maya slid backward until the handcuff halted her, but kept trying to crawl farther, twisting her foot around.

"Exactly," Genna wheezed. "It's just a unit insignia. Ain't my fault it looks like a Brigade symbol. Got this shit in Korea years ago."

"Show of loyalty," Headcrash muttered. "Proves her dedication. No turning back. Authority will execute you if they see it—and us for being with her."

Icarus's flailing leg caught Moth in the groin, launching a trail of spittle from the giant's lips, making his grip falter. The skinny man slipped loose and sprinted toward Maya, shrieking like a banshee.

"You're going to kill us all," Headcrash shouted and fired at him, missing twice.

Maya flattened herself on the mattress as Icarus dove at the wall, smashing a fist again and again until he found the switch, flooding the apartment with light. He writhed around to put his back against the cinder blocks, grinning at the ceiling.

"The shadows are gone," he whispered. "I can see..."

Moth dropped Genna and lunged at Head before he could throw more bullets in the general direction of a nuclear device. The hacker backpedaled behind his barrier and held his arms up in a gesture of surrender.

"Th-the d-drones will find us now. It's dark outside." Headcrash shivered.

Icarus slid up behind Maya, kneeling on the bed and holding her like a hostage taker. His breath ran hot down the back of her neck; she hung like a rag doll. He edged to the side as if to carry her to the door, but her bound leg stymied his escape.

"Icarus," Maya whispered.

Genna, Moth, and Head argued in the background, their shouting blurred into a circular session of blame-throwing.

He leaned forward, cheek warm against the side of her head. "They won't shoot me with you in the way."

"You're right." Maya put her lips to his ear. "You did have more Vesper. I saw Head steal it."

"W-what?" He sniffled into her hair. "No..."

"Silver plastic sheet with black hexagons?" She pointed at Head and kept her voice low. "He's got it in his jacket. He said you'd compromise the mission if you got high again."

Icarus dropped her in a heap on the bed, stood on the mattress, and yelled, "Crash!"

The argument screeched to a halt. All three looked at him.

"You scavved my stash!" shouted Icarus.

The hacker babbled; his jowls flapped in a head shake of vehement denial.

"Jacket. Pocket." Icarus stepped over Maya and jumped to the floor. "Now."

Headcrash patted himself down. "I don't have"—he froze, glancing at where his hand touched his coat. "W-what the hell?" His face twitched; he laughed, cried, and kept saying no over and over as he pulled the silver plastic film out of his pocket and held it up.

Icarus drew another pistol from his belt, howling with rage. "Fuckin' traitor!"

Maya sprang at the wall. Her fingertips passed close enough to set off the switch sensor before the chain cut her flight short; the lights went out. She fell on her chest, seconds before a blinded Icarus opened fire. She rolled on her back as rapid muzzle flashes illuminated the moonlit apartment and saturated the air with the reek of cordite.

"You're all working for *them!*" Headcrash ducked and snapped off a shot that caught Icarus in the thigh. "He's the traitor and you're Brigade."

Collapsed in a heap, Icarus grabbed his leg and wailed.

Headcrash swiveled to aim at Genna, but she fired from the hip. The shot caught him in the shoulder and knocked him to the ground out of sight behind his junk pile. Icarus screamed as Moth stepped on his wrist, pinning his gun to the floor.

The behemoth leveled off his hand cannon at Genna's head. "Drop it, bitch."

Genna didn't look at him, continuing to aim for where Headcrash went down. "Brigade ain't your enemy. We're trying to take down Ascendant. Besides, this ain't a sanctioned op. I signed on hoping to score some Xeno."

Maya slipped over the railing at the end of the bed and landed tiptoe on one foot. Her chained leg dangled in the air behind her as she strained to hop closer to the terminal. She cupped her hands over her mouth, hissing in a loud whisper.

"Persephone, access AuthNet educational archive. Password 'quantum reach.' Display 2081-May-18, Siege of Songnim, news drone footage. Max volume, loop repeat."

"Processing," said an electronic voice.

"Wha—?" Headcrash whimpered, looking up at her with horror in his eyes.

Screams filled the room, shouting in Korean over machinegun fire and the thunder of aerial bombardment. Other voices yelled in English, commands to get down, fire, or run. Splats and shrieks interspersed with the roar of missiles and explosions that shook plaster off the ceiling. Holo-panels erupted with images of men running and dying while ground fire tore aircraft from the sky, sending them down in spiraling fireballs.

Moth went pale and sweaty, glaring at Icarus. The big man hyperventilated. Interlocking steel ingots on his arms rippled like a mass of angry locusts, a wave that ran from wrist to shoulder. He leaned back and bellowed, "They're inside the line!" at the ceiling before driving his right arm downward, impaling the prone man in the chest with five metal fingers.

Icarus gurgled and wheezed, blood spraying between his teeth; with a twist of his arm, the augmented soldier crushed the doser's heart.

"We're overrun!" Moth roared, slinging blood onto the wall as he swung Icarus around and threw him at Genna. She dove to the floor, avoiding the body that went sailing out the missing wall.

At a deafening long burst of machine gun sound from the terminal, Moth ducked, shouting, "Foxtrot Alpha, three-nine. Request immediate drone support. We're pinned down and cut off!" He yanked two massive handguns from his belt.

Maya scrambled back onto the bed and crawled over the side away from Moth. The chain went taut as her hands hit the floor, leaving her hanging upside down by one leg. He opened fire at anything that moved: shadows, rats, waving bits of sparking wires, and people.

"Moth!" Genna's shout was weak compared to the sounds of war from the terminal. "It's not real."

Genna screamed; puffs of white foam blasted out of the couch with each shot at her. Maya clawed at the rug, trying without success to drag the bed against the wall as her nightie gathered at her armpits. Somewhere behind her, Headcrash wailed in rage amid the noise of bullets clanking against his equipment. The recording of a ten-year-old war ceased. A brief window of oppressive quiet afterward broke with the *snap* of a smaller gun firing twice. A dull *clank* of metal on metal preceded a splintered gouge bursting from the floor near Maya's hand.

Three shots from Moth's cannon ended with a gooey gurgling in Head's voice.

Maya twisted like a caught fish on a line, locking upside down eyes with Headcrash for an instant. Blood welled out of his mouth and nose, the gun dropped from his fingers, and he fell backward off the ledge. A few stories down, he found the strength to let out a scream that cut off when he struck the ground. The *squish* echoed back over the silence.

"Where are you? Come get it, you commie bastards!" Moth crept toward the terminal, swiveling left and right.

Maya froze. The slightest rattle of chain would draw attention.

Genna jumped up, aiming over the back of the couch, and let off a series of shots at Moth. Dull *thuds* slapped into his back; slugs stalled on implanted dermal armor. The attack knocked him to one knee, wheezing for breath.

"57129," yelled Genna, yanking a vibro knife off her belt.

Maya gave the woman a confused look. Hypersonic noise filled the air with the flick of a switch. Genna let off a war cry and ran at Moth. Maya gritted her teeth, letting all her weight hang on one ankle for as long as it took to squirm around and grab the chain. She pulled herself up and keyed in 57129. The hasp popped open, dropping her on her butt.

Genna roared. Moth cursed. The floor bucked from the heavy impact of a body. Without looking behind her, Maya scrambled on all fours to the nearest hallway, finding the bathroom rather than the way out. She ducked inside and slammed the door. When she tried to lock it, the metal slider broke off in her hand. A massive impact smashed into the wall; she jumped, swallowing a shriek while cringing from a shower of plaster dust falling from the ceiling and walls. The broken lock slipped from her hand, clattering to the floor at her feet as she edged away from the door, looking around for anywhere to hide. The cabinet under the sink was too small, even for her. A window fifty-stories high above the toilet, useless.

Moth's roar bellowed over the apartment.

With a clipped shriek, Maya leapt into the still-damp bathtub and curled in a ball.

ELEVEN
AND ONE REMAINS

Another heavy crash rattled the building, followed by a series of dull thuds that could only have been Moth's boots pounding the floor. He screamed, as if in pain. Genna let off another war cry; the hypersonic whine of a vibro-blade slicing the air ended with a surprised woman's yelp.

"Gotta do better than that, dink," he growled.

"Shit!" yelled Genna. The floor bucked with a series of rapid *thumps* and heavy impacts.

The rattling of empty handcuffs against a metal bedframe accompanied a deep *whoosh*. Moth groaned with exertion before another *whoosh*. Metallic clattering and breaking glass preceded another loud thud and a second wave of dust falling off the bathroom ceiling. A few seconds passed in silence before a distant smash announced the bed's arrival at the ground floor.

Maya cringed in time with a series of screams, grunts, and howls of anger, both male and female. She held her breath at a long, loud wail in Genna's voice. Moth's deep laughter cut short to a gurgle after three breaths.

Silence.

Four seconds later, a distant *whump* echoed outside.

Knees to her chin, Maya huddled tighter and shivered. Tub mold tainted the air, the taste of decades' neglect mixed with the soapy scent of Genna's hours-ago shower. Crunching in the living room approached. Footsteps. She swallowed. A creak emanated from the door. Wood scraped over ruined tiles. Someone walked in. Hard breathing hovered over her.

Pat, pat, pat. Droplets hit the tub wall, streaks of crimson slid down toward her face.

Maya looked up at the tip of a combat knife. Her shivering stopped. Another droplet swelled and fell. She forced herself to lift her gaze higher.

Genna stood in an odd sideways lean, her beautiful face marred with a swollen left eye, bloody lip, and trails of blood. Some of her ropey hair lay twisted around her throat as though Moth had used it to strangle her. Her right arm hung at an unnatural angle, broken. The loose camo shirt was gone, the tank top ripped. She stared down with a weary, defeated expression.

Maya grasped the edge of the bathtub and sat up, putting one hand on her left ankle where the handcuff had been. "Are you going to sell me to the robot dealer?"

Genna pulled her hair away from her throat and let it fall behind her. "I've got a better idea. You tell another lie. Tell your momma I saved you. Reward would buy a lot of Xenodril for those who need it."

"I'm sorry you had to lose your son because Vanessa is mean." Maya looked down. "I don't like her either."

"I've been so angry for years." Genna spat blood into the sink on her way to use the toilet for a seat. "I hated every Citizen for being vaccinated. Sam lingered for eight months. When he rasped his last breath, he was the color of that wall from head to toe, blind, hallucinating. He didn't even know who I was. He kept whispering for his mama, even though I was right there."

Maya pulled her hand away from the line of bruise around her ankle. "When did you know?"

"I saw the look in your eyes when that bitch said she'd just make another kid." Genna exhaled with a slight shake of her head. "Well played, baby. You beat us."

"She doesn't want me. I don't want to go back." Maya buried her face in her hands and cried, at last able to let her emotions out.

"Come here, girl." Genna slid the knife into a sheath behind her back with a *click*, the same knife that had cut the tape off her. "Moth never saw that one coming. They didn't implant no armor in the groin."

Maya sniffled, stood, and climbed out of the tub before taking two tentative steps closer to Genna. "No witnesses, right?" She stared at her toes. "I suppose it's better than starving."

"I'm not gonna hurt you." Genna brushed a finger over Maya's cheek while silent tears slid down her own. "How can that bitch throw away such a beautiful gift?"

"All she loves is power. I'm just for holo-net commercials." Maya fidgeted.

"Do you think Sam would mind if I stayed with you?" She wheezed as a one-armed hug squeezed the air from her lungs.

"I don't think he'd have a problem with it."

Maya reached up, threading her arms around the woman's back, finally returning the embrace after a minute. Genna got up and carried her, staggering across the trashed apartment to stand at the huge hole in the wall. Maya squinted into a breeze that lofted her hair. A crowd of curious Frags gathered about the bodies of Icarus, Headcrash, and Moth fifty stories below, next to the shattered remains of the bed. Maya watched them for a little while, then looked up and frowned at the gleaming lights and intact walls of the far-off Sanctuary Zone.

Genna backed away from the dangerous precipice.

"Mom?" Maya rested her head on Genna's shoulder.

The question—the title—brought tears.

"Yes?" whispered Genna.

Maya pointed at the destroyed terminal. "We should leave before they trace the calls."

PART II
BLOCK 13

TWELVE
THE LADDER

Alien shadows lengthened across the vast field of ruin, drawn by a hesitant morning sun that dimmed the glow of scattered fires among the rubble. Maya had kept her face hidden against Genna's chest on the way out of the building and for some moments after. The sight of dead people was not one she wished to remember. She peered up over the woman's left shoulder, still unsure how to process the feeling of human contact.

Fragments of standing concrete hinted here and there at the presence of former skyscrapers. Wind, laden with the ill scent of mildew and dirt, pushed her hair forward in a gust and sent a brief chill through her nightdress. Soft rattling emanated from the trinkets and wooden bits in Genna's hair. Maya looked to her right, the direction they moved, at a far-off indigo murk staining the sky.

No stars showed from beyond the tainted atmosphere; a band of deep, dark blue separated the ground from a sky a shade paler. Maya stared until a hint of shapes appeared within the gloom: buildings. Reading about the Dead Space on the AuthNet hadn't been a tenth as scary as being out in it. She clung tighter.

Genna's gait slowed to a stagger. A few steps later, she stopped.

"I can walk," said Maya, her voice a few decibels over a whisper.

Genna swayed on her feet, but got her hand under Maya's butt and hefted her up an inch. "You ain't got shoes."

"Neither do any of the kids climbing on the buildings." She leaned forward to study the ground. Dark dirt, littered with the occasional stone, metal fragment, or bit of electronic debris didn't look *too* bad.

"Yeah, well. They used to it." Genna swooned to the left, but controlled her fall such that she ended up sitting on a white metal box that would've been about waist high if it hadn't fallen over. 'Baltimore Sun' adorned the side in black block letters. Maya withdrew her arms from around the woman's neck as she leaned back against a two-story triangle of concrete that used to be the corner of a massive building. "I ain't wanna take no chances."

"Do they have hospitals out there?" Maya pulled her legs up, knees to her chin, and sat sideways across her new mother's lap.

Despite having one eye swollen closed and a broken right arm, Genna chuckled. "Not like the kinda clinics you're used to, but we got somethin'."

"You're in a lot of pain." Maya reached up, but hesitated before touching the purple lump on Genna's face. "You don't have to carry me."

"You ain't used to bein' out here." Genna rested a warm hand atop Maya's foot, then squeezed it. "I never shoulda done it. Taken you outta that nice comfortable life. It ain't your fault what they do."

Maya clenched her jaw when Genna's finger traced over her bruised left ankle. "That woman never had time for me. I wasn't lying. I really only did see her when she wanted me to pose for an ad. Vanessa can't love anything other than Ascendant."

Genna leaned her head against the concrete behind her. "Got a confession to make, kid. That whole mess"—she exhaled—"was my idea. Thought I'd take that woman's child away like she'd done mine... Killin' you wasn't a real part 'a the plan. Moth took somethin' I said sarcastic to heart. Barnes didn't think they were gonna pay. Backup Op was to bring you to the Brigade."

Maya stared down. "I was angry at you for a bit. I have a confession too."

"I bet you do." Genna forced a smile through her pain. "When did you go from tryin' ta play me to hopin' I felt like changin' my mind? Or you still playin'?"

Maya looked her in the eye. "Are you still doing a mission?"

Water gathered at the corners of Genna's eyes. "No, baby. I can't give you the kinda life you're used to, but you got yourself a momma now if that's what you really want."

"I didn't really have a life. That place was so dark and lonely." Maya shied away from a foul-scented breeze and snuggled close. "Don't you mean *new* momma?"

Genna smiled. "That woman never been yo' momma."

Go ahead kill her. I'll make another one, said Vanessa Oman in her memory.

Silent tears crept down Maya's cheeks. "I decided to trust you when you figured I wasn't a robot and didn't say anything to the others. I saw you crying." She looked up; her expression started a quiver in the woman's lip. "I'm not lying, but I am manipulating you a little since I want to stay with you."

"You gonna be some kinda scary when you grown. Where'd you come up with all that shit? How you know about android power cores?" Genna took a few breaths. "'Nother minute and we'll keep on."

"I made it up. Sounded technical enough. I spend a lot of time on the AuthNet reading."

Genna let her head sag back and chuckled into a wince.

Maya yawned. Much of the fear she had kept hidden had waned, allowing the weight of being up all night to settle heavy on her brain. An involuntary squirm came over her at the memory of a roach crawling on her foot. She closed her eyes. "Isn't it silly to get a tattoo they will kill you for?"

Genna brushed at Maya's hair. "There ain't no Brigade tattoo. Can't believe Head bought that. This from my time wit' the 494th." She sighed. "The Night Terrors. Unit insignia."

"Oh. Hey, if you're a veteran, you're not a Non." A distant *crunch* in the rubble scared away the onrush of sleep. "What was that?"

"Someone movin' around." Genna grunted, adjusted her one-armed grip on Maya, and stood. "Oughta get going."

Maya wriggled loose and slid to her feet, her toes sinking into the damp soil. "You're hurt. How far is it?"

"I can't let you get sick." Genna grabbed at her in an effort to pull her up again, seeming in the throes of a panic.

Maya held the woman's hand in both of hers. "Fade can't hurt me. I'm vaccinated too. If you carry me, you're not going to make it. It looks far."

Genna gave up trying to pick her up and tightened a grip around Maya's right wrist. "Stay close. Watch where ya step. It's about two miles."

The sun had gathered strength in the time they'd been resting. What had once been a strip of dark resembled a city, a sprawl of buildings that lacked the gleam of her former home as well as the everpresent whine of Authority drones. Amid the dull concrete-colored monoliths, a few scattered signs of civilization manifested as gleams of neon or traces of motion.

Maya twisted left to peer at the shining silver edge of the New Baltimore Sanctuary Zone. "I've never been this far out before."

Genna tugged and pulled her up to a steady walk. "'Bout ten miles of Dead Space 'tween Citizen land and where we goin'."

Maya's gaze lingered on the shining cluster of modern buildings behind them, a city full of sad people living sadder lives. Despite the comfort of a perpetually climate-controlled apartment, she'd felt like a rat in a sterile cage. Thinking of all the times she stared at the roof deck waiting for a helicopter that never came, or all the times she'd been scared stiff to attention when an Ascendant drone glided too close to the window got her heart heavy. The drones assumed her an intruder before they scanned. One bit out of place amid millions of ones and zeroes, and it would've shot her. Vanessa wouldn't have cared. She'd have *made another one.* Maya turned her scowl downward, placing her steps with care around chips of concrete and pieces of broken civilization, wincing every so often at the inevitable buried rock.

The Dead Space had once been a thriving metropolis before the war, though Maya had only seen it in images on the AuthNet educational archives. She squirmed her arm around, trying to pull back so she could grasp Genna's hand, but the woman refused to let go of her wrist. The 'you're not going anywhere' grip comforted her as much as it annoyed her.

"Is it as dangerous out here as it says in the archives?" Maya took a long step over a patch of spilled chemical.

"Can't say. Been a while since I read anything online. Bet they make it sound worse'n it is. Citizens gotta be 'fraid so the Authority can keep control. Long as they think they *need* protection, they stay in line." She remained quiet for five or six strides. "Won't say it's not dangerous out here. Dead Space is worse. Ain't as bad in the Hab. Only dangerous there if ya look like an outsider."

Maya looked up and blinked. "Hab?"

Genna filled her lungs and lifted her chin before speaking in a grand tone. "The Baltimore Habitation District." She gestured forward with her left arm, lifting Maya's. "Where we goin'."

"Oh. I read about that. Never heard it called 'Hab' before though. The AuthNet says that people kill each other in the streets and fight for food all the time there."

"And... you still didn't want me to turn you in at the gate?" Genna sniffled.

Maya shrugged one shoulder, yawned, and cast a bleary gaze over smashed buildings. In the light of morning, a handful of scattered tents caught her eye. The color of concrete, only fluttering gave them away as not. "It was on the AuthNet, so I figured it was a lie... or at least not as bad as they make it sound. I don't mind going there."

They crossed the debris field in relative silence for about an hour. Maya looked up every few minutes, growing worried when Genna had both eyes closed and the character of her walk seemed more like a series of random almost-falls and catches rather than planned steps. She shook Genna's arm, startling her unhurt eye open.

"It's not much longer." Maya pointed. "I can see people now. How far inside do we have to go?"

"Block thirteen," said Genna, sounding delirious. "Find Barnes..."

"You're bleeding." Maya walked faster, pulling her along. "Hurry up. Don't slow down. This city looks as big as the Sanctuary Zone."

"It's bigger. More ah us than them." Genna released Maya's wrist long enough to reach across her chest and squeeze her broken right arm. She growled with a clenched jaw and took a few breaths. "Okay. I'm awake. Pain says I'm still alive."

Maya grabbed Genna's hand. "Why do so many people live here if they hate the Authority so much? Wouldn't they want to be far away in the Dead Space or in the wilds?"

"There ain't 'nuff room in the Sanctuary Zone. They only let so many people inside, an' it's a bitch to become a Citizen if ya ain't born into it or serve in the military. Lot of these poor bastards drag their sorry asses into paradise every day to work."

"Why?" Maya blinked. Did all those miserable people she'd watch from the penthouse day after day really live out here?

Genna shook her head. "They hopin' someone on the rung above 'em falls off." She stopped perhaps thirty yards from a pair of rectangular metal signs bearing the words 'Baltimore Habitation District' on either side of a street opening. A handful of locals milled about, some hurrying along while others stood around talking. "You sure you wanna hop off that ladder, kiddo? You were near the top."

Maya looked from the people ahead to Genna. Almost twelve hours ago, this woman wanted to kill her. Now she could barely stand, her body half-broken to save Maya's life. Going home meant being a mouse in a cage all over again. Always alone, only tolerated when necessary for Ascendant business. *Too soft*, said Vanessa again in her mind. *You'll need to understand how the world works if you think you'll ever have a position in my company.* "Yes. I'm sure. I'm sorry you got hurt protecting me from Moth."

"I should probably ground you for a month." Genna resumed walking and cocked a half grin. "Little girls shouldn't trigger post-traumatic stress induced psychotic rampages in veterans."

Maya smiled. "I claim self-defense, but I promise I won't do it again."

THIRTEEN
WELCOME HOME

The **Baltimore Sanctuary Zone looked more like an** abstract blur of lighter color on the distant horizon than it did Maya's former home. Feet accustomed to soft carpet found the texture of a paved road coarse. She turned away and glanced at the buildings flanking the street. To her left, an old red brick structure, reinforced with armor plating, held the trappings of an Authority command post, though no one occupied it. A prominent sign announced 'Firearms regulated by drone enforcement.' Below the text, a stick figure leaned back in death, a dotted line connecting its head to a tiny drone silhouette.

On Maya's right, a cracked storefront window bore three huge Chinese characters in gold paint over red. Inside, it appeared to be a restaurant where a handful of people crowded around tiny tables.

Maya took a breath and let it out while pressing a hand into her belly to stall the torrent of butterflies. *Vanessa told them to kill me. Was she faking?* As scary as the dingy street littered with people was, the lonely penthouse apartment didn't feel any more welcome. A lush cage remained a cage.

She leaned forward, pulling on Genna's arm. "Wake up. Where are we going?"

Genna's hair decorations rattled as she shook her head. "Doc Chang." She blinked, gathered a wad of phlegm in her mouth, and spat a bloody glob to her left. "C'mon."

Maya cringed at the *pat* hitting the street. The idea of being a barefoot waif seemed far less romantic at the wonder of how many people did things like that to the ground she had to walk on. Of course, except for one pair of slippers more like socks with rubberized treads, all the shoes sitting in her old bedroom were tiny versions of a grown woman's high heels. Not the sort of thing that would do well out here. Nothing practical to wear because she was never allowed out except to record ads, attend the occasional tour of a facility, or conduct a 'walk around and smile at the peons' trip to the Ascendant office. She narrowed her eyes. *Only bought me what the photo shoots required.*

"You okay?" asked Genna at a hand squeeze.

Maya yawned. "Yes. I'm tired."

"Me too, kiddo." Genna stumbled but caught herself. "Won't be long."

People—for the most part in grey shapeless ponchos, a few in threadbare rags—seemed to come in two varieties. Those late for something important and those who had nowhere to be and all day to get there. A man in an olive drab jumpsuit that looked like it lost a fight with barbed wire started to approach Genna. His expression implied he planned to beg, but he backed off after making eye contact with Maya.

Along the first street, the ground floor of each building contained stores. Some appeared abandoned, nothing in them, others offered consumer electronics or gadgets the locals either couldn't afford or wouldn't bother spending money on. The pervasive smells of over-salted soup, grade D meat, and a bizarre piss-beer mixture tainted every breath. A handful of cheap food places seemed to do most of the business around here, as well as three bars and two other buildings with black paint all over the windows. Maya narrowed her eyes and vowed to herself that she'd never wind up working in one of *those* places.

Two blocks passed. She caught glimpses of a few kids, most of whom looked like they'd been wearing the same clothes for months. Younger ones played with improvised toys and one group of five teens prowled an alley. Maya didn't like the way they stared at her. Of the lot, only one boy had shoes, and he seemed to be running away from two others who wanted them.

A stick-thin woman, lost in a grimy grey coat that covered her to the shins, shambled out of an alley at them. She reached up to tug at a circular wall of cloth around her head, pulling it down from her face. "Hey, got a couple NuCoin I could have?"

Maya peered up with a neutral expression. *Guess she doesn't feel as guilty as that man.*

Genna mumbled something incoherent.

"Come on, I got a kid too." The beggar twisted around to show off a backpack-turned-papoose containing a maybe one-year-old boy.

"I'm dry, Lynn." Genna looked about to fall forward but caught herself. "Things went bad."

The woman took a half step back and leaned to her left as if measuring Genna's coherence. Once Genna resumed staggering, the beggar fell in behind them, eyeing the knives and handgun. Maya kept her attention on Lynn as she got closer, gaze jumping between an outstretched hand and the weapons.

Genna whirled at the last possible second, drawing her knife and pressing the edge to Lynn's throat. The smaller, pale woman froze with a strangled gargle. "I may be in a bad way, but I ain' no blind bitch. What you tryin' to do, girl? You know I help ya sorry ass out if I had any shit."

Lynn jumped back, grasping her throat in both hands. The baby toppled out of her backpack and careened headfirst at the pavement.

Maya screamed.

Bonk.

The boy bounced on his head and wobbled around onto his back, still moving and cooing as though nothing happened. Lynn wheezed apologies, collected the artificial infant, and ran off with it under her arm like a football.

Maya, gasping for breath with her hands pressed over her heart, peeled her gaze off the street and looked up at Genna. "That was a doll? I thought it was a real baby!"

"Now that's irony for ya." Genna started to chuckle, but winced, and trudged on. "Yeah. She thinks it'll make her more sympathetic or some shit."

"Does it?" Maya ducked around to Genna's left and took the hand of her unbroken arm.

"It did... for the first week."

Past four more blocks they walked, heading deeper into the forest of tall buildings. Every so often, a metal signpost bore a square steel plate with numbers. The first one read 03, the next 08. Eventually, they reached 13. Genna turned right down the cross street. A few e-cars sat about, parked with one set of wheels up on the sidewalk. Most buildings in this area looked at least ten stories high and had more or less the same design. Children's voices called out with the occasional shout or laugh, though echoes made it impossible to tell if they were ten feet or ten blocks away.

At the ninth high-rise on the right, Genna stopped. She almost fell over while attempting to turn her body to face it. Motionless, she stared at the place as though she couldn't quite remember what a building even was.

"Mom?" asked Maya, after a yawn. "Is this it?"

Genna nodded. "Yeah. Them endorphins are wonderful."

A dead identity-scanner, a hexagonal white box on the wall by the entrance with a red lens-eye, offered no reaction as they walked up a short strip of paving that divided a miniscule front yard in half. Genna nudged the door open with her boot and shambled into a hallway lined on both sides with tiny metal doors bearing keyholes and little numbers. Judging from the amount of grime on them, mail service hadn't bothered to stop by since before the war.

Maya glanced down at the cold, smooth floor. She couldn't quite tell what material the tiles were made of, smears of deep emerald green with lighter squiggles. The hallway opened wider fifteen paces farther in, revealing a stairway on the left, a red door on the right labeled 'employees only,' and a lounge with three elevator doors straight ahead that led to another corridor deeper in.

A fair-skinned man with light brown hair in a short military-inspired cut sprang to his feet from behind the stairs. Aside from a compact assault rifle across his back, barrel pointed down, his grey coat and pants looked much the same as everyone else around here not stuck wearing scraps. Squiggly thin black hoses dangled from his filter mask, loose around his neck.

"Damn, Genna... what the fuck happened?" He rushed over and held her by the shoulders.

Genna managed a half breath of laugh. "Mission went to shit. That jarhead you found flashed back hard."

Maya looked off innocently. *He had a little help.*

"Damn," said the man. "Once you're no longer half dead, I need to hear what happened. I don't want to risk using him again if you think he's too erratic."

"You won't," said Maya. "Moths aren't very good at flying."

Genna made a noise like she tried to laugh, but cringed.

The man looked down at her. "Who's that?"

"Kid," said Genna, fighting to keep her head upright.

"No shit it's a kid." He looked at a small door past the elevators. "Weber, get your ass in here."

"Don't worry about her. Found her out there; takin' her in. Bring her up ta my apartment. I need to see Doc." Genna tried to push past him.

Another man, younger in the face than the first but with grey hair, rushed out of the small door. He had a similar oversized grey coat, though his pants bore a blue-charcoal city camouflage pattern. Both of them looked like they spent more time in the sun than this place got.

"Get her to Chang," said the older man.

As Weber attempted to collect Genna by the arms, the other man took a knee by Maya and smiled. "Hello, sweetie. What's your name?"

Maya kept her head down. "Lisa."

He tucked a finger under her chin and lifted. As soon as they made eye contact, his already pale face got two shades whiter. "Holy shit, Genna... you did it. You got her."

"Mom!" yelled Maya, clamping her arms around Genna's waist.

"Barnes, don't. No." With one usable arm, Genna couldn't evade Weber's grip. "Get offa me, Bill."

"You gotta get looked at," said Weber. "Damn miracle you're still even upright."

"We'll sort this out once you're coherent." Barnes's fingers dug into Maya's ribs as he grasped her under the armpits. He didn't seem to be trying to hurt her, but he wouldn't let her squirm loose. "Weber, get her to Doc, ASAP."

"Yes, sir," said Weber. "Come on, Gen. You look like you got run down by an Authority transport."

"No!" screamed Maya.

Barnes hauled her slight body into the air with little apparent effort. Maya kicked, screamed, and flailed as he lifted her away from Genna and carried her past the elevators. She got a handful of leaves from a plastic plant, then tried to grab for a fire extinguisher on the wall but missed. Barnes continued through the small door.

"Put me down!" No matter how she tried to twist or squirm, neither fist nor foot could find contact enough to dissuade him.

"Calm down, kid." Barnes held her out at arms' length like a piece of radioactive debris. "No one is going to hurt you."

"Genna's gonna kick your ass when she wakes up," shouted Maya. "Let me go!"

She pried at his fingers clamped around her chest. He carried her kicking into a small room with a dark grey floor and white walls. Her attempt to cling to the doorjamb slipped away under his much greater strength. Barnes set her on her feet at the approximate center of the room, facing the wall. Maya whirled around and ran after him to the red-painted door, which closed in her face. The knob clicked, as did a pair of deadbolts, one above and one below it. Maya stared at keyholes. Someone had mounted an exterior door backwards to create a prison cell.

The knob refused to turn. She rose up on her toes, grunting and fighting with it.

"Let me out!" She thumped her fists on the steel, filling the ten-by-ten foot room with weak, hollow *booms*. "Mom!"

She went still and quiet at Genna's shouting in the distance. Hope became worry in seconds when no footsteps approached. Soon, worry became anger. Again, she rattled the knob and beat on the door until her hands ached.

Defeated, she slouched. Not getting what she wanted (aside from Vanessa spending time with her) within a matter of seconds was a new experience—and one she did *not* like. If these people knew who she was, they wouldn't treat her so badly. Maya stomped; a sharp *clap* reverberated off the bare cinder block walls. She sighed.

"That's exactly why I'm in here," she whispered. "They know who I am."

Giving up on the door, she pivoted to face the room. A plain steel table sat on the right with two chairs. Her throat tightened when she noticed a pair of handcuffs padlocked to a ring on one edge and bloodstains on the floor under one chair. On the left, a military-style green cot occupied the corner farthest from the door, mercifully lacking anything that looked like it could tie her down. An olive drab shower curtain draped over a rickety metal frame blocked her view of the near right corner. The space had no windows and a single naked light bulb in the middle of the ceiling.

Maya paced, fuming. She clenched her hands into fists, squeezing and releasing them while walking in a tight circle. On her fifth orbit, the lure of the toilet hiding behind the tarp grew too strong to ignore. Once she finished, she attacked the door for another ten minutes.

No one answered her banging, her demands, or her pleas.

Angry, she stomped over to the cot and fell seated, folding her arms across her chest and swinging her feet back and forth while staring doom at the red door. *Genna's gonna kill him.* Her anger faded with the unusual thought that her new mother would actually care if someone mistreated her. Maya's legs swayed to a halt. *She wasn't lying, was she?* A lump formed in her throat. *Is this what she wanted to do the whole time? Kill them all and take me for the Brigade?* She scooted back on the cot and curled on her side. Trembling lasted a few minutes, until the memory of the look on Genna's face the first time she called her Mom came to mind.

No. Genna would be pissed at them for locking her up.

Maya relaxed and smiled the same smile Vanessa Oman usually wore soon before something bad happened to an idiot. It didn't take long for the exhaustion of being up all night to drag her over sideways, and off to sleep.

FOURTEEN
NO REGRETS

Yellow lens eyes opened in the darkness over Maya's face and a crushing metal hand pressed down on her mouth. At the instant a frigid gun touched her temple, she snapped awake with a scream. She huddled in a ball, shaking and sniveling for a while. The grip of the nightmare weakened as the reality of finding herself in a stark holding cell sank in.

She sat up and rubbed the bruise around her left ankle, grateful that no one had tethered her to anything while she slept. Windowless, bare cinder block walls left her clueless to the time, though it felt like it ought to be evening. She stretched before shooting a frown at the door. Her lip quivered from fear. The last time she could remember wanting to sob had been three-ish years ago when Vanessa broke a promise to take her out in person and spend the day with her. The woman had never even apologized. As the daughter of the CEO, she had been expected to accept the company was more important than her feelings.

Maya had never bothered asking again.

Assuming Genna hadn't lied—truth be told, at first Maya only seized upon her guilt as a survival mechanism—the woman represented the mother figure she had pined for. Maya dragged herself again to the toilet, wondering how long these people would leave her shut in here. After flushing, she paced about for some time over a smooth floor neither cold nor warm. Every now and then, she took breaks from pacing to grasp the doorknob and rattle it, or bang on the steel barrier. A faint trace of voices from outside made it through the cinder blocks occasionally, hinting the back of her cell was an outside wall.

She contemplated screaming for help, but doubted anyone would care.

Her orbit resumed, still keeping a wary distance from the blood on the floor or the cuffs on the table. She doubted they'd chain her down and hit her until she revealed some mysterious secrets of Ascendant. No, they kept her locked up for the same reason Genna had originally kidnapped her: money. She sighed, hoping it didn't take them too long to realize abducting her for ransom did nothing but waste time.

Two circles around the room later, she approached the door and twisted the knob. Still, it moved barely a millimeter in either direction. Maya hit it with a halfhearted fist and sank to her knees, slumped against the metal. Somewhere in the back of her mind, she remembered a little white dog sitting by the patio glass, desperate to be let out. She had to have been six or so. The dog had messed one of the rugs and disappeared days later. Thinking about him got her crying all over again.

Her mood swung back and forth between anger and sorrow, manifesting as a steely glare at her lap or a pathetic pout at the door. A tiny warbling noise came from her belly, and she scratched at her nightdress. Chances are, nothing had changed back in the penthouse she used to call home. Vanessa would leave it as is until her replacement daughter grew old enough to be left on her own.

The scuff of boots echoed outside, growing louder. Maya leapt to her feet and took three steps back. She debated attempting a run for it, but figured a panic-driven dash would only make them use the cuffs on her. She held up her hands, staring at her delicate wrists. *I might be able to escape. They'd slip right off.* No. She would act docile and wait for a good opportunity. Make them think she'd given up hope, and as soon as they let their guard down, she'd find her mother.

Deadbolt one clicked.

Maya balled her hands into fists.

Deadbolt two clicked.

"Don't be afraid, sweetie," said Barnes.

The knob emitted a weak metallic *snap* noise and turned. She held her breath as the door opened inward. The older of the two men she'd seen the previous day followed it, carrying a white plastic plate and cup. A patch of sunlight on the wall at the end of the corridor made her feel tired all over again. She'd thought it nighttime, but it didn't even look late in the day. She stared at his eyes, wrinkled at the corners, though he didn't seem *that* old. Thirty-something, with a short, light brown brush cut.

Weber, behind him, pulled the door closed, leaving her alone with Barnes.

To her relief, he didn't lock it.

He set the food on the table and offered a curious smile.

"No." Maya backed up. "You're trying to trick me over there so you can chain me up. I want my mom."

He sighed. "No. I'm trying to offer you food." He took the plate from the table and held it out to her. "She's still in paradise."

"That woman isn't my mother." Maya narrowed her eyes. "I mean Genna."

"She's resting. Doc's patched her up best he can, but she's gonna be in bed for a while." He leaned the plate closer. "Eat."

Maya sniffed at fluffy yellow stuff and a meat patty between two slices of toast next to it. Hunger overwhelmed caution, and she accepted the meal before backing up to the cot to sit with the plate in her lap. Barnes dragged one of the chairs closer and eased himself into it.

"Never saw spray can eggs before?"

"No. I've never eaten anything yellow." Maya lifted one piece of toast to examine the meat disc.

"It's cheap, but it supposedly has all the necessary nutrients."

Maya dropped the toast and attacked the sandwich.

He remained quiet, watching her eat. The meat had a strange, piquant flavor that made her tongue tingle.

"Is this poison? It tastes funny."

Barnes chuckled. "No, it's sausage. Might be a little spicy."

She chomped down the rest of the patty-and-toast, barely chewing before swallowing. When he offered the cup of water, she didn't hesitate and drained it in a continuous series of gulps before handing him back the empty cup.

"It looks like things have gone a little off plan. There's no need to be afraid, Maya. No one here will hurt you. As soon as Ascendant pays—"

"They won't." Maya stared down at her feet, which didn't reach the floor.

Barnes cocked an eyebrow. "Oh, I'm sure they will. Your mother wants you home safe."

Maya's head snapped up with a glare. "No. She doesn't. They were going to shoot me on a live video call, and she said, 'Go ahead. I'll make another one.'"

He blinked.

"Ask Genna. I'm not lying." Maya tested the 'eggs.' Salty foam with a trace of some other flavor, possibly cheese—not too unpleasant.

"What happened to Genna then? You're saying she didn't get injured while exfiltrating you?"

Maya huffed and crossed her arms. "The word you're looking for is *kidnap*, and no. Moth did that. He went crazy. Genna saved me. There is no ransom. They don't care."

Barnes rubbed a finger back and forth across his lips for a few minutes. Quiet settled over the room, enough for the dying wails of Maya's meal deep in her belly to make themselves known. "So, what happened?"

She sighed before rambling through as much as she could remember of the abduction. However, according to her re-telling, Icarus had a drug-induced freakout, Headcrash, a paranoid breakdown, and Moth flashed back to Korea and tried to kill everyone when Vanessa laughed at him. Little Maya, of course, cowered on the bed and watched it all unfold.

"Hmm." Barnes leaned back and let his arms drape across his lap. He tapped his foot while making contemplative faces. "So what you're saying is, Genna didn't kidnap you?"

"She did." Maya rubbed the bruise on her shin where she'd slammed into the pipe while trapped in a black nylon bag. She added some 'child' and a dash of pout to her voice. "But I don't wanna go back there."

"Well." Barnes ran a hand over his hair. "That is a wrinkle no one was expecting."

"Can I go to Genna now or are you going to keep me locked up?" She bit back anger and acted ready to burst into tears. Not that they were too far away—one thought of Moth pointing a gun at her head and out they'd come.

He mulled for a few more annoying minutes.

"Whatever you're thinking, it won't work." She scratched the fork in figure-eights around the empty plate, drawing lines in the grease. "Vanessa doesn't care."

"Would you be willing to record some videos to counteract Ascendant propaganda?" He pinched the bridge of his nose. "Sorry, I forgot you're like what, eight? Videos to—"

"Nine, and I know what propaganda is. I had nothing to do at home but run e-learns and play games, and even a kid my age will eventually get bored with games." She pulled her hair off her face and tucked it behind her ear. "If they believe it's really me, they'll want to kill me to shut me up. But, that would cost too much, so they'll probably just accuse the Brigade of being desperate and using doctored video. I think it will backfire after the ransom demand."

He stared at her, lip twitching, but words seemed to elude the grasp of his brain.

Maya buried her face in both hands and cried for real. "I don't mind if you think it will help. I guess having her *want* me dead isn't going to be worse than her not caring if I die."

Barnes leaned forward, elbows on his knees, head down. He mumbled a few nonsense things and wiped a hand over his mouth. A moment later, he lifted his gaze to meet hers. "So you don't want to go home?"

She wiped tears from her cheeks. "Does Genna live here?"

He nodded.

"Then I *am* home. I don't want to go back to that place. Everyone is sad there all the time. People only smile when they want to sell something. Vanessa threw me away and Genna almost died to protect me from that guy with metal arms. I want to stay with my mom." She slid off the cot to her feet. "Please let me see her."

Eye contact lingered another few seconds before he shook his head with a chuckle. "Well, damn. This is going to ruffle some feathers on up the flagpole."

He offered a hand, which she took. When he pulled the door open, Weber startled. The white-haired man held a small assault rifle as well as wore one over his shoulder. He gave Barnes a confused look when Maya followed him into the hall.

"Change of plans." Barnes took the rifle from Weber's hands and slung it over his back on a strap. "It's a long story. I'll explain later. Kid's not a guest. She's moving in."

"I thought she believed she'd found Sam again." Weber blinked. "You're sayin' Gen wasn't delirious?"

"Apparently not," muttered Barnes.

Barnes led her out of the short hallway that connected the holding cell to the elevator lobby and around a corner to a door she hadn't noticed before. Beyond that, another hallway stretched past three doors on the left and a large box on the right that contained a folded-up firehose behind a transparent panel. At the end of the corridor, a set of glass double-doors offered a view of a parking lot full of trash, surrounded by a fence. About ten paces past the fire cabinet, Barnes pushed open another red-painted door, which led to a bare concrete stairwell.

Dusty child-sized footprints inside made her feel a little safer, and she followed him up the switchback stairs. On the fourth floor, a stylized black spray-paint rendition of an Authority helmet peered out of a circle above the caption 'We are watching.' Maya felt an odd urge to shy away from it, despite thinking of the officers as fools or annoyances before. Vanessa certainly had no respect for the blueberries. On paper, the Authority had the power and

Ascendant was only a company—though at least in Baltimore, they did whatever Vanessa wanted.

She kept her gaze down, mindful of stepping on painful things, though the floor here looked better kept than she'd expected. On the seventh story, Barnes went left to a door instead of right to the next flight of stairs. He pushed it open and entered a blue-carpeted hallway. Bare patches of concrete peeked out from random tears in the rug among numerous stains. Maya put her free hand over her nose at the scent of moldering sweat socks hanging in the air. Six steps down the corridor, her foot mushed into a patch of cold wetness; she cringed, barely managing not to shriek.

The stairwell door closed with a *whump* behind them. Seconds later, a pale, freckled, redheaded girl a little older than Maya stuck her head out of a doorway at the farthest apartment on the left. Her hair dangled well past her waist, and a dirty once-white garment draped loose around her, hanging in several tiers as though someone had wrapped the girl up in a curtain.

Maya's breaths shortened. She couldn't remember ever having other children around her, and a sudden spate of nervousness pinned her gaze to the floor. She'd grown used to being surrounded by adults who either treated her like a short grown-up or ran away from her in fear of saying the wrong thing and invoking Vanessa's wrath.

Barnes stopped at the fifth door on the right side, tapped it twice in a rudimentary version of a knock, and walked into a living room containing a simple rectangular table with fake wood grain in front of a couch covered in sand-brown cloth. Like the hallway carpet, it bore numerous stains. At the far left corner, a short passage appeared to lead to a bedroom. Nearer on the left sat a tiny kitchenette stuffed with debris. Maya hesitated at the door, peering down the hall at the other girl who had continued staring at her. The redhead raised a hand to wave hello, but Barnes tugged Maya into the apartment.

"Genna?" asked Barnes.

A fatigued moan emanated from the inner corridor.

Maya broke away from his grip on her hand and darted across the room. A bathroom shot by on the right, and she two-palmed the bedroom door out of her way. A desk sat straight ahead, littered with papers, old books, and a trio of brown plastic pill bottles. Genna lay on her side facing the entrance on a bed all the way against the left wall. Gauze and bandages covered her injured eye, and blue plastic lattice surrounded her right arm, a 3D-printed cast. Her loose-fitting black shirt bared one shoulder, the rest of her covered by a sheet.

"Mom!" yelled Maya. She raced to the bed, climbed on top of it, and flopped on Genna.

The woman hissed and gasped, abandoning her attempt to sit up. "Maya..."

Barnes appeared in the doorway. "Hon, don't squeeze her so hard. She's in a lot of pain."

Maya sat back on her heels, kneeling next to her on the thin mattress. "I'm sorry."

"Well shit. If you're acting, you're damn good at it." Barnes set his hands on his hips and shook his head. "Just in case you are, I wouldn't go running off. It ain't safe out there for a kid alone."

"She ain't fakin'," said Genna, sounding half-awake. "'Cendant shits on everything it touches."

"I'm two rooms down on the other side. Number 137. If you need anything, come get me." Barnes hovered in the doorway. "Oh, Gen... Don't worry about gettin' down to see Mason. I dealt with your rent this month."

Maya blinked. "Wait... you have to pay rent to live in this place? It's falling apart."

"Probably a pittance to what you're used to seeing for rent," said Barnes. "What's your mo—I mean Vanessa pay for the place they found you?"

She stared at him. "I'm nine. I don't know. Didn't you just take this place over? These are ruins."

Barnes laughed. "Naw. It's not quite as feral as they tell you inside the Sanc. There's still civilization in the Hab. You're thinking of the Dead Space. We have some Authority patrols, but not the tons of armed drones like inside the wall. Landlord will eventually kick people out who don't pay." He smiled at Genna. "You've been busy with us past couple weeks, so we figured you hadn't been doing much else. Harlowe's got you covered."

A doped-up grin formed on her lips. "Brigade's good to its people."

"Whatever you're paying for this place, it's too much." Maya frowned.

"Beats a plastiboard box." Genna cringed, gasping.

Barnes saluted her and left.

"Does it hurt?" asked Maya.

She smiled when Genna reached up with her good arm and took her hand.

"I'ma be okay. Little loopy for a couple days. Doc fixed the bone, but it'll take a while for the fusion to harden." She cringed and rolled flat on her back. "You okay?"

"Yes." Maya eased herself against Genna's left side. Human contact still felt strange—comforting and frightening at the same time.

Genna coughed and stifled a groan of pain. "Not scared?"

"A little. I had a bad dream."

Fingers stroked through her hair. Though not tired at all, Maya closed her eyes.

"What did you dream about?"

Maya gulped. "Moth."

"Yeah." Genna made a wheeze that seemed like an attempt not to laugh. "I think I'ma have nightmares 'bout his ass too."

She fidgeted. "I'm not afraid of his ass. I'm afraid of his robot arms."

"Ow. Stop making me laugh." Genna wheezed.

Maya grinned and snuggled closer.

FIFTEEN
COMMUNITY

The whine of drone fans tugged Maya out of sleep. Disorientation left her thinking she woke up back in her old room. She clambered out of bed and rushed the five steps to the sliding patio door on autopilot, standing at attention with one eye closed. A trio of small lights, two red and one green, drifted across the predawn sky. She stared past a haze of eye crumbs at the unmanned craft slipping among the forest of near-identical skyscrapers.

Unable to hold it in, she let out a yawn. Her former life, and new reality, faded back into memory. The flyer had no markings other than the lights. Relief let her breathe again. It didn't make sense for the Authority to send a patrol unit out this far. Authority drones never swooped in on people and scanned them the way the Ascendant units did—they responded to active crimes or hung overhead as deterrents. The machine glided along in a gradual leftward turn, gleaming as it entered a patch of moonlight. Six long wires with tiny pods every few feet, three per wing, trailed after it.

It's testing the air.

Maya yawned again and stretched. The room had nothing resembling a clock, but signs of blue lightened the sky between the buildings across the street. She backed away from the patio door and approached the desk, idly kicking at flimsy plastic bowls littering the floor. Stacks of old papers lay strewn around a long-dead computer terminal. Despite the battered condition of the electronics, she prodded the power button anyway. As expected, it did nothing.

She sighed. The AuthNet had been her lifeline for so long that the idea of being cut off from it got her heart to beat faster. Technology had been her teacher, babysitter, friend, and timekill for as long as she could remember. A frown started to form, but dissipated when she glanced left to the bed, where Genna remained in a medicated slumber. Maybe she could give this 'other people' thing a chance. She thought back to that red-haired girl watching her and shivered. How was she supposed to react to other children? What if that girl didn't like her? Maybe she could hide in here and avoid her. Ascendant executives had nothing on the intimidation factor of having to deal with kids. No article she'd ever read on the AuthNet prepared her for social interaction with peers.

Her gaze settled on a handgun at the left corner of the desk once the spike of worry faded. The same weapon that might've shot Headcrash, though Moth had finished him. It fascinated as much as horrified her. She leaned close, keeping her hands behind her back since she didn't trust herself touching a firearm. Children shouldn't handle guns, and despite being smart, she remained nine years old. Besides, in case Genna woke up, she didn't want her to freak out and hurt herself pouncing to take the gun away. Safely away from touching it, but still fascinated, Maya studied all the little buttons and moving parts.

With nothing else of interest aside from a closet with a few pairs of black military pants, some woman's shirts, and another set of combat boots, Maya crept into the hall. A short distance from the bedroom, the bathroom on the left offered welcome relief. Black stuff smeared on the white tile walls near the ceiling made her feel like she'd slipped into a horror movie. The tub at least looked clean and even had a few bottles of peach, white, and pink hair care products that looked as out of place as she felt. Alas, it didn't have a machine in the wall to do her hair.

A short while later, Maya hopped off the toilet, flushed, and grinned at the tub. This place didn't have an annoying computer in the walls that would shut off net access and make alarm noises if she tried to skip bath time. Of course, it's not like she had net access anymore anyway. Her smile faded to a smirk and she trudged out to the dark living room. Based on the condition of the terminal, she didn't even try the TV. The flat panel hung on the wall to the right of an open archway leading to a kitchen. She wandered in, rounded a small table with four chairs, and headed for the fridge.

Opening it required both hands and a couple of tries flinging all her weight into pulling. The door peeled away with the crackle of failing rubber, exposing a room-temperature chamber filled with a stink so pungent it drew bile into the back of her throat before her brain consciously processed the foul stench. Gagging and coughing, Maya stumbled back and kicked it closed. Whatever had once been in the bottles and boxes behind that door had ceased being food and counted as weaponized.

She hurried up to the sink and hung her face over it, heaving. Nausea passed in a few minutes, with little more than a tendril of drool coming up. Faint scratching from within a tiny vent fan by the two-burner stove caught her attention. Maya froze, staring at the grease-stained slats and the short length of pull chain. *It's a vent. The wind is blowing something around.*

Maya took a step closer, leaning forward, trying to peer into the darkness of the air duct.

A tiny pink paw gripped a slat a split second before the nose and whiskers of a curious rat emerged.

She screamed and ran to the living room, jumped on the couch, and pulled her feet up off the floor. Without being surrounded by people eager to kill her, she didn't need to swallow her disgust at rats. Her fear of ick (roaches and rats among them) had paled to the terror of Moth, so she hadn't even twitched when the roach walked over her foot. Feeling relatively safe and calm in here, if anything shiny, black, and a few inches long moved across the rug now, she'd scream.

Genna moaned from the back room.

At a knock, she twisted to look at the door. It opened, and a Chinese man entered. His expression of concern eased to a smile when he spotted her. He lacked the voluminous grey poncho-coat that everyone out here seemed to own, instead wearing a plain white tee and blue BDU-style pants. He set a small case on the coffee table and approached.

"Hello, little one. I'm Doctor Chang." He smiled. "You must be the new arrival Barnes was talking about. Are you all right? I heard a scream."

Maya sat straight. The man seemed friendly enough, and if he was the same person who helped Genna, she owed him at least being pleasant. "I saw a giant rat."

"Ahh. Alas, this building has some furry neighbors. You should avoid touching them, but they are not aggressive. He's more afraid of you than you are of him."

She fidgeted. "I'm not *afraid* of it. I don't want it touching me."

Doctor Chang took a knee and gave her a brief once-over, peering into her eyes, holding her wrist, and looking over visible bruises. He grasped her left calf and lifted her leg, tracing his thumb back and forth over a discoloration on her shin. "What happened here?"

"I hit a pipe or something."

He let her leg drop against the cushion. "You don't know?"

Maya shrugged. "I was tied up in a bag at the time. I couldn't see."

"What?" He gasped. A second later, the surprise left him. "Oh. Right. Wow. I can't imagine what things must've been like for you to decide to stay here. Guess the grass isn't always greener. If... you ever need to talk about anything, I'm a good listener."

"There isn't much grass there." Her serious expression lasted another five seconds before she smiled.

He chuckled and stood. "I'm going to check on Genna."

"How long is she going to sleep?" Maya slid forward on the cushion until her feet touched rug.

"Well, it's not like we get the latest meds out here. The best thing I've got on hand for pain is Dendritin."

She scrunched her eyebrows together. "That's a surgical anesthetic. It's not for pain."

He laughed. "You're right, but it's the best I've got. That's why she's so sleepy, and also why I'm stopping in three times a day. Dose management is critical."

Guilt settled in her gut, displacing her forming appetite. Good medicine was for Citizens. Not that Ascendant refused it, but Nons could rarely afford it. Jobs with decent pay seldom went to those without Citizen credentials.

Doctor Chang patted her on the head and walked off toward the bedroom.

A *squeak* emanated from her left. Maya startled and whipped her head around. The porcelain-skinned redhead she'd seen the other day brushed the door out of her way, still wearing the same dingy off-white wrap of cloth. Without her half hiding in a doorway, it looked like a gauzy shirt made for a massively fat adult wrapped several times around her into a multilayered sorta-dress. Here and there, the glint of safety pins stuck out, proving the garment had been made of a single strand of fabric wound about her. Grime covered her feet, caked in around her toenails. The only part of her even close to clean was her face. Up close, she seemed definitely older than Maya, but had to be under twelve. Her stark blue eyes widened with curiosity.

"Hi," said the girl. "I'm Sarah, but everyone 'round here calls me Faerie on account o' me bein' Irish. Can I come in?"

Maya stiffened with discomfort, picking at her fingernails in her lap, studying the flaking raspberry-glitter nail polish. "You're already in." She kept her gaze down until the other girl's feet slipped into view. "I'm Lisa."

"Hi." Sarah smiled. A small brown pouch on her left hip rattled with metal *clicks* and *clanks* as she sat. "Heard Genna took in someone new."

"Yeah." Maya filled her lungs, held the air for a second, and let it out her nose. The urge to shrink away from another child felt strange for a girl who'd thought nothing of prancing about in front of a boardroom and even changing clothes surrounded by a film crew, makeup people, and Vanessa's entourage. The Maya of a few days ago adored attention wherever she could get any. How intimidating could *children* be? *What's wrong with me?* She looked up, trying to think of something to say. "I am not used to being around other kids. Uhh. How old are you?"

"Eleven."

"I'm nine. Parents?"

"Dad." Sarah pointed over her shoulder with her left thumb. "He's down the end. Mum disappeared. You?"

"Sorry." Maya ground her toes into the rug. "Mine didn't want me, but it's okay because Genna's my mom now."

"She's nice." Sarah smiled. "A little scary, but nice."

Maya bit her lip at the memory of her first impression of the woman. Her contempt at the other child's slovenly attire faded when she remembered she wore only a spaghetti-strap nightdress. Worse still, the thin garment was all she even owned. "It's bad to meet someone and lie to them right away, so I don't want to do that. If we're going to be friends... I'm guessing you want to be friends since you came to see me. Can you keep a secret?"

Sarah's eyes widened with excitement. "Ooh. Okay."

"You gotta promise or people could get hurt." She made a finger gun. "Serious hurt."

"'Kay."

"My name isn't really Lisa. It's Maya."

Sarah covered her mouth and gasped.

She cringed, whispering, "Yes. *That* Maya."

"Ooh." Sarah eyed the door before leaning close and muttering in a low voice. "I thought you looked just like that girl on the ads. Oh crap... is the Authority looking for you?"

"I don't think so. Genna and some people kidnapped me, but Vanessa didn't want to pay. She told them to kill me. When Genna saw that, she felt bad for me. She's my mom now."

"Oh..." Sarah grabbed her in a hug. "That's awful!" After a moment, she let go. "I won't tell anyone, uhh, Lisa."

Maya giggled.

Doctor Chang reentered, waving at Sarah as he approached. "Maya, your mother is going to be out for a while. I gave her a nutrient shot, so she won't need to worry about eating today. It will probably be six to ten hours before she wakes up. If she needs any help getting to the bathroom, come find me or my wife in apartment 112. That's one floor down on the sixth."

"Okay," said Maya.

"I've also taken her weapon." He patted his bag. "I don't feel right leaving it lying out and about with you here alone."

Maya shrugged. "I understand. I wouldn't have touched it, but you're right."

"How's that eye of yours, Faerie?" He stooped close to Sarah. "Hmm. Don't see any trace of bruise."

"It's fine now, Doc. Thanks." For a few seconds, her sparkle seemed to fade and she studied her lap.

He nodded and walked out.

"Your father?" asked Maya.

"No. Dad would never..." Sarah glanced at the door, waited a moment, and lowered her voice near a whisper. "There's a man living on the ground floor. Mr. Mason. It was him. He's mean and he lies. Stay away from him. He'll try to hurt you. Even Emily doesn't like him, and she likes everyone."

"Who's Emily?" Maya tilted her head.

Sarah took a deep breath. "Okay. There's only a couple of people in this building. Doc and Zoe are Emily's parents. She's seven. Book lives on the ninth floor with Anton and Marcus, they're both ten... twins. Book's old though, like older than the building. He's not their dad; he took 'em in like Genna and you."

Maya's stomach growled. "Book's a strange name."

"He always tells us stories. They're all in his head, so he's like a book." Sarah held up her hands, counting on her fingers as she spoke. "Arlene and Brian live on the third floor. Arlene's gonna have a baby. Pick, he's six, lives with his big sister also on the third floor. That new guy Weber is on the fifth. Mr. Barnes is across the hall, and me an' my Dad are at the end." She thought for a moment. "Umm. Don't talk about Fade around Anton and Marcus. Both their parents, uhh, died to it."

Maya clenched her fists in her lap. "Okay."

Sarah rubbed her shoulder. "It's not your fault. Hey, did you eat anything?"

"No." She stared at the empty kitchen counter. *There isn't even a Hydra.*

"C'mon." Sarah stood and grabbed Maya's hand. "I'll get you some food. It's kinda random here, but you get used to it. Where us kids eat rotates based on who's got food to spare."

She glanced at the passage to the bedroom where Genna still slept. As uneasy as she felt about being around new people, the woman would be out cold for hours and the apartment contained nothing to eat. Maya got up, followed the other girl out into the hallway, and walked down to the last door before the corridor turned left, near the fire stairs in the corner. Sarah pushed it open and went in.

The layout appeared similar to Genna's apartment, though the patio attached to the living room instead of a bedroom, and the kitchen looked much cleaner. A ginger-haired man in his later thirties, wearing a tank top and shorts, sat on the couch, attention glued to some sports thing on the TV involving armored men colliding with each other. Coppery fuzz covered the exposed parts of his pale legs. Maya stared at him as Sarah pulled her to the side and into the kitchen. Something happened on the screen, a change in the pitch of the crowd roar, and the man raised his right arm—a crude metal prosthetic from shoulder to fist. Far removed from what Moth had, it bore no resemblance to the normal silhouette of a human arm. An inch-thick strut with slender hydraulics on the outside and gears that whirred in the three-fingered grippy claw at the end offered the most basic of function.

Maya gasped and covered her mouth.

"Dad got lucky," said Sarah, as she stood on tiptoe to reach into a cabinet over the counter. "He was in the hospital away from his outpost when an enemy missile strike hit." She slid a plastic plate from the cabinet and walked it to the table. "If he hadn't lost his arm and been sent to the rear, he'd have been killed."

Maya offered an apologetic expression.

Sarah crouched and opened a cabinet under the sink, from which she took a plastic-wrapped white square. A faint crunch came from it when she squeezed, followed by a weak hiss. Maya stared at the too-white material expanding inside like inflating foam. Sarah peeled the wrapper off and set a sandwich on the plate. The eerie scent of fresh-baked bread wafted from it.

A quarter-inch-thick slab of some dark yellow substance sat between the two pieces of 'bread.' She poked it with one finger.

"It's a cheese sandwich." Sarah slid into the chair catty-corner to Maya. "Dad gets boxes of them from the VA once a month."

After a sniff that didn't smell like anything but bread, Maya lifted the sandwich to her mouth, and hesitated. "This is cheese?"

"Useless bastard," yelled The Dad. He lapsed into a coughing fit and threw an empty bottle at the wall. It missed the TV by a few inches and bounced away. "Couldn't gain yards with a fuckin' armed escort." At a buzzer from the TV, he growled and pounded his flesh fist into the seat several times. "Sons ah bitches! Open yer damn eyes!"

Maya shivered.

"He's harmless," whispered Sarah. "He makes a lot of noise, but he won't hurt you... unless you're a piece of furniture or an empty beer."

A test nibble of her sandwich confirmed bland but not awful. Sarah remained quiet while Maya ate, idle save for when the man in the living room yelled again.

"Oi, girl. Grab me another brew, what?"

Sarah stood. "'Kay, Dad."

He grunted. "'Ang on. Belay that. Gotta let the last one out."

Maya glanced to her right as he threw his weight forward in an effort to pull himself out of a well-indented spot on the sofa. The spindly metal arm glinted in a thin stream of sunlight coming in from the sliding glass patio doors. Light coppery hair had gone white above his ears, and the stubble around his cheeks resembled cinnamon sugar. He wobbled for a few seconds, managed to pause the TV, and ambled off after smiling at Sarah.

Something about the man unnerved her. She couldn't peel her stare from the mechanical arm until he'd moved out of sight behind the wall. Maya took another bite of the cheap cheese and forced it down. Sarah lowered herself onto the seat again, still smiling. Drunk plus cybernetic arm seemed like a dangerous mixture. She ate faster, devouring the last half of the sandwich in three huge bites that gave her hamster cheeks.

"Come on." Sarah bounced to her feet. "I'll show you around."

Maya, mouth still full, slid to the edge of her chair and jumped down. Having to deal with other children frightened her less than being around a drunken guy with a metal arm.

Sarah paused a step past the archway connecting kitchen to living room and leaned to her left. "Goin' upstairs, Dad."

The sound of a stream of liquid hitting water got louder as an unseen door opened. "Be careful."

"Will," yelled Sarah.

The red-haired girl went out into the hall and to the fire door at the corner. "We always use the fire stairs 'cause the main stairs stink like a million babies all threw up bad milk at once."

Maya cringed.

She descended one flight to the sixth floor and strolled through an opening missing a door. Junk littered the hallway straight ahead, while to the right it looked abandoned. Thirty or so feet away, the carpet ended at a small rolled-up bit; from there, exposed concrete stretched along below smashed fluorescent bulbs dangling on wires.

"Don't go that way." Sarah pointed right. "It's not safe. This building was damaged during the war... it's why there aren't too many people in it even with cheap rent." She took three steps forward and paused. "Watch your step. I stepped on a screw once here. It hurt."

"Why aren't you wearing shoes?" asked Maya.

Sarah smiled. "Why aren't you?"

"I was kidnapped out of my bed in the middle of the night." Maya blinked. "But all I have are heels."

"Heels?" asked Sarah. "Everyone has heels."

"High-heeled shoes."

"Huh?" asked Sarah.

Maya explained.

"Oh. Those sound annoying." Sarah's continuous smile weakened briefly. "Sorry. Umm. Well. His VA pension doesn't pay much. After rent, his money goes to food and beer. I can get by without shoes, but he can't get by without his beer."

Maya thought back to a dozen pairs of fancy high-heeled shoes on her closet floor. She blinked. "You can't afford shoes? They can't cost that much."

"'Bout eight NuCoin... or fifty cans of beer. Rent's like sixty-five."

The girls stepped among old pipes, machine parts, wires, and boxes of circuit boards and unidentifiable metal scraps.

"They might get stolen too."

"Really? By other kids?" Maya hopped over a minefield of nuts, bolts, and screws.

Sarah shook her head and came to a halt at a door. "No, their parents. Or some doser who wants money for drugs, or someone who just wants to be mean. I was out with Anton and Marcus a couple of weeks ago scavving, and we got robbed. I used to have green camo army pants with all sorts of pockets, but they took everything we found and all of our clothes too."

"Why would they steal clothes?" Maya gasped. "You didn't run?"

"They had guns, and they'll take everything they can to sell. Bet they got at least six NuCoin for my pants. That's enough to get a couple hits of Fume." Sarah pulled at the fabric of the pitiful garment wrapped around her. "Only a real desperate doser would take this. I made it out of an old curtain I found on the tenth floor. You should be safe too." She regarded Maya's nightie. "They won't steal that rag."

Before Maya could decide if she wanted to be terrified or offended her $400 designer nightdress had been dubbed a rag, the door opened. A girl about her size with shoulder-length black hair, green eyes, and pale skin waved at Sarah. Her bone-colored dress looked like something out of a previous century, frilly and with a giant bow tied at the small of her back. She too lacked shoes, though was far cleaner than Sarah and still smelled faintly of soap. The child had an exotic look Maya couldn't quite place until a Caucasian woman with brown hair in a pixie cut came up behind her.

"Hi, Sarah. Who's this?" asked the woman.

"Lisa. She's new. Genna's taken her in." Sarah looked at Maya. "This is Mrs. Chang and Emily."

Emily flashed a huge smile and blurred her right arm back and forth in a wave. "Hi."

"Sarah, please call me Zoe." The woman smiled. "Mrs. Chang makes me feel old."

Maya lifted her right hand and offered a weak excuse for a wave. "Hi."

Beyond them, the apartment appeared to be a combination workshop/clinic. Their living room held several large folding tables littered with tools and parts on one side. Farther from the kitchen sat a wheeled hospital-style bed and several metal carts with trays as well as a medical computer. All of the equipment looked old and well used.

"Zoe fixes stuff," said Sarah. "Mostly the building."

Why's she stuck out here if she's a tech? Maya nodded.

"Can I play?" asked Emily.

Zoe squeezed her daughter's shoulder. "Okay. I don't want you going out of the building, understand?"

Emily nodded.

"Are you sure you don't want to change first? That dress is—"

"No." Emily pranced into the hall.

Zoe gave Sarah a meaningful look. "Okay, you girls be careful."

"We will," chimed Sarah and Emily at once.

As soon as the door closed, Emily looked at Maya. "You don't talk much."

"You talk a lot," said Maya.

Sarah laughed and headed for the fire stairs.

Emily rambled on and on as they walked, explaining how faeries lived in the walls and they talked to her. According to Emily, if the faeries liked you, they'd bring good dreams and ask the rats not to crawl on you at night. "Sarah's not a faerie, but they're not mad at her 'cause people call her that."

"Em's the only one who calls me Sarah." The older girl picked Emily up to carry her past the minefield of sharp things.

"Well you're *not* a faerie." Emily folded her arms. "They told me."

Maya regarded the girl with confusion. Sarah noticed the expression and gave her a 'what?' look. Maya pointed at Emily and twirled a finger at her head. Sarah giggled. She set Emily down at the entrance to the stairs, and the little one zoomed up.

As the pat of her feet on the concrete steps faded, Sarah leaned over with a conspiratorial whisper. "She's seven. She makes stuff up. Kids do that."

Maya squinted with suspicion. "Why?"

Sarah seemed sad, a strange reaction as far as Maya was concerned. "Oh, damn. No wonder you aren't trying to go home."

"What's that supposed to mean?" asked Maya.

"You've never made up imaginary friends or pretended anything?"

"No." Maya thought of the little white dog. It didn't make much sense how ephemeral the memory of him was. Could she have imagined him? "I don't think so. How does it work and what's the point?"

"You coming?" yelled Emily from overhead.

Sarah exhaled through fluttering lips. "We have a lot of work to do." She took Maya by the hand and led her upstairs. "Sounds like you need to learn how to have fun."

"I used to play video games."

"That's cool. I had a system, but it broke. Zoe's trying to fix it, but she needs some part she doesn't have." Sarah sighed. "I never played it much so I don't miss it."

Maya shrugged.

Emily waited for them at the landing on the ninth floor, toes hooked over the top step, dress flaring as she spun side to side in an exaggerated display of impatience. They exited the stairwell and walked into a mass of damp air laced with the smell of outside and mold that brought a hand to Maya's mouth. The carpet squished underfoot, cold and clammy. She went stiff at the sensation like walking over used tissues. Emily held her arm up as if to let a songbird land, though nothing did, and she spoke to thin air about an upcoming party.

"There's a big hole in the wall," said Sarah. "Zoe said if it happened two floors down, the building might've fallen over sideways. Since it's only a ten story, it's okay."

Sarah turned right at the corner, her gait natural as though the ground wasn't nasty. Emily moved like a rabbit, jumping in short hops and reveling in the *squish* her feet made on impact. Maya crept after them, disgusted at the clammy, slimy carpet. A little less than halfway down the length of the corridor, the walls ceased existing. Perhaps a third of the floor had been reduced to a single wide-open space interspersed with metal support beams, exposed pipes, and a handful of broken toilets and sinks where apartments had once been. Numerous piles of plaster rubble gathered at regular intervals along the interior wall like swept-up leaves. A stretch of sixty or seventy feet on the right yawned out into the wide open air, except where three thick pipes stood welded in place as emergency supports. About at the middle of the huge open room sat a shallow but wide metal bowl, blackened by fire.

Maya's brain replayed her upside down view while tethered to a bed, of Headcrash teetering over and falling off a similar ledge. She clamped onto Sarah without thinking.

Emily let off a shout of "Hiiiii" as she ran ahead, leaving wet footprints on dusty concrete.

Three boys lay flopped in a clear spot among the rubble, surrounded by at least a hundred small plastic figures and toy vehicles. Two appeared to be twins, short curled hair and skin as dark as Genna's. Both wore plain white tee shirts a few sizes too big for their bone-thin frames. One had black shorts that looked close to new, while his brother's beige pants ended in shreds at the knee.

The third boy seemed the youngest of all, five or six perhaps. A spherical explosion of dark brown hair hid his eyes from view. Shirtless, he lay on his belly in a pair of green camo shorts, using one hand to stick some of the figures into a plastic tank. His right index finger sank two knuckles deep in his nose.

At Emily's approach, they all looked up. She flopped on the floor, tucked her feet under herself, and selected a toy that looked like a space ship. The smallest boy went back to what he'd been doing, while the two older ones spotted Maya and watched her with curiosity.

"This isn't safe," said Maya. "It's open. We could fall."

Sarah kept holding her hand and walked her closer to the others. "We're not allowed to get too close to the edge, so don't."

The twins stood. Both were taller than Maya, but not quite as tall as Sarah.

"That's Marcus and Anton." Sarah looked at them. "This is... Lisa." She gestured at the caramel-skinned boy. "That's Pick."

"Guess it's obvious why you call him that." Maya forced herself to look at the twins. "Hello."

"Hi," said one.

"Allo," said the other.

Both of them seemed fascinated by her, their stares a little too intense for comfort. She started to bow her head but got angry with herself and gave them a stern look.

"What?" asked Maya.

They smiled at the same time.

"I seen you before," said the one on the left.

"Doubt it." Maya glanced over the plastic people. "I've only been here a day. What are these?"

"Dolls," said Emily.

"Action figures," said Pick, a touch of irritation in his voice.

"What are they for?" Maya squatted and picked up one that resembled a man covered entirely with brown hair holding a crossbow.

"For playing," said Emily. She made the toy space ship fly around, adding sound effects with her mouth. "Sometimes the faeries play when we're all asleep. That's why they move."

"It's wind," said Pick.

Emily stuck her tongue out at him, not that he noticed.

"We find stuff," said one of the older boys. "When we go hunting."

Maya turned the tiny ape-man over in her fingers, unable to imagine how a lump of plastic could be entertaining. All it did was sit there. Sarah knelt nearby and pointed out names for some of them. After a few minutes, Maya dropped the one she had and picked up a golden man, though the metallic shine had scuffed off in numerous places to a pale tan.

"That's Pee Three Cee Oh," said Pick.

"You named them?" Maya blinked.

"No." Sarah bumped her with an elbow. "They're from the stories."

The boy with the new shorts turned out to be Marcus, though he and his brother Anton took their time keeping her guessing who was who. Maya lost the ability to make eye contact with them for a while, wondering if they'd known Sam, Genna's son. While they appeared in good spirits, the few times she'd gotten a good look at their faces, a mark of deep sorrow showed clear.

She abandoned the gold man to investigate another, larger, figure that seemed to be half airplane and half robot man. According to Sarah, it worked like a puzzle. She manipulated its parts, not focused on making either a jet or a man, too distracted by guilt. Hearing people in fancy suits talk about acceptable losses in order to remain profitable hadn't carried a tenth of the weight of seeing the faces of those expendable 'scruffy poor people' who'd been affected by the expense of Xenodril. The more she thought about what Sam and the two boys four feet away from her had gone through, the worse she felt. The one time she'd dared suggesting to Vanessa that she should make Xenodril cheaper, she'd gotten a look as dire as though she'd tried to kill the woman. Had that been the moment Vanessa decided her worthless?

Sarah wiped a tear from Maya's cheek, startling her. "What's wrong?"

Not wanting to say anything about where she'd come from or who she was or bring up Xenodril in front of the boys, Maya rolled a few lame ideas around in her head before settling on one. "I'm worried about Genna."

"She'll be okay." Sarah patted her on the back.

"Dad said she got beat up." Emily didn't look up from the two action figures she'd been making swordfight. "He said she's gonna get better."

For an hour and change, Maya watched the others play with the toys, unsure what to do with herself. An occasional raised voice from outside made her look at the massive hole, though in the full light of day, the non-Citizen city area didn't seem quite so bad. Primitive, but not as awful as the AuthNet archives made it sound. Her mood improved a bit—until a few distant gunshots preceded a howl of pain.

The children got quiet for about two minutes before they resumed playing as though nothing had happened. Maya squinted into the humid breeze sweeping in from the gap. Her head filled with images of Icarus and Head falling. She trembled, gripped by fear. An odd realization dawned, something she'd never considered before: she had a mother she could run to for comfort. She started to stand, but remembered Genna lay in bed, out cold and unable to offer the solace she craved.

Loud whirring from the breach in the wall stalled the breath in her throat. A pack of four-fanned Authority drones streaked by the opening, banking left and diving out of sight.

Maya ducked her head, hiding her face behind a wall of hair. She shivered, terrified at the thought of being located and 'rescued.' The others didn't react if they noticed her sudden terror. Sarah got into speaking lines from one of the stories with the twins, and they re-enacted some scene where little hamster men captured Pee Three Cee Oh. Pick got upset when Emily involved one of the robot-puzzle men and yelled that they weren't from the same story. That error finally got him to look up enough for Maya to see his eyes for the first time, and missing front bottom teeth. The more his finger migrated from nostril to toy and back again, the less interested Maya got in touching any of them.

"Ruben, *¡Almuerzo! Ven a casa ahora.*" A female voice echoed off the walls outside.

Pick sprang to his feet and ran close enough to the edge that Maya gasped. He cupped his hands around his mouth and yelled, "*¿Puedo traer mis amigos?*"

"*Si.*"

"Ooh." Anton scrambled upright, dropping the toys as if they'd become poisonous. "Pick's sister cooks great food."

Marcus and Emily made noises of agreement and hurried upright. Sarah stood but didn't follow the others who ran off. Maya looked up at her.

"Hey." Sarah spoke in a low voice. "I should probably tell you…"

"What?"

"Stay away from Mr. Mason downstairs. He's dangerous. Emily doesn't even like him, and she likes *everyone*."

"You said that already." Maya took note of a trace of blush on the older girl's pale cheeks, which hadn't even happened when the girl described having all her clothes stolen.

"He's not home now." Sarah headed for the hallway. "He goes to the Sanc in the day 'cause he's got a job, even though he's the super. If Genna sends you to bring him the rent payment, don't do it alone."

"Why?" asked Maya.

Sarah's cheeks tinted redder, and she turned away. "Just don't."

They made their way back over the slimy carpet to the stairs and to the third floor. Pick's sister Naida looked old enough to be his mother… if she had him at seventeen. She met them at the door, barefoot and in a pink babydoll sleeper that didn't leave much of her slender figure to the imagination. Frayed denim shorts threatened to slip to the ground with each step she took back inside. This place also had one bedroom, hot pink at the end of the hallway leading off from the living room.

Naida escorted the kids to their places around the kitchen table and seemed happy to host them all for lunch. She chatted on and off while upending a metal can and squeezing yellow foam into a pot. Though it didn't much resemble eggs at first, once it started to cook, it looked and smelled close enough. Based on how fast it went to plates, Maya assumed the 'cooking' part served mostly to make them warm, as well as to add whatever seasonings the woman threw in a pinch at a time.

Maya smiled up at the young twenty-something as she set a plate of eggs and sausage down in front of her. "Thank you. It's generous of you to feed everyone."

"Naida makes a lot of money," said Marcus.

Pick punched him in the arm.

Marcus rubbed the spot, looking confused. "What? She does."

The woman looked embarrassed for a few seconds but brushed it off. She gave Maya's shoulder a light squeeze. "Go on and eat. You're too skinny."

Naida prepared lunch for everyone before sitting down with a plate for herself. Despite the eggs coming out of a can, they had more flavor than Maya expected. Pick seemed blasé to the meal, though the twins and Sarah attacked their food as if they hadn't seen any in weeks. Naida smiled at everyone and fussed with Pick's hair while she ate with the other hand. The first two times she reached for him, he ducked, but he tolerated her attention after that—though he refused to make eye contact with any of the other kids. The twins didn't react to his being mothered, Sarah smiled at the display of affection, and Emily covered her mouth to suppress laughing at the faces Pick made.

Maya lost a few seconds feeling jealous. A tiny inkling of desire to do something nasty to Pick to pay him back for having such a loving family reared up and died. *I'm not Vanessa.* Sarah reached over and held her hand under the table, offering a warm smile.

A knock at the front door silenced the table.

Naida looked up with a mixture of annoyance and resignation. At a second knock, she excused herself and went to the door.

Maya leaned back in her chair, peering at a man standing out in the hall. They muttered a few words too low to hear before she muttered about a short wait and let him in. The face visible under the shrouded hood of his grey jacket/coat looked old enough to be Naida's father. He offered a pleasant wave at the kitchen full of children and flopped on the couch in the living room. She flipped on the TV for him, then hurried back to the kitchen with her head down. Once everyone finished eating, Naida ushered the kids to the exit, apologizing, saying she had to clean up the apartment for someone important who was coming. She told Pick she loved him and made him promise to be careful. When she closed the door, he got a look on his face as though he wanted to get into a fight.

Maya stared at the floor.

Anton, seeming oblivious to Naida's profession, clapped once. "Hey, let's show Lisa the basement."

"I'll be there in a little bit. Gotta make sure Dad eats," said Sarah with an apologetic look to Maya. She lingered a few seconds more, and hurried off.

The idea resonated among the group, and soon Maya found herself pulled along by Emily on one arm and Anton on the other. They had to use the main stairwell to get to the basement since the fire stairs stopped at the ground floor. Maya held her breath on the way down so her food didn't come back up. Sarah had described it well: the entire stairwell reeked of spoiled milk. Waist-high trash collected in the landing at the bottom, mostly empty cardboard boxes, plastic cartons, and soda cans. Marcus waded up to the dark-blue door first and shoved it to the side.

A room full of dusty junk, dangling wires, and eerie shapes covered in plastic sheeting made Maya lean back on her heels. The air here carried a dry smell tinged with something chemical, like a lesser cousin of rotten eggs. It didn't seem like a great place to go. The other kids showed no fear of the creepy, abandoned basement and plowed right in. She hesitated in the doorway, battling between venturing into the darkness ahead or being alone in the 'poor' area. The worry of how many street drugs a designer nightdress would trade for got her moving. Granted, someone who stole the shirts off the backs of children for drug money would likely not recognize a Dori Kavan nightgown.

Maya navigated a windy corridor formed of old washing machines, kitchen ranges, and other giant boxy cabinets that might've been refrigerators. Chairs, ceiling fans, and an assortment of smaller appliances had been stacked on top of them. Her feet turned grey from all the silt on the floor, though at least dry beat slimy.

Beeping and digital explosions came from ahead.

She emerged from the junk maze into an area covered in dark red and brown carpet. From the look of it, someone had used long rugs intended for the building's halls to create a lounge. An enclosed area covered in several uneven layers of rug sat inside square walls of still-rolled carpet. Five ancient arcade games lined the left wall, one of which had Emily's attention. Anton and Marcus occupied themselves with a physical game where they used plastic paddles to knock a flat disc around a white surface. On the far right, a huge table with a green interior held a number of balls as well as two long, tapered sticks. Feeling like she'd invaded someone else's sanctuary, Maya stood at the entrance watching them play for some time without taking a step farther in.

"You can go in." Sarah startled her by coming out of nowhere at her left.

"Zoe set this room up for us. She got all the games working. It's nice, except when the heating machines come on and it gets loud... but it's summer now so they won't."

"Oh." Maya looked from the twins to Pick, flopped on his chest inside the square on a pile of pillows, reading a thin book full of colorful pictures. Two massive cardboard boxes next to him had tons more. The corner of the carpet roll wall at his right held a bunch more plastic people, only these were about three times the height of the ones upstairs and most looked like the same too-skinny blonde woman in various outfits. Three resembled false babies, though nowhere near as realistic as the one in Lynn's backpack. "Wow."

"There's video games there, but I'm already kinda bored with all of them. The driving one's the only one I still try, but it's hard." Sarah pointed at the twins. "Air hockey, and a pool table over there. Comic books there, but Pick will give you a hard time if you don't wash your hands before touching them."

Pick made a raspberry noise.

"There's dolls too if you wanna play with them." Sarah indicated the pile.

Maya stared at them. "I don't understand why people play with dolls."

"They're fun to put different clothes on and make their hair." Sarah pulled her over to them.

Kinda like me. Standing on a platform while a throng of attendants dressed and redressed her, did makeup, and got her hair perfect for an ad shoot sure felt like *being* the doll. She flopped on the mound of spare couch cushions and watched Sarah demonstrate 'playing with dolls.' It didn't pique much interest, though this whole having friends thing had gone from scary to might-be-fun. Maya tolerated the pointless plastic people to humor Sarah's good mood.

The rest of the afternoon went by in a blur. A few hours got sacrificed to video games, she tried playing pool but wound up either miscuing or hitting too weak to sink anything. Frustration got the better of her and she stormed away from the table. She did better at air hockey, though Anton still won three in a row. A bit of Vanessa came out and she refused to accept total defeat. Maya kept going for five more games, eventually winning by one point.

Hours after they arrived in the basement, Pick led a migration out and they spent a while exploring the second floor where every apartment was abandoned. One, which had frightening marks on the walls the twins claimed to be blood, triggered nine different versions of 'what happened' stories, everything from an accident, argument, dosers fighting, and monsters. Emily told everyone how she had talked to the faeries about the dead man's ghost, and assured the others he wouldn't bother them. When Emily said the faeries wouldn't talk about how he died, Maya figured the girl had no real answers and made it up to help the others feel better, then felt stupid for almost believing the girl had talked to faeries. They spent several hours climbing through cabinets and holes in walls, before the twins wanted to go outside.

Pick shook his head. "Nai said she heard people gonna fight when it got dark. I tol' her promise I wouldn't go out." He reached across his chest to scratch his shoulder. "Not safe for kids outside now."

"I'm not allowed out today either," said Emily.

Anton's disappointment faded in seconds. "Book's gonna feed us tonight. It's probably time to go up anyway."

"Is it ever?" asked Maya while they trudged up the stairs. "Safe, I mean."

"Not really," said Sarah. "You should never go outside alone. We always go together. Most people won't bother kids, but there's bad ones too."

Maya looked down, making a game of not stepping on stains. "What's scavving?"

"We find stuff," said Anton. "Sometimes we keep it. Sometimes we can sell it to Foz."

"He owns the Emperor," said Emily.

"Emporium." Marcus gestured at the wall. "It's a store outside, 'bout two blocks down past the big blue car."

"Like stealing?" asked Maya.

"Nope. It ain't stealin' if it's just sittin' there." Marcus grabbed an aluminum can from the ninth floor landing and dropped it down the narrow space in the center of the stairwell, sending it rattling and clanking to the ground floor.

"Sometimes Sarah steals a door." Emily giggled.

"How do you steal a door?" Maya looked up at the redhead.

"She means I unlock it." Sarah stuck her tongue out at Emily. "It's not stealing if no one lives there."

They returned to the ninth floor, the large chamber with the missing wall. It had gotten dark out, though few stars managed to appear behind the smog. Intermittent *pops* echoed off the buildings, gunshots so far away they sounded fake. Maya hurried over to the sprawl of toys and sat on the floor, eager to get low in case of a stray bullet.

The others gathered in a cluster too close to the edge for comfort and reclined while gazing up at the sky. Maya kept her distance for a short while until the feeling of being an outsider grew too awkward. She crawled over and took a spot at Sarah's left. Emily stared out a spot at the corner of the building where the destruction wrapped around and offered an open view to the north. In the early evening, the distant whitish glow of the New Baltimore Sanctuary Zone shone as obvious as the sun.

"She thinks her parents will move there some day," said Marcus.

Pick laughed. "What'd the faeries tell you?"

"It's pretty." Emily crept closer, her toes less than her height away from the end of the slab.

"Em, get away from the edge." Sarah waited five seconds. "I mean it. *Now*."

"Aww." The youngest girl backed up. "I wanna go there."

Maya looked at the floor in front of her knees and traced a random squiggle in the damp grime with her finger. "You don't. It's not nice there."

The other kids, except Sarah, perked up with sudden interest. Soon they all crowded around her.

"What?" asked Emily, looking heartbroken.

Marcus raised an eyebrow. "How you know?"

"What he said." Anton pointed at his brother.

Pick jammed his finger up his nose.

Maya took a breath and sighed it out. "Everyone there is sad all the time. I used to live there. Whenever I looked outside, all the people were always in a hurry, always in a bad mood. There's Authority everywhere, watching everyone. People never look up because they're so many drones."

Emily glared. "But it's so pretty!"

"It's a lie." Maya lifted her gaze from the floor and glanced at Emily. "It's like being locked up. Even when I was home, if I was too close to a window when a drone went by, it would think I was breaking in. If I didn't stand totally still and let it scan me, it would kill me."

"Whoa." Anton's eyes widened. "You're a Citizen?"

"She don' look like no Citizen," said Pick, finger still digging.

Maya shook her head. "Not anymore. It cost too much money to have a kid, so I got thrown out."

"Faerie's mom 'bandoned her too," said Pick.

"She did not!" yelled Sarah. "She... disappeared. Someone hurt her."

"So your parents didn't want you 'cause of money?" asked Marcus. "That's fucked up."

Emily gasped and pointed at him. "Ooo. He said the eff! You made the faeries cry!"

Marcus recited a litany of bad words at random until Emily stopped cringing and burst into tears. He frowned. "Come on, Em, it's just words. Don't cry."

"Mommy says only bad people talk like that." Emily sniffled. "An' if you talk bad, the bad faeries will crawl into your head. They'll steal your dreams and turn you bad like them."

A whiny, laboring mechanical noise echoed up from outside. Sarah's smile faded and she stiffened. Maya glanced from her to the gap. The noise cut out, followed soon by a car door slamming. Sarah pulled some of her hair away from her face and tucked it behind one ear. Her smile radiated falseness until the building's front door clanked shut, reverberating off the faces of buildings across the street.

Maya took Sarah's hand. The older girl averted her rich blue eyes downward.

Scuffing noises came from the right far too soon to have been the person who'd just driven up. Maya looked over and up at an old man with long pewter grey hair streaked with traces of black in spots. He walked on sandals made from chunks of car tire, carried a large plastic bag in one hand and a round, black cauldron in the other. Most of his body hid beneath a grey wool wrap and several long wood-bead necklaces. His dark pants, patched and re-patched, looked as old as their owner.

"Book!" yelled Emily, her mood back to over-happy in an instant.

Anton and Marcus seemed to shed their detachment and took on the normal energy of ten-year-old children. Sarah smiled at him as well.

Book ambled over to a spot closer to the inside wall where a concrete slab had fallen over a small pile of chunks into the general shape of a table. Someone had positioned a few metal folding chairs around another blackened bowl. He set the cauldron and bag on the makeshift table. The boys plus Emily scrambled over like a pack of dogs at feeding time.

Sarah's smile regained its authenticity and she tugged Maya upright. "Dinner time. And he's gonna tell us a story."

The cauldron contained brown goo that smelled strange but not unpleasant. Over the course of the next fifteen minutes, Maya learned about tacos and struggled not wear more of it than what she ate. Both twins looked at the old man in a way that made it evident he'd assumed the role of caretaker. She avoided giving Book a clean view of her face, fearing he'd recognize her.

Once the old man finished his portion, he cleared his throat. Maya peered up through her hair at him, her eyes widening at the presence of metal bits grafted to his head and the back of his neck. One stripe of dark steel followed the curve above his left ear, flickering with a row of cobalt blue LEDs. The outward image of the kindly old person gave way to the worry that a Moth-like monster would tear the wrinkled brown skin away and strangle them all with metal hands.

Book coughed, swallowed, and cleared his throat again. "You're here just in time." He smiled at Maya. "Tonight we're starting a new story. *Harry Potter*."

Emily and Pick cheered and clapped.

Maya's eyebrows crept together. "Never heard of it."

Sarah looked at her as if she'd announced she'd arrived from outer space.

"Well, sit back and listen." Book settled in to a cushioned chair facing the others, and began to speak in a well-practiced cadence, suggesting he read the words from a page.

All the tiny lights around his ear and neck winked on and off in a continuous, mesmerizing pattern. Maya's worry faded as the soothing tone of his voice drew her in to the story. Occasional bursts of wind from the missing wall blew warmth over the room with a hint of evening chill. Her eyes snapped open wide when a woman's voice came out of the old man to speak a line of dialogue. It took her a second to think of electronics in his throat being responsible, but soon, the oddity of it wore off. Maya closed her eyes and imagined the characters, helped along by each having a unique voice. Book must have been doing this for a long time, as she had no trouble believing different people surrounded her.

For the better part of an hour and a half, Book managed to keep all six kids silent and enthralled.

"Daddy," yelled Emily.

Maya frowned at being torn away from the story world, and looked up at Doctor Chang peering around the corridor at the far end of the open space. Emily sprinted over to him and leapt into his arms.

"Looks like it's time for bed," said Book. "We'll keep on tomorrow."

Pick and the twins whined the sort of whine that protested without having much hope of changing anyone's mind. Book shooed the twins off to bed and set about gathering the remains of dinner. Doc waved Pick over as well.

Sarah grabbed Maya's hand. "We should probably go home too."

Maya jumped up, hopeful Genna might be awake. They walked down to the seventh floor, and Sarah followed her inside.

"Mom?" asked Maya.

"There you are," said a still-sleepy-sounding Genna from the bathroom.

Sarah seemed satisfied all was well, waved, and walked out. Maya trailed after her far enough to close the apartment door. She turned the deadbolt and hurried into the back hallway. Genna emerged from the bathroom in a t-shirt and panties, scratching at her right arm through all the gaps in the spider web plastic cast.

Every ounce of fear, awkwardness, and unease that had plagued Maya during the day faded away as she clamped on to Genna's side. She sniffled and cried a little, but smiled the whole time.

"What happened, baby?"

Maya grinned up at her. "I'm glad you kidnapped me."

Genna shook her head. "This world gets stranger every damn day. Did you eat anything?"

"Yes." Maya nodded. "Sarah gave me a sandwich for breakfast, Pick's sister fed us lunch, an' Book made us tacos."

"Good. Sorry I been elsewhere." Genna stumbled to the bedroom, keeping one hand on the wall to steady herself. "Doc gave me another shot. Pain's still... yeah. Damn walls are movin' on me."

Maya held her hand and climbed up next to her once Genna sat on the edge of the bed. "Your eye looks better. It's getting smaller."

"Should be okay in a couple of days." Genna picked at the nightdress and yawned. "We need to get you somethin' more than that to wear. Ain't payin' these vultures out here. They charge way too damn much for everything. Say onna count a bein' a 'long ride' ta the Sanc. Be 'while 'fore I can head to the city."

"Okay."

Genna leaned back and swung her legs onto the mattress. Maya scrambled around, pulling the sheet up and over them both. "Goodnight, Mom."

"Night baby." Genna already sounded half-asleep.

SIXTEEN
ZOE THE SUPER

Maya awoke in the middle of the night, ran to use the bathroom, and crawled back in under Genna's arm. In what felt like an instant, a loud *bang* knocked her awake again. Weak daylight shone in the sliding glass patio doors, though the interior of the apartment remained dark as night. She reached up under the blanket until her hand found Genna's side, and she pushed and squeezed until the woman stirred.

"What was that?"

Genna moaned and wiped at her eyes. "What was what?"

"I heard something explode."

The stink of scorched silicon wafted into the room.

"Oh. Probably the damn fuse panel again." Genna clenched her teeth and stifled a scream. "Oh, damn."

"Mom?" Maya sat up.

"I'm... pain meds wore off."

She hopped out of bed. "I'll get Doctor Chang."

Genna, eyes closed, nodded and flapped her left arm in a rapid wave as if to say hurry the hell up.

"Okay." Maya sprinted to the front door and out into the hall. She opted for the fire stairs—dusty beat spoiled milk—and raced down one floor and over to the door with 112 on it, knocking with both fists. "Doctor Chang?"

A minute or two later, the door opened to reveal Doctor Chang in the full glory of rumpled white boxers and a pale blue lab coat. He didn't seem all the way awake yet.

"Sorry." Maya looked up with urgency brimming out of her eyes. "Mom's in a lot of pain. She said the meds wore off."

He wiped a hand down his face. "Okay, okay. Come in for a minute."

She ducked in when he leaned the door wider. After closing it behind her, he trudged over to the kitchen area and assaulted a small appliance on the counter. Emily streaked from the second bedroom to the bathroom, yelling, "I want the dress!"

Zoe followed wearing a look of resignation as well as blue fatigue-style pants and a black tank top. She skidded to a halt at the notice of Maya, a tiny denim skirt in her hand. "Oh, hi. Is something wrong?"

Maya flashed a brief, polite smile. "Mom's hurt."

"I'm going, I'm going," Said Dr. Chang.

Burbling noises came from the kitchen, followed soon by the scent of coffee.

Emily emerged from the bathroom, spotted Maya, and started walking over, still with nothing on. "Hi!"

"Em, clothes, now." Zoe pointed at the second bedroom with a no-nonsense face.

The girl hung her head and trudged under her mother's arm into her room.

Maya wandered about the living-room-slash-work-studio, peering at the tables a little below her chin level. One had pliers, wire cutters of various sizes, hammers, screwdrivers, soldering tools, and bunch of fancy-looking boxes with wires and needle-meters on them. The next table held a number of partially disassembled electronic devices and a scattering of fuses.

Doctor Chang appeared in the archway between the kitchen and living room with a steaming cup in hand. He sipped and smiled.

Maya huffed. "She's in pain. Please hurry. Coffee can wait."

"I'd rather not give her the wrong dosage." He sipped more. "This is critical." He carried the cup with him to the larger bedroom. "I'll only be a minute."

Zoe glided over to Maya. "Have you had any breakfast yet?"

"No."

Emily zoomed out of her room, once more in the frilly dress. Zoe ushered the girls to the kitchen and filled two bowls with cereal. After setting them on the table, she took a squarish carton from a cabinet and poured soymilk into the bowls. Maya poked at the multicolored puff balls smelling vaguely of fruit. Emily dug right in, eating with surprising care given her age.

"You look like you've never had cereal before," said Zoe.

Maya swung her feet idly. "That's because I haven't." She considered the substance for a few seconds before trying a spoonful. She'd definitely tasted worse things. "It's okay. Thank you for the food."

"Wow, you sure are a polite little thing." Zoe patted her on the head before pouring herself some coffee. "I'm guessing you didn't pick that up out here."

"Mmm." Three spoonfuls later, she looked up. "Can you fix fuses?"

"Unless it exploded, yeah, not a problem."

"It might have." Maya munched a little more. "It went boom, real loud, and all the lights are out. And it stank."

"Hmm. I'll check it out once I'm done fixing something downstairs. Brian's been on my case about that heater unit."

Doctor Chang returned to the kitchen having changed into the same outfit she'd seen him in yesterday, staying only long enough to leave the empty cup on the counter before he hurried out with his bag. Zoe had a bowl of cereal as well, then wandered off into the back for a few minutes. When she returned, she'd donned boots, a tool belt, and carried a large over-the-shoulder canvas bag.

"All right you two, come on." Zoe put the empty bowls in the sink and started for the door.

Maya hesitated.

"We can't stay here 'lone." Emily grabbed Maya's wrist in two hands and pulled. "Too much stuff can hurt us. An' Sarah an' everyone won't be 'wake yet."

Zoe seemed to share Maya's opinion on stink and took the fire stairs down to the third floor. Every minute or so, Emily would stop and squat near the wall and whisper some variation of good morning before hurrying to catch up. The red-painted door required two hip bumps from Zoe to break free of the frame and let off an ear-piercing squeak when it gave way. Dingy green carpet filled the hallway with the fragrance of wet dog, and three plastic buckets caught drips falling from rot holes in the drop ceiling. The third floor looked as though someone had attempted to turn it into a level from a first-person shooter game.

They walked down the hall to the elevator lobby where upturned tables riddled with bullet holes suggested a shootout occurred over a distance of about twelve feet. Plaster bits and broken glass glittered around the elevator doors. Zoe kept going into the hall on the other side and stopped at the fifth apartment on the right.

Maya jumped when Zoe banged on the door. "Brian? Arlene? It's Zoe."

A few seconds later, faint thumps approached from inside. "About damn time."

The door flung inward. A thin, youngish guy with short, blond hair and hazel eyes grinned at her, making his grumble seem more like a joke than a serious gripe. Numerous stains adorned his plain tee, and self-adhesive bandages wrapped three of his toes. "Hey. 'Mon in."

The air hung thick and stale, warm enough to cause sweat within seconds, even with only a thin nightdress on. While Zoe followed him to the far corner of the living room on the right, Emily beelined for the couch where a heavily pregnant twentyish woman sat with her legs covered by a huge ratty blanket. A bright orange shirt sat scrunched up under her breasts, exposing her rounded belly. Maya felt another twinge of jealousy at the woman's somewhat darker skin and frizzy hair.

Emily leapt onto the next cushion and had both hands on Arlene's belly before the woman had opened her eyes. "Hi, little baby." She leaned her left ear against the swollen womb. "The faeries told me you're going to be a boy."

Arlene smiled, running a hand over Emily's hair while waving at Zoe with her other hand. "Did they now?"

Zoe dropped her bag on the rug near a boxy component set into the wall, knelt, and took out a few tools. "How are things going?"

"I can't wait to fit into my clothes again." Arlene laughed. "You gotta send yo' hubby down here an' check my shit out. Shoulda popped by now." She sent a loving look up at Brian. "Your son's just like you. Don't wanna get outta bed in the morning."

Metal clattered from the heating unit. Within minutes, Zoe wound up elbow deep in hoses and dirt.

Emily seemed more excited about the prospect of a new baby in the building than even Arlene did, and her random chattering held the adults' attention. Maya remained near the middle of the room, tapping her toes into the rug while watching Zoe work, content to be left out of the conversation.

"Hey, hon," said Arlene once she finally noticed her. "You be new here?"

"Yes," said Maya.

"Now y'alls in trouble." Arlene winked and nodded at Brian. "Three sistahs in the house."

Brian chuckled. "That girl isn't black, she's like, uhh, Dominican or something. Maybe a little Japanese in her."

Maya broke her stare from Zoe to squint up at him.

"Oh, shit." Arlene chuckled. "You shouldn't have said that. She's looks pissed."

He winced. "Sorry kid, just tryin' to be funny."

"Keep trying," mumbled Maya.

"Ooh," said Arlene. "I like this one. What's yo' name, girl?"

"Lisa," said Maya. "Genna's my mom."

"See." Arlene gestured at him.

"I thought her kid, uhh…" Brian scratched at the back of his head.

"Sam is dead." Maya looked down. "Genna took me in."

A loud *buzz* from the corner made everyone jump. Smoke puffed up past Zoe's face. Coughing, she waved to disperse it. "Found the short."

"Wow." Brian leaned closer. "She looks like that Ascendant kid… the one on all the ads. Genna's gonna have her hands full in a couple years, keepin' the boys off you." He chuckled. "Bet she goes through a lot of ammo when you're sixteen or so."

Maya's heart almost stopped. "I… get that a lot. Guess it's the shape of my face."

"Damn, girl." Arlene attempted to lean forward, but gave up with a fatigued sigh. "He right. You do."

"I wish." Maya glanced sideways, trying to make Zoe work faster by sheer force of will. "If I was her, I'd have all sorts of nice clothes and money, and food."

"I'll bet." Arlene clucked her tongue. "My sorry ass can't even 'ford no maternity dress. That little woman can prob'ly buy this whole building."

Maya shrugged. "It's not so bad. All that money doesn't mean she's happy. Maybe she lives alone in some penthouse and doesn't have any friends because Ascendant is worried someone might try to kidnap her, so they never let anyone near her and keep her locked up."

Everyone got quiet… even Emily.

Crap. She looked up with a plastic smile. "Or, maybe she's got like so many friends she's gotta hire a personal assistant to schedule who can come over on what day. I dunno." The room seemed more stifling all of a sudden. Maya flapped at her nightdress to get some air moving under it.

"They had that thing onna TV t'other night." Arlene pointed at the currently off slab hanging opposite the couch. "Someone started up a rumor 'bout a ransom. Dat mean Ascendant bitch was all like Brigade this."

Maya stifled the urge to cringe. She'd watched the same news broadcast while chained to a bed, listening to Vanessa tell the whole world her daughter hadn't been kidnapped. In a way, the woman had been right. She never had a *daughter*.

A battery powered tool whirred and chirped.

"It *ain't* true. *Theys* not lookin' for no one." Maya folded her arms. "Place would be swarmin' wit' drones if they was."

Emily shot her a confused look.

Brian scratched at his chest. "Yeah, kid's got a point. Doesn't seem like anything's going on in the city." He drifted toward the bedroom. "I gotta get goin'. If I'm late again, I'm screwed."

After an awkward silence, Maya edged over to the couch and leaned against the cushions more than sat on it. Emily broke the quiet by asking what they were going to name the baby. When Arlene confessed they hadn't even thought of a name yet, Emily and Zoe launched a battery of suggestions, which Maya eventually joined in on. Brian, having put on one of those body-engulfing grey long-sleeved ponchos and black sneakers, rushed from the bedroom straight to the door, a filter mask hanging from his fingers.

"Shit," he whisper-yelled outside.

He ran back in, kissed Arlene, and sprinted out.

Loud mechanical rattling came from the corner ten minutes later. Zoe pounded metal on metal for a while, but the banging soon settled to a tolerable background noise. Within seconds, fresh air—cold by comparison to the room—fell on them from vents in the ceiling. Maya pulled the neck of her nightie away from her chest to let the breeze in and fanned herself.

"Oh, you're an angel," said Arlene, reaching both hands up to Zoe. "That sounds like air. Sure hope they pay you good. Don't want you leavin' on us. You do me a solid and help my fat ass to the can?"

"You ain't even close to fat." Zoe stowed her tools back in the bag and stood before pulling Arlene to her feet while making a passable attempt at keeping the blanket around her. "Meh, they pay me by not chargin' rent, but I like it here so don't you worry."

Once upright, Arlene gathered the cloth at her hip and shambled with assistance into the inner hallway.

When the adults were out of sight, Emily squinted at Maya, whispering, "Why did you talk funny? Were you making fun of Arlene?"

"No." Maya kept fanning herself. "I didn't want them to think I'm that stupid rich girl."

"If you didn't want them to think you were stupid, why did you talk like you were stupid?"

Maya sucked in a breath, ready to shout at her, but the question hit her funny and she wound up laughing. Emily giggled along. The girls had settled into a staring contest to see who would laugh again first by the time Zoe guided Arlene back to her spot on the couch and eased her down.

"I'll send Mike down later on to check up on you," said Zoe.

Arlene cringed as if in pain, but nodded. "Great."

Maya stood.

"Nice meetin' you, Lisa." Arlene reached over.

Maya tolerated a cheek pat. "You too. Good luck with the baby."

"Thank ya, darlin'." She settled back and closed her eyes. "Pardon if I don' bother walkin' ya to the door."

Zoe chuckled. "Not a thing."

Maya exhaled in relief with her tongue hanging out as soon as they reached the hallway. She flapped at her nightie, adoring the coolness of moving air on sweat. Dampness in the silk reawakened the fragrance of taco sauce stains. Four flights of stairs later, she'd dried off. *This will need to be washed soon. Do they even wash clothes here?* Zoe walked in to Genna's apartment after a cursory knock.

"Genna? Mike?" Zoe stopped a few steps in and looked around.

When no answer emanated from within, Maya ran to the back bedroom. Genna appeared comfortably asleep, but she found no sign of anyone else. She fast-walked to the living room. "Mom's asleep. Doctor Chang isn't here."

"Oh. I see the problem." Zoe pointed at a patch of kitchen wall that had been scorched black. Smoke peeled out from under the refrigerator as well as a metal panel on the wall. "Fridge went and took the breaker panel out with it. Damn. There goes the rest of my day."

"The fridge was on? It wasn't even cold." Maya looked up. "Can you fix it?"

"Yeah. I can lift a panel from an empty on the second floor. That fridge is going out the window. I'll bring a new one up from the basement. You got anything in it you need to keep?"

"No!" screamed Maya. "Do *not* open that."

Zoe laughed.

"I'm serious." Maya cringed. "I almost threw up."

Marcus or Anton—she couldn't tell which—walked in. "Hey Lisa. We're goin' out to scav. Wanna come?"

"I dunno."

"Come on." Emily pulled on her. "It's fun."

"I don't want you kids going too far," yelled Zoe from the kitchen.

"We won't, Mom." Emily rolled her eyes.

Against her gut instinct, Maya allowed Emily to drag her down the hall to the fire stairs and to the ground floor. She went right at the bottom and out the double glass doors into the parking lot/backyard. A few feeble bits of grass squeezed up from cracks in the blacktop, wavering in a mild but steady crosswind that carried the fragrance of Chinese food. Brown slats in the chain link fence surrounding it made it feel a little safer. Men's voices murmured in from the alley running along the side of the building to the street out front. She glanced in that direction, though the sign of people so close didn't seem to bother Emily or the boy with them.

Pick stood on the front end of a dead limousine that had seen much, much better days. Considering the amount of weeds and grass growing around and into the wheels, the thing hadn't moved for years. The other twin perched in the rearmost seat, moving his arms in pantomime of steering an ancient pirate ship.

As the trio approached, Pick freaked out as if watching them walk on water. Emily got the hint and pretended to swim. The twin with them pantomimed paddling a small rowboat, but Maya felt it far too silly a thing to bother with at all and simply walked.

"Come on, Ant. Scav time," said the boy who'd fetched them from the seventh floor.

The navigator yelled, "We're about to plunder. And stop teasing her, Anton."

"Don't listen to him," said the nearer twin. "I'm Marcus."

"Arrrr," yelled Pick. "Ship full of gold ahead."

A ripple of distant gunshots went off, sounding like firecrackers.

"Cannon fire," yelled Pick. "Bring it about."

The boy in the back seat windmilled his arms. "Aye aye."

Maya stared at them, shaking her head. Emily declared herself a mermaid and ran in circles around the limo. This continued for a few minutes before Sarah emerged from the back door looking paler than usual.

"'Kay, Faerie's here," yelled the twin not in the car. "Come on you two, time to scav."

Pick looked ready to protest, but when his navigator crawled out through the window, he slouched with resignation. Sarah stopped nearby, adjusting the way her hip satchel rested against her leg.

Maya glanced at her. "What's wrong? You look scared."

"Dad didn't want me to go out today. Said there's too much shooting. He's gettin' one o' his bad feelin's and all."

Pick ran to a jagged breach in the fence on the far side of the limo and waited. The twins and Emily followed. Maya looked up at Sarah, hoping she decided not to go. Alas, with a defeated sigh, Sarah started after them.

Maya grabbed her arm. "We don't have to go. I'll stay too."

"I gotta." Sarah frowned. "They're gonna do something stupid without me."

"What's out there?" Maya clung to Sarah as they approached the hole in the chain link.

"Couple blocks of Hab, then Dead Space mostly. We don't go that far away though. Besides, there's nothing in the DS worth taking."

"Is it dangerous?"

Sarah squeezed her hand. "Yeah. There's stuff that can collapse, sharp things on the ground, and dosers. The gangs won't bother with kids like us, but the dosers might chase us."

"To steal our clothes?" Maya ducked through the hole to a relatively normal looking city street. It seemed bizarre to see sidewalks not packed with an endless throng of grey-clad bodies. She turned in place, gazing with awe up at the skyscrapers and lack of drones. The Hab reminded her of history e-learns, what cities had looked like sixty years ago, before holographic signs and 3D-printed construction took over.

"It depends on how high they are. Some might be scared of us, some might think we're monsters and want to hurt us. This one bitch tried to grab Emily 'cause she wanted a kid." Sarah guided her up to a jog to catch up to the others. "I can tell you're scared. Stay close."

"Okay." Maya glanced back at the distancing gate, not wanting to leave the place that already felt like home. The other kids all seemed so excited, and Sarah held her hand, so she kept quiet and followed.

SEVENTEEN
ONE OF THE GANG

aya hovered at Sarah's side as the group walked in the middle of the street. Patches of double yellow line remained in short strips. She thought it stupid to walk in the road until Sarah mentioned anyone in the place who owned a car was already in the Sanc and wouldn't be back until it started to get dark. That, and far fewer nasty things to step on sat in the middle of the road.

Pick led the way, flanked by the twins. They discussed where to go and where they'd been in the past, pointing at and reconsidering several old residence towers. Trash and old cans shifted in an alley between two dumpsters as a moaning skeletal-thin man lurched upright. Maya clamped on to her nightdress, pulling it tight around herself.

A few people walked by in the other direction. Most looked too old to work, and the one man not elderly kept talking to an invisible person next to him, his eyes shifting side to side, never focusing on the same place longer than two seconds. Sarah pulled Maya to the side, against the wall, and held her there until the guy passed. He didn't make eye contact with any of the kids.

"Don't bump him," whispered Sarah. "He's got a knife, and I think he's blind."

"He's not blind. He's crazy. Probably hallucinating and hearing voices. Neutradine or Serenomil might help."

Sarah squinted and whispered, "You can stop trying to sell drugs now."

Maya tickled her.

"Let's try the bird again." Pick pointed down the street.

"Okay." Anton rubbed his hands together with anticipation gleaming in his eyes. "We still got more than half that place ta check."

A few minutes later, repetitious buzzing on the left sounded in time with flashing pink-purple letters spelling out 'Emporium' over a door with grimy windows protected by metal bars. Similar bars guarded a storefront to the right, where a handful of small electronic devices sat on display next to a stack of Hydra packets. Maya stared at the octagonal plastic trays, fully understanding the desperate, eager longing in the little white dog's eyes whenever he saw one.

"That's the Emporium," said Anton.

Maya smirked. "Obviously. That's what the sign says."

Emily giggled. Anton seemed less amused.

"We can sell stuff there." Marcus headed left at the next cross street. "If we find something worth selling."

"I want a Hydra." Maya smiled.

The boys all whistled.

"Good luck with that." Anton shook his head. "Ol' Foz has one and he wants like a thousand NuCoin for it."

"They don't cost that much." Maya glared. "A hundred or two dollars for a nice one."

Sarah gave her a hand squeeze.

Maya cringed. "Uhh, yeah. That's what Genna said. In the Sanctuary Zone."

"That's there; this is here." Marcus clucked his tongue. "Less'n you got a ride to the big city, you gotta give Foz what he wants."

"It probably doesn't work anyway." Sarah frowned. "An' a Hydra's only good if you got the packets for it."

A gust of wind swept down the street, fluttering curtains trailing from smashed high-rise windows and knocking Emily back two steps. Maya closed her eyes and basked in it. The awkwardness of being outside with only a nightdress on had died somewhere between Headcrash and Moth. A hint of fried food got her eagerly sniffing, though a cruel twist of the breeze replaced it with rotting trash. Maya coughed.

The kids all swerved to the right to give a stumbling older man room. He paused long enough to ramble a greeting with a dopey smile at them, though not a single sound out of his mouth came remotely close to a word. He capped his greeting with a whiskey-laden belch that would've uncurled Maya's hair if it hadn't already been straight. Maya frowned to herself, thinking of Vanessa's complaining about her hair. The woman always had treatments done to make her hair straight, and had envied her daughter that one little petty thing.

I'm not your daughter.

Four buildings later, Pick sprinted to the left and up a few steps to the main entrance of a crumbling apartment building. He ducked the push bar and slipped in through a panel where glass no longer existed.

"Be careful in the lobby," said Sarah. "There's broken glass."

The twins went in next, followed by Emily, who hiked her dress up to her thighs as if wading into a pond. Maya cringed away from the edges of the opening, reacting to a few bits of safety glass like a ring of flaming razor blades. Inside, the red-tiled floor startled a squeak from her for being so cold underfoot. True enough, flecks and glimmers—tiny glass fragments—sparkled in the darkness. Even reckless Pick advanced with his gaze locked on the ground.

At the center of the lobby, tile gave way to a rounded silvery emblem with a bas-relief likeness of an eagle under some kind of transparent coating that made it smooth to the level of the floor. Light streamed in from a row of small rectangular windows near the ceiling that encircled the entire lobby. Almost all had been smashed out, the likely source of all the glittering shards on the ground.

"Think it's a big quarter?" Pick got down on all fours at the seam between emblem and tile and tried to get his fingernails in it. "Would Foz buy it?"

"We couldn't lift it if it was." Maya squatted at the edge and traced her fingers over the clear material. "It would be hundreds of pounds, but it's not a coin. Probably silver paint on wood or something."

Sarah shook her head. "We don't have the kind of tools it would take to dig that thing outta there anyway. And who would buy it? It doesn't do anything."

The twins headed for the elevator chamber beyond an information desk covered in black lacquer with three thin gold bands near the top. A handful of rats went zooming away a few seconds later, at which Maya let off a shriek of surprise.

Sarah grabbed her from behind, clamping a hand over her mouth. "Shh!"

Maya whimpered.

All three boys looked at her, the effort to fight off the urge to laugh or tease her clear in their expressions. Emily hid her face in her hands, though her body shook with mute giggles. Maya reached up and grasped Sarah's arm, trying to pull it down from her mouth. Two years didn't sound like much of an advantage, but the girl overpowered her with ease.

"Mmm!" said Maya.

"Done screaming?" Sarah's breath puffed into her left ear.

Maya nodded.

The redhead let go and spun her around nose to nose, speaking in an agitated whisper. "One. They're just rats. They won't hurt you. Two. Do not scream. The less noise we make, the safer we are."

Maya gulped and whispered, "Okay."

At the entrance to the elevator area, Pick grunted and shoved at a door, though his feet slipped over the faux marble floor. The twins watched for a moment before they snickered. Maya, still feeling sheepish, crept up with Sarah holding her hand. Pick glared at the twins and strained even harder. Anton... or maybe Marcus doubled over laughing into his hand.

Pick gave up, winded. After a few breaths, he glared. "It's stuck."

One of the twins grabbed the door handle and *pulled* it open. Pick's grumbling followed them up a few flights covered in old papers and wrappers. The twins stopped short, staring at a magazine page showing a nude woman ascending the ladder of a swimming pool.

Emily tilted her head at it. "Who stole her clothes?"

Maya exchanged a knowing glance with Pick of all people, who seemed ashamed. Sarah kicked the magazine into the trash pile and herded the twins plus Emily upward. One of the twins hustled up ahead of everyone. Of the two, Marcus seemed more given to action and Anton more pensive. Marcus, she assumed, halted two and a half landings up, listening at the door leading to the fifth floor. Evidently hearing nothing frightening, he grinned, opened it and walked in.

A steady breeze carried down the corridor from broken windows at either end. The boys proceeded to the first door on the left and entered an empty apartment. Maya stood in the middle of the main room while the others spread out and searched cabinets, closets, and interior rooms. In a back hallway, Sarah opened a panel and took several fuses, which she put in her hip bag. Pick returned from a distant bedroom with a knife in a battered army-green sheath. Emily pranced over showing off a curtain rod, which she tossed aside with a forlorn sigh when no one seemed impressed.

A tickle caressed the outside edge of Maya's left foot. She looked down at a roach too big to fit in her palm a second before it scurried up and over both of her feet. Maya jumped and danced about, trying to get away from the feeling that bugs crawled all over her. In her haste to back up, she stepped on another one, which burst under her heel like an armored packet of mayonnaise. Disgust paralyzed her. A moment later when she managed to open her eyes, she counted fourteen more at a quick glance. The urge to scream welled up, but she bit it back to a whimper thinking of Sarah's warning. Without the fear of a room full of kidnappers, she wanted *nothing* to do with such disgusting creatures.

Pick crawled out from the kitchen cupboards with a half dozen of the giant bugs on his back. He brushed them off and went for the fridge. Maya shivered and looked away. Two seconds after the rubber door gasket peeled open, he coughed and backed away, fanning at dust in the air. Anton staggered out of a side hallway looking ashen.

"Don't go in the back." He waved his hand past his face a few times. "Whole lotta bad food in the closet."

"Who keeps food in a closet?" asked Sarah with a scrunched up face.

Maya wiped her foot on a roach-free patch of rug while spinning in a constant circle to watch for any others getting close. Having bug guts touch her bare sole made her want to jump in a bathtub *now*. Sarah left the electrical panel open and walked over to put an arm around her. "You okay?"

"Bugs," said Maya in a tiny voice.

"You're such a *girl*," said Pick. "They're just roaches."

Emily glared for a second before pouncing on one of the foul things and grabbing it. She snuck up on Pick and stuffed the insect down his shorts from behind. He squealed and jumped around until it fell out.

"Now who's a girl?" Emily stuck her tongue out at him.

Looking about as apt to cry from embarrassment as hit her, Pick grabbed a roach and stomped over. Emily folded her arms, clearly unimpressed as he put the insect on her head. She didn't flinch or flick it away until he wandered off muttering.

Maya forced herself to follow along as the crew went from apartment to apartment. By the sixth one, she managed not to feel like standing on a table or chair to get away from the bugs, though not every space had an infestation. Most of the rooms offered little in the way of anything interesting to take, so the searching didn't consume much time. By the fourteenth apartment, Maya stopped standing around and joined in the scavenging. She found a box of four Hydra packets in a cabinet over a fridge, though an empty spot indicated the Hydra unit itself had been liberated already, perhaps the same one Foz now wanted a thousand NuCoin for. Maya rolled her eyes. The boy had to be exaggerating. Asking that much money for a Hydra from people who had to choose between shoes or food seemed ridiculous.

Apartment fifteen had a locked door. The twins, Pick, and Emily gathered around it, casting expectant looks at Sarah.

She bit her lip and muttered, "I dunno. Maybe we should get back before something happens. Dad had a feeling."

"Do it," said Pick.

"Do it," said the twins in unison.

Emily got down and tried to peek under the door. "I don't see anyone moving."

Sarah sighed. "Fine." She opened her hip bag and pulled out a small nylon case with a zipper around three sides. From it, she selected two thin metal tools and stuck them in the keyhole. "Everyone be quiet."

Such stillness settled over the hallway, the scratching of the implements seemed loud. The girl wiggled one while trying to twist the other one around like a wrench. A little while later, Sarah turned the knob and pushed the door open an inch. The twins went in first. Pick waved the sheathed knife over his head and mumbled a pirate's "arrrr" before following.

Maya looked from the hip bag to Sarah's face. "Where'd you learn that?"

Sarah put the tools away. "My dad. He's strange. The last time he bought me clothes, he went a week or two without beer and decided I *needed* to learn how to pick locks. A couple months ago, he showed me how to clean and cook rats. Couple months before that, how to escape if 'the Koreans' captured me."

"Eww." Maya shivered. "You ate a rat?"

"It wasn't bad."

"Eww!"

Sarah shrugged. "If you didn't have anything else, you'd eventually get hungry enough to eat it." She gathered Maya with an arm around the back and ushered her inside before prodding the door closed with a foot. "We're easy to spot in hallways, better to stay inside."

Maya headed for the kitchen while Sarah roamed in search of the fuse panel. The boys sat crowded around the coffee table, devouring still-edible Chinese food they scooped out of white cartons with their hands. Maya halted, staring at the recent-looking containers, dead beer cans, and the stink of an unflushed toilet. *Someone lives here.* Before dread eased its grip on her throat to let words of protest out, the boys finished their hurried feast and zipped about, tearing through cabinets, drawers, and closets.

Maya ran to where Sarah extracted circuit breakers and pulled at her arm. "Someone's staying here. We have to leave."

Sarah nodded. "Okay, won't be long."

"No I mean we're stealing from someone's home."

"Oh." Sarah hesitated, sighed, and pushed the breaker box closed.

The twins discovered a few gadgets. Old personal electronics from the look of it, a media player and two flashlights. Emily stomped triumphant out of the secondary bedroom with a scuffed laptop computer held over her head. All were disappointed when it wouldn't turn on, and lost interest until Emily suggested her mother might be able to fix it.

Maya bounced on the balls of her feet. "We need to get out of—"

Thump.

Everyone froze and faced the door. More banging in the hallway grew louder, accompanied by a man attempting to scream despite something covering his mouth. Sarah grabbed Maya and darted to the kitchen, ducking around the wall separating it from the living room. She huddled on the floor, pulling Maya down next to her. A key rattled in the knob. The others scampered in. Pick went straight for the cabinets under the sink, as did the twins and Emily. A nervous whine leaked out of Sarah's nose for a second while indecision radiated from her eyes. She seemed to change her mind that the kitchen wall would make enough of a hiding spot and started to shove Maya toward the cabinets, but yanked her back not a second before the apartment door slammed open.

Sarah scooted to the right, away from the opening between kitchen and living room, butt on the floor. Maya tucked up to her side, unable to tell if the terrified redhead clung to her protectively or if it worked the other way around.

"You fucked up, Dave. I gave you another chance, and you fucked it up," said a raspy male voice.

A meaty *smack* preceded the floor-shaking *thud* of a body crashing down.

Two different men chuckled. The *mmmm*-ing of a desperate man grew louder.

Sarah stared wide-eyed at Maya and held a finger to her lips in a gesture of 'shh!'

"Either you're an idiot, or you did it on purpose," said the first voice. Boot steps thumped around in a lazy orbit. "Which is it, Dave, eh? Whimper once for idiot and twice for on purpose."

One whimper.

"Jackass," said a deeper voice.

Maya twitched at the *thump* of a foot slamming into a gut with a subsequent muffled "oof." Silent tears streamed down Sarah's cheeks. The sight got Maya trembling. If these guys found them, they'd do a lot worse than steal their clothes.

"How am I supposed to trust you to make this right?" asked Raspy. *Whump.*

Dave mumbled incomprehensibly between moans of pain.

For a few seconds, it seemed men took turns kicking and hitting Dave. Pick peeked out of his cabinet door, staring at the open archway between kitchen and the other room. He glanced at the girls and held up three fingers followed by a finger gun, then three more fingers before ducking out of sight.

Sarah looked down at Maya as if she really wanted to speak but couldn't force herself to. When the *thumps* and *pops* of a beating stopped, her hug crushed all the air out of Maya's lungs.

"What's that, Dave? I didn't catch that?"

Dave emitted a wounded moan.

"Need that again a little louder," said Raspy, along with the rattle of metal.

Dave emitted a terrified scream from his nose, and the thumping of a struggling tied-up body rumbled the linoleum under Maya.

"Good night, Dave."

Sarah's foot slipped forward an inch as she trembled; her toe hit an empty piece of pistol brass, sending it rolling across the floor. She cringed at the noise.

Dave emitted a long, muffled scream.

"What was that?" asked the deep voice. "Fink I heard somethin' in the kitchen."

"Rats," said Raspy. "Where do you want it, Dave? Head or chest? Whimper once for head."

The gagged man moaned in a pleading tone, likely begging for another chance.

Maya held her breath. Her heart pounded in her head.

"Hold up," said the deep voice, sounding far too close. "I smell…"

Dave's screaming subsided to sobs.

A head with dark violet color airbrushed across the eyes hovered in the doorway, quite far up off the floor. Its owner leaned farther in, a black leather coat over a bare chest marked by copious scars and a tattoo of a grinning horned skull over his sternum.

"Whatcha got?" asked the raspy man.

The tall thug stepped all the way into the kitchen and set his hands on his hips by a pair of pistols. A heavy, blood-caked chain hung along the length of his left leg atop jeans covered in marker-drawn images of stylized words, more skulls, knives, and other unidentifiable squiggles.

"Couple of little girls," said the tall man. "Thought I smelled kid."

"Juicy," said a new voice.

The tall one stared at Sarah, who hunched over Maya, trying to hide her.

After a moment, he glanced into the living room. "Naw, ya sick fucker. Too little. Actual *kids*. Ain't ripe yet."

Maya couldn't breathe. She threaded her arms around Sarah and held on.

"We d-din't hear n-nothin'." Sarah leaned back. "P-please don't k-kill us."

Another man in a similar jacket but with a dark shirt on under it walked in. He had short black hair in an array of spikes and kept a handgun pointed into the living room. "For fuck's sake, man. Get rid of 'em." He moved out of sight with an annoyed head shake.

Maya stared at his hands, committing herself to take off at a sprint as soon as he twitched and went for a gun.

"G'won. Get outta here," said the tall man, pointing.

Sarah glanced at the cabinets and forced herself upright. "R-really?"

"Yeah. Skeleton Crew don't kill kids... 'less you pointin' guns at us."

"Uhh," said Raspy. "Only problem I got wit' shooting kids is tryin' to hit 'em when they're runnin' sideways. I hate small targets."

Sarah made a gurgling noise while the other men laughed.

"Come on, come on," yelled Raspy. "Dave here ain't getting any deader. I can't get it up with goddamned kids in the next room."

Dave wailed and moaned.

Maya pushed Sarah forward. "Go. He's just trying to scare us."

Sarah reached behind her and took Maya's hand. The big man backed out of the door, forming a living wall between them and a squirming man nearly mummified in duct tape on the floor. Maya looked away before his face came into view. Sarah emitted a faint squeal when the tall man put his hand on her back, but he only urged them out into the hall and closed the door.

"Shit." Sarah fell to her knees. "I-I d-don't believe it."

Maya glanced at the door, sucked in a breath, and knocked.

"What?" screamed the younger sounding guy. "You two little bitches have a freakin' death wish?"

A man with maraschino-red hair whipped the door open. He blinked at Maya and spoke in the raspy voice. "Damn, this one's tiny. Probably take five or six tries to hit her on the run."

"I'm sorry for interrupting your shooting Dave in the head," said Maya, "but I left something in the kitchen. Can I please get it?"

The Skeleton Crew gawked at her for a few seconds in silence before erupting in laughter, and the tall one with the purple band across his eyes waved her in.

"You got a pair, kid." The guy with too-red hair motioned his pistol at the kitchen. "Sure." He kicked Dave in the face, putting an end to the muffled screaming.

Maya didn't look at anything but her feet as she scurried into the kitchen and crouched by the cabinets. "You really don't want to be in there when what's about to happen in the other room happens."

Marcus pushed the door open and climbed out, pulling Emily along behind him. Pick and Anton waited another three seconds before following. Maya marched back out to the door, again without a look to the side.

"God dammit." Cherry Red braced the side of his head with his gun hand. "Where the shit did all these rugrats come from?"

"That little bastard in the camo shorts looks quick." The young ganger pulled his gun and winked.

Pick screamed and took off at a sprint. Maya shrieked and tripped over herself on the way out the door, falling into Sarah's arms. The older girl grabbed her by the wrist, and they ran as fast as they could to the stairway door all the way at the end. Emily brought up the rear, lugging the laptop. They stopped running three blocks later in an alley. Even there, the *crack* of a gunshot from the fifth floor apartment reached them.

Anton and Marcus stared down. Maya gulped. Sarah looked about ready to pass out. Emily's expression could've been contemplative or bored. Pick fell on all fours and made gagging noises amid coughs. He stopped short of throwing up, but remained bent forward for a minute or two, breathing hard, before he sat back on his heels and wiped his mouth on his forearm. Emily set the laptop on the ground and sat on it.

"Damn," said Marcus. "Faerie's ol' man got some skills."

"Yeah. Truth." Anton leaned forward, hands on his knees, and gasped for air.

"I had you wrong." Marcus patted Maya on the shoulder. "Thought you was a fluffy bit, but you got some balls."

Sarah wheezed, breathless. "I can't believe you did that."

Maya tried not to think about Dave. "I couldn't leave you guys in there when they were gonna shoot someone."

"Sorry." Sarah sank to a seat on the pavement. "I didn't know what they were gonna do. Didn't wanna give the others away in case they hurt us."

Pick jammed his finger up his nose.

"Can we go home now?" asked Emily. "I'm hungry an' I'm scared."

"Good idea," said Anton.

"Yes." Sarah jumped up.

Marcus glanced at Emily. "Wow, those guys let you take that thing."

"It didn't turn on," said Maya. "They probably thought it's junk."

"It *is* junk." Marcus frowned.

Pick gathered saliva in his throat and spat a giant wad to the side. "Shortcut." Before anyone could protest, he ran off.

"Pick!" Sarah's nerves tamped her intended shout down to a normal speaking volume. She let off an exasperated sigh, grabbed Maya's hand, and rushed after him. "Ruben!"

The twins and Emily ran behind them. At the end of the alley, Pick zipped around the left corner. They chased him down two more alleys and through a parking lot with about fourteen dead cars. He seemed to be cutting as diagonal a line as possible across the city blocks, using alleys and open doors whenever he could.

The group ducked into the ground floor of a different building, which led them to the street on the other side. They dodged a group of begging vagrants, ran two blocks, and came to a halt at the edge of a courtyard in the hollow of a C-shaped building where two four-story wings sprouted like hugging arms from a nine-story tower. Pick had stopped at the base of a broken statue in the middle, poking a crashed Authority drone with his foot. His toes left dust prints on the dark blue hull, but the machine didn't react.

"Pick!" Sarah whisper shouted. "Get away from that right now."

He ignored her.

She let go of Maya's arm and stormed up to him. Curiosity overwhelmed the twins and they hurried over with Maya jogging along behind them. Emily waited alone, clutching the laptop by the brick wall at the courtyard's mouth for five seconds before darting in with a fearful glance at something down the street.

On the ground, the killing machine was larger than Maya expected, not quite the size of a compact car. The crash had mangled its front-left fan shroud to an unrecognizable tangle of metal. Small silver streaks appeared over the dark blue central body where paint had scratched off. The generally aerodynamic shape reminded her of a giant motorcycle without any wheels, windscreen, or handlebars.

Pick squatted and stared with awe at the huge gun on the bottom. "That's a big'un."

"Fifty caliber," said Sarah "We shouldn't be anywhere near this thing. Come on, Ruben. Now!"

Maya leaned away. "Home?"

"We shouldn't be seen next to a dead drone," said Sarah after she grabbed at and missed Pick. "If someone thinks we did this, it won't matter that we're kids."

"Who'd think we did this?" asked Marcus. "We ain't got no guns."

Pick twisted his finger back and forth in his nostril. "You coulda farted it down."

"Yeah." Anton backed up. "Maybe this is what her dad was worrying about, not those losers in the building."

Maya crept up to the front end, where Pick stuck his nose-cleaning finger knuckle deep in a bullet hole. "Please get away from it."

Marcus startled a yelp from Sarah when he jumped onto the drone and perched in the middle of the fuselage, riding the motorbike it wasn't. He braced his feet on the struts connected to the rear fan enclosures and leaned forward. "How awesome would it be to ride one of these things?" He made flying sound effects and rocked about as if airborne.

Pick scurried away from Maya and crawled under the drone, attracted to a red arrow labeled 'danger,' which pointed at a small hatch.

"That's it!" Sarah lunged at Marcus, grabbing him by the left arm and shoulder. "Get off that thing right now! We are going home."

"Hey!" Marcus shouted and flailed. His flailing leg kicked into one of the open panels, causing a flash and a *beep*.

The drone's flashing police lights came on, along with its three remaining fans, though it didn't leave the ground. A distorted electronic voice warbled a jagged buzzing mess no longer even close to speech. Marcus leapt in the direction Sarah pulled and landed on top of her. Pick shrieked and sprinted for the safety of the empty basin surrounding the nonworking fountain. Anton dropped where he stood, arms and legs out in an X shape. Maya wound up the only one standing—two feet in front of it.

The drone's autocannon trained on her.

Sarah wailed a noise half Maya's name and half the word no.

Old instinct locked Maya at attention. A grid of green laser lines lit her up from a small black lens on the nose, which swiveled back and forth. Maya kept her arms tight to her sides, hands balled into fists, eyes pointed straight ahead, and held her breath. Three seconds later, the drone emitted a pleasant sounding *chirp* and its weapon broke target lock, swiveling to neutral forward.

Her hair whipped around in a fury when the three remaining fans spun up faster. Sparks shot out of its sides from tiny explosions that knocked hatches and body panels open. The whine of fan motors kept increasing in pitch, making her take two steps back.

Maya scrambled to the right and dove to the pavement a split second before the machine lurched into the air, careening in an arc like a giant had kicked it in the back end, bright blue sparks lapping from its hull at the darkening sky. She rolled onto her back, guarding her face with both arms from the rain of debris bits falling on her. The roar and fury of electric motors stopped with an abrupt *boom* when it crashed upside down a distance away and exploded in a plume of blue-green fire. A spinning fan whizzed off like a shuriken and smashed a fourth-floor window.

One by one, the kids rose to their feet, leaving Maya the only one on the ground. Authority drones didn't do random scans; it had to be in arrest mode and locked on to the nearest person after it rebooted. Being that close to a huge machine gun likely to fire if she so much as wiggled a finger wrong kept her paralyzed. Anton and Marcus appeared at her left. Pick peered straight down at her, his feet on either side of her head. Sarah stood on her right, next to Emily.

A short period of stunned silence passed where no one moved even to blink. Sarah reached down and helped her up.

"Whoa." Pick blinked.

"Damn." Anton pointed at her. "You really are a Citizen, aren't you?"

Marcus's jaw hung open. He fished paper out of his back pocket and unfurled a print ad for Loftin-CX, one of Ascendant's designer antidepressants. Crisscrossed by wrinkled creases, the face of her seven-year-old self—bright purple lipstick and all—flashed that perfect smile. "It *is* her."

"Lemme see." Pick ran around to stand between the twins and tugged the paper down to his level. "Wow."

Maya shrank in on herself, wishing she could disappear into a hole. She hadn't felt that embarrassed since she snapped a heel off her shoe on the boardroom table and took a pratfall into Jerry Michaels' coffee on live AuthCast. The junior VP of marketing *still* called her klutz three years later. The tears she wasn't allowed to show then came now. "I... Please don't tell anyone."

Emily touched Maya's cheek. "You're pretty."

"Please don't tell." Maya wiped her face. "They'll hurt everyone. I don't want to go back. I wanna stay here. Genna's my mom now."

"Lisa?" asked Pick.

"Her name is Maya," said Marcus. He fidgeted.

Anton chuckled. "My brother likes you."

Marcus shoved him.

"Like a lot," said Anton.

Marcus shoved him harder.

Sarah seemed to find her confidence—and smile—again. "We're not gonna tell anyone. We all know what kind of lying bitches the Authority are."

"That stuff you said... about it being sad there." Anton looked in the direction of the Sanctuary Zone. "You sayin' that 'cause you knew."

Maya reined in her tears. "Yes."

Emily tucked the laptop under her left arm. She crept closer, poking and touching Maya as if examining a doll in a toy store.

"I think she's lying. Why would the richest kid in the world *want* to live with poor people?" Anton shook his head.

Emily kept touching Maya's hair. "She's not the richest kid in the world. My dad says there's people with lotta money in a place called Ell Ay. Way far to the west past the wilds. So far 'way Authority don' even go there."

"Maybe the richest kid on the East Coast then." Anton shrugged.

"They treated me like a thing. I wasn't allowed to go outside or do anything but sit on the computer all day long. I only saw Vanessa once or twice a month, and for, like, only an hour." Maya brushed her hands down her nightdress in an effort to clear some of the char from the dying drone.

"I still think you're dumb," said Anton. "I'd take a fancy apartment, all the video games I could get my hands on, good food, and money over this... even if I was alone."

"Research showed people responded better to a female child as a marketing tool. They wouldn't use you." Maya took a deep breath before muttering a quick summary of how she came to be out here. "And Vanessa wouldn't even talk to them. She didn't even try to get me back."

"Man." Marcus looked down and shook his head. "Genna wouldn't have killed you, no matter how mean she was at first. She ain't like that."

"How could your mother not want you?" asked Emily, hugging the laptop like a security blanket. "That's so sad!"

"She's *not* my mother." Maya glowered. "I don't think they'd even want me back... but if they do, they're gonna kill everyone that knows I got kidnapped. That woman has power issues. Anything that makes Ascendant seem weak, she tries to get rid of. You *can't* tell anyone."

"But 'Cendant only makes drugs. Authority's the law," said Marcus, still fidgeting.

Maya held her hands up. "They do whatever she wants though."

"Book said 'Thority is different in Boston. Not as mean as here, and they don' like 'Cendant." Anton poked his brother and glanced at Maya.

"Well, we ain't in Boston." Marcus folded his arms.

Sarah hugged her from behind. "No way any of us will say a damn thing."

"Yeah." Pick stuffed his finger up his nose. "I don't like it when I get killed."

Emily bounced on her toes and clapped, beaming.

Marcus's teeth showed in a wide grin. He held a fist out to Maya. "We good."

She gave him a quizzical look. Anton grasped her arm, folded her fingers into a fist, and guided her to touch knuckles with him. She smiled and fist-bumped the rest of the group one after the next.

Marcus patted her on the back. "You one of us now, Sanc girl."

"We should get out of here. That blow up was loud," said Sarah.

"Yes." Maya grinned. "Let's go home."

EIGHTEEN
THE ENEMY WITHIN

The sun had almost vanished from the sky by the time Pick led the way through the breach in the fence, slats in the chain link clattering and rattling with the single-file procession. Maya frowned at the four Hydra packs she carried. Without the machine, they'd be useless. At least they'd last forever… or at least well past her lifespan.

"Mommy's gonna be mad," said Emily. "I stayed out too long." She looked up at Sarah. "Can you tell her we had to hide from bad guys?"

"It's not a lie." Sarah ruffled the girl's hair. "We did."

Everyone got quiet for the short walk across the lot. Maya cringed as a camera-flash snapshot of Moth punching the Authority officer out of her old bedroom appeared in her mind. Having been close to people getting killed didn't make the idea of being one wall away from Dave taking a bullet any less scary. Dozens of articles and e-learns referenced the war, but seeing pictures of dead people, soldiers and civilians alike, had a certain detachment to it that being ten feet away from a murder couldn't compare to. Maya shivered at the thought of what it must have felt like for the people caught up in the front lines. She couldn't wait to get upstairs and be with her mom.

She beat the group to the back door, but it took two hands and a foot on the wall for her to haul the heavy thing open. The others trooped past her into the hallway that connected from the rear exit, past the non-working elevator area, to the front lobby where all the old mailboxes stood forgotten. Needing both hands to keep the door open, Maya shoved the Hydra packs in with her foot before letting the door slam behind her.

"Where's dinner tonight?" asked Pick.

Marcus rubbed his stomach. "Is Naida working? Can she cook?"

"I dunno." Pick ground his toe into the linoleum. "I can ask."

Anton shrugged. "What about Genna? It's her turn to feed us."

"She's sick." Maya pointed at her right arm. "She's sleeping all the time because she's on medicine... and you do *not* want anything that was ever in our fridge. It's so gross we need a new one."

The kids laughed.

"I got cheese sandwiches," said Sarah, earning a chorus of groans. "Oh, come on. They're not *that* bad."

Pick stuck out his tongue. "VA gives 'em 'way 'cause no one wants ta buy 'em."

"I'll go ask my dad to make us food." Emily zipped into the stairwell.

"Hey, good idea," said Marcus.

The twins shoved the fire door open and ran up the steps two at a time.

Sarah sighed. "No one likes the sandwiches."

"I do." Maya smiled.

"I suppose—" Sarah froze as a pair of headlights flashed over the front doors. Her mouth hung open, and the hand she'd been about to point at the door with shook. The groaning whine of an electric motor out front grew louder over a span of two seconds and cut out with a brief squeak of tires.

"Sarah?" Maya tilted her head.

The redhead trembled. Without a word, she backed through the fire door and curled up in a ball under the first flight of stairs. Maya started to follow, but hesitated as a thick-bodied man with shaggy, curly brown hair stormed in from the street. He pulled his hood down once the door slammed and fumbled with a keyring on his way in.

That must be Mr. Mason.

Maya stood her ground, curious as to exactly how bad this man was. He didn't seem obese nor particularly athletic, though he didn't look like he shared the other residents' problem of having to scrounge for food and clothes. His drab grey poncho looked in good repair; two thin spiral hoses ran up the front to a breathing mask over his face. Anyone with a condition like asthma, a diagnosed susceptibility to Fade, or sensitivity to poor air quality often wore the powered filters even when the bacteria forecast showed low levels. Hard brown eyes focused on the floor as he trudged along. His gaze flicked in her general direction for an instant, then returned with interest.

Her initial impression that he'd be as likely to backhand her out of his way as say hello faded. The sense of constant rage melted out of his expression. He reached up and pulled the mask away from his mouth and nose. Thick lips stretched to an over-friendly smile, surrounded by wrinkled, pale skin.

"Hello there, sweetie." He stared at her. "What a nice surprise. Usually you kids run."

Maya kept a neutral expression. "Hello. Is it true that you're mean?"

Mr. Mason loosed a phlegmatic chuckle. "Naw, sweetie. They usually see me after a day's work of dealing with stupid people. Leaves a man in a bad mood." He took a step closer, smiling. "I love kids. You look like I've seen you somewhere before."

"Everyone says that." Maya tensed up. This man made her uncomfortable.

He traced a finger across her bare shoulder, over the spaghetti strap of her nightdress to the base of her neck. The contact sent an unpleasant shiver down her back. She leaned away when he moved to touch her cheek.

"You're really pretty. Perfect even." He gestured to his left. "You hungry, kid? I got a Hydra for those packs of yours. Only working one in the whole building."

Maya took another step back. "No, thanks. I only wanted to say hi."

"Are you sure? There's a Daisho-X with about thirty games waiting 'til I have someone to play with. Would you like to play some games?" He offered his hand. "The washing machine in my place works. I can clean that dirty little nightie of yours while you play. You could even take a bath if you want."

"No." Maya backed up again and narrowed her eyes. The way Sarah had blushed made perfect sense to her now. "I know exactly what you want. You're one of *those*. How stupid do you think I am? I'm not going anywhere alone with you."

Mr. Mason chuckled, coughed, and swallowed. "You *do* look familiar. What are you doing here?" The way he stared at her made her think he tried to imagine away her nightdress. "You're so damn pretty. Bet you don't got nothin' on under that, do you?"

"Stop it." Maya's courage took a dent at the notice he'd gotten between her and the fire stairs. "I read all about people like you on the net."

"You know what else is on the net, sweetie? Famous little thing like you... all sorts of pictures. Do you know what gets done to that fine little body of yours?" He licked his lip. "Maybe I won't recognize you if you behave yourself, huh? You look hungry. Come on, I'll cook you something."

"Hey, where are you two?" yelled Marcus from the stairwell.

"Right here," yelled Maya. "I'm just talking with Mr. Mason."

He chuckled in a low, barely audible tone. Maya backed into the cinder block wall when he made to walk past her, staring defiance up at him. He reached two fingers for her chin, but she lifted her head up and away, squeezing herself against the cold wall, toes whitening on the floor as he leaned over her. Despite the warm air in the hall, she shivered. He grasped her shoulder in a rough, calloused grip.

"Don't touch me."

"Heh." He winked. "Looks like we both got secrets, princess. I might need some help rememberin' to keep them. You're even prettier for real. You sure we can't be friends?"

"I'm sure." Maya would've given anything for Genna to appear out of the fire stairs at that instant.

He brushed a thumb over her cheek before walking off, dragging his hand across her chest. Maya dropped the Hydra packs and folded her arms over herself, shivering once he no longer looked at her. Nausea and fear lasted another two seconds before anger kicked them to the side. She scowled at the door to his apartment, gathered the dehydrated food, and hurried into the stairwell, straight to the hollow under the first flight.

Sarah was gone.

Maya ran up to the seventh floor. She didn't slow down until after she kicked the door to her home closed and flipped the deadbolt. Sick to her stomach from fear, she dropped the silver meal packets on the coffee table, sprinted down the hall to the bedroom, and jumped on the bed. Genna woke on impact and muttered incoherently before sitting up.

"Mom!" Maya shivered from the conflict between anger and her physical inability to vent it on a grown man.

"What's wrong?" Genna sat up.

"Mr. Mason tried to get me to go inside his apartment. He said dirty things and grabbed me."

Genna's dark brown eyes almost bulged straight out of their sockets. The rage and pain radiating from them made her cry, not for what Mason had done, but out of joy that someone actually cared. She cradled Maya's cheeks in both hands and touched foreheads. Her voice quivered with dread. "You tell me everything that happened, okay? It's not your fault."

"I know." Maya sniffled. "Sarah ran away when he walked in, but I didn't. I thought the others might only be picking on a lonely old man." She scowled. "But he's one of *those*."

"What did he do?" Genna's tone got dark. "Son of a bitch. He *did*. Oh, Sarah. No one believed her when she told us he'd tried to drag her into his apartment.

That piece of shit said she made it up when he caught her stealing food."

Maya patted her chest. "He grabbed me here for a couple seconds but walked away. I told him I knew why he wanted me to go to his apartment and I wouldn't go with him." She relayed everything he'd said to her.

"I'm gonna—" Genna raised both arms, her right still in a cast, and inhaled with a hiss. "Ow, fuck." She fell flat, teeth clenched. "As soon as the god damned floor and ceiling stop switchin' places, there gon' be an empty 'partment on the first."

"Are you going to kill him?" Maya lay on her side and tucked herself under Genna's good arm.

Genna pulled her fingers through Maya's hair. "Damn right. An' I ain't gonna use no gun."

"Okay."

"Be a couple days yet 'fore I can deal with that issue. You stay the hell away from him."

"I will." She kept quiet for a few minutes, listening to air swirling in and out of the lung under her ear. Genna squeezed her, muttering random swear words. Never had she felt so secure. So wanted. So *loved*.

Maya burst into tears.

Genna stroked her hair while making comforting sounds. Once bawling gave way to subdued sniveling, she kissed Maya atop the head. "He won't lay a damn finger on you again."

"That's not why I'm crying." Tears kept flowing, though she grinned. "You're a real mother. Vanessa wouldn't have cared." *She would've told me to ask him for money first.* Maya shivered.

"Listen here, child." Genna gave her a look like she'd been caught doing something wrong. "You go on an' forget that woman. She ain't mean nothin' to you no more."

Maya snuggled in close and let out a long, relaxed breath. "Night, Mom."

NINETEEN
LESS THAN WORTHLESS

The exit from her former home replayed upon the canvas of her dreams that night, but Moth seemed even larger than last time. Genna's contemptuous anger had changed to a look of resigned determination. Maya found herself eager to be taped up and stuffed in the duffel bag, though whether she wanted to hide from Moth or because it represented her escape from that lifeless existence, she couldn't tell. She rolled on her front before Genna ordered her to and put her hands behind her back.

Her calm remained only as long as it took for the swaying bag to become still. The bottom hardened as though it had been set down on concrete with a gentle touch. She mumbled despite the duct tape gag, trying to call out for Genna.

Somewhere out in the darkness, the raspy insectoid hiss of Icarus chuckling faded to silence.

She waited for a little while before struggling. The dream had gone off script. This wasn't what happened. Why did they decide to leave her in a bag in the middle of an old sewer tunnel?

Maya grunted and strained, but couldn't break the tape binding her. A few seconds after she gave up and tried to catch her breath through her nose, the zipper tore open to reveal Mr. Mason grinning down on her like a little boy who'd opened the ultimate holiday present.

Her scream erupted in the real world.

Genna woke seconds later and pulled her into a one-armed hug. As the barrier between dream and not solidified, Maya calmed. She clung for a while before the fear passed, then straightened up and yawned.

"I'm gonna wound that man." Genna pulled Maya into her lap and swung her legs around so she could sit on the edge of the bed.

"Just a bad dream. Are you still hurting?" Maya rested her head against her mother's shoulder.

"I feel pretty damn good today."

Maya smiled. "Your eye isn't puffy anymore."

Genna tried to move her right arm. "Still sore, but I think the nanobots are done. Just gotta get Doc to take this damn brace off."

"You should wait another day." Maya leaned over and poked one finger at the irregular shaped holes in the latticework cast. "The nanobots build a framework for new bone to grow on. It won't be strong yet."

"Now you sound like Doc. Where you learn all that?"

A spaghetti strap slipped past her one-shoulder shrug. "People talked about drugs and medicine stuff around me a lot. Sometimes, I'd go with Vanessa to the office and sit there all day because she wanted me to be seen at a function later. I used to have to do intro bio and stuff, but I don't think she wants me to take over Ascendant anymore." Maya frowned. "I told her Xenodril's too expensive. Why make medicine to cure people when the people can't afford it?"

"Oh, baby." Genna hugged her. "You don't gotta worry 'bout none of that now."

The last vestiges of trembling at the nightmare faded from her muscles. She swished her feet back and forth, smiling.

Genna picked at the nightdress. "First thing I'ma do is go scare up some real shit for you to wear." Her expression waxed sympathetic. "Wanna talk about that dream?"

Maya draped her arms in her lap and fidgeted with her fingernails. "I dreamed about you taking me again. Only the bag stopped in the middle of the underground, like everyone left me there alone. I couldn't get out. Then Mr. Mason opened it."

Genna drew her into a near-painful squeeze. "Oh, honey. I'm so damn sorry. Maybe someday you gonna be pissed off at me for that, and you got every right to be."

"No." Maya squirmed free and landed on her feet. "It's Moth I'm having nightmares about. He's the only one who really wanted to hurt me. There's no food in here. I'm gonna go ask Sarah for some sandwiches."

"Okay." Genna wiped at her eyes and got out of bed. "Damn. Feels like I've been on Bed Patrol for a week. I need a damn shower."

"It works?" Maya blinked.

"'Course it works. Why you think it didn't?"

Maya tilted her head forward, eyebrows a flat line. "Have you *seen* the walls in there?"

"Heh. Ain't as bad as it looks." She waved at the hallway. "You want me to come with?"

The color of the sky visible from the glass patio doors hinted that they'd both slept into the early afternoon. Mr. Mason would be in the Sanctuary Zone now, far away from here.

"I can go. He's not here now." Maya put a hand on her stomach to still the grumbling, and walked to the front door.

"Okay. Come right back."

"I will," yelled Maya, while jogging down the hall.

She unlocked and opened the door. Barnes sprinted by and forced his way into the broken elevator down the hall. Seconds later, a faint metal clanking emanated from the shaft.

"Mr. Barnes?" She stared at the battered metal, wondering how he managed to open them at all—they looked beyond smashed. Interest waned in seconds; she rolled her eyes and headed left down the hall to Sarah's apartment. "That's weird. The elevators don't work."

Two Authority officers in full armor came barreling out of the fire stairs at the corner while three more emerged from the main stairwell in the elevator chamber—the one that smelled like sour milk and puke. Maya gasped and darted back in her door. She stumbled to all fours for a few seconds in the living room and crawled up to a run. Genna stood next to the bed, attempting to get her bra off with one hand.

"Mom!" Maya raced into a hug. "We gotta hide. Authority is here!"

Genna scooped Maya up with her good arm and looked around as if searching for something to stuff her in. "They're in the hall? Can we get to the elevators?"

"They're right outside... and the elevators are broken." Maya pointed at the patio. "Can we hide there?"

Disregarding her current state of dress—half a bra and panties—Genna speed-limped for the sliding glass doors. "Nowhere to go out there but jumpin', and I ain't know how ta fly."

The front door flew open with a loud *bang*. A pair of large blue-armored men shuffled in, pointing rifles at them.

"This is an Authority lockdown," said an electronically boosted voice.

"Noncompliance will result in death. On the ground."

Genna sank to her knees, right arm stiff forward, left wrapped around Maya. "Please don't hurt my daughter. She's only eight."

Maya kept her head down.

"Two contacts; one adult, one juvenile," said one of the blueberries. He advanced, waving his rifle to the side. "On your faces."

Genna rolled onto her chest and spread her arms and legs out, but didn't let go of Maya's hand. Maya whimpered and mimicked the pose. Three more Authority officers walked in. Heavy boots *thunked* on the concrete slab floor as they spread out into the other rooms.

Maya stifled an angry yell when black gloved hands grabbed her forearm and jerked her hand away from Genna's. The officer pinned her arms behind her back and secured her wrists with plastic ties before cinching another set around her ankles. Genna got similar treatment, though the officer fixed her bra in place once she had been restrained.

He rolled Maya onto her back and held a brick-sized device over her. A bright flickering light from the underside made her squint. She caught herself firing an indignant glare up at him and tried to act frightened and timid. The man swatted the device a few times, grumbling. A few seconds after the light became steady, it turned pale blue. Maya shut her eyes and looked away.

Beep. Beep. Beep.

An angry tone emanated from a similar device hovering over Genna's face. The officer near Maya forced her onto her front again and added another tie, connecting her wrists to her ankles behind her back. Before she could gasp at the rough treatment, he picked her up by it. She screamed as the bindings bit into her skin, all her weight hung by four plastic loops. He hauled her out the door, carrying her like a briefcase made of person.

"What the fuck is wrong with you?" shouted Genna. "She's a kid!"

Genna let off a grunt in time with a meaty *thump.*

"Mom, help!" screamed Maya. She thrashed, unable to see anything but her hair and the carpet gliding by below. "Ow!"

Sarah's father shouted in the distance to the left, sounding furious. A loud smash preceded the delicate clinking of broken glass. Maya wriggled, begged, and screamed all the way along the hall to the stinky staircase and down to a fifth floor room where six Authority officers milled around a trio of portable computers. He set her down flat on her chest atop a desk only long enough to get an actual grip on her body before maneuvering her around more or less upright. A hard plastic strip proved a rather uncomfortable thing to sit on, and kept her heels wedged against her butt.

"What's your name?" asked a different armored figure. Little of his face showed through his visor, save for some black traces of a poor shaving job.

"Lisa," said Maya. *They'll expect me to be bossy.* She added a sniffle, trying to sound anxious and harmless. "I'm scared! I want my mommy. We didn't do anything wrong."

"No one said you did." A gravelly voice came from the far side of the suitcase computers. "This is a routine security check. We'll be gone in a half hour."

A more gentle gloved hand brushed over the side of her head and forced her to look up. This blueberry appeared to be female. "Kid does look an awful lot like her. How credible was the tip?"

Maya cringed, bringing her right shoulder up to her head, hoping to hide the designer tag on the thin strap. If any of them noticed it, game over.

"As good as anything these bottom feeders come up with." A man with 'Baxter' on his nametag paced about. He looked as eager to get out of here as Maya.

The female officer waved another device over her face. "Goddamned uplink error. Local WiFi's probably down. Nothing in the onboard database."

Baxter shook his head and gestured at the wall. "These animals probably shot it too."

"Was working three minutes ago," said the woman.

"No one can hurt you now." A different male officer approached and set his hands on his hips. "If you've been kidnapped, you can tell us. Whatever they threatened you with is a lie."

Maya peered up between strands of her hair at him. *Yeah. I'm being kidnapped all right... by you assholes.* She swallowed the venom that wanted out, and looked down. "No, sir. I live here." Worry made for a passable fear substitute and allowed for believable trembling.

"That ain't her. M.O. would be goin' nuts." An armored man patted the woman on the shoulder. His nameplate read 'Hammond.' "I'll put her with the other juveniles."

"You're so sure?" The woman fiddled with her machine for another few seconds before giving up with a sigh.

"Yeah, I met the little precious angel once. She's like a smaller version of her mother. Thinks we're like her personal servants or something. Threw an epic shit fit when I wouldn't give her a ride to Emperor's Plaza." Hammond regarded her with a mild frown. "If this *was* her, she'd be telling us all about how much trouble we'd be in for treating her like this."

"How adorable." Baxter rolled his eyes and walked out. "She looks so sweet and cute in the ads. Guess *everything* on TV is a lie."

"Hey," said the gravelly voice. "None of you nobs forget that Oman owns Ascendant, and Ascendant provides eighty-six percent of our operating budget in this area. Official or not, she *is* your boss... functionally anyway."

"Man, that's such bullshit," said the female blueberry. "We used to be something more than corporate enforcers."

"Feel free to complain, Warren... but it's your pretty ass that'll be hittin' the pavement," said gravelly man. "And you ain't got the body for strippin'."

The female officer glared off to the side, muttering "dick" too low for him to hear.

Hammond put his hand on Maya's head and turned it so she looked at him—or at least at his shiny visor. "Last chance, kid. You sure you're not Maya Oman? Someone seems to think you are."

Maya grunted, trying to shift her weight off the painful plastic digging in to her backside. "No, sir. My name is Lisa."

"She's at least a Citizen," said Officer Warren. "Hey, wouldn't Maya have a tracking chip? Flip her over so I can scan her hand."

Oh, no. Her mind raced. She couldn't remember if she'd been chipped. Her breath seized in her throat. *If they figure it out, maybe I can order them around? No. They'll want a promotion for 'saving' me.* Bile crept up into the back of her throat as Hammond rolled her onto her belly. Though the plastic strip connecting her hands to her feet stopped gouging her rear end, the riot ties bit into her ankles, making her whine. The officer waved a small object around her hands, and then her butt.

"No signal," said Warren.

"Wouldn't get one even if that was Maya," said the man behind the computers. "Our dear little princess does not have an identity chip. Her mother figured it would make it too easy for abductors to pick the real one apart from the decoys."

Maya slouched with relief. One of Genna's friends must've done something to mess with the facial recognition. She didn't care *why* the blueberries failed to recognize her, as long as they did.

"Couldn't they chip them all?" Warren held her arms out. "Reckless not to chip a kid you *expect* will be abducted."

"Five grand a chip," said a distant man. "Probably failed the cost-benefit analysis. That or she thought anyone stupid enough to try and abduct M.O. would be stupid enough to fall for a decoy."

"Great." Hammond scooped her up, holding her at least like a person with a soul might carry a child. "I suppose harassing Nons beats getting shot at."

"Why's that kid scanning as a Citizen?" The female officer caught Hammond's arm before he could carry her out.

"My mother is a veteran," said Maya. "But she can't afford to live in the Sanctuary Zone."

"Oh." Warren seemed satisfied and put the scanner back on her belt.

Hammond carried her out into the hall. Maya squirmed in a halfhearted protest, frowning at the thick grey plastic around her ankles. He brought her into a disused, grungy apartment two doors away from the Authority's temporary command center, where the other kids had all been lined up on their knees facing the wall. Pick on the far right in the corner, the twins, Emily, and Sarah closest to the way in. All had been trussed up the same way as Maya. Pick looked frightened, but seemed to be able to hold himself together. Anton and Marcus trembled in silence. Emily wailed as if she'd skinned both knees. She alternated between begging to be untied and calling for her parents. The look on the redhead's face made it seem like a good thing she'd been restrained, or she might've wound up shot. Her hip bag of tools was gone, hopefully hidden in her apartment and not confiscated.

The blueberry eased Maya down next to Sarah. She shifted around and sat back on her heels. Sarah leaned against her, as close as she could get to a hug while hogtied. Hammond muttered a few words under his breath and glanced at a massive armored man near the window. Maya's eyes widened; this guy could've probably gone head-to-head with Moth and had a chance—if he had metal arms under that suit.

Several minutes passed in tense silence with the blueberries talking amongst themselves about sectors.

"Are they gonna shoot us?" whispered Emily. She sniveled. "I'm scared."

"No," said Maya. "They're just searching."

"Then why are we bein' 'rested." Emily coughed on snot she couldn't reach to wipe.

Sarah sighed, not even bothering to struggle. "They always do this, Em."

"Always?" whispered Maya, twisting at her wrist.

"Like once a month at least." Sarah huffed, attempting to blow a strand of hair off her face.

"They linin' us up like they gonna execute us," said Marcus.

Emily wailed again. "I don' wanna be ex-cuted."

"Quiet," barked Baxter. "Eyes front."

Maya gave up trying to get her hands free and glared at the wall.

Hammond grumbled. "Hey, Sarge. Is this necessary? They're just kids."

Emily stared at one of the assault rifles pointed in their general direction. She wriggled and wailed, begging to be cut free, promising to be good. Maya scowled at the floor in front of her knees. Her heartbeat pounded in her ears. This frightened her far more than being taken by Genna and her crew. At least she'd been valuable to them. The Authority would consider her another worthless Non no one would miss. Being a child only stopped them from going out of their way to hurt her; if something happened at random, oh well.

"Em, be quiet," whispered Maya. "Do what they tell you and we'll be okay."

"You didn't serve in the Iraq campaign, did you, Hammond?" Sarge continued gazing out the window. "Sure, they look harmless. That tiny one dressed up like a doll almost makes you feel sorry for her. Out here, you can't trust anyone. They're all cuteness and innocence until you turn your back, and then one of the little bastards throws a grenade at you... or runs and grabs a weapon. You wanna shoot a little kid, Hammond?"

"No, Sarge." He offered Maya an almost apologetic shrug.

"You feel bad enough hearin' that one carry on." Sarge tapped his foot. "That's the kind of guilt you can get over. An hour after we leave, she'll forget us. Now imagine that little angel running at you with a grenade. You think the kinda guilt you'd have puttin' a bullet in her heart is gonna go away with a beer or two?"

Emily scrunched herself down, trying to keep quiet. Maya eyed the handful of rifles not quite pointing at them. At any second, one of the blueberries could get sick of hearing Emily carry on and silence her for good.

"It's okay, Em. We'll be fine. They won't shoot us," said Maya. "Please just stay quiet."

Screams in the distance sounded like Naida, or maybe Arlene. An angry man bellowed and a heavy *whump* reverberated in the floor. The female voice stopped screaming.

Pick sniffled. His face reddened and his fists turned purple from trying to break the zip ties.

Baxter walked over to Hammond. "Seen it too many times, Chris. Soon as you let your guard down, even the children will stick a knife in your back."

"Maybe you wouldn't have to be so paranoid if you stopped treating us like garbage. Assholes. She's seven and terrified." Sarah twisted around to glare at them. "Are you really so scared of little kids you gotta cuff us so tight we can barely move, or does it make you feel like a big tough man to terrorize children?"

Baxter cracked her across the face with the butt of his rifle, knocking her sideways to the floor. Sarah's mouth hung open, her eyes unfocused. A trail of blood crept down over her forehead, another from her lip. Maya stared in horror for a second at her helpless friend, hogtied and unconscious, before looking up at Baxter. Emily closed her eyes and trembled, emitting a steady whine.

"Sarah!" Maya struggled to move closer, desperate to wrap her in a hug. That she couldn't with her wrists locked together infuriated her past fear. She glared up at Baxter. "What did you do that for? What's wrong with you?" Venom pooled at the tip of her tongue, rage at the way they treated a harmless girl threatened to launch a tirade. She bit her lip; if she acted like her old self, all of these kids would be in trouble… as would everyone in the building. Tears of shame and anger leaked out of her eyes, followed by a genuine squeal of fright when Baxter raised his rifle again.

Hammond shoved Baxter before he could give Maya a whack. "What the fuck was that? God damned kid's in restraints. You can't take a fuckin' wisecrack from a twelve-year-old? You get off on that or something? You could'a broken her goddamned neck."

"She's eleven." Pick narrowed his eyes at the man who hit Sarah. "Asshole."

"Fuck you, Chris." Baxter pushed Hammond away and took a step toward Pick, who cowered.

Hammond grabbed the other blueberry and yanked him back with enough force to make him stumble. "You hit another kid, I'm going to break my Hornet off in your ass."

Baxter rolled his shoulders and took on an aggressive lean at Hammond. "Bunch of Nons. If we don't kill them now, we'll wind up doing it in five years when they're older."

"They're not *all* criminals," muttered Sarge. "Just most of them."

"Still a fucking kid." Hammond shoved him again. "This ain't what we signed on for."

Baxter took a swing, which Hammond ducked. The two men collapsed in a heap of writhing armor and blurry fists. A third Authority officer in the room standing by Sarge watched with mild interest. Maya cringed away from the fight going on less than an arm's length behind her. Blood continued to seep down Sarah's porcelain face, threading in a trail that dripped from her nose. Maya seethed in silent fury, but no matter how hard she strained, the plastic cuffs refused to snap. Unable to get her hands loose to embrace her friend, Maya stooped forward and pressed her forehead to Sarah's.

"Please be okay," whispered Maya. "I'm sorry…"

Sarge stomped over, hoisting Baxter and Hammond up by the necks of their armor like a pair of kittens. He tossed Baxter one way and Hammond the other.

"Knock that shit off. If one of you is going on report, you're both going on report. Either one of you got a complaint?"

Hammond fumed, staring at Sarah. "Maybe I do."

"No, you don't." Sarge pointed at Baxter. "And neither do you. Both of you get the fuck out of here and go do something useful. Check the ninth and tenth."

Maya shifted sideways, struggling to reach Sarah's head to put pressure on the bleeding cut over her left eye. Her fingers teased at hair, but nothing more. Anton whispered to Marcus.

"Quiet," said the smaller officer. "Face the wall, don't talk. At the moment, none of you are in any trouble. This is a routine security check. Obey the rules and no one gets hurt."

"Tell that to Sarah," muttered Pick.

If they knew who I was, they'd wet their pants. Maya tried to burn holes in the wall with a glare.

"Hey, hey, hey!" yelled Brian, somewhere outside. "I didn't do anything. Get offa me."

The tromp of boots went down the hall. A few minutes later, Maya cringed at the echo of an armored vehicle hatch closing outside. At the tromp of more heavy footsteps approaching, she twisted around to look at the door. Two blueberries carried a struggling, hogtied Genna down the hall toward the stairs. Maya tried to jump upright, but wound up rolling onto her back when the binding jerked her to a halt.

"Hey. That's my mom! Why are you taking her?" She scooted in a series of short hops for the door until not-Sarge grabbed her and dragged her back to her place against the wall.

"If your mother's got nothing to hide," said the blueberry, "she'll be back in a couple hours."

"Why?" Maya shook her head to fling away a streamer of snot from crying. "Why are you taking her?"

"Got flagged. She probably looks like someone on the wanted list. If she's clean, she'll be back in a few hours." He patted her on the head.

Sarge walked out while talking to thin air. "Floor nine, status. Good. Ten?" He grumbled to himself for a few seconds. "Well then *finish* it."

One blueberry left.

I could tell him who I am. I could order him to let her go. She exhaled, feeling defeated and helpless. *No. They'd still take her, and take me too.* Maya wanted to cry but wound up getting furious instead. Vanessa loathed being backed into a corner and having no way out. That woman never allowed herself to become helpless. Of course, she also wasn't nine. Maya slumped, hiding her face behind a curtain of hair. The more she wanted to hold Sarah in her arms, the tighter the plastic around her wrists felt.

Emily whined to herself, desperate to cry but terrified to make a sound. Anton and Marcus grimaced and gasped while attempting to free themselves. Pick had curled up in the corner, staring past his knees with a wide-eyed, heart-rending expression of pleading fear. Maya fumed in silence. Every second of being treated like this made her hate Vanessa a little more.

About ten uncomfortable minutes later, the remaining blueberry said "Copy" and walked out.

Maya looked around, her panic building. Too-fast breathing left her dizzy in seconds. At the rapid *thunk* of several heavy vehicle doors closing, and laboring electric engines whirring off to silence, she stared in horror at the still-unconscious Sarah.

Her heart raced as she struggled to move. "A-aren't they gonna let us out?"

Pick twisted himself around and fell flat on his stomach. "Nope." He squirmed and grunted.

"No?" Maya gasped. "They're just gonna leave us tied up?"

"Yeah. They always do," said Marcus. "Guess they wanna run away before we go after 'em with grenades."

Anton shook his head. "Last time they was here, they left Faerie in the wrong 'partment. No one found her for like a whole day."

"W-what do we do?" Maya flopped on her side and nudged Sarah with her head a few times.

"Don't scream." Emily sniffled before answering in an eerie whisper. "We hope someone nice finds us. If you scream for help, someone bad will come."

Maya peered up from the floor at Emily, still kneeling where the Authority had placed her, looking pathetic in her costume doll dress. With the threat of violence out of the room, Emily surrendered to crying and calling for her mommy and daddy, though not too loud.

Go ahead, shoot. I'll even watch if it will get you to stop pestering me.

Vanessa's voice in her memory filled Maya with disgust. How could that awful woman allow people to be treated like this for no crime other than being too poor to become Citizens? She rolled onto her back and used every muscle in her body in an effort to break the tie linking her wrists to her ankles. The harder she struggled, the more they hurt, and the less she believed she could escape.

Pick gave up his fight as well and lay still, looking a mixture of bored and nervous. Marcus knee-walked around the junk, heading for what had been the apartment's kitchen. Gritting her teeth, Maya pulled with all the strength she could find in an effort to stretch her legs out and snap her way free. Pain overwhelmed fear, and she sagged limp a few seconds later.

A glint of sunlight flickered from the broken window by where Sarge had perched. Maya figured it about noon. Her nightmare swooped in on wings of terror. The Authority had taken Genna. Silence said every adult in the building had been arrested, and Mr. Mason, away in the Sanc at his job, hadn't been here. He'd be back in a few hours.

And the Authority had gift wrapped her for him.

TWENTY

CLEANUP

ooden thumping came from the kitchen. Maya stared at the ceiling while trying to twist her hands out of the tight plastic loops. Anton, who she assumed to be stronger than her, had failed to break loose. Emily had curled up on her side, her constant pleas for her parents having faded to tiny whispered mewls.

Maya rolled her head to the right, staring past several roaches at the shivering, crying doll. She blamed Vanessa for this. Angry resolve sidestepped the onrush of panic caused by the bugs crawling closer. Standing around them had been scary enough, but now she couldn't even get up. Having her face at floor level with enormous insects made her draw in a breath to scream, but she remembered Emily's warning and choked on it. With an uneasy whimper leaking from her nose, she swung her legs side to side in an effort to rock herself off her back while trying to resist the urge to shout for help.

"Swear it ain't none of us what told," said Anton. "Them bugs won't bite you long as you're moving. They only have a taste if'n they think you's a deader."

"I know." Maya grunted as her body surrendered to gravity. She straightened herself out on her belly. "Mr. Mason did it."

"Blueberries didn't take you though. Guess you got lucky." Anton settled in, looking as though he expected to be stuck all day.

"Why'd he do it?" asked Pick. He shifted on his side, tucked his knees against his chest and rolled onto them.

Maya snarled from the plastic biting her skin, but she wobbled until she mimicked his technique. Without carpet, the concrete slab floor hurt her knees, but she felt less helpless as close to upright as she could get. She frowned at Sarah, who hadn't yet come to. At least the bleeding had stopped. Sarah knew what Mr. Mason wanted too. Maya bit her lip while staring at Emily. She couldn't say it in front of her. "He's mean and greedy. I bet he thought he'd get a reward."

"Shit," said Marcus from the kitchen. "Ain't nothin' in here."

"Shut up," whisper-shouted Pick. "Don't yell for help or bad people will come."

Maya glanced at the window. *Bad people are gonna come anyway.* The thought of Mason finding her helpless got her shivering, but that his 'revenge' had wound up taking Genna away made her furious.

"Whatchu lookin' for?" said Anton.

Marcus emitted a grunt as if trying to lift an object too heavy for him. "Broke pipe or something wit' an edge. These shits are plastic."

Maya blinked. *Zoe's workshop! Wire cutters.* She knee-walked to the door as fast as she could move, which wasn't fast at all, wincing whenever her bones hit the ground too hard.

"Hey, what are you doing?" yelled Pick. "Don't go out there. Someone will 'nap you."

"That's what I'm afraid of if I just stay here too." Maya stopped at the door to catch her breath. "Stay quiet."

Ignoring his protest, she leaned her head out and looked both ways. Aside from a haze of smoke and the smell of some chemical she didn't recognize, the hall appeared empty. The stinky stairwell had no doors, and she'd never be able to reach the knob on the fire exit while hogtied. She had bigger things to worry about than an unpleasant odor. With a grunt of determination, she got her weight up on her knees and toes, and shuffled out the door, ignoring the whispered shouts of the other kids telling her not to.

Huffing and gasping, she scooted down the hall. The blueberries had taken her to the fifth floor, probably because the middle of the building made the best central command post. Except for that one guy Hammond, and maybe Warren who'd been nice, the experience had dulled the horror of watching Moth kill blueberries. A tiny part of her psyche wanted Moth to still be alive so he could twist Baxter's head off for hitting Sarah, and beat the snot out of the one who tied her up.

Maya yelped with each strike of her knees upon the smooth concrete floor on her trek to the stairwell. She didn't even notice the stench, her brain spinning in too much of a whirlwind of anger and fear to register it. She dragged herself to the first step, turned around, and got a grip on the edge. The tether between her hands and feet allowed barely enough room, and between pushing with her toes and lifting with her arms, she pulled herself up one step. She repeated the process again and again, stopping for a few breaths as soon as her backside had a solid purchase on the landing.

She stared down past her legs, and the tenuous grip her toes had on the eleventh step, at a fall that would probably break her neck since she couldn't protect her head with her arms. *Sarah needs help.* Maya forced the terror of a fatal somersault out of her mind and kept going. She rolled backward and wriggled over to the next set of steps. One stair at a time, she made her way up. The urge to get herself free before Mr. Mason came back and found her friends surged, allowing her to ignore the growing pain from where the bindings bit into her skin. No one remained behind to save them.

Sweat soaked her by the time she reached the sixth floor. She dragged herself away from the stairs before trying to roll onto her knees, not wanting to risk a fall. Inch by inch, she hopped and shuffled down the corridor. A sudden, horrifying thought sent tears streaming down her face. What if Zoe's apartment door was closed? The mere worry it might not be open got her as sick to her stomach as if Mason had found her. A steady stream of determined grunting came from her with each shuffle forward to the corner.

Joy burst from her chest at the sight of the workshop/clinic door hanging wide. It took a somber turn when she shuffled in and found Zoe unconscious on the floor, also hogtied with plastic strips. Small scratches on the woman's arms suggested Emily had been torn away from her mother.

They didn't take everyone. Where's Doctor Chang?

"Hello?" asked Maya.

Silence.

Out of breath, she knelt in place for a few seconds glancing at the bottoms of tables, trying to remember which one had the wire cutters. "Sorry, Zoe. I'll help you clean up."

Maya hopped forward and slammed her shoulder into the nearest table leg. She rocked side to side, shaking the table until stuff started falling from all sides. Something hard bounced off her head, making her cry out, but it looked like a spool of solder. Snarling, she flung herself against the table until she ran out of breath, then looked around the rug.

She bit her lip to keep from cheering at the wonderful blue plastic tool four feet away. Maya let gravity take her down on her side and inchwormed up to it, fingers grasping at the carpet until she got a hand on the cutter. After a moment of fumbling, she managed a decent grip and twisted her head around to look at her feet. The blueberry had pulled the strips tight to the point of being cruel, and the wire cutter hurt when she tried to slip one of the points under the plastic.

Maya growled and forced the tool between her skin and the painful strap before squeezing the grip with both hands. Growling with effort, she strained with all the strength she could muster. Eventually, a loud *click* broke the silence and her right leg shot straight out, leaving her left still tethered to her hands. With a little more mobility, she shifted her weight to one knee and repeated the process to free her other leg. She sat upright, rubbing at her raw ankles with opposing feet while trying to work the snips around to attack the plastic encircling her wrists.

Each time Maya slipped and dropped the cutter, her frustration grew. When the tool hit the rug for the fifth time, she let off an angry scream, but gave up on the impossible task and crawled to Zoe. It took some creative wriggling to work the snips behind her back, but she snipped the riot ties off the woman and tried to wake her up by patting her on the cheek with a foot. Alas, Zoe didn't react.

"Did they give you a tranq?" Maya grumbled and wobbled up to stand.

Keeping a death grip on the wire cutter behind her back, she ran down to the fifth floor. Marcus had dragged himself once more into the living room and rocked side to side, still trying to free himself. Pick's calm had broken, and he sniveled into the lack of rug. When Maya *walked* in, everyone went silent and still, staring.

Everyone except Sarah, who remained unconscious.

Maya hurried over to Marcus and twisted around so they could all see the wire cutters behind her back. Emily smiled and bounced in place. Pick looked awestruck.

Anton smiled. "Nice."

She sat on the floor and cut Marcus loose, who then freed her hands and snipped the riot ties off his brother. Maya swiped the cutter and cut the bindings away from Sarah before handing it back to Marcus. He set Emily free while Maya patted Sarah's cheek and shook her. As soon Marcus untied Pick, he ran out, screaming for his sister.

"We gonna go check on Book." Marcus waved the cutter. "Might need this."

"'Kay," said Maya. "It's Zoe's."

"Mmm." Sarah stirred. She opened her eyes, looked at Maya, and threw up.

Maya patted her on the back until she stopped vomiting, then grabbed her in a hug. Though she cried, inside she seethed. "Are you okay?"

"Dizzy." Sarah sat up, holding a hand to the side of her head. "Ow. That bastard hit me, didn't he?"

"Yeah." Maya brushed Sarah's hair away from her face. "You're bleeding."

Sarah convulsed again, but didn't vomit. "Doc?"

Maya shook her head. "Gone."

"Daddy?" Emily burst into tears.

"They always take him for a little while." Sarah got to her feet, holding on to Maya for balance. "Got some kinda problem with a doctor wanting to be out here with Nons, I guess. Probably."

"You're technically a Citizen too," whispered Maya. "Your dad's a vet."

Sarah glowered as if she'd been called something nasty. "So?"

"That officer hit you. You're not eighteen yet, and a Citizen. He could get in a lot of trouble if your dad filed a complaint."

"And then they come back here an' give it to us worse." Sarah grabbed Emily's hand. "'Mon."

Maya followed them back to the Changs' apartment. As soon as they entered, Emily wailed "Mommy!" and jumped on top of Zoe, sobbing. Maya walked over to the medical station and hunted through two cabinets' worth of pill bottles and disposable prefilled injectors until she spotted a box of slender green tubes. She plucked one out and turned it in her fingers to read the lettering melted into the plastic housing: ATQ-110C. *Hmm. This is the stuff, but how much Placinox did they give her?* She held the syringe up to the window light, noting it held about 2ccs.

"What's that?" asked Sarah. "You shouldn't be touching Doctor Chang's medicine stuff."

"It's the antidote to the standard Authority tranquilizer shot. They use Placinox as a chemical restraint. I bet she put up a fight when they tried to take Emily, so they knocked her out. This will wake her up, but I'm not sure how much to use."

Sarah looked back and forth from the drug to Zoe a few times. "How long will she stay out if you don't do anything?"

Maya blinked. "I said I don't know how much they gave her, but it would be at least a few hours." She marched over to the unconscious woman while twisting a selector ring at the top end. "One cc shouldn't be a problem. That little won't do anything even if they didn't give her any tranquilizer, and I'm sure they did. The worst thing it'll do is fail to wake her."

Emily stared up at Maya with an expression that could've been hope or mortal terror. Maya pulled down on Zoe's belt to expose a few inches of butt, and jammed the autoinjector home. It let off a weak hiss. Maya held it up again to confirm 1cc remained in the tube.

"Why'd you hit her in the ass with it?" Sarah picked Emily up and held her.

"Intramuscular." Maya bounced up and put the injector back where she found it.

The girls stood in silence for about forty seconds, all staring at Zoe until she moaned.

"Mommy!" yelled Emily.

Sarah set her down and edged to the door. "Maybe you should bring one of those for my dad. He always gives them a hard time."

Maya glanced at the cabinet. "Okay."

Zoe sat up looking groggy. "Emily? Where's Em..."

"Mommy!" wailed Emily as she clamped on to her mother.

"Baby..." Zoe sniffled, patting her daughter on the back while rocking her. Eventually, she looked up at Maya. "What happened?"

Maya explained everything she knew. Authority conducted a 'security check' and left everyone in restraints. Zoe grumbled about bullshit protocols.

"They do it to be assholes," said Sarah with a scowl. "They ain't afraid of us. They're cruel."

Maya rubbed the lines of fire around her wrists. "They got Genna."

"Where's Mike?" Zoe kept rubbing a hand up and down Emily's back. "Did they drag him to the Sanc again?"

Both Sarah and Maya shrugged.

"Bastards," said Zoe. "He's as clean as you can get."

"He'll be okay," said Maya. "Maybe he hid like Mr. Barnes."

Anton ran in and handed the wire cutter to Maya. "Book's okay. Sarah, your dad's pretty pissed off, but he's not hurt. He wants to you help him put his arm back on. I couldn't find Mr. Weber or Mr. Barnes. They took Naida for her shots. Brian's gone. They left Arlene on the floor but didn't cuff her. She couldn't get up, so me and Marcus helped her to the couch." He fidgeted. "She looked bad. I hope Doctor Chang comes back soon."

Maya glanced between him and Zoe. "Shots?"

Zoe blushed. "Uhh. Naida's job is, uhh, and—"

"I know what a prostitute is," mumbled Maya.

"Well..." Zoe sighed. "They round them up and force vaccinations and other things on them... kind of like keeping up on rabies shots for a dog."

"That's horrible!" Maya gawked. "It's... it's..."

"We're not even people to them," said Sarah.

Anton gestured at the door. "That's everyone. Mr. Mason's door is locked and he didn't say anything when I banged on it."

"He's not here," said Maya. The coldness in her voice got a raised eyebrow from Zoe. "He's at work."

Sarah shivered and stumbled to the side, woozy. "I... should go help my dad."

Maya grabbed Zoe's arm. "They took Genna. We gotta go help her."

Zoe ran a hand over Maya's hair. "Oh, Lisa... there isn't anything we can do but hope they decide to let her go. I'm sorry, but it's the Authority."

"But..." Maya scowled. *I'm Maya Oman. I can order them to set her loose.* "I can..."

"Don't go getting any wild ideas." Zoe's light brown hair turned near blonde as she leaned into a shaft of sunlight coming in from the patio doors. "You saw how they treated you when you weren't in trouble. Being a kid isn't any protection. All we can do is keep our heads down."

Maya's lip quivered but she refused to cry. "Sorry about knocking your stuff all over."

"Forgiven. You had a good reason." Zoe traced a finger over the bloody lines around Maya's ankles. "You fought like a little tiger. Come on, let me clean that up."

Sarah wobbled to the doorjamb and clung. "Gotta go. Dad needs me."

Zoe carried Maya to the exam table and worked an alcohol-pad around where the riot ties had drawn blood, making her hiss and squirm from the stinging. Zoe grasped Maya's left heel and raised her leg, spritzing around her ankle from a white spray can. The raw skin tingled for a second before it felt like it caught fire.

Maya dug her fingers into the cushion on either side of her butt. "Ow!"

Pain lasted less time than the yell. Zoe sprayed the Epi-seal (made by Ascendant) on Maya's other leg and both wrists. Clear liquid flashed to white foam, and new skin faded in over the cuts like she'd never been injured.

"I'm sorry, sweetie. You don't want an open wound out here. It'll get infected."

Maya folded her arms over her chest, shivering. "I know. Thank you. It just hurts. Doctor Chang needs to check Sarah. One of them hit her with his rifle on the head, and she threw up. That's not good after a head injury. She might have a concussion."

Zoe scowled, looking angry and worried at the same time.

Barnes walked in and approached Maya. "There you are. What happened?"

She narrowed her eyes. "Where the hell have you been? Thanks for leaving us tied up on the floor for an hour!"

He showed little reaction to her outburst. "Securing the area and avoiding notice by the Authority. You weren't in any danger, Maya."

"Maya?" asked Zoe. Recognition dawned. "Oh, my."

"Thanks." Maya smirked. "The blueberries didn't recognize me."

"They came for her?" Zoe picked Maya up and set her on her feet before putting Emily on the table. The younger girl hadn't struggled as much and only had red marks, no bleeding.

Barnes scratched at his head. "Hard to say. That was our initial thought, but seeing as how they left her here, I'm not so sure."

Emily clamped onto Zoe, refusing to let go.

"They were looking for me, but I told them I wasn't who they thought I was. I scanned as a Citizen, but I said my mom is a veteran."

Barnes chuckled. "Damn lucky thing we got those signal jammers up. Well, I suppose some good came of this. They've been here and decided you aren't who they think, so any future tips will probably get ignored."

"It's *not* good," yelled Maya. "They took Genna. We have to go save her."

He rubbed his chin, his expression grim. "Damn. That's a problem."

Maya grabbed his hand and shook his arm. "Bring me to the Sanctuary Zone. We have to help her."

Barnes walked out. Maya ran after him.

Once in the hall, he went down on one knee and whispered, "If they took her, that means they don't know she's with us. If they did—"

"They'd have shot her." Maya looked down at her feet. "They're gonna find out. We have to help her before they do."

"It's not that easy. We can't just run off and save her like they do in the movies. We don't know what facility they brought her to. An operation to break someone out of prison isn't a small thing. At best, it would take weeks of planning."

"What if she doesn't have weeks?" Maya scowled. Anger didn't seem to be working, so she drew her hands together under her chin and tried to look pathetic. "Please? They're going to kill her. I just got a real mother. I don't wanna lose her already."

Barnes cringed. "I'll see what I can do, but don't get your hopes up, kid. Good chance the only thing we'd do is get ourselves killed or captured too. Genna would want us to carry on and not waste everything we've accomplished over a poorly planned rescue attempt."

"How do you know she'd want that? Sounds like you're just saying that because you don't wanna go."

His resigned expression showed no signs of change. Maya stormed off, stomping all the way up to the seventh floor where she ran to Genna's bed, flopped on her chest, and bawled.

When tears ran out, Maya stared at the wall while drifting through moments of crippling sorrow, murderous anger, and shivering fear. Crumpled sheets stretched out before her face like a mountainous arctic waste. Would Mason try to grab her like he did Sarah? Without Genna here to protect her, what could she do?

Maya pushed herself up and wiped her tears with the front of her nightdress. Fear of Mr. Mason morphed into hatred. He'd done this. He'd taken her mother away. How convenient the Authority showed up while he wasn't here. Of course they'd spare their informant the humiliation of being 'processed' and left to the mercy of whoever found him. A slice of Vanessa surfaced in the back of her mind. *No one messes with me like that and gets away with it.* The Authority would be back… soon if any truth existed in the rumors they would release any of the people they'd taken. She didn't hold on to much hope that Genna would be one of the ones they simply cut loose a few hours later, but perhaps Doctor Chang, Brian, or Naida would come home.

She'd give the Authority what they wanted—a Brigade terrorist.

It would only take a bit of setup and a little luck. She jumped from the bed and rummaged Genna's desk, pulling open each drawer and rifling among junk, boxes of bullets, gun cleaning kits, knives, and wire scrap. The big drawer on the bottom left held two bras and several pairs of women's underpants. Despite the awkwardness, Maya rooted around in case—for some strange reason—something to write on had been hidden beneath.

Finding nothing of use, she ran out and back downstairs to Zoe's place. Maya hesitated at the door, listening to the echoing voice and sound of Emily in the bathtub. She peeked inside the empty living room, searching back and forth until she spotted a notebook and a pen on one of the tables she didn't knock askew. The door made a tiny *creak* as she brushed it aside and crept closer. Better for Zoe if she didn't know anything about this plan. Maya would steal one page and borrow the pen. The slosh of bathwater came from the back hall, accompanied by Emily's echoing sniffles. Maya locked her gaze on the hall as she snuck in.

"Hey, you doing okay?" asked Zoe from the kitchen, behind her.

Maya let off a yelp; she jumped and whirled to face her. "Uhh."

Zoe wandered over, a cup of coffee clutched in two hands. "You look terrified. Are you sure you're all right?"

"Yes." Maya flashed her Ascendant smile. "I felt bad about messing up your work table. I wanted to help you pick up."

"Oh, don't worry about it." Zoe winked. "But I appreciate the thought."

"Is Emily okay?" Maya stooped and grabbed tools, circuit scraps, and such from the rug, which she set on the table.

"She'll be okay. I think she wanted to wash the Authority off."

"Are *you* okay?" Maya peered up at the woman with a rehearsed-cute head tilt. "You look sad."

"I'll feel a lot better when Mike comes home. Thank you. You don't have to pick up if you don't want to. I'll get to it eventually. I needed to sit down and try to remember how to breathe. Still a little foggy from that shot they gave me." Zoe trudged to the kitchen.

"I don't mind, Mrs. Chang." Maya hurried picking up as many tools, electronics parts, solder, and other stuff she thought fell from the table.

Splashing continued to emanate from the bathroom. Emily seemed happy, or at least distracted, by whatever she played with.

With Zoe out of sight behind the kitchen partition, Maya edged over to the notebook and removed a blank page. She nabbed a pen as well, and headed for the door.

"Bye, Mrs. Chang. I got all the stuff off the floor."

"Call me Zoe," yelled Zoe. "And be careful, *Lisa*."

"I will." *Somewhat.*

Maya raced back upstairs and leapt into one of the kitchen chairs in her apartment. She flattened the paper out on the table and wrote down all nineteen addresses for Vanessa Oman's homes. Everything from the decoy places she never bothered to set foot in to the three top-secret ones that only six or seven people in the world knew existed. Maya dug the pen into the paper on number seven. She hated that underground bunker. Vanessa had only taken her there once because she got stuck with her by virtue of travel plans. Even the rug was super-expensive, so Maya hadn't been allowed to leave the small, undecorated bedroom. "Kids break things" had been Vanessa's explanation for why Maya's room was so empty. "You can have things when you're older."

She daydreamed about spilling ink and stuff all over the white sofa and chairs, the expensive rug, and knocking all those stupid, hideous sculptures off the wall. For most of her life, she'd been so quiet and obedient, but even that failed to make Vanessa love her. Now, she didn't care anymore. She had a real mom, and nothing would stop her from getting Genna back.

With both sides of the paper filled with sector addresses, building numbers, and a couple of door access codes, Maya held it up to admire. A twinge of guilt and hesitation danced in her belly, but the memory of Mr. Mason touching her lessened it. Thinking of how Sarah had gone from tough and protective to a terrified child cowering under the stairs at his approach cemented her resolve. After folding the paper up small, she ran to Zoe's apartment only long enough to put the pen back, and rushed down the fire stairs to the ground floor. Mr. Mason would be home soon and she did *not* want to risk him seeing her again.

She crept out of the landing into the first floor hallway. Mason's apartment door, blue and dented, sat halfway between her and the exit to the parking lot. He'd taken over the superintendent's spot, but he didn't really do anything here other than collect rent money for the building's owner. Zoe did all the work fixing stuff.

Maya scurried to the door and tried to open it, but the knob wouldn't budge. She looked around for a vent to crawl in—the movies always had one of those—but didn't see any way in. A short distance deeper in the hall, an open door led in to a dirty room where two massive metal beasts, industrial hot water heaters, slumbered. The sight of them sent a shock of unease down her spine. This room looked like the stuff from which nightmares were made, and the idea that Mr. Mason lived right next to it caused a lump to swell in her throat. He'd keep her prisoner in here amid all the rusty pipes and old machines, do unspeakable things, and probably kill her so she couldn't tell anyone... and no one would ever know.

Despite feeling terrified that she'd spot a skeleton or signs of a previous victim, she forced herself to walk inside. Steel shelves flanked the door, laden with cobwebs, sections of pipe, wrenches and two toolboxes. A metal stairway at the far right side led down to the basement and the furnaces for the heating system. Breathing left the taste of metal and oil on her tongue. Grit crunched under her feet, a large part of it looked like rusted metal flakes. She stopped three steps in when she got a good look at the wall that separated the room from Mason's apartment. No vents. Not unless she risked going to the basement, crawling into the boiler, and hoping the ductwork somehow connected. Maya tiptoed to the stairs down and lost a few minutes staring at the grill door on the front of one. It looked like a monster that wanted to eat her.

She shook her head. "No way."

Sarah!

Six flights of stairs later, Maya skidded to a halt in front of apartment 139. She knocked.

A man rambled drunken incoherence inside. The angry tone of it made her consider coming back later, but she stood fast.

Sarah opened the door in a few seconds, looking weary, but smiled once she recognized Maya. "Hey."

"I need your help. Get your lock stuff." Maya bounced on her toes.

"Are you hungry?" Sarah took her hand and pulled. "C'mon. You gotta eat something."

"Later." Maya dug her heels in. "Please. This is important. We don't have much time."

Sarah bit her lip and looked over her shoulder. "Okay, be right back."

She left the door ajar and ran into the apartment. Maya waited in the hall, listening to an unending tirade of linguistic masterpieces such as: "sons a' bitches," "who them fuckers think they is," "I'ma bust my boot off in a dozen asses," and "fuck 'em all, bloody idiots," interspersed with several loud burps.

The redhead reemerged from the back room with her hip bag on and adjusted the many folds of her wrapped-around dress to hide it. She came to the door by way of the kitchen and retrieving a beer for her father. His angry rant faded to some affectionate mutterings. He kissed her on the top of the head and settled in to watch TV. Sarah slipped out the door and pulled it closed.

"What's going on?"

Maya smiled and took Sarah's hand. "Trust me."

She led the older girl to the fire stairs and down to the ground floor. As soon as they entered the hall, Sarah got tense. When Maya walked straight at Mr. Mason's door, Sarah recoiled.

"No. Don't." Sarah shook her head. "Get away from there."

"Sarah." Maya spun around. "I know what he did to you."

The girl's snow-white face turned as red as her hair. "He didn't. I got away. He grabbed me and tried to get me to take my clothes off. He told me what he wanted to do to me. I kicked him in the balls, so he punched me. I started screaming and he let me go." Sarah wiped at her left eyebrow. "He lied. He told everyone he caught me trying to steal from him."

Maya stared into her friend's dark blue eyes. "He tried to trick me to go inside with him. Offered to wash my nightie and give me a bath. I believe you."

Sarah sniffled.

"You're afraid of him too. He's the one who told the Authority about me. He's responsible for what happened today, like a little boy mad at me for not getting his way. I am going to make sure he never hurts anyone again."

"H-how?" Sarah leaned forward and stared at the front doors. The look on her face suggested the tiniest noise would've sent her sprinting up the stairs.

"I have a way. It's better if you don't know, but I need to get inside his apartment."

Sarah furrowed her eyebrows. "You don't trust me?"

"I do!" Maya hugged her. "I don't want you getting in trouble if it doesn't work."

"I've done worse than break into this pig's apartment." Sarah looked around again before whispering. "I help the Brigade sometimes."

"You're eleven." Maya blinked. "Genna said they don't involve kids in war."

"I don't war. I sneak around and bring messages."

Maya sighed. Arguing wasted time. "Okay, fine." She held up the paper. "I wrote down Vanessa's addresses. Most of them are secret. If the Authority finds this in his place..."

Sarah's eyes widened. She almost shoved Maya on her ass to get to the door. "They'll totally kill him!" She rummaged for her tools and attacked the knob as if ten million NuCoin waited on the other side.

Maya flailed her arms to keep balance. "Uhh, yeah."

The doorknob lock clicked in about thirty seconds. It took Sarah another sixteen to get the deadbolt open.

"Don't touch anything," whispered Sarah.

Maya rolled her eyes. "They're not going to look for fingerprints."

She walked into a disaster of a bachelor's home. Cups, plates, take-out food containers, and random cardboard boxes stood in piles so thick they formed islands with definable paths between them. The place was at least twice the size of every other apartment she'd seen, with two bedrooms, a kitchen, a small area with a table, and another room at the far back end holding a desk with a computer terminal. Being half-underground, it lacked a patio.

Maya tiptoed around the junk, careful not to step on anything other than exposed carpet. In an alcove between kitchen and bathroom, a tiny washer/dryer combo supported a small army of soda cans. The sight of it made

Maya feel sick.

Aluminum cans clattered as her foot plowed forward through the junk at the doorway to the computer room. Sarah followed close behind, refusing to let go of Maya's shoulders. Two wastebaskets to the left of a rolling chair overflowed with crinkled-up tissues.

"Wow, he must get sick a lot," said Sarah. "Look at all of 'em. They're on the floor too. And that one's stuck to the wall."

"Eww." Maya tiptoed among a minefield of paper wads on the carpet. "Vanessa had an assistant like that... she was always sniffling."

The component stack next to the monitor looked like a mixture of routers, high-end enthusiast gaming computer cases, and a satellite net uplink from hell. She smiled at the Takeshi-Imura logo on the main computer box.

Maya leaned forward to stick the folded up paper between the components, but froze. "I got a better idea."

"What?" asked Sarah in a strangled whisper. "I don't like it in here. Let's get out of here."

"They're going to think it's suspicious if it isn't on his computer somewhere." Maya took one look at the dingy grey chair and decided to stay standing. She hip-bumped it aside and moved up to the keyboard. The machine seemed to be on, so she tapped a random key, which brought up a password prompt.

"Crap," said Sarah.

"It's cool. I know a trick for the TI machines. They still haven't patched it. If ya hold both shifts, and hit the number keys in alternating order from right to left toward the middle, it's a backdoor." She tried to hit both shift keys with her pinky and thumb, but her tiny hand couldn't manage it. "Hold down the right shift, please."

Sarah reached around her and poked her finger into the key.

Maya pressed left shift and typed 0192837465 on the number keys. The screen flashed and went bright blue. "We're in."

The blank screen faded to reveal an image of a cartoon version of Maya, tied naked to a chair with the shadows of several men looming over her. Much to the real Maya's horror, her illustrated doppelganger looked eager and happy. Along the left edge of the screen, a column contained a list of disturbing categories with numbers next to them, presumably counting images that fit each one. 'Sexy_Maya,' currently highlighted, had 5721 entries. Domx_Vanessa was in the sixty-thousand range.

Sarah clung to her from behind, shaking. "Holy shit. That's disgusting. Sick freak. Who would draw that?"

Maya clamped her jaw, trying not to throw up. As much as she wanted to close the page, she had to leave it open or he'd know someone was here. She did *not* want to see anything else, figuring the image she'd stumbled on was probably the tamest thing there. The cartoony scene made her almost as sick as Mason grabbing her chest. She braced her right forearm to her mouth to hold in puke.

"Don't look over there," said Sarah.

Of course, Maya glanced to the right. A number of dolls lay on the floor around two video game consoles with pink controllers. Any lingering doubt or regret at what she planned to do vanished. She minimized the awful image and got into the file system where she created a folder and named it 'work expenses.' After that, she created about a dozen blank spreadsheets, titling them with dates ranging over the past two months. In one of the spreadsheet files, she entered the addresses and passwords from the notepaper, and hid the tab.

"Why are you hiding it?" Sarah squeezed her, whined, and looked back at the door. "I really, really, really do not want to be in here when he comes home. He'll keep us."

"I'm hiding it because I don't want it to look too obvious. I could stick it to his fridge, but then they wouldn't believe he did it." She closed the file, closed the folder, and—with great reluctance—tapped the screen to return to the porn site. Cringing not to look, she hit the lock button, which replaced the revolting cartoon with a pleasant, innocent password prompt. As a final touch, she wedged the folded notebook paper between the bottom component and the desk. "Okay, let's get out of here."

Bang.

Both girls jumped and clung to each other at the noise out in the hall. Footsteps grew louder.

"Cabinets," whispered Maya. "Hurry!"

Holding hands, they speed-tiptoed through the junk toward the kitchen. Maya about lost her bladder when a blur of dark swept past the door, but whoever it was kept on going into the fire stairs. At the squeak of shoes on concrete steps, they shared a sigh of relief. As soon as total silence returned outside, Maya ran out into the hall. Sarah pulled the door closed and started for the stairway, but Maya grabbed her dress, nearly ripping two safety pins out.

"Wait!"

Sarah, tears in her eyes, whirled around. "What?"

Maya pointed at the door. "Make it locked again or he'll know."

It took her about twice as long to re-lock the door with shaking hands, but soon, Mr. Mason's apartment—and the horrors inside it—didn't appear to have been tampered with. Sarah put her tools away and took a few deep breaths. Her cheeks glowed red and she dripped with perspiration. Maya shared the trembles of adrenaline, but nervous giggling started.

A moment later, Sarah looked worried and a touch sick. "Does he have drawings of me too?"

Maya shuddered with rage. "No. He didn't make those." *How many people hate me enough to wanna imagine such awful things happening to me?* She sniffled.

Sarah comforted her with a hug and a back pat. "We got him."

"He deserves it." Maya grabbed her friend's hand. "We shouldn't be seen here."

"Right." Sarah backed up to the fire door.

"Are you hungry?"

"No." Sarah shook her head. "I think I'm gonna chuck again."

Maya hurried up the stairs behind her. "Me too."

TWENTY- ONE
NO COMING BACK

Crumbs fell onto the thin plastic plate between Maya's elbows. After sitting around Sarah's apartment for the better part of an hour, ravenous hunger came out of nowhere. Even the shitty Veteran's Benefits Center cheese sandwiches tasted like a feast. Honestly, the bread *was* pretty good, even if she knew the 'just baked' fragrance/flavor came from chemicals. The cheese, not so much.

Sarah sat catty-corner, having finished hers in six bites, clearly eating to survive and not to taste. She hooked one heel on the chair and leaned her head against her knee, watching Maya eat. Her father grumbled at the television, decrying how unrealistic whatever war movie he'd settled on was. Whenever *anything* happened, he'd pause the movie to go off on a bitching rant about how one particular vehicle couldn't do that, or that specific gun couldn't hold that much ammo, or the armor the character wore wouldn't do shit against 6.55 millimeter armor-piercing explosive bullets.

As threatening as he sounded, Maya believed Sarah's opinion of him being all noise and no threat. Any time the girl got close to her father, his whole demeanor changed. With trust that he wouldn't turn violent (at least toward them), the verbal rampage seemed humorous instead of scary. She smiled at Sarah, who still looked somber.

Maya stared at her.

"We killed him," whispered Sarah.

Maya studied the last inch or so of sandwich, admiring the pattern of small bite marks. "They might not kill him, but they'll interrogate him. He won't know anything about the addresses, so they'll think he's lying."

Sarah covered her mouth to muffle a burp. "Good for him."

"Yeah." Maya gnawed her sandwich to death. "Genna was gonna kill him anyway."

"You can stay here."

Maya looked up, fear in her eyes.

"Uhh, for now." Sarah fidgeted. "'Til Genna comes back. Most people they keep this long don't come back."

Maya shot a sullen glare into the plate. "I'm not gonna let them kill her."

"Maybe they'll let her go. They've taken Naida like twenty times."

"That's different." Maya crossed her arms.

Sarah leaned forward over the table. "You shouldn't be alone. You're too little."

"You're only two years older than me." Maya glared. "And I'm smarter."

"Nuh-uh." Sarah shook her head.

"Am too," said Maya, adding a raspberry. "But you're stronger."

The whirr of an e-motor outside stalled the breath in Maya's throat. She ran from the chair to the living room and out to the patio deck, where she grabbed the flimsy metal railing and peered over at the ground seven stories down.

A large blue van with white Authority markings had pulled up out front. One officer sat behind a machinegun in the middle of the roof while two others got out and moved to the side. They pulled open a thick, armored double-door with a deep metal scraping noise that echoed down the street. Maya shoved away from the railing and darted back across the apartment.

"Where are you going?" yelled Sarah. "Stay out of sight."

"Plan part two," shouted Maya, not slowing.

She headed for the fire stairs and ran down so fast she had to catch herself on the walls to make the turns at each switchback without falling. On the ground floor, she emerged into the hallway seconds before two Authority officers dragged Brian in the main entrance. She tried not to breathe too hard and ruffled her hair up to better hide her face. One of the officers snipped plastic ties off Brian's wrists.

"Thanks for the ride," said Brian, with almost enough sarcasm to earn a punch to the head.

The officer lowered his fist and pointed at the hallway instead of hitting him.

Maya kept her hands at her sides and crept out of the late afternoon shadow, bare feet silent on the smooth concrete floor. Brian tromped by, giving her an incredulous look, almost walking into the wall. He hesitated at the door to the fire stairs, watching her approach the officers the way someone about to witness a horrible plane crash would stare, unable to look away.

When she got close enough, Maya stopped, gaze down, feet together. "Umm, excuse me?"

Both officers pulled guns and aimed at her.

"Don't move," yelled one.

"Against the wall, now," shouted the other.

Maya obeyed. As soon as the cool cinder blocks touched her chest, black-gloved hands forced her arms out to the side and slid up and down her body. He patted down from armpit to knee and around her hips.

"She's not armed," said the man right behind her.

"Really?" asked the other. "You had to frisk a tiny little kid in a nightie to figure that out? Where would she hide anything?"

"I dunno, but kids don't walk up *to* us unless they have bombs. Maybe she had a clicker or something."

"I want to report a crime." Maya kept her palms flat against the wall, arms outstretched. "You are the Authority. My mother said I should go to you if I see something bad."

"Okay kid, whatcha got?" The man who seemed friendlier put his weapon away.

Maya didn't move. "There's a man here who's working for the Brigade." She spoke the last word in a half whisper.

"Whoa." The officer who frisked her put a hand on her shoulder and tugged her around to face him. "You Nons never turn on each other. This don't feel right. What gives, kid?"

Maya clasped her hands in front of her and kept her face hidden behind her long, straight hair. "My mom's a veteran, so I'm a Citizen. You arrested her on accident 'cause someone lied to you. I know who the real Brigade spy is. I want you to let my mom go."

"There was a dark-skinned woman brought in from here a few hours ago," said the nicer man. "No suspicion of Brigade activity, she flagged as a person of interest. Probably be back to you in a day or two once she's processed."

"I want to do the right thing." Maya ground her toes into the floor, perhaps overacting a little. "He lives in the super's apartment. Mr. Mason. I was playing hide-and-seek with the other kids and I was hiding in the machine room. I heard him talkin' onna call. He's going to give information to the Brigade tonight."

"What sort of information?" The nearer officer finally put his sidearm back on his belt.

"Can you bring my mommy home please?" Maya tried to sound cute and endearing. She fidgeted at her nightdress and swished side to side.

"Oh look at this one." The nicer officer chuckled. "What are you, like eight? Already trying to play the game."

"I'm sorry." Maya acted a sniffle. "You're right. I shouldn't play games with you. A person is supposed to report crimes because they're crimes, not to get something. Mr. Mason is helping them. They wanna kill Miss Oman. I heard paper crinkling and he was typing on his computer."

Both officers coughed.

"Horseshit," said Frisker.

"He said stuff that sounded like addresses. Something about the Shroud at Double Rock." Both men twitched at her name-drop of Vanessa's most secure dwelling, the underground one Maya loathed so much. "There were a lot of names. I don't 'member everything." She peeked up.

The men exchanged a glance. Her heart pounded. They'd either believe her or realize she *was* Maya Oman. She bowed her head before they looked down at her again.

"I dunno," said Frisker.

The other man took a knee and grasped her shoulders. "You sure you heard that exact thing, kid?"

Maya forced herself not to tremble, and made eye contact with—according to his nametag—Officer Kumar. "Yes, officer. The Shroud at Double Rock. He called it a pain in the ass 'cause of underground. What's a double rock?"

"Nothing you need to worry about if you want to stay healthy." Frisker shifted his weight back and forth.

"This could seriously bite us in the ass, Cortez." Kumar glanced at Maya for a few seconds more before standing. "If this kid misheard some dude and we go crazy..."

"Yeah. But if we don't... and... fuck."

Maya unclasped her hands and let her arms sway idle at her sides. "So, you search his place. If you don't find anything, all you do is waste time. If you do find something, you get big promotions and stop them from killing Miss Oman."

Kumar tapped his fingers on his helmet, thinking. "Okay. What if this kid's right? We'd be off this shit detail for life. Where's the apartment, kid?"

Maya pointed at the chamber of dead elevators. "This way." She raised her hands to dissuade them from getting it in their heads they should put her in binders, and walked up to Mason's door. "Here. It sounded like he was playing a computer game before he got the call." She debated making up a story about Mason doing stuff to her, or giving a truthful account of him trying to get her to go inside his apartment, but decided against it. If they thought her vengeful, it might ruin the plan.

"I don't like this," said Cortez. "Heard about shit like this up north. Kid could be leading us to a bomb or an ambush."

"I'm not." Maya looked down. "There's no bomb. Can I go now please? If they see me talking to the Authority, I might get in trouble. People here don't like snitches... even little ones."

"So why are you snitching?" Cortez leaned over her.

"Because... my mom said that society is only as good as its laws, and people have to do the right thing." She summoned her most idealistic wide-eyed expression.

"Right. They're cute when they're clueless." Kumar waved at her. "Go on home."

Maya backed to the fire stairs while Kumar pulled a small device from his belt, which opened both locks in a matter of seconds. They peered inside, muttered a few curses, and radioed out for backup.

She turned around to start up the stairs and almost screamed at Sarah being less than a foot away. Without a word, the older girl took her by the hand and led her upstairs, back to apartment 139.

Maya sat on the patio, legs dangling through the bars of the railing, feet swaying free. Sarah adopted a similar position on the other side of two plastic cups full of Citru-Shine nutrient drink. The bright orange liquid looked in no way anything of nature's creation. Each sip crashed into her sensorium with the overwhelming strength of eating five oranges in a single bite. A tattered strip of yellowing fabric around Sarah's calves fluttered in the wind from where her curtain-dress showed signs of unraveling. The sun sank into the murk in the west, darkening the city. None of the Authority vehicles had turned on any lights. Before long, they became imperceptible from the general gloom below.

"I can't believe you walked right up and talked to them." Sarah still looked terrified over an hour later. "I thought they were going to arrest you."

"I had to." Maya leaned her head between the bars and peered down at nine Authority vans and a swarm of blueberries. "I can't believe we're not all tied up again."

"It's not a full search and sweep this time. They locked the building. No one can leave their apartments... at least the ones where the doors work." She winked. "'Course, it's stupid to go down there—they'd shoot us."

Maya glanced over her shoulder at the patio door. "But we're stuck out here."

"Yeah. Not our fault. They didn't give us any warning. Besides, it's not like we can go anywhere unless you wanna jump."

Headlights glimmered to the left, rounding a corner a few blocks north. Maya reached over and Sarah took her hand. Mr. Mason, even seven stories down and in a car, scared her. His little beige e-car trundled down the street, slaloming junk and debris. About a hundred yards from the front of the building, he jammed on the brakes when the far reach of his headlights caught the first of the Authority vehicles. He hesitated only a few seconds before pulling up and parking out front as though he owned the building.

Sarah leaned her head against the railing to peer down, clutching the bars.

A handful of lights came on, beams swarming like a sea of angry bees until they converged on Mason, who raised an arm to shield his face. Over a loudspeaker, a man ordered him to the ground.

Mason stood motionless for two seconds before a sharp *pop* went off, and a sparkling fist-sized lightning orb dazzled bright blue on his chest. Mason hit the street convulsing. The blueberries swarmed him, and the *thumps* and *thuds* of a thirteen-on-one ass-kicking echoed up from below. A few comments from the blueberries hinted they'd seen *that* picture—plus found even worse on his computer—and seemed to take umbrage with it.

Sarah gathered a wad of spit on her lip and let it fall. "Go to hell, bastard."

Maya swung her feet side to side, watching them drag the unconscious man into the back of one of their vehicles. "Yeah. What she said."

When the trucks lit up with blue flashing lights and proceeded to pull away, the girls retreated from the edge and sat facing each other. Maya sipped more of her drink and cringed at the punch of *orange* to the teeth.

"Think he'll be back?" asked Sarah.

Maya shook her head. "Nope."

Sarah leaned forward and scratched at the front of her ankle. "Do you feel bad?"

The image on that computer screen would haunt her dreams for months, but the man who put such terror into her friend deserved the worst the Authority offered. "Nope." She shivered and looked at the door. "Do you think they're going to leave us locked outside all night?"

Sarah shrugged. "At least it's summer. It won't be too bad."

They leaned against the warm glass, trading stories about funny things that happened before they met. Unfortunately, all of Maya's stories involved video games, sitting bored to tears in an Ascendant office, or often-painful mishaps while filming ads. Sarah's stories were more interesting; she told of hiding from older kids and dosers while scavenging, followed by one about how an old battery-powered talking teddy bear turned itself on and made Pick wet himself last year.

A few cars slid by in the half hour or so after the Authority departed. Maya leaned her head on Sarah's shoulder and got a protective arm around her back.

"Do you think that woman really wanted you to die?" asked Sarah.

Maya flexed and relaxed her toes a few times, pondering. "I… no, probably not. She hates losing control more than anything. The only power they had over her was the threat to kill me, so she wanted to take that away." A lump started in her throat, but she was beyond done with letting Vanessa Oman hurt her anymore. "I bet it wouldn't have bothered her if they did, but she was bluffing."

Sarah let her head lean to the right, atop Maya's. "Sorry she hates you. It's awful to think she can't love anyone."

Maya scratched at the crook of her neck where Sarah's hair tickled. "There's a picture of a man on her desk. It looks old. She told me once 'they' killed him when he wouldn't do what 'they' wanted. I think the old government tried to take over Ascendant. Maybe she loved him and doesn't wanna get hurt again."

"Do you think that's why she left you alone all the time? So she didn't get attached?" Sarah shied into her at the sound of a distant drone, too far away to see except for a patch of light on buildings two blocks away.

"Maybe." Maya scrunched her hands into the silk of her nightdress, choked up by Genna's promise to find her better clothes. "Or maybe she's just a bitch. Nothing I ever did was good enough for her. I used to try and call her to say goodnight, but she never answered."

They clung to each other in silence for some time, glancing down at the street whenever a car pulled up or an Authority transit bus dropped off workers.

"He won't come back, will he?" asked Sarah.

Maya shrugged. "Not if they believe me."

Buzzing erupted throughout the building from dozens of tiny speakers, followed by a loud *bee-woop* noise. A sharp *click* emanated from the door above their heads and a recorded voice played, "Lockdown lifted. Thank you for your compliance."

Maya stood and pulled the patio glass open with a grunt. "Guess they believed me."

"Yeah." Sarah's long-absent smile returned.

TWENTY-TWO
A GAME UNFINISHED

ook's voice bumped against the edge of Maya's consciousness. She reclined on the concrete in the story room, less than two feet from the edge by the missing wall. Two days had come and gone. Doctor Chang had been the phantom they mistook for Mr. Mason coming home early. Naida showed up earlier that morning, in a bad mood but seemingly healthy. Pick hadn't joined them for story night, preferring to stay with his sister.

Every so often, a word crept in past the swirling storm of worry raging in Maya's skull. Book continued to narrate the story in character voices, using his own wheezy tenor only for the narration. Maya wondered what sort of life the man had led to require a cybernetic implant capable of changing his voice to such a degree that he could sound like everything from a little girl to a demonic creature. Maybe he worked for the pre-war government, a spy or something... or maybe he had been an actor. Few people got cybernetics these days. The expense and risk were unheard of out here in the Habitation District. Only Citizens had the money for implants, and only clinics inside the Sanctuary Zone were safe.

Maya wondered how much of what she'd read on the AuthNet was, as Sarah's father liked to say, 'boo-shee.' The articles did portray the conditions out here far worse than they seemed to be. Granted, it *was* bad. Except for Genna's stash, most people she'd met had only the clothes on their backs, or at least they appeared to as they wore the same stuff every day. She had yet to see Pick with a shirt on, though he did have at least four different pairs of pants. Emily owned a second outfit consisting of a loose white top, skirt, and black tights, but Maya didn't want to take the girl's clothes. That costume dress would fall apart eventually. Maybe she and Sarah could sell Mr. Mason's computers to Foz for some outfits—provided the Authority hadn't impounded them. There had to be *something* worth scavving in there. Not like he would need them again. Maya squirmed. She didn't really want to touch them... or anything else in that place.

She squinted as the wind picked up, whipping her hair about and brushing warmth over her bare shoulders and legs. It reminded her of her first hours away from the Sanc, chained to a damp mattress in a room full of people ready to kill her. While a trio of magical children searched for a secret under the school in Book's story, Maya gazed out at the murky ruin of a city and tried to make Genna come home by sheer force of will. She'd cut the tape within minutes of arriving at their hideout, which made her kinder than the Authority. Officer Baxter would've left her in the bag the whole time.

Her mother was the only person the Authority hadn't brought back. Maya rolled on her side toward the edge, propped her head on her left hand, and traced lines in the concrete dust with her finger. None of the adults wanted to do anything to help. Even Barnes and his Brigade friends had given up. She peered out at the smear of light in the fog where the Sanctuary Zone glowed. Vanessa couldn't know that Maya had come to truly despise her. Maya had spent most of her life being the embodiment of lies, smiling for the camera. She could lie more. Maybe if she traded herself back to that life, she could ask not-Mom to set Genna free.

She doubted Vanessa would believe Genna really helped her escape her kidnappers, but what that woman believed often had little impact on what she did for appearances. If they could turn it into a media circus and make money out of it, she'd do it. Maya sniffled at already thinking about leaving her new friends and never coming back. Genna had saved her life; she *had* to return the favor.

That's what family does.

Maya sat up and moved away from the edge. The other kids, sans Pick, sat in a close circle around Book. The old man's forehead still bore a purple mark from the Authority security check. Apparently, they liked lip even less from old men than they did from little red-haired girls. Maya plopped down next to Sarah, who seemed like herself again. With Mason gone from the building, she'd returned to her carefree bravado.

Most of Maya's raspberry glitter nail polish had flaked off. While pretending to listen to the story, she helped the rest of it along by picking at it. Sarah gave her a 'I know something's wrong' look, but didn't try to talk over the narration. Maya wanted to run off right that second, but with Book there, not to mention Barnes, Weber and who knows how many other adults up and about, someone would grab her. If they knew she wanted to run off to save Genna, she'd wind up in a locked room or under constant supervision.

Perhaps she could share her plan with Sarah. That would end in one of two ways: either the girl would want to go with her, which would be too dangerous... or she'd tell her dad, which would circle right back to her being trapped here.

Maya didn't want to run away, but she couldn't let Genna rot in jail. If, hopefully, she hadn't been executed already. She hid her face against Sarah's shoulder and sniffled.

"It's not even a sad part," whispered Emily. "Shh."

Maya tried not to think about Genna, but couldn't get into the story despite the perfect imitation of multiple character voices.

Eventually, Book stopped. "Okay, kids. Time for dinner."

Food plans had been arranged earlier. Anton, Marcus, and Book would eat with the Changs. Sarah and Maya would dine at home, likely on a feast of self-inflating cheese sandwiches. Pick, presumably, would eat whatever Naida cooked him. Had Maya's gut not been in knots over Genna, she would've envied him. His sister was an awesome cook.

She trudged behind Sarah down to the seventh floor and back to their apartment. Sharing a bed with Sarah was cool, but she'd rather have her mother there to protect her. That also explained the patio being on the living room; that apartment had two bedrooms unlike Genna's. For all she'd seen so far, Sarah's dad was a screaming heap of uselessness. If something bad happened, he'd throw a tantrum and shout, but more or less sit there *doing* nothing about it. Maya felt a little cheated. She'd wanted Genna to get the chance to smash Mason in the face.

Maya locked the door and deadbolt once inside Sarah's apartment. The Dad was in the bathroom, pissing from the sound of it. Two huge men frozen on the TV screen grimaced at the exact instant their boxing gloves caught each other's faces.

"Eww." Maya rushed into the kitchen. "Why can't your dad close the bathroom door?"

Sarah shrugged. "It's just the way he is. Too much time in the military." She stooped, took a pan out from the cabinet, placed it on the stove, then set out three small metal canisters with lids and generic white labels marked 'beef stew' in a line on the counter nearby.

Maya sat on the edge of a chair, forward enough for her feet to touch floor. "Why are you doing the cooking?"

The Dad tromped back to the couch, fell into his divot, and belched. He unpaused the TV, and within a half second, erupted in a cavalcade of obscenities directed at the man winning the boxing match.

"Oh, Dad's not very good at it." Sarah opened a canister and poured the chunky brown sludge within into the pot.

"All you're doing is warming up stuff from a can." Maya didn't flinch—much—when a suspicious roach-like tickle swept over the top of her right foot. She jumped, but relaxed at the sight of a scrap of plastic wrapping drifting across the floor.

"Some people really are that bad at it." She dumped the second canister into the pot, but struggled with the twist lid on the third, grunting and making faces.

Maya twisted left as Sarah passed behind her, then whipped her head around to track the girl on her way into the living room. In flagrant disregard of the seemingly violent drunkard on the couch, the redhead walked up to him.

"Dad?" shouted Sarah over the TV.

He paused it, fury evaporated in an instant. "Oi, luv?"

"Can you open this?" She held up the metal canister.

The Dad gripped it in his living hand and clamped the rickety metal one on the lid. Unpadded fingers scraped around without any sort of grip. He switched hands and strained, face reddening. Two seconds later, the metal claw hand crushed the canister with such force beef stew exploded over them both. He made a sheepish face and handed her back the twisted ruin.

"Thanks, Dad." Sarah stood for a second, brown goop dripping from her face and chest, then walked back to the kitchen. "See?"

Maya blinked at him. He licked at his arms and lifted his tank top to his lips, slurping up every trace he could find. When he started jamming his tongue into the cracks and crevices of his prosthetic arm, Maya cringed away. Sarah slapped the bottom of the smashed canister, urging the rest of the stew out of it into the pan.

Eventually, the smell of beef broth permeated the kitchen and pulled The Dad away from his TV. He stumbled in, muttering as if in the midst of a debate about the merits of 'benevolent dictatorship' versus 'socialism by committee.' He plopped himself in a chair opposite Maya at the square table and squinted at her. "Damn, you gettin' a lot of sun, Faerie."

"I'm over here, Dad." Sarah sighed.

He glanced at her, at Maya, and back to Sarah. "Dammit girl. You're too young to have kids."

A bubble of mirth almost managed to rise past the sludge in Maya's heart.

"She's not mine, Dad. For shit's sake, I'm only eleven. I'd have been two when she was born."

"Oh. Well, that's not possible then." He tapped his three metal fingers on the table. "Hmm. I don't remember you."

"Genna's her mom," said Sarah.

The Dad chuckled. "I don't remember ever puttin' the moves on 'er. Sure would like—"

"You didn't," said Maya. "Sarah said I could stay here 'til Genna comes home."

"Oh." Several missing teeth showed in his grin. "Nae problem. Where she be?"

"Authority got her." Sarah turned off the heating element and doled stew out into bowls.

"Bah. 'At's boo-shee." The Dad grumbled. "Ain't they no respectin' anything."

He drinks too much. Maya leaned back from a blast of beer breath and managed a weak smile when Sarah set food in front of her. "Thanks."

Aside from Sarah's father rambling about the Authority overstepping its supposed legal rights, no one spoke over dinner. He mumbled something incomprehensible and winked at Sarah.

"Thanks." Sarah smiled.

A few seconds after he got up and walked into the living room, Maya whispered, "You understood that?"

"Yeah. He just said the food was good." Sarah stacked the empty bowls and carried them to the sink.

"Srah! 'Mere." Dad wagged his metal arm from the living room. "What a dark one's name 'gain?"

The girls exchanged a glance that wordlessly agreed on playing it safe.

"Lisa," said Sarah.

"You too." He waved. "'Mere. 'Mon back." The Dad trudged off to the larger bedroom.

Maya blinked.

"It's okay." Sarah put the bowls down, wiped her hands on a towel, and walked down the hall.

Maya hesitated a few seconds before getting up and following. In the bedroom, he pointed at the bed and murmured indecipherable words again.

Sarah sat on the edge, evidently understanding him. Maya hopped up next to her. While The Dad rummaged among a pile of old boxes in the big closet, she looked around. A thin wire came in from a hole in the ceiling, ran along the wall to a crude electronic box over the bed. It had two buttons and a big speaker, but she couldn't imagine what it did.

The Dad surfaced a few minutes later with something that looked like the baby produced from a wasp mating with a handgun. It had the overall shape of a pistol, with a rubberized grip. Two metal studs protruded from the squarish front, above and below the barrel. Diagonal yellow and black lines covered the rest of it. He looked the device over before nodding at it.

"'Kay." He held it up. "Ya two nee' learn 'ow ta 'fend yerselves. Nae need killin' f'ya got one o' dese 'ere Hornets."

"Is that a gun?" asked Maya.

"Stunner." The Dad moved closer, holding the weapon in his palm. "This"—he pointed at a sliding switch where a right-handed shooter's thumb would be—"be the power switch. Thing won't work if it's back. Push forward wit' yer thumb." He demonstrated.

The device emitted a faint *bwee* noise like a capacitor powering up. Sarah leaned back, looking uneasy.

"This one be jes like what dem 'Thority shits 'ave." He patted it. "Two modes o' use. This"—he pointed at a button in the middle of the pistol grip—"releases the magazine." He withdrew a narrow magazine from the handle and tilted it to let the girls look in the top. It contained thirteen metal rods about an inch long each, tipped with needles. "Microcell battery inside each dart will knock a man on his arse fer a couple o' minutes. Donnae work on armor." He reseated the magazine and held the Hornet so they could see the front end without it being pointed at them. "S'got two prongs." He indicated the pair of metal studs on the front end. "Mode two." He demonstrated the selector above the trigger, which rather than firing darts, would send power to the electrodes.

He turned the power switch off and handed it to Sarah.

She took it with an unsteady hand and looked it over. At his prodding, she worked the various buttons and controls, unloading and reloading it, switching modes from shoot to zap, and repeating it all with her eyes closed. After, he made her do everything over again with the weapon held behind her back. Once Sarah finished, he had her turn it off and made Maya do the whole routine. Twenty minutes later, both girls could recite the optimal range of thirty feet for the dart, knew not to aim for the face (since it could cause brain damage), and that the in-magazine battery could power five zaps from the electrodes before running dry.

"Ye did good." He patted them both on the head. "Donnae shoot kids wit' it. Tae small, might do real 'arm." The Dad put the Hornet back in the closet and reburied it.

Maya raked the carpet with her toes as he walked out. A moment later, the boxing match resumed in the living room, and with it, shouted curses. "Wow, he really does come out of nowhere with random stuff."

"Yeah. Next month he'll teach us how to rig a proximity mine or kill a Korean soldier with dental floss and two potatoes."

Maya giggled into her hands.

Sarah got up. "We should get out of his room before he forgets why we're here."

They walked out, hooked a hard left, and went into the other bedroom, about two-thirds the size. Sarah pulled a shoebox out of her closet and set it on the bed. Maya flopped on one side.

"Wanna play a game for a bit? I'm not really tired yet."

Maya tried to sound interested. "What is it?"

Sarah lifted the lid to reveal stacks of old cards with fanciful pictures. "Dad tried to get rid of them 'cause he thought it was real magic, but that's just the name of the cards." She explained how the game worked—each player had a pool of points, and the first person to run out of them lost. Some cards were lands, which somehow translated to power, and the players used creatures, spells, and enchantments to do various things.

They sat cross-legged on the floor and played for a little more than an hour, though by that time both had amassed a huge field of cards. Neither had taken a single point of damage, and Sarah had wound up gaining ten more from where she'd started.

"This is impossible," said Maya. "Are you sure we're playing it right?"

"Yep." Sarah showed off a card. "The rules are right here."

Maya felt a little embarrassed at her surprise Sarah could read. The twins had mentioned between video games in the basement that Zoe and Doc tutored them almost like school, but for some reason took a break over the summer months. Book made it a point to ensure his boys could read and offered to help anyone else who wanted to learn. The e-learns Maya had finished had gone up to grade twelve, stuff intended for eighteen-year-olds—one benefit of total boredom while locked in a lavish penthouse prison.

Despite their gap in institutional learning, Maya had in Sarah a friend she could relate to for the first time in her life. Her heart grew heavy at the thought of leaving. Staying here with Sarah and letting Barnes and the other adults worry about Genna made logical sense, but she couldn't get over the guilt. Abandoning this growing friendship felt like an awful thing to do. She meant to come back—with Genna—but didn't know if she'd be able to. The worst thing that could happen would be to wind up stuck in the penthouse again. It didn't seem likely at all that Vanessa would hurt her; after all, she hadn't actually *done* anything but be kidnapped and decide to hate the woman.

She distracted herself by staring at the pretty pictures of monsters and elves on the cards.

"Go ta bed," yelled The Dad.

Maya gathered her cards.

"Wait. Don't you wanna leave it so we can keep playing tomorrow?" Sarah blinked.

"Uhh." Maya almost burst into tears. She wouldn't be here tomorrow, but maybe she'd make it back. She slid her hand the other way, laying the strip of cards back on the thin rug. "Okay."

Sarah hit the light switch by the door, darkening the bare bulb at the center of the ceiling, and crawled into bed still in her curtain-dress. She scooted all the way across against the wall to leave room. Maya thought it odd the girl didn't change into a nightgown, but had too much on her mind to bother questioning anything. *Duh. I've only got one thing to wear too.* She climbed in to lay beside her friend, but focused on staying awake. Before long, heavy snoring rumbled the wall behind Sarah. The Dad had passed out. For a little while, Sarah lay flat. Eventually, she rolled on her side up against Maya. Warm breath puffed over the back of her neck. A moment later, a pale arm slid across her chest and held on.

Great. I'm a stuffed bear.

Maya stared at a patch of moonlight on the rug, cast from a tiny two-foot square window in the wall at the head of the bed. *I'm supposed to be smart. Running off in the middle of the night doesn't seem very smart.* Her mind wandered around what Genna might be doing at that moment. Pacing in a jail cell, punching the wall, possibly delirious on interrogation drugs. Maybe fate would have a sense of humor and Mr. Mason would end up in the same cell. Genna wouldn't want Maya to put herself in danger, but she had to.

Being the pet of the CEO of Ascendant Pharmaceuticals sucked.

Once Sarah's breathing took on a pace that indicated sleep, Maya lifted the girl's arm away and slipped off the bed. She thought about going for the Hornet, but Sarah had mentioned The Dad would pop awake at the slightest noise, something about his having been with a reconnaissance unit during the war. If he was even half as unstable as Moth, sneaking into his room had 'bad idea' written all over it. Maya crawled to the door before standing and looking back at Sarah. Everything about this plan felt like a mistake. Everything except letting Genna die.

"I'm sorry, Sarah," she whispered.

After a lingering stare, Maya bowed her head and made her way across the apartment and out to the hallway.

PART III
DEAD SPACE

TWENTY- THREE
THOSE WHO HAVE NOTHING

**aya crept down the fire stairs to the ground floor** and crossed the parking lot to the breach in the fence. It occurred to her that having a plan first might've been a good idea, but after three days, Genna should've been set free if they hadn't found anything. She didn't have time to plan. All she needed to do was get to the Sanctuary Zone and... well... she'd figure the next part out when she got there.

The coarse paving massaged her soles, surprising her by how much warmth it held even at night. Bright artificial light in the distant gloom shone like a beacon in the dark, a snow-globe silver castle. Finding the Sanctuary Zone wasn't the hard part. She headed in the direction of the glow for a few blocks, but doubt crept in once a glance back over her shoulder couldn't pick out her building anymore. The urge to go *home* to her friend reared up. Maya bowed her head, turned about and took a few steps back toward the building. She stopped, staring down at the road, shivering from fear and sorrow. Without her mother, she couldn't go back. None of the adults seemed to care at all about Genna. If Maya didn't do something *now*, the woman could die. A deep breath gave her confidence; she whirled to face the Sanc again, and set off at a brisk stride.

Fear chipped away at her mind. Minutes later, her gait slowed to a tentative creep. She distracted herself from her worries by trying to keep her feet on the painted yellow stripe down the center of the road. Patches of much newer looking paving filled in wherever the war had dug holes. A while of walking later, she looked up, but felt no closer. Random facts from endless hours in front of the AuthNet told her the Habitation District was 11.2 miles south from where she wanted to go. She frowned at her spindly legs. The most walking she usually did took her between her bedroom and the bathroom, never mind eleven miles outside barefoot.

This is stupid.

"Hey," said a gurgly male voice at the same instant his hand patted down, grasping her shoulder.

Maya let out a short, high-pitched squeal.

A shaggy-haired man, who likely looked far older than his true age, flashed a yellow-toothed smile. "Can ya spare any change?"

"Uhh." Maya clutched her chest. "You scared me."

"Sorry." The stink of his presence ripped the air out of her lungs.

Eyes watering, she tried to walk off, but he didn't let go of her shoulder. "I don't have any money."

"Aww, come on. We're in this together." His fingers slipped down, his fist closing around the nightdress between her shoulder blades. "I don't need much. Ya can spare a bit?"

Maya shivered. She didn't sense the same unease that Mason radiated, but the tightening cloth about her chest made her worry he'd steal her only possession. If she fought too hard to get away, he'd rip it right off her. Walking eleven miles barefoot sounded like a bad enough idea, but naked? She'd have no choice but to give up and go back to Sarah's place. "I'm just a kid. I don't have any money. Please let go of me."

He jogged her with a gentle shake. "You don't know how hard it is out here, missy. Everyone's gotta help each other."

Maya struggled, twisting side to side in an attempt to get him to release her nightdress. "Please let me go. I swear I don't have any money." A weak ripping sound from behind her right ear made her freeze.

The man rambled about how people who don't help each other ain't worth nothin'.

Maya reached up behind her head and tried to pry his fingers away. He kept jostling her about. Desperation peaked, and she drove her heel into his toes. "Get offa me!"

The man blinked as if waking out of a stupor. He stared vacantly at her for a few seconds and let go. Maya stumbled forward three steps and whirled to face him, clutching the garment to her chest.

"Oh. Just a kid. Damn. S'pose I was sleep-begging." Breath from an alcohol-laden chuckle made her gag. "Sorry if ah scared ya."

She backed up against the wall of a building, hands clutched to her chest, watching him amble across the street and crawl into a battered box. Once sure he wouldn't bother her again, she squirmed around and examined her nightie. Without taking it off, she couldn't see any damage, and didn't feel like checking that badly out in the middle of the street.

Fear battled with her need to help Genna. *I am Maya Oman. The blueberries will do what I tell them.* She sucked a breath in her nose and marched forward. It felt like she'd gone far enough to leave the Habitation District and enter the Dead Space, but the area hadn't changed much. In the middle of the night though, she couldn't tell if the buildings around her were occupied or abandoned. She felt like a squirrel lost amid a forest of high-rise concrete and glass. In every direction, tall buildings appeared endless. Only the light from the Sanctuary Zone provided any indication of direction. Nothing looked the least bit familiar, as best she could remember from her arrival here less than a week ago.

Wind brushed her hair to the side, warm and tainted with the scents of the city. A wisp of food, a dash of urine, and a whole lot of wet dog smell. Maya felt surprised she didn't gag on it and wondered if she'd already gotten used to this place. She yawned, but kept going, ignoring her increasing desire to run back and jump into the nice safe bed with her new best friend. More than fear, guilt at how Sarah would react to waking up alone almost changed her mind.

The shadows danced and swayed around her. Fragments of conversations came from the dark, whispers carried on the breeze. Her rational side thought of vagrants, dosers, or gang thugs, but her child-brain conjured up images of magical creatures and monsters from the card game she'd been playing. She hurried up to a run until she found a gap where a missing high-rise let the moon paint the street in a brilliant ghostly light. Maya crouched behind a chunk of concrete, too frightened to step into the well-lit area lest some troll or bogeyman find her. An unseen object overhead scraped at stone in a rhythmic back and forth that kept time with the breeze. Her brain told her a giant winged reaper raked its scythe on the dead building, sharpening it for her.

Maya let out a whimper of alarm and scurried off to the left. She navigated the shadows amid the rubble and sprinted away from the patch of moonlit street. Soon, she felt silly for being afraid of magical creatures, and slowed to a determined walk, punctuated with irresistible yawns.

"Those things aren't real. Like Emily's faeries. They don't exist. She *wants* to imagine them. I *don't.* Get out of my brain. I'm not a silly little child who needs to make things up. I'm not afraid of—"

Maya shrieked when a large alley cat shot out of the shadows in front of her and ran off back the way she'd come.

Hands on her chest, she sank to her knees, shivering and trying to catch her breath.

"Okay... maybe I am scared. But, I'm scared of the Authority. Not made-up monsters."

She hated how the darkness felt alive. She hated being nine years old and having a child's mind that couldn't help but imagine things that didn't exist. As much as she *knew* such creatures were impossible, she couldn't shake the fear that one of them chased her.

Two blocks later, the road glimmered with so much shattered glass and debris she had to turn left down a side street to avoid it. For once, she missed her high heels. Shitty shoes beat no shoes. Though, she couldn't run in those... and out here, having to run away from something bad went beyond a maybe.

The first opportunity to head north again took the form of an alley. At first, she didn't pay much attention to the mountains of garbage all over the place, instead focusing on wherever she stepped to avoid glass, jagged shards of concrete, nails, or anything painful.

Someone coughed.

Maya froze again, looking around in the scant light that made it between the tall buildings. Along both sides of the alley, twenty or thirty boxes of various sizes had become shelters for men, women, and children. They all huddled under blankets of plastic tarps, some scraps of fabric, and slabs of plastiboard. *There's so many empty spots in our building. Why are these people out in the street?*

Many appeared to wear garments made of scrap cloth or plastic sheets. Some of the smallest—and one wrinkly old man—didn't bother with even that. She spun right and left, horrified at the conditions these people lived in. A metal barrel topped with a grill held the skeletal remains of several rats as well as a shish kebab skewer of eight fat roaches.

A child coughed, another murmured in their sleep. One man snored, a bizarre wet noise that echoed in the nocturnal stillness. Voices emanated from up ahead where a street crossed the alley. She crouched low at the corner of a crumbling building and peered around. A handful of men loitered in a group, though one with cherry red hair stood out as familiar.

Maya gulped.

They looked too far away to notice her if she moved slow. She got down on all fours and crawled past two cars and a broken concrete lane divider. When she reached the dark on the other side of the street, she jumped up and ran into an alley. From there, she headed east two blocks until the highway to the Sanctuary Zone came into view. The entire strip of road glowed with the light from countless Authority drones. Curfew existed even among Citizens, and the drones didn't have any sense of sympathy. Not for a mugging victim only trying to get to a medical center, and certainly not for a little girl outside past bedtime.

She couldn't take the easiest path. Even during the day, the route would be a hornet's nest of drone activity. A solitary kid would attract attention. Maya grumbled to herself. Vanessa would laugh if she asked her to set Genna free. The woman could read people like text files and would sense Maya's disloyalty. She'd never let her leave, and would probably consider her self-stealing property.

With a scowl, Maya headed to the northwest, into the Dead Space and away from the road. Moonlight filtered in past large gaps in the walls of buildings, illuminating airborne dust in long, cascading beams. Every so often, the breeze knocked a piece of debris loose, creating a clatter of stone on pavement or the rattle of plastic swept out from an upper floor. Sharp *clanks* of small metal objects falling made her jump and gasp every time. She didn't know what time it was, or how long she'd been walking, but her head swam and her feet hurt. Another alley crammed with people sleeping in boxes provided too much temptation. She ambled along, barely able to keep upright, until she found an unclaimed black carton that already had a thin blanket arranged along its bottom. Since it appeared empty, and didn't smell *too* bad, she crawled in. Once she pulled the plastiboard flaps closed, she curled up on her side and used her arm as a pillow. Dizzying exhaustion dragged her under before she could feel too foolish for spending the night in a box rather than in a real bed with Sarah.

Oppressive heat woke her. Sweat ran in trails down her face and back. Maya pushed the box flaps open with her feet, gasping at the rush of cooler air. No wonder no one slept in that box; intelligent people didn't spend the summer in a jet-black shipping carton. She scooted out, stood, and stifled a yelp after stepping on the scorching pavement. A hopping dance moved her a few yards away to a patch of shade.

The scent of cooking meat drew her attention to a fire in a barrel, over which a woman wearing a dress of plastic bags and wires handed pieces of what had to be rat to four children, three Hispanic and one as pale as Sarah but with blonde hair. The oldest looked about Pick's size, and the group all wore skirts made from the same set of purple rose-patterned curtains. Between young age, long hair, and distance, she couldn't tell girls from boys.

Maya stared at the meat for a few minutes. The woman took notice of her and beckoned her over. Hunger pushed fear aside, and she navigated a patchwork of shaded strips to avoid burning her feet again. The oldest child, probably a girl, handed her a knitting needle with a half-rat impaled on it.

"Thank you," said Maya.

A short distance away, five men emerged from the ground floor of a building. One carried a pistol, the other four crude spears. They set off southwest and soon vanished among the decrepit former city. Maya nibbled on the tough, stringy meat. Two of the kids tugged at her nightdress, feeling the silk and gasping with awe.

She examined one child's curtain-turned-skirt with the same degree of appearing impressed, hoping to forestall the sort of jealousy that resulted in theft. Her rat meal died a quick death, and she handed the empty skewer back to the woman.

"Thank you for feeding me."

The woman smiled.

Maya regretted looking at her teeth. "I... uhh, gotta go."

She waved, evaded curious small hands, and headed north at a light run. The Sanctuary Zone stood out against the horizon much less during the day, but remained visible in the haze. Off to the east, the continuous whirr of drone fans warned her away from the road. She looked back to the south and considered going home. No doubt, Sarah would be in a panic at waking up to find her missing.

Every street looked the same. Even if she gave up on Genna and tried, she had no idea if she'd even make it back home in one piece. Everyone had warned her how dangerous it was to go outside alone. What if she'd gotten lucky making it this far? She'd probably get hurt trying to go back. At least north, the route was unmistakable... and she couldn't give up on her mother.

Maya held her arms out to the sides for balance as she walked up a section of concrete lane divider that had flipped onto a car, becoming a narrow ramp. She stood at the tip and squinted into the wind. A tiny dot of cyan light blinked atop the Ascendant tower, barely visible behind a dense fog of pollution.

"Please be alive, Mom."

She jumped to the car's roof, hopped to the trunk, and lowered herself to the road before jogging north into the Dead Space.

TWENTY-FOUR
BAD MEMORIES

aya walked for hours, ignoring the building sense of hunger in her belly, the pain in her feet, and the growing sense she'd been foolish for running off. Whenever the ground offered a patch of dirt instead of paved surface, she took the opportunity for comfort. Little by little, the glimmering city of white and silver drew closer. The abandoned parts of old Baltimore housed dangers she'd only read about on the AuthNet—Fade, other diseases, dosers, roving gangs, and territorial militias that supposedly got into routine turf wars.

Some gangs even turned cannibalistic according to the Authority. Many shot down drones, even the bioassay units, which only tried to help everyone by monitoring Fade levels to provide early warning. She peered straight up as she walked, wondering if aliens sent such an awful disease to Earth to scrub the planet of humans before taking it over. No one she could remember from the company took that theory seriously, but everyone accepted Fade fell from the sky. It had to be a weapon left over from the war. Which side had made it, no one could agree upon, though everyone blamed old governments.

Ascendant's way, the rule of Vanessa Oman, offered a much better society.

Or so they said.

Maya stuck out her tongue. "Bleh."

A massive pile of concrete blocked the road ahead, five or six stories of some building's face, which had fallen. She glanced up at the naked girders and gaping wound in the high-rise for a few seconds before climbing through a window hole. It had collapsed long enough ago for no trace of glass to remain. She jumped down on the inside and landed on all fours.

"Hey. Check that out," said a man.

Maya snapped her head up. Two thin figures in ragged pants and jackets mixed of brown and black leather sat on either side of a metal basin repurposed to a fire pit a short distance to her right. A feral-looking woman with a shock of purple hair, so skinny she didn't seem to have breasts, knelt on the far side, jabbing at smoldering wood with a longer stick. Her outfit looked like armor made from old tires, and she had lots of knives tucked in sheaths wherever she could tie them on. All three had skin as pale as ghosts, smeared with thick grime.

The woman grinned at her. "Looks delicious. Kill it, eat it, or fuck it?"

"Three, then two, then three, then one," said the man on the left.

"I ain't gonna two it after ya three it," said the other man.

Oh, shit. Maya abandoned stealth and took off at a full sprint. The metal basin clattered behind her as the trio leapt to their feet and gave chase. She curved left, heading for a maze of smashed debris, hoping for a place too small for an adult to follow. Tears streamed out of the corners of her eyes, driven into her ears by the racing wind past her face. Whooping noises and cheers rang out behind her. Footsteps got closer. She yelled with clenched teeth, trying to milk as much speed as she could out of legs used to lounging.

An angled section of fallen building offered a ramp. She scampered upward, heading for another window hole. One of the men seized her ankle with a *slap* and dragged her back. Maya grabbed the edge of the sill and glanced down at a wagging tongue, horrified that he tried to pull her foot to his mouth and lick her. She stopped trying to haul herself up and lunged backward, stomping his tongue into his teeth with her heel. The man stumbled away, abandoning his hold on her leg to grab his face with both hands, emitting a pained howl past his fingers. The skinny woman raised a bow and drew an arrow back.

Maya let off an "eep" and dove through the window. She landed on her chest a few feet below as an aluminum razor-head arrow struck the dirt six or so inches to the right of her head.

"Shit." Maya shoved herself up. "I'm such an idiot. Why did I run away?"

She snagged the arrow and scrambled ahead over the avalanche of debris. Office chairs, old copiers, desks, and large slabs of drywall created a maze that forced her to belly crawl in some places and jump to climb others. She headed for a patch of daylight about forty yards away at the end of a narrow tunnel no adult could fit in. Silence gave her confidence during the long crawl, hoping the freaks had lost track of her in the rubble. Still attempting to be quiet, Maya scooted to the end of the junk labyrinth and crawled out into the light.

The skinny woman came out of nowhere and grabbed her by the hair, screaming, "Gotcha!"

Maya growled and jammed the arrow into the woman's thigh hard enough to sink the entire bladed point to the shaft. "This is yours." She gave it a twist, which caused the woman to wilt down to one knee, screaming.

The Frag abandoned her grip on Maya's hair to cradle the wound. Maya scooped up a double-handful of sparkling concrete dust, hurling it into the maniac's face before swiping a giant combat knife from the freak's belt sheath. While the Frag howled and grabbed her eyes, Maya ran down a long section of street with minimal cover, the two men chasing. Buildings on both sides had been reduced to rubble fields and the occasional scrap of steel girder that stuck up like a middle finger to the society that had devoured itself.

Raging obscenities spilled from the woman's mouth. An arrow clattered to the ground somewhere off to the left. Maya hoped the glittering in the dust meant pulverized glass. Three blocks away, a cluster of still-standing skyscrapers with heavy damage offered a place to hide. She didn't look back to see if the men continued to chase her or tended to their wounded sister/wife/whatever, and darted in a broken street-level window. She stuffed herself in the bottom drawer of an old office desk and pushed it closed. Tromping boots went by outside, came back, and went by again.

"Ya'in 'ere, tasty rat?" shouted a man, his voice filling the room around her.

She pictured him sticking his head in the window, scanning the room for any sign of her. Maya buried her face in the bend of her elbow so she didn't make any noise. Even the act of breathing in a tiny metal box seemed so loud that Vanessa could hear her from the Sanc. Realizing those people would've killed her brought irresistible tears, but Maya managed to weep in total silence.

"Aha! Gotcha!" shouted the man.

Maya refused to move since the shout didn't sound any closer. *He's trying to trick me.*

Eventually, enough time passed without any audible sign of them chasing her. Hopeful they'd given up, Maya pressed her hands against the metal overhead and pulled the drawer open. She climbed out and crept across the room to the window. Listening to total quiet for a moment convinced her the Frags had given up. Maya slipped back out the window to the street. Fear shifted to anger at those people for costing her time. Time that could kill Genna.

Scowling, Maya crossed left over a four-lane road, jumped the concrete divider, and hurried over a parking lot crisscrossed with grass-grown cracks.

A building in the shape of an L rose some sixty stories overhead, with numerous sections of the exterior wall missing. In what had once been a courtyard, a giant pile of slabs and debris had collected, almost deliberate in its effort to be a monument. Laughter and chatter of childish voices far overhead sounded familiar.

She crawled into a space far too small for a grown up to fit and spent a few beautiful minutes on all fours catching her breath. When she finally looked up, her heart skipped a beat. Not far from the end of the debris tunnel lay the mangled frame of a metal bed with an electronic handcuff dangling from one end.

After a few minutes' more rest, she crept out from under the mountain of debris and stood. A dark blotch to her right stained the pale stone in the rough shape of a flattened rat. The body was gone, likely someone's dinner. Maya gazed from the splat mark up to a yawning hole near the fiftieth floor. She cringed as she looked back down, but the only trace of her abductors was a large swath of discoloration on the ground, plus a gouge where Moth's arm probably hit.

She eyed the spot where the rat landed again, cringing at the memory of Head's reaction to Moth hurling it out of the building. No guilt existed for Moth—in fact, his death rather comforted her. The Chinese guy, meh. She didn't feel much of anything for him. Head, though, she regretted a bit. She'd only wanted to create enough chaos to escape... though she should've known how things would've ended. Maya sank to a squat and sobbed, feeling horrified that her plan might've killed Genna if circumstances worked out even a slight bit differently. Poking a crazy cybered-up veteran square in his mental disorder ranked up there on a list of dumb things to do with juggling live hand grenades.

"Stupidity and desperation often look the same," said Maya, quoting Jerry Michaels, the Ascendant VP she disliked. A sly grin formed on her lips. The man had refused to stop calling her klutz after she tripped accidentally once. Three months after that, she'd rather purposefully swatted his coffee into his lap and said, "Oops. Guess I *am* a klutz." That had been one of the few times she got a genuine smile from Vanessa—for a show of vindictiveness.

Maya sighed.

In a moment or two, she gathered her composure and set off again, wiping her eyes and sniffling. She didn't look back at the building where she'd been held captive; for all she cared, the whole thing could collapse and the world would be a better place. A few children's giggles echoed from high overhead. Another thing she didn't want to look at—kids her age walking on steel beams. Watching one of them slip would be a nightmare she did *not* want repeating in her head.

She followed a curving driveway out of the courtyard and took a left where it met the street. Still headed in the general direction of north, she walked past the slumped corpse of a parking garage, an old strip mall, and a scorch mark where some kind of shopping center existed before the war. Next to it, a field of chest-high grass offered not only a break for her tired feet, but also the fear of emerging covered head to toe in bugs. Four-inch roaches horrified her, but at least she could *see* those. Tiny ones she wouldn't notice before they bit her everywhere skeeved her out more.

She opted to stay on the pavement.

Buildings crept by, and again the daylight weakened. Maya plodded on until it became dark and the city grew dense once more, but these high-rises creaked with every breeze, seeming as if they might topple at any second. Far more than the Habitation Block, this place looked *dead*. Light from up ahead cast long shadows from a pair of thin figures seated on the sidewalk in front of a building bearing a 7-11 sign. Inside, shelves toppled to the side like a giant's game of dominos. Emptiness and white paint turned the old store into a giant lightbox. She crouched behind the rusting hulk of an old black pick-up truck covered in anti-Korean graffiti and watched the people fiddling with a small device on the ground between where they sat.

"Come here, child," said a placid male voice. The figure on the right waved at her.

He sounded friendly enough, and after the fright with the creepy trio, it seemed a decent idea not being alone when it got darker. Maya changed course and crossed a small, empty lot to where the two men sat on concrete bars at the far end of parking spaces. Both had shaved heads and unusually pale skin, and wore robes made of red and burgundy fabric with a trace of periwinkle blue at the neck. Maya made no effort to hide the enormous knife, but the men didn't show any reaction to it.

"Welcome, child." The second man pulled his hands out of his sleeves and held his arms out to the sides. "Please, sit and be welcome."

"Be welcome," said the other.

Maya approached, squinting at the intense fluorescent glare from inside the building. Eight hot dogs sizzled over the electric heating element of a little grill the men had set up, powered by a wire running back into the store. She eased herself to sit with her legs to the right, then smoothed her nightdress down to within an inch of her knees. Not putting weight on her feet felt awesome. She left the knife on the ground by her rear end, hidden from view of the men, but still in easy reach.

"What is your name, little one? I am Var, and this is Fud." The slightly smaller man gestured at his companion. With the robes, white stuff on their faces, and shaved heads, they could've been brothers.

"Lisa."

"Behold the innocent wanderer," said Fud. "We see that you are alone and in need, and offer our aid."

"You're not going to hurt me?"

"Of course not, child." Var tilted his head. "We have eight nutrient tubes. You are welcome to two of them."

"Thank you."

Both men bowed their heads in unison.

"What fate has set you loose upon the world with no one to guide you?" asked Fud.

"My mother was kidnapped. I'm going to get her back."

They made the same sorrowful face at the same moment.

"Poor child." Var leaned forward and lifted the lid from a plastic cooler case. He opened a cloth inside and withdrew a tortilla, in which he cradled one of the hot dogs before adding some shredded cheese and wrapping it closed. "Here. Take this nutrient tube with Jeva's blessing."

Fud bowed his head and made an odd noise.

Maya's eyebrows crept closer. "Uhh, thanks."

He wrapped another hot dog and handed it to Fud before taking one for himself. Maya waited for them to start eating before she took a bite. They munched in silence, their expressions a creepy mixture of meditative calm and joy.

"Have you considered allowing Jeva into your heart?" asked Fud. "Your unfortunate circumstances are not suffered by his children."

"Not really." Maya nibbled. "I never thought about it."

"Jeva sees all," said Var. "He protects those who follow the one true path."

"So, you're Sons of Jeva?" Maya fought the urge to roll her eyes.

They smiled.

"We are his children," said Var.

Fud bowed his head. "This world is an evil and broken place, and he has promised to rebuild from it a paradise in which humanity will thrive." He made a grand sweeping gesture. "He protects and guides us, his humble servants."

Var handed out another round of hot dogs. "He provides us with everything we need, such as these nutrient tubes. As protected Sons of Jeva, we are allowed entry to the city as often as necessary to spread The Word."

She winced. The checkpoint at the gate hadn't occurred to her before. Perhaps a silly robe and make up would get her in without notice. She vaguely recalled something about freedom of religion from the old government. Perhaps one of a few things the Authority had kept. No way would she let them shave her head though. "So, what's it like?"

"The Ceremony of Universal Welcome is beautiful," said Fud, with a starry-eyed upward stare. "For three days, the supplicant meditates alone in the spirit dome, with nothing between them and Jeva but the sacred embers."

"Naked?" Maya squirmed. "Is that really necessary?"

"It is a representation of one casting off the trappings of the Earth." Fud brought his hands together, smiling. "The sacred embers burn, covering you with Jeva's wisdom and love. The supplicant is safe and protected within the spirit dome. Upon the Third Day, Jeva shall bestow upon you your sacred vestments." He patted his robes. "The only possession you will ever need."

"So you guys don't own anything?" Maya shifted a bit of hotdog from one side of her mouth to the other.

"We give everything, all worldly possessions, to Jeva." Var bowed with reverence. "Our tasks may produce NuCoin, which we lovingly surrender to the furtherance of his needs."

"If he's a supreme being, why does he need money?" Maya raised an eyebrow.

They made faces at her like a cute child who'd inadvertently said something offensive.

"There are mysteries we dare not question." Fud tucked his hands in his sleeves and bowed his head. "Jeva commands the discarding of wealth and material possessions. The Great Unmaking was brought about by the unrestrained pursuit of such things. He does not himself possess—he separates the material from the world and guards our souls."

"When you experience the sacred smoke, all will become clear." Var gazed off with the expression of a small child seeing his mother.

Great. They're want to lock me in a sauna with hallucinogens for three days. No wonder these two are broken. "Umm, so you've seen Jeva? Like, not from the smoke, but really?"

They nodded. "He dwells not far from here in the Grand Temple at Adelphi. A vast underground palace."

"Does it have tunnels and metal rails going through it?" asked Maya.

Fud's eyes popped wide. "You have seen it? Truly, a sign."

No. But I know what a subway station was. "Uhh, I heard someone talk about it. How do you know Jeva's a god?"

"It is The Word," said Var.

Both men bowed their heads.

"So, this guy just says he's a god, and you believe him?"

Fud looked hurt. "Child, please guard your words, lest Jeva hear."

"She does not know, brother." Var raised a placating hand. "Soon after the Great Unmaking, Jeva was as you are now, a mere mortal wandering alone across the vast nothing the world has become. It was then that he came upon the Sacred Speaker, and it bore unto him The Word."

Both men bowed, quiet for a long moment. They chanted a syllable that sounded a bit like 'Oman,' which made Maya clamp her hand over her mouth to hide a snicker. She managed to conceal her smile before they looked up.

Var raised his palms upward. "The Sacred Speaker communicated with Jeva and taught him what we must do to prevent our world from spiraling into the Sun. Through the Speaker, he became holy, no longer a mere mortal. Our race has squandered this planet, our most precious gift, and the Distant Watchers were displeased. They sent the Sacred Speaker as a test, and thank Jeva he found it."

Fud bowed, and said the strange word again. That time, it sounded like a mixture of 'ohm,' and 'amen.'

"Who's the sacred speaker?" Maya wiped her hands on her nightdress.

"The Sacred Speaker is a totem given to Jeva by the Distant Watchers." Var paused for another reverent head bow. "He has told of it several times. A lustrous pearlescent purple statue in the shape of a woman in fine robes. Though it is not alive in a way a simple human mind can understand, it bestowed The Word upon him."

The men bowed again.

Maya glanced to her left at the far off *pop* of a gunshot. "Have you seen it?"

"Oh, no," said Fud, hand on his chest. The look on his face would've been appropriate had Maya suggested throwing an infant in a bonfire. "Only Jeva is permitted to gaze upon the Sacred Speaker. He was commanded by the Distant Watchers never to reveal it to anyone else, for they could not bear the magnificence of it and would surely die under the fearsome presence of her voice."

"Riiight," whispered Maya. "So, he's never actually shown anyone the proof he's a god or that there are aliens, uhh, 'distant watchers?' He could just be making this all up to take your money."

Var sighed, eyebrows together in an expression of sympathy. "Oh, child. Faith is something one must accept. When you see him, you will understand."

She eyed the darkness, finding it held a sudden appeal over her present company. The last thing she needed now was to fall asleep here and wake up locked in a stone igloo somewhere naked, head shaved, and high as hell on whatever drugs they burned by the bucket load. So much for priesting her way into the Sanctuary Zone. Of all that, the thought of someone cutting her hair angered her the most. Of what little reaction she'd ever managed to get from Vanessa, the woman had been jealous of her hair. Not-Mom never could get hers quite as straight.

"Thank you so much for giving me food, but I don't think Jeva would want me."

"Do not be so critical of yourself, child." Fud smiled. "All who know the Sons of Jeva respect his power. We have no fear of the denizens of this place. He will protect us."

Maya tucked her feet closer, preparing in case she needed to sprint. The analytical part of her mind wanted to point out that these two had fallen for a con man who may or may not even have a talking statue. Convenient he couldn't show it to anyone. Of course, as placid as these two appeared right now, they might go ballistic if she threatened their faith.

"I'm nine. I don't have any worldly possessions to surrender."

"Of course you don't." Var smiled. "You're still a child. You are innocent in the evils of the world, and need to embrace Jeva before your soul is stained."

Maya clasped her knife and stood, keeping the blade hidden behind her back. "I gotta go. I, uhh, think I hear a Sanctified *Shǎguā* calling me." She curtsied and sprinted for the corner of the building, hoping they didn't understand Chinese. Of course, had her vocabulary been better, she might've come up with something stronger than 'simpleton.'

"Wait, child," yelled Fud. "You shouldn't be alone."

Once she hit the alley along the side of the 7-11, the lack of bright fluorescent light rendered the world impenetrable and black. *They might be nice, but they're so creepy.* Dying grass slid between her toes, and she slowed to avoid a nasty fall until her eyes adjusted to moonlight. Her foot found a can or pipe—which shot out from under her—and she spilled over onto her hands, the knife flying. For a few minutes, she remained still. When the pain in her palms and knees faded, she patted around until she found her stolen weapon. Relieved, she stood and dusted herself off. The Sons of Jeva gave up calling after her and retreated around the storefront, seeming afraid to leave the cone of light emanating from within. She almost felt guilty for running from their apparent kindness... but they'd been so *creepy*.

The radiance of the Sanctuary Zone dominated the horizon a touch off to the right, and now that the sun had gone down, the lights of dozens of drones slid back and forth over the highway. She looked around at a dirt lot with tufts of grass amid patches of bare dirt. A feeble glow up ahead outlined a cluster of box trailers, one with a cloth awning on the side. Faint notes from heavy music leaked out of a tiny speaker somewhere. The shadow of a large industrial complex sat beyond them.

A glint of moonlight to the left caught her eye where a shallow puddle spread out at the base of a corrugated metal tunnel about three feet in diameter. It passed under a road long-ago rendered useless to vehicles. Still, the culvert offered a place to spend the night away from prying eyes and sycophantic cultists.

She eased her way down the embankment, toes squishing in inch-deep mud, and crawled into the tunnel. Lumpy metal made for a lousy bed, but it was dry and felt safer than being outside in the dark. Alone, cold, and frightened, she shivered. Her mind bounced between the want to be safe at home with her friend, and worry for Genna. She pictured the lay of the Magic cards and cried from guilt, her soft sobs echoing in the tunnel.

TWENTY-FIVE
JOB OFFER

Rapid-fire Chinese shouted in a woman's voice startled Maya awake. The tirade flowed far too fast for her to make sense of it, though she did pick out the word for 'idiot' a few times. She sat up and tried to stretch, an uncomfortable prospect at best in a corrugated metal pipe. Her legs hurt from so much walking, her chest ached from worry and guilt, and her throat felt as though it had turned into cotton overnight.

She crawled to the end of the tunnel and tried to coax any amount of moisture into her mouth. The distant argument raged on while she regarded herself in the surface of a muddy brown puddle. Maya touched the water; ripples broke the illusion where the sky reflected as a strip of bright grey glass next to her face. That she felt no urge to add to the puddle worried her.

I haven't had anything to drink in two days.

The shouting petered out to a few quick snapped remarks. Maya emerged from the pipe and stretched a leg to step over the mud. She guessed the time at close to noon with a threatening, overcast sky. People tended to stay inside when it rained out of fear of Fade, though she'd gotten inoculated soon after birth—unless Vanessa lied about that too—but it seemed unlikely. The vac shot cost Ascendant about ten dollars to make, and Maya had been valuable. Maybe.

She tried to swallow the cotton in her mouth, half considering attempting to drink the muck. Disgust overpowered desperation, and she walked away, navigating a patch of rough weeds to the far side of the ditch. She climbed the bank, pausing at the top to peer between strands of wild grass at a collection of wheeled dwellings. A portable town made of four white semi-trailers and a pea-green house trailer sat in the shadow of a distant industrial complex.

A short Asian woman with glossy, tight black pants, heeled boots, and a long-sleeved net shirt that didn't do much to conceal her breasts paced back and forth under an orange awning on the side of the largest trailer. Her black bob cut flared out each time she turned with the sharp twist of a soldier. Dark-blue earrings, wire mesh in the shape of three-dimensional stars, seemed about to fly off. The woman muttered to herself in Chinese while drumming her fingers on a boxy machine pistol hung on a strap over her shoulder.

Maya gathered her courage and pulled herself up out of the ditch. She approached the angry woman and stopped about ten feet away. "Excuse me. Can I please have some water?"

The woman halted, blinking at her as though she'd spoken an alien dialect.

She tried to think back to the handful of Chinese language e-learns she'd dabbled with. "*Gěi wǒ shuǐ*? Please? I haven't had anything to drink for days." Maya twisted her toes in the dirt and added a needy whine.

The woman cringed. "Stick to English. Where did you come from? Who are you working for?"

"I live in Block Thirteen." Maya crept closer. "I'm not a thief."

The woman sighed. "Okay. I can give you some water, but watch your hands." She gestured with a beckoning wave and pointed at a rickety wooden porch on the house trailer before going inside.

Maya scurried up and sat on the second step, facing toward the culvert she came from with her back to the trailer. In the daylight, the store where she'd met the Sons of Jeva blended into the surroundings, becoming another unremarkable square in the landscape. No sign of the men remained. She brushed dried mud off her foot, fidgeted, and searched the cloudy sky for the elusive source of a drone fan's whirr.

A dirt path stretched to her left, leading across a rough, dead meadow to a far distant collection of stacked oceanic cargo boxes and a handful of more solid buildings. She remembered Headcrash talking about stashing her in a place called the Spread, and proceeded to frighten herself by thinking about what it would have felt like had they left her trapped inside one of the containers. Multiple scenarios played out in her mind, each scarier than the last.

A few minutes later, two older teen boys emerged from the tall grass following a curve on the path, walking closer. She ducked and pulled her hair down over her face. The scuff of their shoes grew louder. Maya sat as still as she could and tried to become part of the porch, using her body to keep the knife out of sight. *Please don't steal my stuff.* Her attention drifted to the rumble of a distant green cargo truck with white Nutrimax markings. An Authority van followed close, protecting a shipment of food heading for the Sanctuary Zone from outlying farms.

Maya shivered at the memory of how she used to react to news of Nons and Frags being shot for trying to assault the grow facilities. Of course, the media called them terrorists attempting to compromise the food supply. After living out here, she thought it more likely they had attacked out of hunger, trying to take food. She stared at the convoy until it passed out of sight to the left, sinking into the endless rolling meadow grass.

The boys halted a few paces away. One wore a common voluminous grey coat-jacket with the built-in rebreather, and dark pants. The other had no shirt, and an exposed strip of white underwear ringed his waist above the baggiest pair of drab green pants she'd ever seen. Both had sneakers that looked older than her.

"Missy Hong," shouted the one in the jacket. "You here?"

"Ya, ya," yelled the woman from inside. "Be right out."

Maya sat in awkward silence, concentrating on her want to be ignored. Icarus had wanted to visit this woman to buy more Vesper. She'd stumbled straight into the den of a drug dealer. Fear almost got her running, but extreme thirst won out and she stayed put. Two-ish minutes later, Missy emerged from the trailer and set a large plastic cup of water down on the porch next to her. When Maya looked up with a grateful smile, the woman offered her a blue plastic plate with two doughy pillows on it, each the size of a man's fist.

"You're skin and bones. Poor thing."

"Thank you." Maya set the plate in her lap and drank half the water first.

"Missy Hong," said the shirtless kid. "What's good? Got any Soul-Razr?"

"Dandelion Wine for me," said his friend.

They both held up NuCoins, clear plastic discs with two sides cut flat, which gave them an overall shape like thumbprints. The modern currency shimmered with rainbow holograms embedded within. People in the Sanctuary Zone still spoke of dollars more often than NuCoin, but those existed only as numbers in computers now.

"How much you want?" asked Missy.

"Whatever I can get for three," said the bare-chested kid. He held up three coins.

"Soul-Razr's hard to come by, big boy. Eight per ride. I got your Dandelions no problem. Twenty for ten."

"Pussy shit," said shirtless.

"Maybe, but the ride ain't half bad and it won't make my brain explode."

Maya tuned out the rest of the deal and feasted on the dumplings, getting two bites into the second one before the boys walked away and Missy sat next to her. Maya glanced left and up at her, but didn't slow down eating.

"Yeah, you looked hungry." Missy brushed Maya's hair off her face. "There's a story in those eyes."

Sensing a possible sympathetic ear, Maya explained about her mother being taken by the Authority and how she'd decided to go to the Sanctuary Zone to get her back. She omitted who she really was, which likely made the entire story seem ridiculous, as evidenced by the incredulous—and somewhat patronizing—look Missy gave her.

"That's a hell of a tale. You're going to need more than that knife to beat a city full of blueberries. If you've got nowhere to go, I could use a little runner."

Maya shook her head. "I can't. I have to get my mom back. And wouldn't people just beat me up and steal the drugs?"

"Well, you supposed to be small and sneaky... but once word's out you with Missy Hong, no one dare touch you. Everyone knows me, and the people I work for. You tell 'em you run for me, they leave you alone."

Or kill me so I can't tell on them. "I have to at least try to help my mom. You're really nice." She chomped down on more dumpling, chewed, and swallowed. "I'm too little to have a knife. I don't really even know why I grabbed it. Can I trade it for the food or maybe some pants... shoes?"

"You don't have to trade for it. I not let ya starve. You not gonna get her out of there with or without a knife, and I don't have anything your size."

Maya's throat tightened. "Can you help me? I'll make deliveries for you if you can get my mom back."

"My influence is out here." Missy gestured around. "Inside the Sanc, we operate in the shadows. Authority is easy enough to pay off, but they only look other way. They don't take requests. Cannot order person out of jail like calling a pizza."

Maya held the last bit of dumpling and stared at it. "I'm going to try to get her back."

"Good luck with that kid... good luck with that." Missy patted her on the back. "You got balls for a little thing. If the blueberries don' kill you, come on back here and I set you up. Oh, and if you tell anyone I'm nice, I'll cut all your toes off. Make necklace."

Maya gasped. Missy winked.

She finished the dumpling, even though it hurt to pack even more food into her stomach, and drank more water so fast it streamed around her cheeks and dribbled down her chest.

"Slow down." Missy took the empty plate. "You choke."

"Thank you for the food. Are you sure you don't want the knife?" Maya sipped the water down to a quarter of a cup. Her belly felt ready to burst open.

"Yeah. I don' do the knife thing." She showed off the gun hanging at her hip.

A pair of men stepped out of the next trailer to the right; each wore a long black coat and had an assault rifle over their back on a strap. One pulled out an electronic cigarette and raised it to his lips with a hand wrapped in dragon tattoos. The machine emitted a hiss as he sucked on it, and he leveled a cold stare at her while white vapor oozed from his nostrils. The other threw a sideways nod at her, while muttering something in Chinese. Missy shook her head.

Organized crime…

"I should go." Maya stood. "The dumplings were really, really good."

"You serious about going to bust your momma out?" Missy raised an eyebrow.

Maya nodded. "Yes. Can you help?"

"Sorry kid. Over my head."

"Okay." She smiled.

Three steps later, Missy jogged up behind her and grabbed her shoulder. "Hold on."

Maya looked up at her.

"I can't believe you serious."

"I am."

"Two things." Missy pointed north along the dirt road. "One. There this big-titted blonde in the Spread. Goes by name DeeDee. She ain't to be trusted with a pretty little thing like you."

"Why?" asked Maya.

Missy let go of her shoulder and patted it. "Look, you stay away from her. Don' even let her see you."

"Oh." Maya gazed down. "She's a madam, right? The kind that won't care I'm too little."

"Damn girl." Missy laughed. "You should not be in such a rush to grow up. I can't help you directly, but I know a guy might be able to give you little advice. Follow this road to the Spread. Look for place call Devil's Hangover. Ask for Diego. Everything shady 'round here go through him."

"Diego." Maya rubbed her belly. "Okay."

Missy backed up, pointing at her. "Remember I could use good runner. If things don' work out, you come on back."

Maya's grateful smile faded to a worried stare once she faced the road. While this path appeared free of debris, drones, and offered nice soft earth to walk on, it also led to a place she dreaded going. Between AuthNet articles about gang wars, insurgent groups using the Spread to fire random rockets and missiles into the Sanctuary Zone, Authority raids, a woman who might abduct her for the sex trade, and desperate poor, she gave serious thought to taking her chances with drones. It would be unlikely they'd recognize her. The highway looked a mile or two away to the east across a veritable minefield of destroyed buildings likely to be littered with unexploded bombs from the war as well as equally dangerous Frags.

Few Citizens recognized the difference between Nons and Frags, considering both mindless dreck who would just as soon kill her as say hello. Nons weren't anything like what the 'net said, only normal people guilty of the felony of being poor. They still clung to the trappings of civilization as it had been before the war. Frags, on the other hand, could be dangerous. Frags went *way* off the grid. An encounter with one of them could be as pleasant as meeting Missy or as terrifying as the bitch who tried to kill her with an arrow.

Maya stood in the middle of the path, toes dug into the dirt, leaning forward into a wind that pressed her nightdress against her body and tried to knock her over backwards. Every road led to something scarier than the next. Maybe if she carried drugs for Missy, the woman could help her? No. She'd read enough about organized crime not to trust them. Sure, they'd take good care of her, but if they even suspected betrayal, all that kindness would disappear in a heartbeat. If they realized who she was, it could be Moth all over again... and this time she probably wouldn't escape alive. Not the way Vanessa handled ransom demands.

She glanced back at Missy's trailer for a second before looking ahead down the road. She wanted to scream 'Mommy' until Genna swooped out of nowhere, wrapped her up in both arms, and told her everything would be okay.

Maya stared at the dirt, and let the tears roll while the wind howled.

No. Everything wouldn't be okay.

Not by a long shot.

TWENTY- SIX
THE JIGSAW RIVER

ead down, Maya fought her way forward into the wind. Without the barricade of high-rise buildings, the ocean-scented air protested her every step. The grey sky never quite made good on its threat to open up with a downpour, though a few isolated drops fell here and there. Being out in a field with nowhere to hide didn't seem like a wonderful idea. Even if she carried a knife as big as her arm, who'd be afraid of her? She came close to dropping it for no other reason than her hand got tired, but she decided to keep it as a possible trade item. Maybe the man Missy spoke of would have a store where she could exchange it for better clothes.

One hour melted into the next, yet neither the distant boxy shadows of the Spread on the horizon nor the silhouette of the Sanctuary Zone looked any closer than before. Her pace slowed as her subconscious called her foolish and stupid in Vanessa's voice. Teaming up with Sarah to deal with Mr. Mason had been the most awesome thing she'd ever done. Having that special friendship might make it easier to cope with losing Genna. Maya stopped walking, sank into a squat, and wrapped her arms around herself. *Why is it cold in the summer?* Her teeth chattered with each gust of ocean breeze that seemed to pass through her flimsy garment as if it wasn't even there.

Maya glanced behind her along the road at the faint trail of small footprints. Missy's trailer sat too far away to see anymore. She wondered if the woman might protect her if she asked for help going home to Block 13 instead of the city. Tears raced down her cheeks as her brain teased at accepting Genna as gone. Could she trust Missy? She didn't feel safe trying to walk home from here. What if she ran into those three crazies again—or worse? Asking a favor from a woman connected to organized crime wouldn't be a simple matter. They'd expect something in return, though how bad could doing a few deliveries be?

They'd never let me stop. And when I got too big for the Authority to ignore, they'd make me shoot people or do what Missy does. Maya stuck her tongue out. Upon reaching the conclusion she had only one option—continue to the Sanctuary Zone—she sniffled and wiped her face on the back of her arm. If the Authority grabbed her, she could always lie and tell them she escaped the kidnappers.

However, if she *didn't* get caught...

Vanessa had a terminal in each of her apartments and super-user rights to everything in the Ascendant system. If Genna remained alive, Vanessa—or a sneaky little girl using her terminal—could find her.

Her heart beat with eager determination. Maya sprang upright and marched forward. A short while after the sun crested its peak and began the long slide into the western horizon, a rushing noise grew distinct from the bay of the wind. The thundering reminded her of waterfalls she'd seen in videos, though nothing like that should exist here. She walked faster, heading toward a square of smashed concrete surrounded by a chain link fence that had been knocked flat, the industrial complex she'd seen from Missy's. Strange machines lined up along the back of the former building, a mixture of sea-green paint and rust. Pipes large enough for her to crawl into came up out of the ground about fifteen yards from the machines and connected to huge round chambers.

She thought them pumps of some kind, though by their condition, she didn't think they'd been operational since before the war. Maya couldn't suppress a giggle at how the Son of Jeva referred to the war as the Great Unmaking. She shook her head. "Yeah, aliens are going to throw the Earth into the Sun because we've been naughty. Right." *Hmm. Some people think aliens created Fade.* She squinted at the sky. *Enough plausibility for suckers to believe it.*

The roar of moving water became louder as she advanced. She stepped with care over a broken piece of fence, watching for sharp things on the ground. The entire area behind the building consisted of concrete tarmac well into the process of being reclaimed by nature. Green stuff sprouted from thousands of cracks, and much of the area looked charred. At the sight of a bowl-shaped crater in the ground up ahead, she wondered if a nuclear device had gone off here.

Curiosity got the better of her, and though she didn't want to waste too much time, she walked toward the hole. A metal sign on the ground lay with the words upside down to her. Maya walked around it and peered down.

< COAGULATION POOL

< AERATION TANK

SEDIMENTATION POOL >

FILTRATION TANK 4, B >

Maya scratched her head, shrugged, and kept walking. The rushing noise grew loud enough to require shouting if one wanted to be heard. About fifteen paces from the sign, she peered over the edge of the great opening in the ground. A moss-lined concrete channel, half of a rounded section six feet in diameter, carried a flow of water downward into a subterranean passageway. The splashdown of dozens of streams leaking from a maze of broken pipes around the edges lofted a cool mist that sprayed at her shins and feet.

The massive chute ran about forty yards before it ended, pouring its contents down a short waterfall to another broken section of sewer pipe that took it deeper into the tunnels. She edged away from the hole, having trouble thinking under the burden of the heavy noise. It looked dangerous, though the tunnels did seem to progress in the direction of the Spread, and perhaps even the Sanctuary Zone itself.

A sharp *click* to her left drew her attention to a white mark on the concrete. Before she could wonder who'd thrown a rock at her, a gunshot erupted with a *crack* in the distance. Maya gasped and dropped to all fours. She peered through the fluttering shreds of metal slats in the crushed fence, scanning the area for the person who'd *shot* at her. They had to be quite a ways off if the bullet got to her before the sound did.

Far enough away for people to be no taller than grains of rice, two large crowds gathered on either side of the dirt road where it curved. The ones on the far side of the path fired guns at the ones on the near, who responded in kind. A handful ran at each other with clubs, bats, and even a katana or two. Here and there, blooms of fire erupted wherever the fighters traded Molotovs. Gunshots went off like a fusillade of fireworks, the distance muting them to snaps and pops.

She exhaled a small sigh of relief. No one had shot at her specifically, merely a stray bullet since she found herself directly behind one of the warring groups. Still, she kept low. A bullet wouldn't dodge around her because the person firing it didn't want to hit her on purpose.

Another projectile struck one of the big pumps behind her with a *clank*. Three whistled overhead. Maya looked around in a frantic search for cover, but the only option that didn't involve standing up and sprinting was the hole. When another bullet chipped off the concrete less than an arm's length away from her, she swallowed her fear and leapt onto the incline, intending to hover right below the level of the ground.

Slimy moss-covered concrete took her feet straight out from under her. She slid on her butt for about ten feet, fell three more, and landed sitting in armpit-deep water. The current plus frictionless gooey biomatter beneath her swept her along the forty-yard chute in a matter of a few seconds. She screamed when sliding became freefall at the end. Maya clamped her eyes shut and held her breath before landing flat on her back in the next section of tunnel, underwater.

The torrent churned and swished her side to side, carrying her feet-first down the slippery channel. She slid up against the wall around a tight turn, went under again, and caught air as the captive river dumped her out the end of one broken segment of pipe into yet another chute.

Maya managed a shriek and gulped down air before she splashed into chaos again. Her fingers scraped at ooze and congealing algae, her effort to slow down useless. She rolled to the right, powerless against the current carrying her around a leftward curve; her stomach and thighs brushed the wall. Maya gulped water and air in equal parts, struggling to breathe. The turn abruptly straightened, and she shot off the end into a fall, pedaling her legs and windmilling her arms. An attempt to scream triggered coughing. This drop gave her enough distance that she flipped over in midair and hit the next section of rushing water flat on her chest, arms stretched out over her head.

The landing knocked a bubble out of her lungs; she scrabbled and clawed in a desperate search for breathable air. When her hands touched the bottom of the concrete tube, she realized the current no longer swept her along. Maya pushed her head up, breaking the surface, and gasped. After a momentary coughing fit subsided, she got her knees under herself and shivered in a shoulder-deep bath. Strands of green plant matter dangled overhead, interspersed with daylight leaking in from copious cracks and smaller holes overhead. The deafening rumble of dozens of little waterfalls had faded to distant background noise, and her panicky breathing echoed around her. A current still existed, but this far down, it didn't have enough power to push her along.

Maya knelt in place until her heartbeat slowed to normal. She spat and coughed more, covering her mouth with her hands and shivering. A burp brought the taste of dumplings back. When she finally stood, she cringed at the feeling of inch-deep slime squeezing between her toes. The water almost reached her hips. Her soaked nightdress, smeared green down the front as if she'd slid over paint, clung like a second skin.

She gathered it up into a roll and wrung it out while looking around. The channel she'd fallen from poured a thick stream of water into her current pipe about ten feet behind her, over a clear patch where no algae could grow. The end hung at least four times her height overhead, vines draped from it like a beard, though they didn't look thick enough to support her weight, especially climbing face-first into the pour.

Forward, the crushed sewer pipe continued to a maze of others, crisscrossing like a gargantuan version of one of those novelty waterfalls in a fancy restaurant. She walked along the only route she could follow, flapping her nightdress to help dry it. Gunfire and angry screaming continued outside, easily thirty or forty feet overhead. At least she'd gone somewhere well out of reach of stray bullets.

Her right foot shot out from under her when she encountered a particularly snot-like patch of algae, leaving her flat on her back underwater again. Maya sat up and spat out the foul-tasting liquid, somewhere between rust, dirt, and moss. She gagged, but didn't throw up. After swishing her foot back and forth to rinse the slime from it, she stood and managed another eight yards before stubbing her toe on a chunk of concrete hiding under the muck. That time, she fell forward.

Maya pushed her head above the surface again and sighed. "So much for drying off."

She decided against standing and pulled herself along sorta-swimming, walking her hands on the bottom while kicking her feet in the water. At the end of the pipe, another one a few feet below ran at an oblique angle. It passed from behind and left to forward and right, going about fifty yards to a huge chamber full of more pipes. Maya turned herself around and descended feet first, happy at least to find *one* intersection short enough for her to climb back up if she had to.

The water in the next area only came up to the bottoms of her knees. She tried walking again and made it to the end without falling, though she slipped and skidded on her heels several times. She crouched with her toes over the edge, grabbing the rim of the broken concrete tunnel on either side of her feet. From her perch, she looked out over a gigantic underground chamber full of dangling vines draped among twisted steel girders and lit by shafts of sunlight. A few birds flitted around near the top, where they could easily duck out one of the cracks to get to open sky. She felt like a rhesus monkey high in the trees of the rain forests that now only existed as images on the AuthNet and memories in old people.

"Wow."

Water pressed at the small of her back, flowing around her to spill into another section of pipe. The bottom of the chamber had a green pool, some twenty or so feet below. Momentary temptation to jump in came and went. *No. That could wind up being only a few inches deep and I'd die.* Maya looked left, right, up, and down, trying to figure out where she was and where she had to go. She let her feet slide from the edge and sat. Here, the mild current had no chance of pushing her loose, even with the slimy green stuff everywhere.

She checked herself: feet, knees, elbows, and hands, for scrapes or injuries. Other than sore spots from banging into the pipe, she found nothing to worry about. A relieved sigh escaped her and she slouched. In that moment of stillness, her teeth chattered.

I have to get out of this water or I'm going to get sick.

Maya leaned back, the way Vanessa did to ask the ceiling why things always got difficult for *her,* as if the only person in the world who ever had something go wrong was Vanessa Oman. Her gaze settled upon a scratch in the dark stone that formed the shape of an arrow pointing left.

She raised her arm to touch it, but couldn't reach. Even if she stood as tall as she could stretch, it would be too far overhead. Her mind presented her with two theories: an adult made it, or the rats here were geniuses and could fly. She decided to trust option one, and not trust sticking around until the sort of person who lived down… in whatever this place was found her. With nothing else to go on, and no idea which way led where, she decided to follow the arrow.

Maya lowered herself to the next length of pipe and crept along, doing as much as she could to keep quiet. She'd follow the arrows and leave without ever being spotted by the people who made them. A few minutes later, another arrow on the wall pointed at a left turn. She followed a curved length of still-intact pipe. After so many open waterslides, being in a tube felt strange. The old passageway was huge, tall enough for a grown man to walk upright in. By this point, the water barely made it up to her ankles. At the center of the macaroni-shaped segment, she felt confident no one was around and peeled off her nightdress. Water splattered around her feet as she wrung it out, rolled it up the other way and wrung it again. Once it stopped dripping, she flapped it out a few times and put it back on. The cold, damp fabric made her squeal on contact, and locked up all the muscles in her back for a moment.

She emerged from the end of the curve into a straightaway where big chunks from the top of the pipe had fallen in. Thin streams of water dripped in from most of the cracks; rats teemed around the concrete bits on the floor like liquid shadows. Maya raised her empty hands and blinked. *The knife!* She looked over her shoulder at the way she'd come, unable to think of where along the wet rollercoaster ride she'd lost her grip. She gulped, figuring it a miracle she hadn't cut herself.

Rats in front, nowhere to go behind her, she stared at the little furry menaces and tried to summon up enough courage for a mad sprint past them. Doctor Chang and Sarah said they wouldn't hurt her, but who knew if apartment rats had a nicer disposition than these rats? People living out here got wild and nasty—wouldn't the rats too? Eventually, she darted forward, hopping around chunks of concrete and other debris carried here by the water. Fur brushed across her right ankle. She yelped, terror and tears blurring her vision and thoughts to one thing: *get away!*

Her panic-powered sprint came to an abrupt end when she collided with something much softer than sewer pipe or even a dirt wall. She bounced off and landed on her butt, hands braced behind her, legs apart, sprawled at the lowest part of the curved passage.

A man filled the end of the tunnel where it opened into a sideways passage. His olive-drab poncho wavered in a mild breeze, covered with two straps connected to satchels on his hips. He carried a long sniper-style rifle across his back, topped by a military-looking scope with rubber lens caps. Round goggles hid his eyes from view, and a pewter-colored spray of facial hair poked out around a breathing mask over his mouth and nose. A string of giant mousetraps hung from the back of his belt.

Maya stared at the pistol strapped to his right thigh and the huge knife on his left. Her mind went blank. She couldn't decide if she should scream, run like hell, plead and beg, or say hello.

"Hey there," said the man, his voice scratchy as if he didn't get to use it much. He pulled his goggles up to his forehead, exposing two discs of clean pale skin around hazel eyes. "You fall in?"

Maya pulled her knees to her chest and wrapped her arms around her legs, shivering. "Please don't hurt me."

He ducked the edge of the pipe and took a step closer before squatting. "Easy, kiddo. Whatcha doin' down in the Jigsaw River?"

"Uhh." She slid backward a few inches. "People were shooting at each other and I was right behind one group. Bullets were hitting the ground all around me and I didn't want to get hit."

"Bit tricky down here. Easy to get lost." He offered a hand. "Ye can call me Pope if'n anything."

She stared at his fingers for a moment before deciding to accept the handshake. "Maya. Do you live here? Are those arrow marks yours?"

Pope emitted a wheezy chuckle. "Yep. I don't like people much. I'm happy with my rats."

"I met someone who had pet rats before." Maya cringed at a flash of the upside-down image of Head's face a second before he plummeted over the edge.

"Hah. Ain't pets, kiddo. They're dinner." He winked. "You don't look like no Frag." He lifted her chin with a finger and studied her face before taking a knee, threading his fingers around her left ankle, and pulling her foot up. She swallowed, but didn't move as he poked at her sole. "You run away from home, kid? You don't look like you been out of doors very long."

She stood once he let go of her leg. "I only wore shoes when..." *We're filming an ad or doing a publicity event. I was never allowed outside.* "I stayed inside all the time. Carpet."

"Oh, a Citizen." He clucked his tongue. "What are you doing all the way out here?"

"Are you going to hurt me?"

He put a hand on her shoulder. "Not everyone out here's a bad sort. Course... you right in assumin' it. Better to stay alive that way. But no, I ain't gonna do nothin' ta hurt ya."

"I'm lost. I don't know where I am." She let some of her worry leak from her eyes. "I was from the Sanctuary Zone, but my birth mother got bored with having a kid and threw me out. I found a real mom. The Authority took her away and I'm trying to save her." Pope patted her on the back, a hermit's best attempt to be reassuring. She had to work to keep her embellishment tears from becoming too real. If she let in a thought of Sarah or the unfinished card game, she'd lose it. "Can you help me get to the Spread? I need to find someone there."

Pope scratched around the edges of his breathing mask. "I suppose I might be able to help with that. How's about you do me a little favor in return."

Maya shivered. The list of favors someone like her could do for a grown man came up on a short and *very* disturbing list. The memory of Mason's computer screen leapt to the tip of her brain. Her head shook back and forth in a rapid no before she realized she was backing away and sniveling.

"Hey kid. Easy. What's wrong?"

"I don't wanna." She pulled down on the hem of her nightdress, holding it tight.

"Sweet shit on toast, girl. Did someone touch you?"

Maya gulped. "Uhh, almost. I ran away."

"That *ain't* what I'm gonna ask ya ta do. Not e'en close." His face reddened with a flash of rage. "You point me at that sorry son of a bitch and I'll make sure he don't bother you again."

She stared into his eyes for a few seconds before clinging to him. The fear from the past few days melted out in a short period of uncontrollable shaking. Something about him made her feel safe. It didn't bother her when he rose to his full height, picking her up and carrying her along a series of tunnels. He eventually descended a metal ladder to a square passageway with train tracks set in a groove along the floor. She came close to falling asleep with her head on his shoulder, no longer having to worry about danger coming out of nowhere.

A shift in gravity startled her awake as he set her down, seated, on a green cloth cot. They'd stopped in a rectangular room attached to the subway tube. A grey metal table with three chairs stood a few feet away. Three military-style trunks sat in front of a long locker cabinet to her left. In the far left corner, a toilet jutted out from a pipe, cordoned off only by the hint of where a wall used to be.

Pope left her on the cot and went to one of the footlocker-sized cases. Maya yearned to find Genna, but she'd gotten herself hopelessly lost underground. She pulled her feet up onto the cot and rested her head against her knees, hoping that her sense of this man hadn't been wrong. If he wanted to harm her, she couldn't get away. He returned in a moment and handed her a cooked but cold rat-on-a-stick. It smelled okay, so she nibbled at it. A lump tightened in her throat at the memory of her reaction as 'Eww!' when Sarah first mentioned eating rats while they'd been out scavving. Again, she felt foolish and guilty for running off—but what other chance did Genna have?

"Why do you live down here?"

He took the long rifle off his back and laid it on the table before sitting in one of the chairs closest to the cot. "I came back from the war to everything I'd known being gone. Had a wife, two sons, brother... three sisters. Parents.

No damn idea what happened to any of them. The whole area we'd lived in was in ruins. Wasn't no VA left then... uhh, sorry, Vet'rans Administration. Everything wound up shut down in some transitional period, then the damn blueberries took over. Spent a couple years searching but... best I hope for is they didn't suffer.

"This new privatized government don't have any room for fools like me that did the dirty work of the old regime. They'd just as soon forget we exist. Worse, 'round here, they're little more than hired thugs of Ascendant. Sometimes almost can't tell 'em apart."

"I'm sorry about your family." Maya gnawed on rat meat tougher than the one the woman had given her and a lot saltier. The idea of eating rodent bothered her much less than she expected. Remembering Sarah telling her that she'd eat rat if she had to made her homesick enough to wet the corners of her eyes. "You were in the army?"

"Yeah. Ranger." Pope chuckled. "I had the simple job most of the time." He patted the rifle. "Some people think it's easier to put a target down when you're too far away to hear them scream, but they don't know what it's like. I got to look them right in the eye every time." He sighed. "So. How did a tiny little critter like you wind up all alone out here?"

Maya explained her walk from Block 13, the only omitted detail being her true identity.

"Diego is going to somehow help you?"

"That's what Missy said." Maya pulled a leg off the rat and nibbled on it.

"What d'you expect ta do if you even make it inside the city?"

She turned tiny rat bones over in her fingers, debating how much she could trust him. "I'm going to sneak into Ascendant and hack their computer. I can change the information so they let her go."

Pope laughed until the grim look on her face made him pause. "No shit?"

"No shit." She hesitated, feeling like she'd fallen in way over her head. "Unless you can help me save my mom."

"Ehh." He rubbed at the bridge of his nose. "I don't do Sanc Zones... or people much, for that matter. I'll get you home safe, or take you to the Spread. Your choice. This down here ain't no place for a kid, so you can't stay with me."

She worked the other rear leg back and forth until it snapped off the carcass, and pulled the meat off the bones with her teeth. Asking him to bring her home might be worth it only to watch him beat the hell out of those three idiots who wanted to eat her, but the Spread was so close. Genna couldn't have much time left. One tear slipped down her right cheek. She had to still be alive.

"I gotta try. If I can't do it, will you help me get home after?"

He dragged his hand down over his mouth, chin, and beard. "I suppose. If you manage to not get yourself killed."

He's trying to scare me. "Okay. What was the favor you wanted me to do?"

Pope leaned forward, forearms across his knees. "I found an old survivalist bunker down in the deep tunnels. Door's locked from the inside. Been trying to get inside that thing for a year. Place has got to be loaded. Only way inside is this ventilation pipe I ain't about to fit through. 'Mere a sec?"

Maya set the plate down and walked over to him. "'Kay."

He put his hands on her hips, fingers straight like knife blades, and pulled back to measure her width. "You'll be able to fit easy. You crawl in and open the door. Should be safe. If it ain't, back out and no harm done."

She tapped her foot, thinking it over. Every minute wasted could be the one where they shot Genna in the head. "Okay. Let's go."

Pope led Maya along a confusing network of passageways, including a few stretches of the Jigsaw River. She hiked her nightdress up despite the water only reaching mid-shin at its deepest. He halted in the middle of the chute and pulled himself up to enter a break in the side that led to a square-walled corridor heading perpendicular. Maya climbed the rounded tunnel and braced one knee on the smoothest part where the concrete had long-ago crumbled away. A gap between the outer corridor wall and the section of pipe offered a view down a drop of about three or four stories, rife with exposed rebar, weeds, and jagged pieces of fallen debris. She peered up at Pope, waiting in the square hallway.

He grabbed a dead caged lightbulb at his head level on the wall and reached one arm out to her. Rather than take her hand, he clamped his fingers around her forearm and hauled her into the air like a sack, carrying her safely over the pit before setting her down on her feet. He didn't let go until they'd moved well away from the edge.

"That's why you shouldn't be down here." He winked. "Too easy to get yourself killed. Half of this place is ready to collapse at any moment."

She smiled at his back as he walked ahead, entertaining the thought he might not dislike people—or at least kids—as much as he said he did. No fault existed in his logic, however. This place *was* a deathtrap. After a short walk, he turned right at a four-way intersection and they cut across a room that looked like an electrical switching station for an old subway. Pope headed down another two long, straight passageways full of grime and chemical odors. Maya spent a little while trying to balance-beam walk on a train rail since it hurt her feet much less than the gravel on either side of it. The weak glow of his flashlight hid most of the details of her surroundings other than a thick mossy smell. Despite being close to blind, she had a feeling she'd gotten as filthy as she'd ever been in her life.

He took an abrupt left into a short alcove that stopped at a heavy door, like something out of a starship or maybe an old war movie about submarines. He knocked on it, making little noise.

"Keyhole and a crank. Couldn't get the damn thing to budge... but." He pointed the flashlight to the left, where a hunk of wall crumbled away to expose a dark metal pipe near the ceiling about eighteen inches around. "I think that's the air vent for whatever's in there. It's about eight or nine feet."

She gulped. "O-okay."

Pope clipped the light to his belt and rummaged in one of his satchels. He pulled out a rope, which he tied around her waist. "I'll hold the other end. If you need to get out fast, scream and I'll pull."

"Okay."

He boosted her up to the hole. Maya leaned her head into the pipe, finding only darkness, silt, and metal flakes.

"Can I have the light?"

Pope unclipped it and held it out. Maya aimed it down the tube, expecting to see rats, but relaxed at a ninety-degree turn about ten feet in with no vermin in sight. Against her better judgement, she crawled inside, displacing loose dirt. The rope tugged at her hips whenever the cord snagged at the jagged break. Its presence lent a sense of calm. One shriek and he'd sweep her back out to safety. At the bend, she peered around at another elbow only twelve inches later. She wriggled in, rolled over, and crawled around the second bend into a five-foot section that ended with a curve straight down.

She crawled over and peered down at a square folding table with one empty Hydra tray and a fork on it. Since the opening sat two feet away at the bottom of a stub, she couldn't see much else of the room.

Her surroundings didn't give her enough space to turn around, forcing a headfirst descent. She pulled herself as far as she dared into the drop before gravity took her the rest of the way. Catching herself against the sides, she stopped sliding with her face a few inches from the end of the pipe.

"Pope?" she yelled.

"Aye?" His voice echoed down the tube.

"The pipe sticks out of the ceiling. Lower me slow."

"Roger," he yelled.

Maya wound her right leg around the rope as he pulled it taut, hooking her foot for a grip. With the flashlight leading the way, she let herself slip forward. The nylon bit uncomfortably into her hips, thigh, and calf, but supported her weight. He fed line at a slow but steady pace. Once she emerged from the pipe end, dangling above the square folding table, she squirmed around to examine the chamber.

I feel like the woman in Tomb Explorer... but she's got big guns and bigger... Maya rolled her eyes. *Why do they always make characters like that?*

The room looked small, not even half the size of her old bedroom in Vanessa's penthouse. Two fluorescent light bulbs ran across the ceiling, one on either side of the vent pipe. A hollow cubby in the right wall held a thin mattress. In the left far corner sat a plastic toilet. Shelves full of junk covered the walls, and a pair of metal cabinet doors seemed like they had something valuable behind them due to the presence of a giant padlock. The inside face of the thick door had a large wheel connected via gears to two metal slats. She whistled. Whoever built this place did *not* want anyone getting in here.

She extended both hands and her untangled left foot in preparation for touchdown. The rickety card table wobbled as it absorbed her weight. Her body dangled by the hips until the rope gave her enough slack to kneel. Maya untied the knot and pulled the rope away from her leg. She panned the flashlight around again, making a sour face at a strange unpleasant stink in the air. One of those cabinets must be full of bad meat. She pointed the beam on the floor, finding it mostly clean except for a dark brown/red stain that appeared long-ago dried. Her gaze traced it back under the table she knelt on, and she locked eyes with the half-exposed skull of a dead man.

She screamed.

The rope whistled back up into the pipe. A few seconds later, the *whump* of Pope falling on his ass echoed from the hole in the ceiling.

"Shit!" he yelled. "Girl, you okay?"

Maya dropped the flashlight, buried her face in her hands, and bawled. "There's a body in here!"

Pope grunted. "Can you get to the door?"

"He's under the table!" Maya wailed. "I don't wanna step in him."

"It's okay, Maya. Calm down. Are you sure he's dead?"

"Yes!" she yelled, hands clamped over her eyes. "His face is half gone and I can see his skull!"

"Listen to me, kiddo. He can't hurt anyone anymore." He cleared his throat. The scratchy wheeze in his voice faded a touch. "You want to get away from him, right? In order to do that, you're going to have to open the door. I can't get the rope back to you down the pipe."

Maya sniveled into her fingers, not wanting to look down again and see those horrible, lifeless eyes gazing back at her. The flashlight painted a stretched oval of light before her knees in which dust motes cavorted and shimmered. That *thing* might be looking at her still. It rested only a few feet below. If it reached up it could...

"Maya?" yelled Pope. "Are you okay?"

"No," she whispered.

"Maya?" A heavy *thump* from the door startled a yelp out of her. "Can you open the door?"

She grasped the flashlight and twisted around to point it at the exit. The table wobbled. Maya let off an uneasy whine, terrified it might collapse and dump her on top of a dead body. She braced her hands and shifted her weight from her knees to her toes. The more her perch shimmied back and forth, the louder her whining became. As if one tiny misstep would set off a nuclear bomb, she eased herself upright.

Pope's banging on the door faded away from the forefront of her awareness as she stared down the length of the flashlight beam at the far wall. Her breath echoed in her head. She lowered the spot of light to the floor in search of a patch without a stain. It seemed whatever had leaked from the corpse migrated the same way, implying the ground wasn't level. She crept to the edge, away from the door, closer to where clean space waited.

Five baby steps later, her foot came within three inches of the corner. She tried to think of a way to get down off the table without any chance of touching dead man. If she jumped, the table would go flying. If she tried to climb down, she might touch him.

If—

The leg collapsed... or did the dead man knock it over?

Maya shrieked at the top of her lungs as the table dumped her. She hit the floor and flung herself forward into a somersault before crawling in a blind panic against the innermost corner between the toilet and the bed, where she cowered. The flashlight wound up near the middle of the chamber, directing its beam at a twisted black-purple claw of a hand poking out from behind the upended card table.

"Maya!" Pope whomped on the armored plate. "What just happened?"

She bolted from her hiding place and ran to the door, pulling and twisting at the wheel. When it rattled without moving much, locked in place, she screamed. Why did she do this? This was such a bad idea. Why did she untie the rope? Now she would die in here.

"Let me out!" She pounded on the door. "Help!"

"I'm right outside. You're not in any danger. Forget everything but the door. Breathe in and out. Don't think about anything else."

Maya stared at the wheel, rapid breaths racing in and out her nose. Her heart thudded in her head. She covered her mouth and nose with both hands and closed her eyes. *Calm down. Think. Don't panic.* A momentary daydream of being reunited with Genna eased her fear, but replaced it with grief. She forced herself to turn around and walk back to the flashlight, staring only at the yellow plastic object—not what it illuminated.

As soon as she grabbed it, she sprinted to the door and studied the mechanism. A small hooked latch caught the teeth of a gear. Two whacks with the flashlight broke the grime and let her open the latch, unlocking it, but she still couldn't budge the wheel. She grabbed one of the spars connecting the wheel to the center and pulled herself up off her feet. Even with all her weight bouncing on it, it wouldn't turn.

"It's stuck."

The wheel rattled side to side from his attempt to turn it, but it refused to move. He tapped on a small hatch at eye-level to an adult. Maya dragged one of the chairs over, climbed up, and flipped the metal flap up. Pope stuck a small spray can in and dropped it.

"Use that on any part that should move."

The spray lubricant stank, but she held her breath and applied a liberal spread until she couldn't find anywhere else to add more. "Okay."

Pope struggled with the wheel again. He grunted, and after a few loud bangs, the mechanism broke free of the crud and spun. He whirled it about with ease, retracting the horizontal slats, and the door gave way. She jumped down off the chair and pulled it back. Pope stepped in and swept her up in his arms.

Maya held on and sniffled. He wasn't Genna, but he'd do in a pinch.

With her attached to his side, he searched around the place for a few minutes, fiddled with a switch on the wall, and examined wires running back and forth across the ceiling. One of the shelves held hundreds of Hydra packs as well as the machine itself. He opened an electrical panel and flicked switches one after the next.

"Is the food good? Can we eat?"

"Ration packs look intact, but there's no juice here. Bet the wire's been cut somewhere... I think I know where the solar panels are. Found them a while back, wondered what they went to. Probably take a couple days to get things online." He set her down on the bed and went over to the body.

Maya rolled away and curled up, having less than zero interest in watching that. Rummaging noises continued for several minutes. She cringed and flinched with every squish and crinkle. Eventually, the jingle of keys preceded a triumphant grunt from Pope.

"I'm going to move this poor bastard. Take him topside and give him a proper grave. Be right back."

"Okay." She closed her eyes even harder.

Amid the total silence of the underground room, Maya imagined an angry ghost staring at her. She couldn't bring herself to look, terrified of what he'd do if she made eye contact, and shivered in silence. Her nightdress had finally dried out, but she couldn't get comfortable.

Some time later, Pope returned—without the corpse. She sat up as he attacked the padlock.

"Reckon you don't want to sit around here for three days waitin' on a meal."

"They might kill her. I can't wait." With the flashlight back in the room, enough ambient radiance existed to confirm the body as gone. She couldn't help but stare at the patch of floor where he'd been.

"All right. Wait here a moment while I make sure this key works."

"'Kay."

Pope walked outside and closed the door. The wheel spun, sealing the chamber again. Metal rattled, and the little locking hook flipped over and grabbed the gears. He tested the wheel to verify it had locked, then opened it.

Maya ran to him.

He re-locked the door, stashed the key in his satchel, and picked her up. She held on while he carried her down tunnel after tunnel, up a ladder, and walked along a dry length of concrete piping. Water fell in drops and trickles around them, though he weaved among them without letting any touch her.

Soon, he patted her on the back to get her attention and put her down once she let go. She looked up at him and followed his gesture to a ladder leading to a round metal disc. Maya took a step back to give him room. He climbed to the top and pushed the cover aside, flooding the tunnel with heavy metallic scraping. She pulled herself up, taking one rung at a time. When she reached the end, he grabbed her by one arm and lifted her out of the hole like a caught fish before setting her down in dead grass next to a rectangular white concrete slab a few inches higher than the dirt.

"The Spread is that way. Take us about two hours to walk." He worked the metal cover plate back over the hole. "We're going to pass close to the highway. If you hear any noises you don't recognize or don't expect, drop flat where you are and don't move. The human eye goes to motion. It's better to sit still in an open field than run to a bush."

"Okay."

"There's tall grass; little critter like you can disappear." He winked and pulled the sniper rifle off his back.

He set off at a brisk walk, but slowed when it seemed she had to exert herself to keep up. Soon, a mixture of dead brown and live green wild grass tickled her legs and came up to her shoulders in places. The whirr of drones got louder over the course of fifteen or twenty minutes, and eventually, the glow of flying lights became apparent to the right. Not long after that, the black highway surface emerged at the center of a trail the authority had burned through the field. About twenty yards of bare ground flanked the road, offering little potential cover for anyone trying to set up an ambush for travelers.

When a rumble vibrated the earth, Maya stared down at her feet for a split second, and flopped on her belly. Pope eased himself to one knee and flattened out on his chest, rifle trained in the general direction of the road. The lens caps opened automatically when he touched the trigger, and he leaned his eye over the scope.

"One Authority transport," he whispered. "Looks like they're heading for the Hab District."

She crawled up alongside him, though couldn't see anything but grass. "One?"

"Probably taking a detainee back to the shithole."

Maya gasped. She started to feel like bursting into tears at a grand waste of time, but if that truck carried Genna home, she wouldn't care. She trembled with anticipation until the whirring electric motors changed pitch downward.

"Stay still. They're stopping. That's real weird."

She gulped air.

"There's a civilian car coming in from the south." Pope shifted, pointing the rifle more to his right. "One man inside. Figure him early twenties maybe. Short blond hair."

A terrifying noise became apparent in the distance. It sounded like the straining e-motors of Mr. Mason's car. No way did they let him go. Not after finding those addresses. Worry at what he'd do to Sarah or Emily made rat meat dance in her gut. Then again, all e-cars sounded the same.

The car stopped with a faint squeak of brakes about fifteen yards from the huge blue six-wheeled Authority van.

She couldn't take the suspense anymore, and pulled her legs up to kneel. Inch by inch, she perked higher until she could see over the tips of the grass. Sure enough, it was Mason's car, but not Mason driving it. Brian got out and shoved the door closed. He looked annoyed—not the sort of attitude anyone without a death wish projected when approaching two blueberries.

"We already told you, pal, the info was bogus." The shorter Authority officer pointed at Brian.

"I know how you people work." Brian put his hands on his hips. "That kid vanished. You fuckers snuck in when everyone was sleeping and took her back to her mother. I need that reward since I found her."

Maya's jaw dropped. She started to jump up, but Pope grabbed her and clamped a hand over her mouth. She stared at Brian, trying to give him brain cancer with her eyes.

You asshole!

TWENTY-SEVEN
BEYOND REPROACH

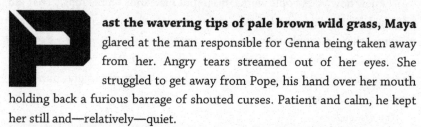**ast the wavering tips of pale brown wild grass, Maya** glared at the man responsible for Genna being taken away from her. Angry tears streamed out of her eyes. She struggled to get away from Pope, his hand over her mouth holding back a furious barrage of shouted curses. Patient and calm, he kept her still and—relatively—quiet.

"There's no reward for Maya Oman because the girl is not missing," said the Authority officer.

"Oh, fuck. Of course not. You bastards already got her." Brian scowled.

"No. The child you identified was not a match," said the second officer. "While I'll give it to you that she looked a lot like her, it wasn't her."

"Yeah." The taller officer chuckled. "The kid's a tiny version of her mother. If that was her, she'd have been trying to order us around, calling us lazy, worthless, that sort of thing."

"Yep." Officer Two shook his head. "That girl kept her head down and behaved herself like any other Non. Besides, if the daughter of Vanessa Oman was missing, don't you think there'd be dozens of us tearing the Hab apart building by building?"

Brian grumbled. "So that's it then? There's nothing? What about that other guy you nabbed? Any reward for him?"

"We can't discuss it. If an informant had been involved, and I'm not saying there was, it would be on them to contact us about any possible reward once criminality was confirmed on the part of the detainee."

Brian wiped both hands down his face and sighed. "Shit."

"Have a pleasant day, Mr. Harper."

The blueberries sauntered back to their APC and climbed in. Maya writhed and squirmed, grabbing fistfuls of grass between gesturing and pointing at Brian.

"Mmm! Mmmmmm!" She clutched at Pope's wrist and futilely tried to pull his hand away from her mouth. "Mmm!"

Brian walked backwards until his ass hit the little beige e-car. He leaned/sat on the hood, rubbing the bridge of his nose. The Authority transport reversed around in a K-turn and lumbered off in the direction of the Sanctuary Zone. Snot flew from Maya's nostrils, launched into the grass from hard breaths with her mouth covered. When the rumble of the Authority van's existence faded from the air, Pope let go of her.

"You asshole!" yelled Maya. She sprang up to a sprint and darted onto the road, pointing at Brian. "You killed Genna!"

She rushed him, landing two or three punches in the approximate area of his groin before he got his hands on her arms and held her at bay. A pair of four-fanned Authority drones glided abreast about twenty feet above, though neither paid them much mind.

"You lying piece of shit!" She tried to kick him while screaming a series of random swear words. "Why? Why did you sell us out? They're gonna kill her."

Brian hoisted her into the air by the arms, his expression of confusion tinged with exasperation. His gaze drifted left to Pope emerging from the weeds. "Uhh." He put her down, weathered a few more feeble punches, and grabbed her by the wrists again. "Stop."

"I hate you!" She twisted and jerked on her arms, trying to get away. "Get offa me, you piece of shit! You killed my mom…" The fight melted out of her. She sank to her knees and sobbed.

Brian let go of her arms, gaze locked on Pope's rifle. "I didn't have a choice. We're having a baby any day now. I… thought you were kidnapped. Thought I was doing something good for a kid. I had no damn idea they'd take Genna."

"Don't!" shrieked Maya. "You're not allowed to even say her name." She continued bawling.

Pope walked up behind her.

"I had no idea… I thought you'd be sent home where you'd be safe and happy and we'd have enough money to give my baby a decent shot at not turning out as a piece of gang trash." Brian bowed his head, scratching at his nose. "That reward was a lifeline I couldn't resist."

Maya cried into her hands for another few minutes. "What if they kill her?"

"I'm sorry." Brian stared at the street, raking a hand over his hair. "I never even imagined they'd go after her. I figured they'd come in, rescue you, and leave. Why would they care about her anyway?"

"You want this guy dead?" asked Pope.

Brian coughed.

She lifted her head and peered up at him. Vanessa's haughty laugh danced across the back of her mind. Maya could kill a man with one word right now. One yes, and no more Brian. Vanessa would do it without a second thought. She'd ordered death for less. Her gut twisted up in a knot at the worry the Authority had executed Genna. It tightened harder at imagining Arlene's reaction to the news Brian had been found dead and their kid would never know a father. She clenched her hands into trembling fists and glared at him.

Brian stared at the street. "I'm sorry."

"No. I don't want him dead." Maya looked down. A second later, an explosion of rage leapt out of her heart and raced down her arm to her fist, which she pounded square into his groin.

Brian wheezed, grabbed himself, and slid off the car hood to his right. He curled up on the road, moaning.

"Vanessa would kill him. I'm not her." Maya scowled. "It's not his baby's fault. Does Arlene know what you did?"

"No," squeaked Brian. He took a few quick gasps of air and found a normal voice. "Thank you."

Maya stepped closer to him. "Don't thank me yet. If Genna's dead... I'm... gonna do something mean to you."

Brian emitted a high-pitched whine.

"Small fists hurt, don't they?" Pope chuckled. "Sooner or later, you'll figure out the Authority ain't to be trusted. They do whatever they want on account o' no one stands up to them."

"I thought it was Mr. Mason who called them." Maya lifted and dropped her toes a few times. She didn't feel too bad over setting him up. He still deserved it for what he did to Sarah, plus none of the kids in the building (or near it) would've been safe with him around. "I'm going to tell Genna it was you. She's probably going to kick your ass."

Brian cringed, but nodded. He dragged himself upright and moved around the car with one hand braced on it as he limped.

Maya glanced up at Pope as the little car pulled a U-turn and sped away. "We should get off the road before the next drone comes by."

"Yeah. They'd probably give me a hard time over this rifle." He hurried back into the weeds.

She ran after him. "I don't think they'd be too polite."

"Probably right." Pope winked at her.

Her rollercoaster of anger and grief leveled off in a few minutes. She wiped her eyes and nose, then looked up at him. "I thought he was nice. He seemed friendly."

Pope shook his head. "Out here, it's everyone for themselves. Hell, even in that fancy city it's the same way. Only difference is they shoot each other in the back with politics or legal bullshit."

"Boo-shee," muttered Maya, thinking of Sarah's father.

Silence save for the rustling of grass gave way to the distant whine of drone fans about fifteen minutes later. Pope steered her farther west, away from the highway and out of easy sight. They stopped once for a pee break and continued on their way until the sun went down a little more than an hour later. With the sun waning, towers of stacked shipping containers bathed in electric lights glowed prominent against the indigo sky up ahead.

The Spread resembled a massive scrapyard run by someone obsessive about order but too lazy to clean anything. A grid of passageways crisscrossed among piles of junk, old airplanes, and hundreds of clusters of trans-oceanic shipping containers. Some still sat on frame trailers that converted them from boat boxes to trucks, though the majority had been there so long they'd been built up to permanent structures with awnings, flowerpots, lawn chairs around grills, even small gardens.

An area about a quarter mile away from the end of the meadow had light and activity, a small town nestled within the endless collection of forgotten scrap. Had Moth and his crew decided to leave her trapped in one of these boxes while they waited for a ransom, she might be dead now. After Vanessa told them to get screwed, they might've gone their separate ways and left her there. Maybe someone would've heard her screaming, but then she would be truly abandoned. Maya closed her eyes and breathed in the smell of rusting metal, dirt, and a weak trace of food.

I shouldn't think about that. It didn't happen. No point giving myself more nightmares.

"You sure this is what you want, kid?" asked Pope.

"I'm this close. I can't give up on her." Maya looked from the settlement to him. "Will you take me inside?"

"Sorry, girl. I don't do the whole people thing. It's this or back to your Hab block."

She tapped her foot. "Are you trying to scare me into going home or do you really not want to go in there?"

"Let's just say I've got a few 'friends' there who'd not take kindly to seeing me waltz in. I'm probably still faster than them, but I don't think a gunfight would help your cause out too much, considering you won't be able to *talk* to Diego when I get done with him."

"Uhh. Anything I should know?" She blinked. "Is he dangerous?"

"To you? Probably not. He's elbow deep in everything going on out here that people don't want the Authority to know about. That tends to make a guy paranoid. Don't gamble with him though. Bastard cheats."

"I won't." She took a few steps forward. "Thank you. Will you help me back to the Hab if... if... she's... umm. Yeah."

Pope put his hand on her head, patted her, and ran it down onto her back. "Can you find your way back to that manhole?"

"Yeah." She sniffled.

"I s'pose I could relocate to a safer spot. If you need someone to watch out for you, maybe I could. Perhaps there's an order to the way things work after all."

Maya hugged him. "I have to try and help my mom. If I can't, I'd like it if you could take me home. Maybe you could stay there. I've got a friend who's probably really mad at me for running off." She sniffled.

"I'll sit around here for a while. Somethin' goes wrong in there, you holler."

"Okay." Maya felt stupid for the second time since Genna went missing, but Pope would be waiting right here. It shouldn't be too dangerous to go talk to someone. "I'll come back if he can't help me."

Pope nodded.

Maya stared at the lights of the settlement, gathered her courage, and ventured in among the scrap.

TWENTY- EIGHT

THE DEVIL'S HANGOVER

The dark had never really been frightening to Maya. Something about this place, however, made her jump at every fleeting shadow and lent haste to her gait. At home, she seldom bothered with lights. Not that they'd have come on if she wanted. Vanessa liked to save on power.

It hadn't mattered much though. The ambient glow of the city outside provided enough illumination to function, and the dimness offered a quiet comfort contrary to the frenetic blaze of lights she associated with advertising shoots. Invisibility compared to the spotlight. Vanessa would've turned every light in the place on had she been there, but she almost never showed up. Why visit the closet where you store your advertising materials.

Maya scowled.

Okay, now I'm feeling sorry for myself. F—forget Vanessa.

Metal creaked and groaned with each shift in the wind. She looked up and around at the cargo boxes piled eight and nine high in places, wondering if enough of a breeze might send them crashing down. Each one as big as a cargo truck—a whole stack falling on someone wouldn't leave much to scrape up. Repetitious squeaking emanated from somewhere overhead in a woman's voice. A man groaned. Maya cringed and hustled up to a jog, passing an emaciated man who lay against a blue cargo box under a white symbol that resembled a poppy. He looked at her, though his gaze seemed to go *through* her, not seeing her. The man raised a plastic straw to his lips and sucked on it. A faint trace of mint in the air made her cover her mouth. She didn't want to breathe in any drugs.

The Spread felt much bigger inside than she expected. From every scrap, stack, or trailer, thick shadows crept outward, cast by the brilliant glare emanating from the Sanctuary Zone less than a mile away. Any one of them might hold a dangerous wild dog, a desperate doser, someone like Mr. Mason, or maybe a guy like Cherry Red who talked about his game of target-shooting kids. Even if he had only said it to scare them off before they shot Dave, it was still mean.

She swiveled to glance back to the south, feeling stupid for not staying with Pope as well as annoyed with him for not coming inside with her. Maybe he thought the place safe enough, or figured she'd chicken out.

Maya allowed herself to relax a little. He'd held her down when she tried to storm out in front of the Authority. He wouldn't let her do something foolish. Because he'd let her go on her own, this place must be at least *mostly* safe.

She emerged from a deep shadow into a courtyard formed by a ring of trailers and a few ramshackle buildings made of welded sheet metal and old truck parts. The overall aesthetic of the settlement reminded her of an Old West movie where everything had been made out of rusting metal, appliances, and repurposed machines.

A hand-painted sign reading 'The Devil's Hangover' swayed on short chains over the door to a long, grey-walled building. It looked like someone had welded a number of cargo boxes together and added extra walls made from cinder blocks and corrugated steel. Two doors taken from a tractor-trailer cab, one white and one metallic purple, hung in the opening, an end-of-the-world version of a swinging saloon entrance. She walked up three dusty wooden steps onto a porch made of plywood sheeting atop more cinder blocks.

The trip through the Jigsaw River had left her filthy, as though she went for a roll in a pile of mud and charcoal bits. She swatted at her nightdress in a feeble attempt to clean up a little. Men's voices inside laughed and joked about 'stupid Koreans' and stuff they'd seen overseas during the war. Another man insisted the Koreans didn't really start it, and the entire conflict furballed out of something that happened in the Middle East over oil. A new voice blamed religion and got into a shouting match defending Koreans against the guy who hated them. Another man insisted governments in general bred corruption. A woman shouted in agreement that all government can go to hell.

"Who cares who the hell started it? It's done." She grumbled. "You're already into it for five beers, Vance. I better see some cash or I'm going to have to get Diego involved."

"Come here, darlin'," said the guy who had an issue with Koreans.

Maya shoved herself into the white truck door and forced it open. It yielded with a grating squeal of metal that had the stereotypical effect of causing everything going on inside the place to halt dead. Five men, two women, and one skinny longhaired Hispanic guy behind the bar all stared at her.

She pushed the door out of her way, grunting from the weight. Two steps in, she let go and dodged as it swung closed. The continuous *reek-reek* of it swaying back and forth seemed loud enough to hear all the way back in Block 13. One of the women gave her a pathetic 'aww' stare. The other didn't bat an eyelash and continued walking two drinks to a table where a pair of middle-aged men sat.

The bartender gawked at her; he seemed caught in a struggle between yelling 'get out' and wanting to hear the punch line of a joke starting with 'a little girl in a nightie walked into a bar.'

One of the men at the table of three broke out in a cold sweat, staring at her. Maya kept still until everyone except for the man behind the bar and the sweaty guy went back to what they had been doing. As soon as she started walking into the room, the terrified man jumped to his feet and pulled a gun.

"Run! She's gonna explode!"

Maya shrieked and sprinted to cover behind the corner of the bar. He almost got the weapon pointed at her before his two friends tackled him. He screamed 'it's a bomb' and 'get away' repeatedly while his buddies shouted at him to calm down, reminding her of the way Genna brought Moth back from the brink. As pathetic as she felt, she understood how he'd mistaken her for one of those androids. She looked like she'd crawled out of a wasteland.

The bartender shook his head, causing a long, thin moustache and goatee to sway. Between his slender build and long, black hair, he could pass for a woman from behind. He stared at her with a mixture of incredulity and annoyance. A red cartoon demon on his black tee shirt held up one hand with the index and pinky finger raised while licking the knuckles between them.

Once it seemed the crazy man would no longer shoot her, she climbed a stool and plopped herself down, swinging her feet while gazing up at the bartender. "Are you Diego?"

"Little young for your fan club, *ey vato?*" yelled a man behind her.

The bartender used his middle finger to pick his eye at the man. "Who's asking?"

"I need to get into the Sanctuary Zone without being noticed by the Authority. No checkpoints, no scans." She crossed her arms on the bar and leaned on them. "Can you do that?"

His grin became a chuckle in a few seconds. "Well, damn. Come right out and ask in the open then. You a mule?"

"No. I'm a girl." She blinked at him. "What kind of question is that?"

"Hey kid," yelled a man in the midst of the struggle on the floor. "You real?"

Maya rolled her eyes. "Yes. I'm not a walking nuke."

"You want a drink, kid?" Diego cocked an eyebrow. "Sounds like you already had a few. No way you should do whatever it is you're thinking."

"No, thanks. Alcohol has deleterious effects on the body, especially to someone my age. There's enough that'll kill me out here without me doing stupid things... well, at least dumber things than I already am doing. Missy Hong said you can help me. My mother is in a lot of trouble, and I have to get inside the Sanc to help her."

Diego reached around to the shelf behind the bar and set a bottle of water down in front of her. "Who the heck do you think you are, little one?"

Maya picked up the bottle, examined the label, and opened it. Once a sniff test confirmed ordinary water, she drank about half of it in one shot, then stared at him for a few seconds. "Who do I think I am?"

"Yeah." He sighed. "I guess I need to hire a guy to check ID. You're a bit young for a bar, never mind the whole secret agent stuff."

Maya pulled her hair off her face and leaned in close, staring at him. "Look at me. Look *real* good. You tell me who you think I am."

His amusement lasted another three seconds. His rich tan faded to a deathly pallor; sweat melted out of his face. "No fucking way."

Maya smiled. "You're not as dumb as you look."

"Linda," yelled Diego. "You've got the bar."

The woman who'd given her the sympathetic glance hustled over. "Sure thing, boss."

Diego gestured at a doorway a few feet away to the left marked 'private.' Maya swiped her water bottle and hopped down from the stool. He nudged the door open and she slipped under his arm into a back room. To the right sat a desk, two sofas facing a giant TV, and a ratty round carpet. On the left, two plain steel shelves held cases and cases of beer, wine, and freeze-dried bar food like chicken nuggets and hot pretzels.

He brushed past her and paced back and forth. "What the hell are *you* doing out here? Do you have any idea of the shitstorm that'll roll in on us? No way I'm helping your mother. No offense, but that's a frozen cunt if there ever was one."

"Yes, I know." Maya sipped her water. "But that's not my mother."

"What?" He stopped in place like paused video, his belt-length hair wavering in the breeze from a tiny electric fan. "She's not?"

"Well. I suppose on a genetic level, thirty-seven percent of my chromosomal make up is hers. But, the bitch isn't my mother in the real sense. My *mother's* name is Genna."

"Oh damn. I heard some mercs mighta nabbed you, but word is they got themselves one of the decoys." Diego covered his mouth and sank backwards, half sitting on the desk edge. "You're not an android, are you?"

"No." Maya picked at the water bottle. "I don't think so."

Diego got up and rummaged the top left desk drawer. He returned and held a box up to her, white plastic tube at her lips. "Breathe into that, and keep doin' it."

Maya bit down on the straw, inhaling and exhaling. A little arm extended out of the top of the black box and held a lens in front of her right eye. After about ten breaths and some flickering blue light, it emitted a series of chirps.

Diego pulled it back and studied a LCD screen on the underside. Both of his eyebrows shot up. "Well shit. You sure you don't want anything stronger than water? And whiskey tango foxtrot."

"I don't want alcohol, and I'm not in the mood to dance." Maya drained the bottle. "Thanks for the water."

"Uhh, right. So, yeah. You're real. What the hell are you doing here?" He tossed the device in the drawer again before running his hands down the thighs of his jeans in a repetitious, nervous motion that caused the gun on the back of his belt to tap on the desk.

"Missy Hong said you could help me." Maya let her attitude down a notch. "I need to get my mom out of jail, and to do that I need to get inside the Sanctuary Zone without getting picked up at the gate. If they catch me, they'll ship me back to Vanessa, and I'll be basically in jail too. Can I trust you?"

When he nodded, she rushed a summary of getting kidnapped, the ransom going to hell, Genna fighting off Moth to prevent them from killing her, and then winding up taking her in. Diego didn't seem surprised that Vanessa told them to shoot her while she watched, and gave her a sad stare.

"So. I gotta get her out of there. If I can get back to the penthouse, I can use Vanessa's terminal to get in to the system and find out where she is. I should be able to send an e-mail posing as her to order Genna's release... or something."

He stroked his goatee. "Hmm. That might work. Assuming they haven't pieced together that she kidnapped you and executed her already."

Maya scowled.

"I see your point about sneaky. Your plan won't work as well if they know you're back."

"They refuse to admit I ever left." She frowned.

"It's late. I'll see what I can do. Please tell me you didn't tell Missy you'd owe her a favor."

"I didn't."

He pointed at the nearer couch. "You can crash there. Hungry?"

She dragged her feet on the way around the armrest and flopped down. "No. I'm too worried. I should eat something, but I don't have any money."

"I'd make you wash dishes, but you're too grubby." He winked. "Sit tight. I'll need some time to make arrangements... if I can swing anything."

Maya fired a sour stare at the floor as he walked out. The couch smelled like wet dog, though it didn't feel damp to the touch. She shifted to the side and tucked her feet under her on the cushions. A few minutes later, he ducked back in with a bowl of 'chicken' nuggets infused with cheese. She couldn't tell what the meat came from—other than it not being chicken—but it tasted okay. Finally, she'd found someone who agreed to help. She settled into the couch and forced herself to eat.

With a spot of warm inside her belly, and a spark of hope in her heart, Maya closed her eyes.

TWENTY- NINE
MOMENT OF DOUBT

aya awoke curled on her side. She yawned and stretched, taking note of a coarse wool Army blanket that hadn't been there before. Sleeping on a padded sofa made her sore, or maybe the aches came from all the walking she wasn't used to. Another long stretch made her feel better. After laying still for a little while more, one arm draped over the side and cheek smushed into the cushion, she slid off to her feet.

Blinking the tiredness from her eyes, she padded across the back room and tried to open the door to the bar, but it only parted a quarter inch before halting with a metallic *clonk*. She pushed again, soon realizing a padlock on the outside kept it closed. Maya shoved at it few more times with increasing panic.

Son of a bitch!

She spun in place looking for a way out. A small brown door in the back corner hung ajar in front of a lightless room. It bore a sign of a white stick man on a blue field, to which someone had added a black marker arm holding a pistol against the circular head. Windows on the outer wall about the size of cinder blocks might work, but they also sat high, near the ceiling. Maya rushed over and climbed the steel shelving along the outer wall farthest from the desk. The uppermost shelf lined up with the window. Two clear panels flanked a metal bar about as big around as her wrist in the middle. Neither square was big enough to allow her through, even if she could manage to kick out the thick plastic, and judging from the overzealous caulking job, that didn't seem likely.

Maya climbed down, too angry to cry despite being terrified. What was

Diego up to? Would he sell her out to the Authority hoping for a reward like Brian? Her throat tightened. What if Diego wanted to literally sell her, like to that DeeDee woman Missy warned her about?

I hate being me. Why can't I be a nobody?

A quick scan of the shelving revealed nothing she could use to escape or wield as a weapon. She darted over to the desk and pulled open the top center drawer. Beer openers and a nudie magazine. Papers in the top left. Thirteen cans of Tuna Blast cat food in the top right that looked like they'd been in there longer than she'd been alive.

"Eww."

She slammed that drawer and went for the bottom right. Amid a couple of screwdrivers, some fuses, and pliers, she found a black-handled stiletto in a leather sheath. Maya picked it up and stared at the glinting edge. *Come on. I can do it. He thinks I'm like Vanessa. Just gotta threaten him with it so I can get out of here.*

Metal bumped at the door. Maya hauled herself over the sofa back and crawled under the blanket again, hiding the knife. Diego pulled the door open and crept in, trying to be quiet. Maya pretended to be asleep. *Get closer.*

"Hey kid. I know you're awake. I saw the door wobble. Sorry about that."

Maya pushed herself up to sit, scowling at him.

"I didn't know who might've heard what. Didn't want anyone grabbing you in the night."

Maya nursed a nugget of anger to conceal her panic. "Little warning would've been nice. You scared the crap out of me."

"Can's over there if ya need it." He pointed at the little door past the enormous TV. "You're probably hungry. Be right back."

As soon as he walked out of sight, Maya crawled over the sofa and threw the knife in the drawer before running to the bathroom. By the time she returned, he'd heated up another batch of pseudo-chicken. Maya accepted the plastic plate and sat on the musty couch to eat.

"Okay. Got good news and I got, uhh, news." Diego handed over another bottle of water. "Oh, here." He put a folded lump of black cloth on the cushion next to her. "Alls I got, but you look like you need it."

Maya set the plate down and picked up the fabric, which unfolded into a plain black tee shirt. Sized for an adult man, it would fit her like a shin-length dress. Thrilled, she put it on over the nightie and resumed eating. "Okay, you're forgiven for locking me in here. What's the news?"

"I got you a way into the city, but there's a price."

"I am not doing anything disgusting or messed up." She shoved an entire nugget into her mouth. "Exepfft eaffing thiff."

"Nah, nothin' skeevy. Your way in is smuggling some Prime12 to a buyer inside the Sanc. Drugs are comin' from Missy Hong."

"Ascendant doesn't make that one. How dangerous is it? Will the Authority send me to a work camp if they find it?"

"Not really. It's illegal, but it's not a narcotic. It's a cortical stimulant used by net pirates to speed up their brains. It's not chemically addictive, but users tend to get hooked on feeling like a digital superman when they're on it."

"Okay." She ate another nugget. "I'll do it. Do I have to walk back to Missy?"

Diego shook his head. "Nope. It's all taken care of. They're sending it here inside the head of a doll, so no one will think anything about you carrying it."

"They're still going to recognize me at the checkpoint." She glugged water.

"You're not going to use the checkpoint." He grinned. "You afraid of heights?"

Maya swished her feet back and forth. "Umm. Not really. Well, maybe a little. Why?"

"The buyer is going to hijack an Authority patrol drone and fly it out here. You're so damn little you can ride the thing and glide in straight over the wall. He'll land you in a back alley somewhere out of sight, and then you drop the doll off at the Emerald Oasis. The guy you're bringing it to will probably even give you a ride to wherever you want to go after that."

"What's that? Emerald Oasis? Sounds like a prostitute club." She bit the front end off another nugget. "Or like a place dosers go to get high."

"As far as I know, it's a motel." He cringed. "Probably similar kinds of stuff going on there, but all the place itself does is rent rooms. What the people do in 'em isn't their concern."

She huffed. "Fine."

"Great." He patted her on the head twice. "I'll go finish setting up. I know you're in a hurry, so I told them to hustle."

Maya stared at the last three nuggets, unsure if she wanted to eat them. Somehow, Missy Hong got her wish and she wound up couriering drugs anyway. Maybe the woman had no idea who was doing it? She hugged her new shirt tight, counting on Genna being alive and able to deal with any complications that might come out of her working for organized criminals.

She took her time with the last of the food, still having half a nugget left about ten minutes later when Diego walked back in with a doll in a pink dress. It had a somewhat oversized plastic head, glittering blue eyes, and blonde hair down to its butt. Like Maya, it looked like it had rolled in dirt.

"Here you go." He tossed it onto the couch next to her. "All our man needs is what's inside the head. If you wanna keep the doll afterward, I don't think he'd care."

"Why does everyone assume I *want* a doll?" She picked up the toy under protest. "Genna didn't play with dolls when she was little."

"Whatever." He held his hands up. "Show time, kid."

She got up and followed him across the bar and out the front door. Already, she adored the new shirt. The wind didn't go through it as much.

He tromped over the plywood porch and down the steps, continuing for about twenty yards west from the Devil's Hangover before pointing north.

"You see that pile of cargo boxes with the sorry-ass excuse for a ladder thing sticking off the left side? Top one's bright orange?"

She held a hand over her eyes and squinted. The not-quite-noon sun created a lot of glare and made everything that far away dim and the same color. "I... think so."

"It's the tallest pile in the area. Thirteen boxes. You can't miss it. Bright damn orange with Chinese writing on it. Should be a ladder going all the way up the side. Make sure you're on top of that thing in two hours. That's where the drone is going to go."

"'Kay. Uhh. Is it safe?"

"Probably not." He chuckled. "Probably about as far from safe as you can get."

Her teeth chattered as a shiver of fear slammed into a wall of determination to get her mother back.

"Oh, it shouldn't be that bad. Those things are pretty stable. They fly flat, like riding a magic table or something. Up to you. No one's going to give you a hard time if you don't want to do it."

Genna could be in the middle of an interrogation right now. She could be getting beat up or starved or whatever they do to make people talk. "I'm going. Can you give me any shoes?"

"That shirt's one of mine. Got an old pair of sneakers, but they're way too big for you. Don't keep an inventory of kid clothes. People out here tend to make for themselves."

Maya sighed.

She clung to the doll as if it might offer some protection and walked deeper into the Spread. Once she left the clearing around the settlement, it became more difficult to keep track of the specific pile she was supposed to climb. Fortunately, miles and miles of abandonment with few people surrounded her. Chances were high that, except for the settlement, she'd be the only person there. Bad people had no reason to go places where victims didn't live.

The cargo box canyons and debris-packed passageways mutated into a living video game in her head. She'd spent so much time playing games, she'd wound up bored and started hunting down schoolwork over her age rating to have something different to do. She got herself worked up to the point of tears again thinking that the reason Vanessa had never arranged for her to go to school wasn't that Maya sought out e-learns on her own, but that the woman honestly didn't care. She didn't need to be smart to smile for a camera, and not-Mom had already decided her too soft to ever run Ascendant.

Stop it. "That's not true. The house computer made me take schoolwork. Vanessa never mentioned it because the computer did that. She probably paid extra to make me have smart genes. How many kids my age pass high school math? She wouldn't waste it." *Smart genes are no guarantee. Maybe she didn't know. Not like she was around much.* "Argh. Stop."

She marched forward, unconsciously clinging to the doll while she focused on her need to find her real mother. Groaning metal towered over her on every side, slowing her pace to a hesitant walk. She crushed the doll into her chest with both arms, shivering at the sound the wind made among the precarious stacks. Every *scrape*, every *clank*, every *slam* as the wind played with container doors made her jump. All the stacks looked the same.

Step by step, she made her way among the refuse of a prior age, navigating the cool dirt trails. A cat walked by, keeping a wary distance. She offered a halfhearted smile at it, though the animal darted off as soon as she took a step toward it. Perhaps forty minutes after she left Diego, Maya came to a halt in the shadow of a gargantuan tower of oceanic shipping containers. The top two glowed in the noon sun, so fluorescent orange they hurt her eyes. At the near corner along the broad side, a crude ladder made of welded rebar zigzagged its way to the top.

The end looked so high up it probably counted as being on a different planet.

Maya sank into a squat and hugged her doll. The thought of what she was about to do sent shivers down her spine. Her toes dug in to the dirt and she hid her face in the mass of fake blonde hair. Marcus... or was it Anton... had joked about riding an Authority drone, and in an hour, she'd be doing it for real.

I don't wanna.

Closing eyelids squeezed tears out. She pined for Genna. In a daydream, she cuddled with her mother and listened to the woman promise her Mr. Mason would never touch her. Still shaking, Maya opened her eyes and looked up. The woman who would protect her, who almost died to do just that, needed her.

Yes, I'm only nine… but I'm Maya Oman.

She stood and stared at the ladder.

"I'm coming, Mom."

THIRTY
OVER THE WALL

 shift in the wind carried the brackish smell of low tide in from the east. Maya stood stiff as a board, feet together, clutching the doll to her chest while studying the path upward. It looked as if someone had welded multiple separate ladders each about eight feet tall together into the sort of off-kilter backdrop they used in quirky cartoony movies made to scare children. No two sections seemed to line up, each varying a few degrees from straight up.

She crept up to the bottom and grabbed the rung at eye level. Going barefoot up a ladder made of rusting rebar amounted to one of the dumbest things she'd ever considered, but she was short on time, money, and shoes. Diego would have offered if he had any to give her. Though, how many people had she met who hadn't bothered even to give her a spare shirt?

Everyone's out for themselves, said Pope's voice.

Maya again thought of the dozens of pairs of tiny high-heeled shoes sitting in a closet somewhere, waiting for Maya II to reach nine years of age. Was Vanessa serious? Would she 'have another one made' or would it be cheaper to recycle old video of her? Any random girl or even a synthesizer could provide the voice. A sudden thought almost stopped her heart. The marketing team said 'juvenile female' was best. What would Vanessa have done with her when she wasn't small and cute anymore? Would she have become a real daughter then, or been thrown out and replaced?

Stop it. Why make me smart if she was going to just throw me away? Vanessa has no patience for kids. She'd have talked to me if I was grown, probably given me a crappy low-level job or something.

Pissed, Maya forgot her worry and set her foot on the first rung. She tucked the doll in the front of her shirt, hanging out of the neck opening with its head under her chin. Diego said two hours; by her guess, she'd taken less than one to get out here. No need to rush. Rocking her weight into the ladder resulted in no motion at all. Despite the cobbled-together appearance, it seemed solid enough.

She grunted and pulled herself up. The ladder had not been designed with someone her size in mind. Advancing each rung proved to be a gymnastic task as the spacing put the next one at the level of her collarbones while she stood on the one below it. She set both hands on top of the rung and pulled herself up. As soon as she could get her leg up, she braced one shin next to her hand and steadied herself with the side bar before pulling her feet underneath her again. It hurt, both her feet and her legs, but she repeated the process thirty-nine times, keeping count to distract herself from the increasing wind and from any temptation to look down.

Once she reached the top of the thirteenth box, she crawled forward and rolled flat on her back, out of breath. A few minutes later, she got to her knees and looked around. The end opposite the ladder had a metal folding chair behind a barrier of quarter-inch thick steel plate. Spent rifle brass littered the area.

She didn't trust standing on such a high place, and crawled closer to the eastern edge. The Sanctuary Zone jutted out from the middle of an open field that bore the squarish scars of razed building foundations, many of which looked like pits in the earth. Exposed basements collected rusty rainwater, pre-war boilers, and all manner of junk and debris no one bothered to clean up. A veritable moat of open nothingness surrounded the place where Citizens lived. The numerous patrol drones in the air would surely shred anyone or anything trying to cross that field. Even if a person could make it through that, they'd encounter a twenty-foot wall of smooth steel, no doubt packed full of sensors.

The cleanliness of the city mocked her. White buildings with silver windows glowed in the glare of millions of lights and advertisements along with the cyan light radiating down from the pyramid atop the Ascendant tower, which hid behind a murk of gloom in the air. The headquarters of the richest corporation in the world (at least according to the AuthNet) stood at the center of the Sanctuary Zone.

Miles to the southeast, the bulbous white shapes of six inflatable greenhouses rippled in the wind, surrounded by three concertina-wire tipped fences and a dense layer of drones. They resembled gargantuan maggots, and looking at them brought back the stink of chemicals and soil from one of Vanessa's 'meet the little people' tours on which she'd been dragged. After two hours walking around tanks and planting beds, Maya sat in the same limo as Vanessa. She'd tried a new ploy—suggesting they eat together like a tiny adult expressing interest in a corporate meeting. It had worked; though they didn't talk much during the meal, the woman had tolerated being there for the duration. Alas, acting all grown up didn't convince Vanessa to live with her.

She huddled out of the wind behind the hunter's barricade and pulled her new tee shirt down over her knees to her ankles. A shell casing rolled in a clattering circle as the breeze picked up. The sense that the entire stack of cargo containers swayed caused her stomach to do a backflip. Maya glanced down when the empty brass bumped into her foot. She hoped whoever had built the perch used it to hunt deer or some other target that walked on four legs rather than two.

Maya clung to the doll for a while, feeling foolish and lost. Eventually, the idea of sitting here felt stupid. She crawled left and peered around the steel plate at the city she'd spent her entire life minus about a week in. Somewhere in the haze, hundreds of drones whirred about, 'protecting' the Citizens from crime. One of them would be on its way here, broken from routine. The others shouldn't notice her. No programmer would ever anticipate someone *riding* a drone. A person's weight would probably keep them grounded or make them uncontrollable and obviously compromised. She gazed down at her spindly arms and legs. The machine wouldn't feel her. It would fly normally.

The anticipation of waiting caused chicken nuggets and fake cheese to bubble up in her throat several times. When the whirr of fans emerged from the silence, she had to re-swallow her breakfast again. She buried her face against her knees.

"What am I doing? This is so so so so so stupid."

A blast of wind scattered the spent casings and sent them rolling off the side. Maya looked up at the blinking red and blue lights of a hovering Authority drone. Most of her attention went to the .50 caliber cannon underneath, though fortunately, it remained locked forward and offline.

"Greetings, princess. Your coach has arrived." A man's voice crackled out of a speaker.

The drone glided to its left, centered on the cargo box, and touched down on a quartet of unfolding legs. Two seconds later, all four fans stopped dead.

"Do you have the baby?"

Maya held up the doll. "Yes."

"Did you bring anything to tie yourself on with?"

"No. No one said anything about that."

"Uhh, I guess it won't be a problem. Hop on the main body and grab the spars. I'll keep it flat and steady. It'll be like riding a flying bike."

"I've never ridden a bike."

"Whoa, kid, really?"

She grumbled while walking over to it. "Yes, really."

With too much time to consider it, she'd chicken out. Somehow, the thought of riding on top of a drone scared her less than going down that ladder. She felt a bit like a treed cat. Easy to get up, but petrified of going the other way. Maya stuffed the doll into the front of her shirt again before climbing up on the main body the way Marcus had. A moment of wiggling around found the spot that felt the most stable, and she bent forward to grab on to two metal struts that braced the forward fan shrouds.

"Ready?" The speaker hurt her ears that close.

"Yeah." She blinked. "Wait!"

"Waiting. Hurry up."

She reached up and gathered her hair into a ponytail, which she also stuffed into the neck of her shirt/nightie. The last thing she wanted was for her hair to get sucked into a fan in midair. Her hair wasn't anywhere near long enough to reach the blades, but strange things happened when people did stupid things. With no way to tie it, she pressed herself down in hopes of pinning it, and the doll, in place.

"Ready."

Maya hadn't prepared herself for the loudness of the fans that close, and screamed when the drone sprang to life. They went from off to full speed in the blink of an eye. Aside from a faint sense of increased weight, she didn't feel much different from being stationary on the ground. Watching the cargo box tower fall away below did more to prove she'd gone airborne than any sense of inertia had. As the initial fear of doing something so ridiculously dangerous that the Authority hadn't even come up with a plan to stop it faded, she grinned at the awesomeness of flying.

The drone tilted forward and picked up speed. Boxes and junk raced by on the ground. The settlement neared in seconds, and right in the middle of it stood Pope.

He came looking for me. Oh, no. "Pope!" she shouted.

She shot overhead before she could tell if he'd reacted to her yell, though several denizens scattered like roaches in the light. The drone tilted along in a gentle left turn, orienting itself to the east, and climbed higher. Her fingers went numb from the cold air and tight grip. She wanted to close her eyes and wait for it to be over with a safe landing, but terror refused to let her trust not watching.

A field pockmarked with scattered fires glided underneath, probable evidence of recent Brigade attacks on Authority outposts. They used some of these fields for training, and the news often featured stories of the Brigade attacking 'children.' By children, the AuthNet meant eighteen and nineteen-year-old rookie officers.

The drone made an angry sounding buzz.

Maya gasped. *What was that?*

Ahead, the New Baltimore Sanctuary Zone rushed closer at a frightening speed. Her chariot altered course a little more to the left, heading for a swarm of other drones in a perimeter orbit. Three minutes after takeoff, the drone appeared to have resumed its normal programming and entered a lazy patrolling path around the city outskirts. The machine gun on the bottom swiveled back and forth, matching the motion of the sensor ball at the nose end scanning the ground.

"Hey. Mr. Hacker? Are you still there?"

The drone buzzed again. "Unidentified voice print." It tilted back, stopping in midair. The gun spun in a 360 turn, searching for her. "Proximity fault. Unidentified individual, you are hereby ordered to show yourself."

"Hang on, kid. I'm trying to—" The speaker cut out. A second later, the drone erupted with flashing red lights and a warning siren. "Unauthorized access. Unit 1359 compromised."

The fans cut out to an instant stop. She screamed as the drone fell like a brick. Whirring deafened her again in a few seconds; the abrupt midair halt crushed her into the fuselage, the doll's plastic foot stabbing her stomach. Her chariot levelled off and spun in place, hovering for an instant before zipping to the right, clearing the wall by only a few feet. A handful of blueberries walking the top dove for cover.

So many things could go so wrong at that moment her brain blanked from sheer terror. Maya screamed and wailed, begging the hacker to let her down. She held on with all the strength she could force into her hands and thighs, and then some more. Her flying machine swerved back and forth like two men arguing over one joystick.

"... fighting me for control... not sure how long..."

"Stop! Help!" Snot smeared out of her nose, driven around her cheek by the onrush of wind. She didn't dare let go to wipe her face.

"… bail out when… water."

The drone again plummeted in a vertical drop. Her vice-like thigh grip began to slip away from the fuselage, but she managed to hold on long enough for the drone to halt again. Chicken nugget vomit slime went flying as she smushed against the drone for the second time. When the drone stabilized, Maya coughed up more bile.

A flash of fading sunlight at the ground caught her eye. The drone lurched into motion again, careening like a drunken moth toward a huge, rectangular artificial lake of grey, one of the reservoirs of drinking water. Six spherical tanks arranged along the near edge thrummed with machinery; she passed so close, the vibrations of the pumps resonated in her bones. The drone went into a flat spin, bucking like an angry horse, and dipped to within fifteen feet of the surface.

"Now!" yelled the voice from the speaker.

Maya let her legs loosen. Her body glided upward, a meat flag moored by her white-knuckled grip on the thin fan struts, waving as the drone climbed and dropped. It dipped down, closer to the surface. She pulled her knees to her chest, planted her feet on the body, and forced her fingers open. With a thrust of both legs, she jumped clear of the deathtrap. She took a great breath and closed her eyes a second before plunging into the icky-looking water.

The high-pitched whine of fans muted to a blurry swirl of sound.

Once she felt as though she'd stopped going down, she risked looking. Much to her surprise, the water wasn't opaque as it had looked from above. A haze of blonde doll hair formed a cloud at her chin. Steady, mechanical thrumming filled her ears from unseen turbines. The bottom, at least three stories down, appeared farther away than the surface. She kicked to orient herself vertical and reached one hand up.

A series of lances broke the surface, a graceful row of silver icicles plunging past her on the left. Heavy *thudding* slammed into the water from overhead. It took her a second to realize the beautiful sight came from large-caliber bullets entering the water. Maya almost screamed the second time the drone fired, but managed to keep what little air she had inside. She flailed her arms and pulled herself around in a twist. A rapid search locked her gaze on a wide concrete pipe near the surface on her left. She swam toward the distant wall, not going up or down.

When another spray of gunfire hit the water where she had been, failing to correct for her motion, she pulled herself upward, wanting to breathe. Panic rose and fell, dueling with her need to stay alive. More bullets splashed into the pool somewhere behind her. She didn't look. It seemed like only an instant later her body *demanded* air; she found herself climbing. Her head breached the surface and she let out a great gasp. Overhead, the drone circled, evidently having lost track of her. She gulped down two more full breaths, took in another huge one, and ducked underwater again. Skimming about five feet beneath the surface, she swam hard until she had to come up for air again. The drone spotted her and whipped around. Maya got only one breath before she forced herself down.

Spiral cavitation paths rained like the spears of an angry god all around her. She pushed herself deeper and deeper and kicked forward. It fired another volley, again failing to correct for her underwater motion. Proof that it evidently couldn't see her when she submerged gave her a little scrap of hope. Each swipe of her hands pulled her inches closer to the salvation of the great pipe. A shadow shot overhead and she surfaced behind the drone to breathe. Maya managed four long strokes without diving before it came around to face her. She ducked under before the gun could finish swiveling toward her.

More silver spirals streaked by, plunging with muted, whooshing splashes. She kicked and pulled, inching away from where the drone pelted the reservoir. After one more bob up to breathe, she swam down and glided into the great pipe. Its elevation on the wall relative to the reservoir surface let water fill it three-fourths of the way. She skimmed the bottom until she felt she'd gone far enough in to put tons of concrete between her and the drone. Once she felt relatively safe from gunfire, she surfaced inside the pipe and kept swimming. The unexpectedly loud echo of her coughing and sputtering scared her quiet.

A few yards farther in, she swiveled and peered at the opening. The shallow angle didn't let her see the drone, but the angry whirring in the air left no doubt it continued hunting her. Wavering light glimmered along the top of the pipe, reflected off the water. She swam deeper in to a right elbow turn and a T-junction about twenty yards later. To the left, it went upward at a shallow angle. In the distance, a metal grating platform jutted out from the side by a door, with a ladder hanging from the edge into the water. On her right, the pipe angled downward and the water came up to the top a few feet away from the turn. Maya thanked circumstance for such an easy choice of which way to go, and fought to swim against a mild current until she reached the ladder.

She scrambled up out of the water and collapsed on her side. The reality of .50 caliber bullets being fired at her crashed down hard; she trembled, dry heaving and sobbing. Maya curled into a ball, clutching the doll. Minutes later, she got her fear under control—somewhat—and sat up. A catwalk made for work boots didn't treat her butt with much tenderness, so she scooted across the deck and sat on a four-inch concrete curb by the door.

There, she huddled with the doll in her lap. Hiding underground seemed like a *really* good idea at that moment. The drone couldn't have scanned her, or it wouldn't have fired at her. It had to have detected someone too close to it and reacted as if attacked. *They didn't mark me as a criminal, did they?* She closed her eyes and tried to stop shivering. *Of course not. If they did, it would have said my name and told me to surrender.*

Echoes of sirens and warning buzzers continued to drift in from the pipe. Would they find her here? Who would even think anyone would do what she had done? A hacker got into the drone; they'd probably think he'd made it go nuts and sensed a person where none had been. No way in hell would they expect a drone to carry a passenger. The drone's operator might not have even realized he'd been firing on a child in the dark, with only a head poking up out of the water. The reservoir had been grey, the same color as the sky—a giant mirror. No wonder it couldn't see her when she submerged. She'd wait for things to quiet down. Maya held the doll out at arm's length and stared into its blue, plastic eyes.

"Why am I holding on to you? You can't help me." She flashed a wry smile and neatened the toy's hair. "Your head's all full of drugs."

Maya cradled the doll anyway, unable to explain how it made her feel better—but it did. She leaned her head back against the metal door, waiting for her heart to slow down and the shaking to stop. As soon as it got quiet outside, she'd continue. She coughed and wiped her nose. Droplets crept down her back and legs, hitting the water below the grating with faint *plonks*.

She tried not to think about a ginormous machine gun trying to kill her.

She refused to remember jumping off a flying drone.

She forced herself to believe she could find her mother.

She conjured the mental image of Genna holding her tight.

I did it. I got inside.

PART IV
SANCTUARY

THIRTY-ONE
CITY OF THE DEAD

aya continued shaking long after any audible hint of activity ceased echoing down the pipe. Her soaked hair draped like a dead animal against her back, but she refused to move. She cradled the doll the way she wanted Genna to hold her following such a terrifying ride, but stopped short of speaking to it. It wouldn't do any good telling a hunk of plastic everything would be okay, not to mention an echoing voice could attract problems.

Over the course of an hour, her mood eased back from heart-exploding fear to paralytic depression. What if Genna had already been discovered as Brigade and executed? Maya had made it over the wall into the Sanctuary Zone, but that also meant she couldn't easily stroll out the gate and go home. All the entrances had checkpoints, and if the Authority got her, she'd never see Sarah or any of her friends again. She wiped silent tears from her cheeks and concentrated on keeping them quiet while stifling a coughing fit. No trace of daylight remained in the tunnel she'd entered from. Enough time had passed for notice to die down, and yet still, her ass remained planted.

She scratched at the top of her foot. Barnes didn't think she could get this far, and here she sat. Missy Hong thought it impossible for her to get inside the city, yet inside the wall she was. She tilted the doll side to side, listening to the glass vials shift inside its hollow head. Hiding down here in silence for so long, her mind wandered, and the appeal of the Sons of Jeva made some sense to her. Not that *they* did, but she understood how people could fall for it. Hoping that some magic power had control over fate made not knowing tolerable, like an adult craving the security of being a child again with a parent to protect them.

Maya combed the doll's hair with her fingers. "It would be nice if there was something up there. Then I could ask it to make sure Mom's alive. Maybe I'm doing that right now... or maybe I'm talking to a toy." She shook it. "What do you think, doll? Pretty silly of me to talk to plastic."

Bright blue fake eyes regarded her from a lifeless face bearing an innocent, empty smile.

A beep came from above and to the left. Maya peered up at a card-reader box on the wall beside the door she leaned on that had no knobs or handles. Her spike of fear faded at the realization no one tried to open it. Its built-in clock read 22:00:13, so it must've chirped at the hour changing. She'd been down there for hours and not heard its clock beep before. Maybe she'd not noticed due to her fear or because of all the noise outside.

"Well." She stretched her sore legs before standing with a weary whimper. "Mom isn't getting any freer."

Nothing she could think of to do to the panel opened the door, so she crept to the edge of the grating and lowered herself back into the water. A few minutes of swimming brought her to another T-junction. Sounds of traffic echoed to the right and a constant, mechanical whirr came from the left.

One of her e-learns had gone over how the Sanc collected rain into reservoirs, treating and cleaning it before sending it back into peoples' homes. She grinned at having fallen into the brackish artificial lake. That meant she'd hit a pre-treated pool, so this passage had to lead right out to the Sanc via the storm drains that collected rainwater.

She hurried to the right, swimming about sixty or seventy yards to a spot where a narrow rectangle of light shimmered on the water's surface. She set her feet down, the level of the water even with her chin, and stared up a shaft to a street-level drain. Headlight glare washed over the slot every few seconds, casting moving shadows from dangling strands of plantlike muck.

A rotting series of huge metal staples on the wall provided a passable, if not punishing, ladder. Maya pulled herself up and out of the water, scaling the crud-caked rungs. They led to a manhole cover she couldn't budge, so she stretched left to peer out the opening.

The storm drain had a view of an open area, a courtyard between office buildings rather than an actual street. Glowing electric light outside made her squint, but after a moment or two, her eyes adjusted. Men and women scurried back and forth in the shadow of massive high-rise towers bedecked with holographic advertisements. Traffic sounds came from the left, along with the occasional louder whine of an Authority drone flying by.

Miniature umbrella-drones shadowed many of the people. The fist-sized floating spheres kept their transparent rain-shields in place over their owners, so many that all the little fans sounded like an army of bees.

A spray misted her in the face, gusting into the opening on the breeze. Since she couldn't budge the manhole cover, she slithered out through the storm drain onto the road and into the fresh (ish) air of the city and a light but steady rain. She'd already gotten soaked from swimming, so it didn't bother her. Maya sat on the curb by the opening, taking a minute or five to catch her breath and wait for her feet to stop hurting from the metal ladder. People seemed too busy to notice her, and walked by without as much as a look of disinterest.

A pair of Authority drones flew around the corner from the left, two blocks down where the concourse met a street. They glided along at about the level of the fifth floor. She didn't know if their sensors would detect the drugs in the doll's head, but perhaps losing the knife had been a good thing. *That*, they would have picked up. Of course, knives weren't illegal, but a girl her age with one would prompt questions.

Once she caught her breath, Maya stood and chose to walk off to her left at random. The clean metal sidewalks of the Sanctuary Zone felt strange underfoot after so much old-fashioned paving and dirt. At the end of the block, she merged with a stream of pedestrians.

She didn't think much of walking around in the open until a shimmering glow on the left regaled her with an eight-foot tall version of her own smiling face above the scrolling logo of Cendrolex, a liver-restoration medication. Her broad grin sparkled with teal lipstick as her white-gloved hand raised a cup of wine into the scene. A recording of her voice played.

"Cendrolex... live life to the fullest."

Maya remembered tasting the colored water. She wondered if the same person who thought it a good idea to have an eight-year-old market a drug to alcoholics and appear to drink on camera had drawn the line at letting her have real wine, or if someone else had made that decision. With a huff of disgust at her video self, she grumbled and trudged off. Despite looking like a refugee from a battlefield, she kept her head down so no one could see her face.

At the end of the block, she stopped to wait for a red light. Upon a giant video billboard mounted to the fourth floor of a building across the corner, a ten-foot-tall version of her pranced around showing off her shapeless body in a tiny purple bikini—an effort to get women to buy Adimera, a fat-destroying pill that 'blasted the pounds right off.' She squirmed, remembering how much she'd hated that thong, a wedgie she couldn't get away from. One of the production guys called it butt floss. Her aesthetic technician lost her job that day for challenging the request to put such a skimpy thing on a girl her age. That ad, they'd only filmed three weeks before her abduction.

"You can look like this forever with Adimera," said a little-girl voice that sounded too much like hers.

Yeah, Adimera... and two in sixty people suffer potentially fatal hemorrhagic diarrhea, or, if they're lucky, heart failure. Almost no one who saw that ad would know Maya's twig-thin physique came from custom genetics. How many people had Ascendant fooled into thinking a couple of pills could turn them from normal people into supermodels? Watching a giant image of herself prance about and wave her butt made her blush and look down. It had seemed fun at the time (except for the wedgie), but the finished advert mortified her. Had Sarah or her other friends felt that embarrassed after they'd been robbed? Maybe not. The giant Maya had a wholly different feel to it. Her handlers had coached her to act too much like a grown woman, showing off her next-to-nothing outfit. She held her stomach, sick at the thought of Mr. Mason watching that ad over and over.

Please don't let any of my friends ever see that! She blushed at the memory of Anton saying Marcus liked her. Maya closed her eyes and wished for religion to be real so she could ask some deity to make sure he never saw that video.

Embarrassment waned when her mind changed gears, wondering how many people died from consuming the drug. Did that count as her killing them? Some poor person might see her, think Adimera would magically give them a body like hers, and they'd wind up dropping dead of a massive heart attack.

Maya looked up, scowling at herself on the huge screen. The traffic light changed, and she scurried across, eager to get away from the spectacle she'd made of herself. She wanted to run away from the ad, but fast-movers attracted drones. A person running among a crowd, even a child, would draw attention. Only the guilty ran.

A pair of cars trying to nose far enough into the intersection that they could turn even if the light changed caused a delay in pedestrian traffic at the next cross street. Maya hid among the adults, gaze down, hoping no one bothered to take notice of the bedraggled urchin in their midst.

"Attention Citizens." A capsule-shaped drone, yellow-and-black striped, glided overhead with a flashing amber light on the bottom. "We are pleased to announce that airborne bacteria levels set a record low for the second consecutive day. Public advisory to use breathing apparatus remains suspended. Have a nice day."

She crossed with the crowd and turned left. Whenever she'd left the penthouse, she'd always had a driver. Only once had she joined Vanessa in the helicopter. Traffic had been horrible that day and they would've been late for the recording session without flying. Maya spun through a few steps, gazing up at the buildings around her. She had no idea where she was and came to a halt against the side of a dark grey office tower.

Another holographic version of her, about six years old, passed overhead on a drone-mounted screen, pitching a diet aid that promised to let people eat as much as they wanted and never gain an ounce. In theory, the drug bound on a molecular level to food, making it too large to pass through the intestinal wall. Rather than be digested, it went straight out into the toilet. Only, the ad didn't mention how one in every hundred or so people who took it died a horrible, agonizing death from multiple organ failure or how overuse could cause someone to starve while eating tons of food. How many people had bought Nutridyne because of her smiling endorsement? How many people had she killed?

Maya sank to a squat, clutching the doll and wanting to throw up. She pressed herself against a building, cowering behind an artistic flange, hiding from her vapid murdering image. Nervous shakes rattled her body. A person couldn't walk fifteen feet in the Sanc without seeing her face somewhere. Though she'd never been there, she knew her ads ran in all thirteen Sanctuary Zones of the Eastern Commonwealth States, all the way from the Boston Sanc to The Miami Arcology, as well as what remained of Europe. Marketing kept wanting her to visit London, but Vanessa had never agreed to it. The Authority had no influence there. Ascendant executives had a serious hatred for the California-Washington-Commonwealth, as they didn't trade with the East Coast. No money for the corporation.

She sniffled, glaring at the flying billboard gliding off into the distance.

I didn't know any better. I'm only a little kid. I only wanted to make my mother like me.

Maya growled. That woman was *not* her mother. Once the attack of nausea subsided, she crept to the corner of the building and peered around. Warm rainwater ran in the next sidewalk like a river, deep enough to cover her feet.

The street shone as bright as day from hundreds of signs and banners. Vertical swaths of light scrolling with product imagery clung to every building, white, red, blue, green, and every color imaginable flickered and shone with the same general message: buy something. She slipped out into the pedestrian path again, holding pace with a fat man in an ankle-long coat. At least at his size, he kept the rain off her for another two blocks before he headed into a residential high-rise.

Maya spun in a slow turn, searching the sky for the telltale cyan glow of the Ascendant tower. Too many tall buildings formed an impenetrable wall and choked off the sky. She huffed. A glance down at herself made her decide not to walk into any place too well lit. The soaked ragamuffin look would cause trouble; a concerned Citizen or suspicious blueberry would both spell disaster.

She kept to alleys for another few blocks, turning without plan in a desperate search for an Infoterm. They existed, that much she knew, but where they were located or what they looked like was another thing. One of those would be able to give her directions to that place... Emerald Oasis.

At the next corner, she turned right, entering a huge canyon with walls of identical silvery skyscrapers on either side of a four-lane street. Six huge red banners, each spanning at least ten stories, hung from the buildings on the left, wavering in the breeze. Gold writing at their tips mixed in English and Chinese referred to the area as Emperor's Plaza. Rain caught the glow of dozens of advertisements, dancing in rainbow swells wherever the wind caused droplets to cluster. This place, she knew. Vanessa's assistant had brought her here a few times to shop for clothes and games. The bottom ends of the banners swayed, gliding back and forth above the wide outdoor stairway that led down into the shopping center beneath the high-rises.

Maya followed a clump of pedestrians to where a set of painted lines spanned the street between the third and fourth of the six towers, a crossing that lined up with the stairway. In a few minutes, the light gave the green to the crosswalk, and she hustled with the group to the other side. People went left, right, and straight ahead in roughly equal amounts. She stayed with the group headed down into the Plaza.

A wide chrome-plated stairway decorated with giant hanging flowerpots of ivy descended to a recessed square lined with storefronts. Three railings carved to resemble Chinese dragons separated it into four lanes. She hurried along, happy to have stumbled across a familiar place. In the middle of the courtyard ahead, a pack of five blueberries stood by a fountain, sipping coffee and talking. Maya drew in a gasp and dove to the left behind a six-foot video display upon which an Asian woman showed off a black, skin-hugging dress with a high Chinese collar. A diamond-shaped cutout over her cleavage offered quite a view.

Maya scrunched up her nose, wondering why anyone would wear

something like that. The cold could get right in.

The screen shifted, and again she stared at herself circa two years ago. Seven-year-old Maya stood at the side of a hospital bed in a dark dress. Except for her, the entire scene was black and white. A blond boy about her age lay in the bed, wheezing and coughing. She wore a grim expression, this ad being the only one in which they told her not to smile. Maya recited words she'd memorized years ago in time with the recording.

"Michael's parents didn't love him enough to buy genuine Xenodril. They trusted an imitation. Michael is dying to Fade. I'm glad *my* mommy loves me." The Maya on the screen held up a box with a fancy Xenodril logo over a blue swoosh. "Xenodril cures Fade. Does your mommy love you?"

As a giant block of legal 'boo-shee' scrolled across the bottom, she thought of Sam and the implication that he died because Genna didn't 'love him enough' to buy a $200 per dose drug. Maya hated herself for saying that. Even after arguing with Vanessa about it, she'd caved in and recorded the ad. Not that anyone ever got away with saying no to that woman. Had Genna ever seen that ad? Probably. Is *that* why the woman had been so rough with her at first? Had she listened to Maya accuse her of not loving Sam?

Disgusted with herself, Maya punched the screen (not that it cared) and burst into tears.

"What was that?" asked a man.

Fear devoured sadness. Maya froze. Stretched reflections of blue in the silver ground shimmered closer. She bowed her head and walked back the way she'd come, heading for the stairs.

"Hey kid," yelled one of the Authority officers. "You okay?"

"Yes. Thank you." She jogged.

"Stop. What are you running for?"

Crap. She bolted.

"Shit. Runner. Call it in," said another man.

Heavy boots clambered after her up the stairs and into the street. A solitary e-car swerved to avoid hitting her and a woman's shouting joined the commands emanating from the blueberries to stop and get down. A whistle zipped over her head and a brilliant flash of blue lightning sparked off the side of a building.

She thought of the Hornet. The Dad said it had too much power and could kill a little kid if they didn't weigh enough. Maya became acutely aware of her spaghetti-noodle limbs; she fit square into the 'didn't weigh much' category. An uneasy scream/whine seeped past her teeth. Compared to the drone flight, getting chased by blueberries seemed trivial. Maya kept her wits, even as a second stunner dart skipped off the ground too close to her feet. A tingle crept up her legs, electricity carried by the rain-soaked metal. She debated diving flat and surrendering, letting them realize who she was and trying Plan B, but an alley offered escape before they could fire a third dart.

They chased her, but she rounded another corner, which blocked their shot. Her feet slipped out from under her on the wet metal, but she flailed and managed, somehow, not to wipe out. She followed a back and forth zigzag path, keeping to areas devoid of people and passageways too narrow for cars. They would call in drones any second if they hadn't already. Her surroundings grew progressively dingier, making her think she went the wrong direction—closer to the wall rather than toward the city center.

Yellow caution signs flashed at the mouth of another alley a block and change ahead. Both had the same text:

INTEGRATION WARD 04

CAUTION: FADE

DO NOT ENTER

She pumped her legs as hard as she could, weaving behind dumpsters whenever possible to keep the blueberries from getting a clear shot. Another sparking dart skittered across the wet ground, leaving a trail of scintillating sparks. At the next corner, she tried to turn at full speed and her feet slid out from under her. Adrenaline blocked any sense of pain from her mind. She bounced off her chest and scrambled upright in a narrow but bare alley leading to a fifteen-foot chain link fence topped with coils of razor wire.

A pair of Integration Ward signs sat on either side of a locked sliding gate. Large, yellow flashers at their corners cast flickering shadows over distant shambling figures in the yard beyond the fencing. *Fade victims. Blueberries won't follow me in there.* She raced down the alley past the welded-shut doors and boarded-up windows of disused warehouses. At the end, she wedged herself through a gap between the gate and the fence too small for an adult. The Authority officers slowed to a walk near the far end of the quarantine alley, seeming to have given up.

She backed away while watching the blueberries for a few steps, then spun about and hurried down a narrow street between two white-walled buildings. The steps of a former warehouse offered a place to sit and remember how to breathe like a normal human being again. She held the doll in her lap and bent forward. Excess adrenaline trembled off in a nervous shudder. Muffled gasps for air made her cringe, seeming loud enough to echo for miles. Hopefully, her gamble would work.

Citizens, as a rule, didn't get the vac shot. People were expected to buy Xenodril to get rid of Fade once they'd caught it. If taken within the first week (two if the person was super fit) the Xeno would get rid of the disease with no more side effects than if the person had come down with a heavy flu. To those with money, Fade was a nuisance. Ascendant didn't sell the permanent immunity serum. Of course, Vanessa had it, and Maya remembered being brought around a Fade ward as a PR stunt about four years ago. They'd never have done that if they hadn't given it to her. Yes, she was sure she'd been inoculated. Veterans tended to have it too since some believed Fade to be a bio weapon employed during World War Three, the vaccine given to soldiers before Ascendant controlled it.

The true victims were the poor bastards who lived out in the Habitation District. Anyone who couldn't afford to buy Xenodril, or who couldn't get past the security checkpoint to buy some, didn't have a chance. Fade became a death sentence. And, from what she'd heard, there weren't very many worse ways to go.

She resumed trudging along once the exhaustion of her frantic chase faded. At the end of the short street, past a dead forklift, she entered another courtyard with no fancy lights or tempting signs, no shimmering little Mayas gliding overhead or smiling from freestanding signs.

Only death lived here.

Forty or fifty people milled around a series of white tents. Some looked older, some about Genna's age, and a handful of children clustered in the corner. All wore robe-like garments of off white made of long wrapped shrouds. Those who could walk shambled about like zombies, bumping into each other and startling as though few of them could see more than five feet forward.

Patches of grey marred every face she gazed upon. A tiny red-haired girl maybe five years old reminded her of Sarah, only with much floofier hair. She sucked her thumb in the far corner; blotchy grey spots covered the right half of her face, making the skin look dead, and the eye on that side had milked over.

Maya broke down at the sight of such a small child so sick, and cried into her hands.

"Shit, not another one." A wheezing man sidled up to her, long strands of white gauze dangling from his arms and shoulder. He shook his head. "Too damn young."

A woman staggered over. The way her skin hung in folds hinted that she had likely been huge before she got sick. Her death vestments undulated with all the excess flesh shifting underneath. She didn't seem capable of moving her left leg, an effect that made her seem even more like an undead. "Where'd you catch it, kid? You don't look sick yet."

"She's not in Fade bandages." The man coughed. Dark ochre ooze slid down from both nostrils in a wavering double-tendril Maya could not look at.

"Uhh, I'm not sick. I went the wrong way."

The woman's mouth curled into a sinister smile. "Well, congrats kid. You're sick now."

Two more men approached, curious about the newcomer. One old man in the back fell forward, made no effort to get up, and screamed at the ground.

"Fade isn't contagious once the infection has set. After forty-eight hours, the motile pathogen mutates into a host-dependent state that is no longer capable of being a vector for cross-contamination." Maya bit her lip. "You can only catch it if a new batch falls out of the upper atmosphere, or get a blood transfusion from someone who has it."

"What the hell was that?" asked a man who had the features of an African, but a skin tone like dirty plaster. "That sounded like Janus, but in a kid's voice."

"It *is* a kid, Don." The first man leaned close. "Hell of a wrong turn. Didn't you see all them flashing lights?"

"Yes. I was running away from some bad people. I knew they wouldn't come in here because everyone believes the lie that Fade is contagious."

Four more Fade victims crowded around, including the little red-haired girl.

"Will you be my friend?" The child dragged herself closer and offered a creepy half smile. "Doctor says I won't forget everything for another two weeks. I'd like to have a friend before my head stops working."

Maya stared at the girl, sniffling. Shaking from grief, she reached out and let the girl hold her hand. "I... Oh, this is *so* wrong."

"I know you," said the child. "You fly! Can you show me how to fly?"

"I don't..." Maya blinked. How could this child possibly know about the drone?

"Ashley's right." A new woman who only had a few small patches of grey around her lips and nose pointed. "I've seen her in the air."

"It's the Ascendant girl," wheezed a gurgling voice.

Over the span of three seconds, the curious crowd became menacing—except for Ashley, who continued smiling at her new friend.

The once-fat woman grabbed at her. "They'll give us medicine for her."

"Get her," yelled a man.

"No!" shouted Maya. "They won't." She backed up, but the crowd of sick people swarmed around behind her.

Maya walked to her left, deeper into the tent city. Ashley hung on to her hand like an anchor, keeping her from moving too fast. The girl giggled, limping along as best she could behind her. Maya hurried past tents containing those who could no longer even stand. Inhuman voices moaned names. A few, even adult voices, called out for Mommy or Daddy. One woman kept shrilling "Eddie" every three seconds like a stuck cuckoo clock.

Shroud-wrapped bodies closed in. Maya leapt away from twenty or thirty grasping hands. Past the last tent, the brick buildings formed an L-shaped left turn lined with orange-painted garage style doors, each marked with a three-digit number. She firmed up her grip on Ashley's hand and pulled her ahead in a sprint to a left turn a few seconds away.

As soon as she rounded the corner, she skidded to a stop, her heart slamming. Aside from twenty more rolling doors, and a 'Billy's Storage' sign discarded on the ground, only a cinder block wall and more razor wire waited for her. A dead end. She backed up, doll in one hand, Ashley in the other, facing the shambling crowd of moaning, bandage-clad people.

"It won't help. They won't give you anything!" yelled Maya, edging backward. "I was kidnapped already and it didn't work."

Sick people crowded in, all forty or fifty of them that could walk. They filled the passageway, trapping her in an ever-shrinking space. Whispers of "grab her" continued, interspersed with the occasional "it's her fault" or moans of "Xeno."

Maya continued retreating until cool cinder blocks bumped against her back.

"Why are they mad at you?" asked Ashley.

"Please stop," yelled Maya. "They won't listen."

The living mummies closed in, leaving only a small gap between her and the people crowding her.

Maya sank against the wall until her butt hit the ground, and clamped her arms around Ashley. "I'm sorry. I'm sorry." She sniveled and raised the doll-bearing hand to guard her face. "Please don't hurt me!"

THIRTY-TWO
ZERO ICE

aya shivered, waiting for the hands to grab her. Moans continued to emanate from the crowd here and there, though a sense of unease radiated from the people closest to her. She risked a peek and lowered her arm. Four men and two women swayed on their feet, firing stern, accusing glares down at her. Perhaps her tearful apology had confused them. Like the blueberries, maybe they'd never expected the daughter of Vanessa Oman to act so... pitiful.

"Kidnapping me won't help you. Vanessa doesn't care about anything but money." Maya sniffled, scavenging some confidence. She shoved herself upright, back sliding against the wall. "Some mercenaries kidnapped me two weeks ago and tried to make them pay in Xenodril. They're all dead now. Vanessa laughed. She was ready to watch them kill me before giving medicine for free. She won't help."

Murmurs of indecision passed among the crowd.

"Why are you mad at her?" Ashley let go of Maya's hand and faced the group. Her fragile body shivered as a tremor in her right leg threatened to send her to the ground.

Maya pulled her fingers through the girl's wild hair, a futile effort to tame it. She burst into sobs again at seeing such a young girl sentenced to death. "If you help me, I can help you. I promise. I... can't walk away. I don't wanna think about what's gonna happen to her. She's so little."

"Why should we believe anything that comes out of your mouth?" asked an Asian woman. A heavily wrinkled face conveyed great age, though her rickety frame and short stature could've fit an adolescent. "You're always talking about this drug or that drug or this miracle or that miracle. It's all lies."

"You're right." Maya looked down. "I'm nine years old. I grew up in a perfect penthouse apartment and did whatever I was told. I read scripts. I smiled at camera drones. Some of those ads aren't even me; they're computer generated. I told her Xenodril should be free, but she won't listen."

As if on cue, a huge drone passed overhead projecting a giant hologram of Maya. The craft flew too high to hear the audio, but she remembered holding that damn massive bottle of nutrient powder for hours. The producer joked she could've fit inside the thing, and if she'd curled up in a ball, she probably could have. At least they hadn't made her drink any of it. 'Mega-muscle-strength' scrolled below her face.

Who in their right mind uses skinny little me to sell that crap to bodybuilders? Probably the same idiot who came up with the wine ad.

"What are you gonna do then?" A brown-haired woman with a deep tan and Hispanic features forced her way to the front. She looked normal except for her hands, which had gone grey up to the wrists and barely moved, making them appear like false plaster prosthetics. "You say you're just a little kid."

"I... uhh, don't exactly have a plan yet. But I can get into Ascendant. I need to go there to break my mom out of jail." She held her hands up as the crowd's anger rose. "No! Not that bitch. I ran away from home. I have a new mother, a woman who cares about me."

A disturbance at the rear of the throng spread forward, altering their focus. The crowd calmed and parted with a deferential silence, clearing a path for another figure to walk between them unhindered. The silver-haired woman who approached didn't appear to be one of the sick. She wore a dark teal doctor's coat over a tight black sweater and slacks, and looked healthy as well as a bit on the stern side. Her expression of confusion became one of concern once she spotted Maya. Wrinkles around her eyes made her seem sixtyish, or perhaps younger with a load of stress.

"What are you doing here?" asked the new arrival.

Maya blinked. "Who are you?"

"I'm Doctor Janus. I try to do what I can for these people, but on my own time." She collected Ashley and picked her up. "So, Maya... what are you doing in my *Integration Ward*?"

"I've got a friend, Doctor." Ashley grinned and pointed. "I don't want to forget her."

Maya clenched her hands into fists, furious at not-Mom for causing this suffering. "Why did you say integration ward like that?"

"Come." Doctor Janus offered a hand and looked at the crowd. "Please go rest. There's nothing to be gained by threatening this girl. If there is a way she can be of assistance to us, I will ensure the opportunity is not wasted."

Maya looked at the hand. "Are you kidnapping me?"

Doctor Janus laughed. "No. I only want to talk."

She clasped the woman's hand. "Okay."

The doctor carried Ashley to a large, square tent and set her on a cot with a woman who bore a strong resemblance, save for the striations of grey all over her. The little one curled up and smiled.

"Who?" moaned the woman.

"Terri, this is your daughter, Ashley."

"Ashley's gone." The woman thrashed her head side to side. "I don't have a daughter."

"Mom." Ashley poked her. "You are sick."

"This is someone else's kid. Thank you for making me feel better." The woman pulled Ashley into a hug.

Doctor Janus stooped and checked the woman's eyes. "It's your daughter, Terri. Your memory is going."

Maya stared at her feet until the doctor tapped her on the shoulder. She followed the woman across the courtyard to a square tent set up with the trappings of an office. Once inside, the doctor spun around and folded her arms.

"Okay. I'll make you a deal. Spare me the bullshit and I'll listen with an open mind. Play games, and you'll regret it."

Maya glanced down at the doll. "You sound like Vanessa. How do I know I can trust you?"

"Perhaps I share the trait of not liking to be toyed with, but I'm nothing like her. I overheard a little of what you said out there, and I think we may be of a similar mindset." She fished an ID badge out of the doctor coat's pocket and held it out.

Doctor Elisa Kazimierz, Sector 9 Medical Pavilion.

"That's your name?" Maya looked up. "You don't want the Authority to know."

"Yes." She put the ID away. "I go by Janus to keep word from spreading back to my superiors."

"Two faces," muttered Maya.

The doctor smiled. "While what I am doing here is not against the law, showing too much concern for people society has written off would not bode well with Ascendant. If I am dismissed, I would lose access to what little resources I can use to assist them."

Maya took a seat in a white plastic chair facing the table serving as a desk. "Can Xenodril help?"

"It depends on how much damage has been done. Fade is a syndrome, a body's systematic response to internal assault by weaponized nanobots as well as a synthetic viral pathogen. Xenodril halts the infection where it is, destroying the virus. A chemical marker in the medication triggers a shutdown in the nanomachines. People who have suffered neuromuscular degeneration may regain the use of their limbs eventually, but it's not guaranteed without additional nanosurgery these people can't afford. Memory loss, unfortunately, is irreversible. There are about five patients here who are in all probability beyond any help, even if you had Xenodril with you right now. The other fifty-two could survive if they are treated soon."

"Why did you say Integration Ward like that?"

Doctor Janus scowled. "The name makes it sound as though this is some kind of halfway house with the intention of reintegrating them back to society. It's a bold-faced lie. This is a dying ward, a human wastebasket."

Maya wiped more tears from her cheeks. "I need to meet someone at a hotel called the Emerald Oasis."

The doctor did a double take. "What?"

"I made a deal for help getting inside the city. I'm bringing him something. After that, I'm going to go back to where I used to live and I'm going to break into the Ascendant network. I should be safe from the corporate drones. Taking me out of the system is work and effort, and programmers are lazy. Besides, Vanessa doesn't know how much I hate her now. She thinks I was kidnapped and... doesn't care. I can still probably lie and act innocent if I get caught."

Doctor Janus pursed her lips.

"I'm trying to get my real mom out of jail. She was one of the mercenaries who kidnapped me, but she's really nice and she felt bad and I decided to run away from Ascendant and now she's my mom. I'm not going to let them hurt her. When I get her out, we'll steal enough Xenodril for everyone. She'll know how to do it. I swear. I don't want any of these people to die because Vanessa is a greedy bitch."

"That's an optimistic plan you've got."

Maya jumped to her feet. "Please help me find that hotel. If I get caught, I'll do everything I can to talk them into sending Xenodril here. It'll make for great PR. They won't be able to say no."

"Well, I suppose there isn't much to be gained from trying to use you as leverage. I find it plausible that Vanessa would be inclined to risk your life to maintain her appearance of total control. Your plan sounds like a long shot, but probable failure is better than definite failure." Doctor Janus got up and walked for the exit. "Come on."

Maya hurried to follow the long-legged doctor to the entrance. Janus produced a key, opened the gate, and re-secured it once they'd gone outside.

"It's cruel to keep them locked in."

Doctor Janus raised both eyebrows. "Oh, it's not to keep them in. It's to keep paranoid people *out*. There's idiots out there who think it's their righteous duty to bash in the skulls of anyone with Fade, like it's some kind of punishment from a higher power. A 'mark of the beast' or some such nonsense like that."

Maya sighed. She glanced back, tapping her big toe on the ground. "They were ready to hurt me... are you sure they're not locked up so they don't riot?"

"No, Maya. Most of them couldn't walk two blocks without collapsing from exhaustion. Between depression, muscle weakness, disorientation... the worst they'd do is get themselves hit by cars or shot by drones."

Maya frowned.

The doctor led her to a door in the alley between the two sets of Fade warning signs. Beyond it, a small e-car in a garage chirped and lit up when they approached. The driver's side door opened on its own.

"Get in the back seat and stay down."

"Okay." Maya crawled in and huddled in a ball on the floor.

The car lurched forward a few seconds after the rattle of a motorized steel garage door stopped. She kept herself crammed in a tight ball, head down, and didn't make any noise or try to look around. The car stopped a few times, but since the doctor didn't say a word, she kept still. A faint bump rocked the floor a few seconds before the vehicle came to a full stop for the sixth time.

"We're here," said the doctor. "Emerald Oasis."

Maya climbed into the front and slid into the passenger seat. "Thanks."

"Don't forget your promise. Little Ashley is counting on you."

"You didn't need to do that." Maya sniffled, but fought the urge to cry more. "I already feel like shit. I won't forget."

The doctor pushed a button on the console, causing the passenger door to pop open. "Good luck, kid."

"Thanks."

The car sped off as soon as she had both feet on the ground, tires squealing out of the parking lot before the door even finished closing. *Damn. Guess she doesn't want to get caught here.* Maya sighed. She looked away from the road and up at a flashing green hologram of a palm tree over the words 'Emerald Oasis.' A cluster of women on the far right end of a long one-story building had dressed in ways that left no doubt as to their profession. Unlike Naida, these women seemed proud of what they did and didn't try to conceal it.

Maya looked back and forth among plain green doors, each marked with a fake gold palm tree stamped with a room number. *Great. What room? Is he still even here?*

It didn't occur to her how conspicuous a little girl holding a blonde doll at midnight in the parking lot of a brothel-motel was until a man with neon blue hair appeared in a window, waving frantically at her. Two round, dark lenses hid his eyes, connected by a thin spectacle frame.

He disappeared. Two seconds later, the door nearest that window opened. Maya decided to run over there before someone more conscientious called the Authority on a wayward child. His white tank top looked clean enough to pull duty in a surgical ward. Loose, glossy black pants obscured the contours of his legs and gave off an 'I have tons of money' vibe that seemed as out of place here as she did.

"Wow." The guy seized her by the arm and hauled her inside before shoving the door closed a few decibels shy of slamming it. "You are so damn lucky. I spent the past two hours debating if I should get the hell out of here or not."

He sounded like the guy who'd been speaking through the drone's speaker.

Maya glared up at him. "Don't you mean *you're* so damn lucky I still showed up after that bullshit?"

"That was out of my control. I got attacked by an overclocked defprog at a really bad time. It rubberbanded me out of the mini-net in the drone before I knew it was there, and with trying to fight the operator for control so he didn't throw you off to your death, the firewall closed me out. I couldn't get back in. It went full-paranoid mode. Not even the Authority operators could get in on a legit port."

Maya threw the doll at him. "There. Hope none of it broke."

She wandered to the bathroom, took one look at the place, and gave serious consideration to peeing on the sidewalk outside, but wound up standing on the seat with several layers of toilet paper between her bare feet and the plastic seat. As much as she *needed* a bath now, she wouldn't have touched that tub in a heavy chem suit.

Maya rushed out of the chamber of horror as soon as she could and spent a minute wiping her feet on the rug. Four oblong boxes about the size of electronic pianos, all interconnected by a series of spaghetti wiring, sat in a row across a battered desk. Each component had the same word painted across some part of it: 'Zeroice.' The unit on the left had a primitive version, neon blue paint on top of white. With each device to the right, the size and artistry grew.

"What's a Zeroice?" asked Maya.

"You're still here?" The guy looked up from the bed, where he'd laid out ten narrow glass vials containing liquid that radiated a faint pale blue glow. "Oh. I guess you want your dolly back." He reattached the head, fiddled with the back of the dress, and chucked it to her.

Maya caught it, feeling a little foolish for doing so, but didn't drop it. "So, what is it?"

"*I'm* Zeroice."

"Oh. Did your mother write your name on your computers so you don't lose them?"

"Fuck you, kid."

"Considering the kind of motel this is, that's not funny. And no thanks."

Zeroice again looked up from the drugs and frowned. "I wasn't trying to be funny, nor was that an offer."

"Help me get into the Ascendant network."

He didn't look up. "That whole 'not funny' thing? You're better at it."

"I'm serious. It's the least you can do after almost getting me killed."

Zeroice sighed. "The deal was getting you into the city. I did that."

She leaned forward and snarled. "Into the city did *not* mean dumping me in a freezing pool of water while getting shot at by a drone *you* lost control of."

"It looked worse than it was, kid. Four or five feet underwater, the bullets don't have enough energy left to do anything."

"I can't breathe water!" She glared.

His blasé demeanor showed not the slightest dent. Apparently, a raging nine-year-old didn't scare him. Maya smirked. *Getting upset never worked on Vanessa, but she's not human.*

Maya dropped her voice to a neutral tone. "Please? I need help."

"Not my problem, kid. You did your part. I did mine. Deal's done."

She held the doll to her chest, half hiding her face behind its puffy hair. "Please." Sniffle. "It's really important." Whimper.

He loaded the drug vials into a foam-packed case, humming.

Maya worked herself up to a good crying whine. "Please, mister. My mom is gonna die. I can't do it alone. I need help."

He smirked at her, either annoyed or guilty at the crying child. Perhaps playing the tears card might work on some people after all. "Keep it down. This ain't the kind of place people bring kids, and the walls are thin. I don't feel like getting my ass kicked by someone who thinks I'm into little girls."

"Please help me." She opened the tear gates wider and sniveled. "I don't mean that Vanessa bitch, I mean my real mom."

"Vanessa bitch?" Zeroice finally looked at her with eye contact.

Maya pulled her hair back, giving him a good view of her unmistakable perfect cheekbones and glittering gold-brown eyes.

"Oh fuck." He jumped off the bed. "Oh, fuck. Fuck fuck fuck."

She throttled back on the crying. "Relax. They don't know I'm here. I'm running away."

"Head, you idiot. You god-damned idiot. What the fuck did you do?"

Maya blinked. "Y-you're Alfonse, aren't you?"

He whipped about to stare at her again. "How the hell do you know that?"

"You're right." She studied her toes. "Headcrash *was* fucked in the head."

"Stop that shit. You're what, eight? You shouldn't fuckin' swear."

"Nine. And why?"

He shrugged and thrust his arms out to the sides. "Because. You're nine. That language sounds wrong comin' outta a little kid."

"Well?"

Zeroice raked his fingers over his head a few times. "This is bad. This is really bad. I'm fucked. Galactically fucked."

"Only if I scream." She made the most innocent face she could.

"What do you want?" He fell seated on the end of the bed. "I can't believe I'm being blackmailed by an eight-year-old."

"*Nine*. Maybe you should ease back on the drugs. Your short term memory is going." Maya swished side to side clutching the doll. "I want you to help me get my mom back. You're a net pirate, right? Look me in the eye and tell me you're willing to pass up a chance to get root access to the Ascendant network."

Zeroice's head popped up. He regarded her for a second. His upper lip twitched with a nervous tic. "Okay. I'm listening."

THIRTY- THREE
HOLLOW MEMORIES

areful not to step on any unidentifiable stains on the dark green rug, Maya wandered around in an approximate circle while Zeroice tinkered with his rigs. He'd rambled about cobbling together a bit of net code to act as a software bridge. The mother of all ideas seemed to strike him out of nowhere soon after, and he pounced on his hardware.

In seconds, the man went motionless, gazing into nowhere.

"Hello?" asked Maya, creeping closer. When he didn't react, she reached out and poked him on the arm. "Hey. Are you still alive?"

She couldn't tell if he ignored her or if his consciousness had gone down the wires plugged into the back of his neck. He showed no awareness of his surroundings, or her shouting at him. Maya sighed, unsure what she should do with herself or how long to wait here hoping this man did something to help her. She frowned at the disgusting room. Neither the bed, the one other chair, the shelf by the window, or anything within fifteen feet of the bathroom looked safe to touch.

A small black box on a little table next to the bed projected green digital numbers when she waved her hand over it, announcing its opinion of the time at 11:48 p.m. Maya yawned. She hovered on the balls of her feet to minimize contact with the rug. Her mind ran away with the imagined army of viruses and germs crawling over her toes.

"Shoes," said Maya to her feet. "I'd even wear those stupid heels in here."

Zeroice muttered, shook his head as though clearing a fog, and looked back at her. His left eye clamped shut while his right couldn't have been open any wider. "Did you say something?"

"I want shoes."

He rubbed his face. "Nothing's open at this hour. Sack out, we can go somewhere in the morning."

She thought it over. "I don't want to waste more time. Is your program ready?"

"Yeah. You'll need to open the door for me though, in a manner of speaking." He scribbled on a scrap of paper and handed it to her. "Put that address on a net crawler."

Maya glanced down at the note: 00FC.18D4.98A0.0153

On the reverse: 'Headcrash is fucked in the head.'

"Yeah. He was," mumbled Maya.

Zeroice drummed his fingers on the desk. "So where is he? I haven't seen any sign of his mottled ass since he said he got this big job."

Maya folded the paper up and tucked it into the doll's dress. She took a breath, held it, and let it out slow. "He got shot a few times and fell fifty stories. I don't think he made it."

"Oh." Zeroice sighed. "Dude was weird but not a bad guy."

"Yeah." She started to feel a little sorry for him, but chased it away. The man had willingly taken part in a plot to kidnap and kill her. Even if he showed a little kindness, she could only feel so much sympathy for a man who decided it acceptable for a nine-year-old to die as a political statement. "Not bad for a guy who wanted to murder me, I guess."

He cringed. "Okay, so rush mode."

"Yes please. I want to get out of this room before I catch whatever's living in the rug."

"Right." He turned back to the machines and reached for a plug. "I'm going in again. I'll hack an e-car and pull it up outside. You said Ascendant tower, right?"

"Near it." She hurried over to the patch of linoleum by the door. "It's an apartment building two miles south on 60th Street. You'll probably be able to figure out which one because it's on the patrol path for Ascendant-owned drones."

Zeroice snapped the wire into the socket behind his ear and sagged back in the chair as though he'd had a stroke. Maya fidgeted in place, shifting her weight back and forth from leg to leg. About four minutes later, the glare of headlights passed over the windows and lit up the dingy curtains. Maya opened the door and peeked out at a boxy silver e-car with tiny wheels and no people in it.

She crept out of the room, pulled the door closed, and looked around.

Confident no one watched her, she ran to the little car and crawled in. The instant she pulled the door closed, the self-driving taxi lurched into reverse. She yelped in surprise, holding onto the dashboard until the car finished swerving its way out of the parking lot and drove in a calm, straight line along the road. Maya slid down to the floor in front of the seat. Better no one see her at all. Curled up in the space where a person's legs should be, she waited. Fatigue threatened to pull her to sleep while anxiety kept it at bay. Battling exhaustion made worse by the mesmerizing thrum of the e-motors, she picked at tiny rubber nubs in the floor mat. Every few seconds, a band of streetlamp light pulsed over the cabin.

Her body slid around with every turn, acceleration, or slowdown. She clung to the hope that her appeal to a hacker's need for a once-in-a-lifetime chance worked. Riding blind in a car driven by a man she'd known for fifteen minutes could go wrong in so many ways she tried not to think about it. Vanessa would never have taken a risk like that. That bitch also thought her too-compassionate daughter too timid to do anything of the sort, but she didn't have a choice. In truth, she feared losing her *real* mother more than anything bad happening to her.

This close to finding Genna, she couldn't stop fidgeting. She wondered what Sarah was doing at that moment, then felt stupid. *Duh. She's asleep. It's past midnight.* Again, she thought of the unfinished Magic game and hoped that her friend hadn't given up and put the cards away. Did she leave them set up in hopes Maya would come back?

"I'm sorry, Sarah," she whispered. "I should've told you. Please don't be scared."

Tears patted on the floor mat.

Her crying petered out to a forlorn, silent stare by the time the car came to a full stop a few minutes later. The audio system emitted a series of odd chirping noises like someone turning it on and off as fast as possible. She popped up and peered over the door. A cavernous parking deck with pure white walls surrounded her. Silver letters spelled 'Ascendant' here and there along a thick cyan band that circled the chamber. Only six cars remained at this hour, two of which belonged to Vanessa. A twinge of sick danced in her gut at the sight of the $200,000 onyx monstrosity. Bad enough people died so she could buy it, the woman barely used it.

She crawled from the floor to the seat of the little box-on-wheels and looked at the building entrance not too far away. Zeroice had been considerate enough to park her right next to the elevator. With any luck, the security detail would be sleepy as usual. Maya eased the door open and ran to the elevator. The grubby, frazzled urchin staring back at her from the mirror-polished doors was a far cry from the lying monster floating all over the city, and she didn't much mind the new version of Maya.

As soon as she pushed the button, the twin slabs of steel slid sideways, releasing a blast of cold pine-scented air that fell over her, causing a shiver. She darted in and reached up to the penthouse symbol. The system chirped when her fingertip made contact, and the doors whooshed shut.

"Restricted access," said an electronic female voice. "You have five seconds to confirm identity."

Maya stood on tiptoe, held on to the wall, and put her eye in front of the scanner. It emitted a painful flash of amber light, then a pleasant chirp. She backed up, one hand over her right eye, cringing from the brightness.

"Good morning, Maya," said the same voice. "You are up past your bedtime."

"I know. I'll do two extra e-learns if you don't tell Vanessa."

The elevator got underway, making her feel heavier. "Three."

"Three?" She gasped. "But that will take me all day. I won't have any time to play."

"Would you prefer I notify your mother that you are not only awake at this hour, you were outside?"

"Okay, fine." She added fake sullenness to her voice. The building AI would've suspected something wrong if she didn't put up a fight.

When the doors opened, she forgot how to breathe. Her old home looked pristine, as though nothing whatsoever had happened. Before the AI could prod her, she walked in over soft beige carpet. As usual, the air-conditioning ran at an economic seventy degrees, but having spent a week without any AC, the place felt chilly. She hurried deeper into the apartment and glanced around.

The main living area glowed eerie in the ambient light from the city outside. The long white sectional couch, flat-panel television bigger than some cars, and a quarter of a million dollars of furniture showed no sign of any violence. Gunfire and flashes replayed in her mind. Moth had fired his giant cannon at people in this room. Not even one carpet fiber looked out of place.

She bit her lip. Had it really happened? Would she get back to her old bedroom and realize the entire thing had been a dream? The plush carpet warmed her feet as she walked nearer the window and peered out at the roof deck. No sign of an Authority helicopter, blood, spent bullets, or any damage met her gaze. The routine of kneeling in that spot while watching the twilight sky for any sign of 'Mother' coming home brought a bitter glower. She wouldn't let herself cry one more tear over that awful woman. A somber sigh painted a blotch of fog on the glass, hiding her reflected face. After a moment, she turned away.

The sudden whine of a drone startled her paralyzed. A three-fanned Ascendant security unit cruised around the left corner of the building. She prepared to jump back, but it already noticed her and its cannon pointed straight at her chest. Maya went rigid at attention and let the doll slip from her fingers; it plopped on the floor, synthetic hair tickling her calf.

Maya shivered, staring straight ahead. *Please recognize me.*

A grid of green laser light covered her. The scan felt like it took longer than it should. She couldn't stop trembling. One bullet from that enormous cannon would… she didn't even want to think about it. She raised her hands in a slow gesture of surrender and pulled her wild hair back from her face. Emerald glint flickered past her eyes. The drone emitted a pleasant beep and resumed its patrol circuit.

Maya fell to all fours with a hand on her stomach. Had there been any food in her, it would've been on the rug. In minutes, she shook off the fear and found a surge of confidence in that Vanessa hadn't disowned her or marked her as a criminal. One good thing had come from such extreme disinterest. The woman genuinely did not care one way or the other if her daughter was home, dead, missing, or plotting against her.

Fighting off the yawns, she ran across the living room and down the hall to the bathroom. She peeled off the tee shirt and nightdress, stuffing them into the automatic washing machine before climbing into the bathtub. As much as she wanted to soak and enjoy freedom from all the ick she'd collected in that horrible hotel, she washed herself with a focus on speed instead of comfort. When she finished with the soap, she scooted to the back end of the tub, leaned her head into the hair machine, and let it work.

The automatic shampooer would take about ten minutes to finish, so she allowed herself that time to soak and relax. When the dryer stopped, Maya got out of the tub, careful to keep her hair from getting wet, and dried off. After stuffing the towel into the laundry slot, she started to walk to her old bedroom, but froze in the middle of the corridor. The spot where Moth had punched a blueberry so hard the man had embedded in the wall appeared undamaged.

She looked down at herself, noting small bruises, nicks and scrapes from spending a week running around outside in a nightdress. That couldn't be fake… could it? Freaked and angry, she stared at the rug, the wall, the corner molding. Her heart fluttered at a smudge of dried blood in a gap in the parquet floor lining either side of the carpet strip. She crouched and touched it, lifting her hand to examine the tiny flecks of dark crimson on her fingertip.

It really happened.

Maya ran to her bedroom closet and flung the doors open. Rows of small fancy dresses and high-heeled shoes greeted her. She slipped on underpants and grabbed a pair of black leggings before crawling into the oversized beige sweater she'd worn the day they abducted her. Alas, she owned not one pair of practical shoes. The only time she bothered with footwear was on the set of a commercial, or if she got dragged off to some PR dinner. Even for the rare occasion Vanessa allowed her to go shopping, they expected her to dress to the nines. No such thing as sweats and sneakers for the daughter of the Ascendant CEO.

Maya fumed, fighting back the urge to take every last fancy piece of clothing and throw it in the trash. "You never wanted a daughter," she whispered. "You wanted a prop."

Her need to be with Genna grew painful, but sorrow didn't survive long before anger took its place. Not-Mom had built her entire empire on the misery of people like Ashley, and Maya wanted no part of it anymore. *I don't care what Vanessa thinks of me. I hate her.*

After a moment of glaring, she got an idea. Maybe she *could* help Genna escape in a more direct manner. First, she had to find her. Maya pulled a small bag off a shelf and dropped it at her feet. The floppy nylon thing reminded her of a smaller version of the sack Genna had used to kidnap her. She couldn't fit inside this one—too small—but it would hold what she needed. She selected a glimmering teal dress with metallic sheen and packed it. Matching high-heeled shoes followed. She debated hose, but skipped them. Too hard to put on outside, and the blueberries wouldn't think it strange for her to have bare legs with a dress like that... if they even noticed. Only one of not-Mom's aesthetic technicians would. She wouldn't exactly have to deal with Felipe the perfectionist keeping her on the makeup chair for two hours for this performance. If everything worked, she'd never see the idiot again.

She packed another ten pairs of underwear, two sweaters, and her other three sets of leggings before heading down the hall to Vanessa's room. The woman didn't keep much here. Her closet had two suits, one with a skirt and one with slacks, yet more high heels, and a shelf with some underthings. She cringed. Vanessa had the same twig-thin build as Maya. Genna had shape. *Nothing here for Mom.*

Grumbling, she plodded back to her room, dropped the bag at the foot of her bed, and put the doll in it. A few minutes of rummaging around the desk unearthed a small digital recorder. She padded out into the corridor and approached the terminal on the wall. Like a gunslinger preparing to draw, she stared at the slow-blinking red light, wondering if this would be the one time out hundreds of tries the woman would answer. Of course she wouldn't.

"Maya," she said.

"Voiceprint recognized. You shouldn't be awake this early. Please return to bed."

"Outbound call, Vanessa Oman."

She held the recorder up and pushed the button.

"This is the private vid-mail inbox for Vanessa Oman, CEO of Ascendant Technologies. If you have the necessary clearance to contact this number, leave a message. Otherwise, please disconnect this call and await the arrival of Authority Officers."

"Begin message," said a digital one.

Maya poked the end-call button. She walked to the kitchen, set the recorder on the table, and popped a Hydra tray in the machine. While it processed, she ran back to her bedroom and retrieved her personal computer. The well-worn silvery grey portable had kept her in other worlds for many hours. When she returned to the kitchen, the smell of something vaguely resembling beef had filled the air. She never thought she'd be so happy to have a rehydrated meal, but breathing the essence of it got her salivating.

She stood on tiptoe to reach into the Hydra, pinched the thin plastic at the edges of the hexagonal packet, and carried the steaming meal to the table. Maya ate one handed while linking the recorder to the terminal and splicing Vanessa's mailbox announcement to pieces. She devoured most of the meat and half of the beans before attacking the brownie in the middle.

A dot on the screen flashed from yellow to green. Maya picked up the recorder and hit the play button.

"Clearance. Vanessa Oman. CEO. Authorize."

She smiled. Creating 'authorize' out of 'Authority' and 'otherwise' took a little fiddling to make it sound right, but it worked. Her finger traced around well-worn keys as she pondered packing the computer as well. It had provided an escape into video games or movies as much as it burdened her with the drudgery of e-learns. If she could get Genna out of prison, she wouldn't need an escape from reality. She much preferred a real parent to a virtual paradise.

One finger to the power button turned it off.

"Nah."

Two steps later, she stopped. *I really should stop being stupid.* She sighed under the weight of guilt at not telling Sarah of her plan and grabbed the computer. *This is a tool. I might need it.*

After packing the portable computer in her bag, she spun the recorder on the table and flashed a broad grin.

THIRTY-FOUR
HOME INVASION

he door to Vanessa's office was locked as expected. Maya didn't even try to use the access panel as the AI would surely lose its electronic mind if she did something so out of routine. In Vanessa's bedroom, she struggled and strained to drag a table six feet left to position it under an air vent. Once it looked good, she put a chair up on top of it and climbed.

Fortunately, Vanessa, or whoever had designed this place, had put all their security concerns on keeping people who didn't belong here out of the penthouse. A private office inside the apartment wasn't as protected from someone already inside. Compared to the thirteen-story nightmare ladder and a drone flight, standing on a chair on top of a table didn't even register as risky. She plucked the vent cover off and pulled herself up and in. Her fingers went numb within seconds of crawling into the blast of AC. The duct took a ninety-degree right two feet away from the opening.

Steel walls bucked and boomed as she shimmed along the narrow confines. Another reason she didn't worry about alarms or anything—an adult couldn't fit in there. A short crawl brought her to a left turn, and a few feet farther, a spar that carried cold air to Vanessa's private office. She had one in every location she considered a possible home, though Maya couldn't remember the woman ever using this one. Come to think of it, she couldn't even say for sure that Vanessa had ever spent more than four hours in this penthouse over the entire nine years she'd lived here.

Maya pushed the vent cover out and peered down at the floor. It didn't look like an awful jump, but doing it headfirst wouldn't be a good idea. She retreated to the junction, crawled past the vent, and backed into it. After stuffing the recorder into the waistband of her leggings, she shimmied in reverse and slithered into the hole. Her sweater bunched up at her armpits; bare stomach touched frigid metal. She squealed and let herself drop free, landing on the rug in a backward roll.

Burgundy-stained wood shelving took up three walls of the office around a modest (at least for Vanessa) marble-topped desk. The room had somewhat less sparse decoration than Maya's bedroom, with only two functionless items: a morale-boosting award made of a sculpted obelisk of crystal that her employees had supposedly all chipped in to buy her, and a white six-inch pyramid with a cyan base. The company had distributed thousands of them, a bit of promotional swag sent to hospitals and doctors back when Ascendant still had to compete for business.

Maya hopped into the huge leather chair behind the desk and stared at a warped version of her face smeared over the surface of a gold-tinted computer bar. She touched the power button and a holographic screen unrolled like a window shade spooling up from below. Amid a background of swirling smoke in myriad shades of blue, an Ascendant logo—a white and cyan pyramid—appeared above a red blinking light.

She held the recorder out and pushed the button.

The spliced passphrase caused the logo to disappear. The terminal displayed infinite swirling smoke for an arduous long minute. Maya pulled her heels up on the chair and shivered from the air-conditioning—this room had been turned down lower than the rest of the apartment. When a screen full of icons and a standard user interface popped up, she almost screamed a cheer.

Holy shit! It worked!

Leaning forward, she attacked the virtual keyboard. One thing Vanessa hated was inefficiency. She'd labeled and sorted everything in an easy to follow structure. Maya went into the Authority network, pulled up the 'pacification and rehabilitation' records, and got to the database of 'MPRs'—Miscreants Pending Reintegration.

Search: Female, black, age between twenty and thirty.

Over a thousand hits came back.

Maya added a detention date within five days to the search filter.

It dropped to 108. She swiped her hand at the holographic screen, pushing aside picture after picture of women that varied from terrified to furious to so far stoned they didn't seem to know where they were. The fifty-fourth image was Genna, in a bright orange jumpsuit. The expression on her face—pure sadness—made Maya cry. She looked like she knew she'd never get out alive.

The file indicated they held her pending further interrogation in support of an execution order for suspected Brigade activity. They had no hard proof, but her visual similarities to security camera footage from several terrorist incidents came close enough that they decided to err on the side of murder. A freak of bad timing had saved her. Such a 'maybe' situation required the signature of an Authority commander who had yet to review the case due to being out on vacation for two weeks.

Maya's stomach did a backflip. Had 'Sandoval, R' not decided to go on vacation when he or she did, her mother would be dead. She growled, wanting to scream at Vanessa, but also mindful that the terminal could hear her. If she used her real voice, it would lock her out in an instant. Maya poked at the screen, changing Genna's detention order to a charge of food theft, and the expected sentence of execution to the minimum selection available—three months. She grabbed a notepad from a drawer and wrote down the address of the detention facility the system showed in her record.

Maya grinned. *This might really work.*

Oh, shit. She raced to the door, unlocked it from this side, and retrieved the doll from the bag in her bedroom. After pulling Zeroice's paper free from the dress, she hauled ass back to the office and smoothed the crinkled scrap on the desk in front of the virtual keyboard. One finger tap opened a net crawler. She typed in the address and hit 'go.'

The window flashed white, displayed a progress bar for two seconds, and then the words 'site has no content' appeared.

She shrugged. *Guess he didn't program graphics. I hope that worked.* Curiosity got the better of her. A hand swipe minimized the blank window and she opened an internal search prompt into which she typed 'Maya Oman.'

A result panel opened with schedules. A few dozen photo shoots, a handful of video recording sessions, a real-time status application linked to the fourteen false Maya androids. She flung her hand at the screen, scrolling past pages and pages of old appointments. Her unease faded at finding no trace of anything indicating Vanessa had ceased trusting her. Though being worried about a traitorous child would require having a tiny scrap of care.

The scrolling green text bounced to a halt when it reached the oldest entry. The heading of 'invoice' made her blood run cold. She reached out and poked it, opening a screen with an e-mail chain. She swiped down to the oldest message.

From: Kerensky, R, MD

To: Oman, V
Subject: Invoice 15812
Feb 2 2084 3:14 pm EST
Miss Oman,

The genetic material assembly is complete. We have your fertilized egg ready for implantation. To confirm, you are requesting the child be female? All early signs look wonderful. Our simulation has predicted the physical characteristics you are looking for will fall into the desired parameters. In basic terms, she will be exotic and pretty. As for your request to have an IQ in the 140-170 range, that we will not be able to confirm until the child is old enough for basic testing.

Please let us know when you would like to come in for the procedure to implant the fertilized egg.

From: Oman, V
To: Kerensky, R, MD
Subject: RE: Invoice 15812
Feb 2 2084 5:34 pm EST

Yes. Female. I do not have time to set aside for such an ordeal. Grow it in a tank and send me a notice when it's no longer in need of diapers.

From: Kerensky, R, MD
To: Oman, V
Subject: RE: RE: Invoice 15812
Feb 2 2084 5:38 pm EST

Very well.

From: Kerensky, R, MD
To: Oman, V
Subject: RE: RE: Invoice 15812
Jan 28 2088 11:34 am EST
Miss Oman,

Your daughter is nearly four and is beautiful and healthy. Thank you again for settling the invoice. Cognitive testing shows signs of intelligence notably above average. She is ready to go home with you as soon as you desire.

Maya clicked on the attached file and found an itemized receipt for genetic work totaling 650 thousand dollars, or 168,831 NuCoin. She pounded both fists on the desk. The marble slab didn't react. *Grow it in a tank? You bitch!* Despite being more furious than she'd ever been, the tears wouldn't stop. Not being able to make a sound without giving herself away as an intruder frustrated her to the point of gnawing on her forearm while her body convulsed with silent sobs.

She raked her hands at the screen and headed into the Ascendant manufacturing system, wiping her cheeks every few seconds. *I'm not an 'it.'* In a few minutes, she'd gone into the production management system and noted preset lot numbers for both Xenodril as well as A-Profen, a common headache pill that even Ascendant sold cheap. After some manual tweaking of code, she swapped several lot assignments in the distribution control script. The end result should be several batches of Xenodril inserted into packaging for A-Profen. She remembered Vanessa screaming at someone during a photo shoot about the Parkville warehouse security being unforgivably bad. A few more finger taps, and she programmed the system to route the mislabeled shipment there.

She tapped her foot on air, waiting for some sign that Zeroice had made it into the system, not knowing if she should stay here or get the hell out. Still, she couldn't do anything until morning. Showing up at the prison doors a few minutes past 1:00 a.m. would fool no one.

Thinking of bed brought Sarah to mind, along with a healthy heaping of guilt at the unfinished game. Maya went into the Authority personnel database and ran a search on Baxter, the man who knocked Sarah out with his rifle. His file looked unremarkable, but then again, his particular breed of assholedom didn't exactly stand out among the blueberries assigned to the Hab. Maya opened an e-mail client, lifted the address of Baxter's supervisor's supervisor from the system, and sent a message (as Vanessa) to her.

Lieutenant Witt. There is an officer under your command by the name of Baxter whose flagrant disregard for his station made me take notice of him the other day. He caused the delay of one of my people, which resulted in significant losses of time and money. I do not expect your officers to show such disrespect to those who work directly under me. That one of your men's names became known to me should in and of itself be a significant indication of my vexation. See that he is dealt with in the most appropriate manner possible. I do not want to become aware of this man's existence ever again.

-VO.

With a big grin, Maya drove her finger down like a knife into the virtual keyboard to send it. Even if they eventually figured it out as 'boo-shee,' the email would make that prick sweat for a little while. She yawned again, but scooted closer and hunted around for anything she could find about Genna, Headcrash, Moth, or Icarus. The Authority didn't have files on any of them, which surprised her. Granted... had they known for sure who Genna was, she'd have been executed already, likely shot right in the apartment while on the floor next to Maya.

On a lark, she searched for Fade. The usual data popped up, explaining how the bio-weapon came about during the war. Ascendant scientists determined it had been designed in such a way as to allow for contamination on friendly targets to have a long period (one to two weeks) where the correct treatment resulted in a lack of permanent effects. This simplified combat theater distribution as they could throw it all over the place and treat their own people later. The pathogen attacked the central nervous system as well as internal organs; the telltale appearance of random grey blotches varied from one individual to the next, an engineered cosmetic symptom for psychological warfare. Spreading rumors of false high-contagiousness coupled with obvious signs of infection probably caused as much death as the agent itself.

Maya scowled.

The computer had no information on which country had made it, but it did prove that it hadn't been aliens or some dangerous microbe brought down accidentally from asteroid mining. Ascendant, at the time a tiny bio-pharma company, developed Xenodril. Based on the tone of the article, Maya got the feeling the United States had been the target of Fade since they had to scramble to make the cure. Then again, Ascendant might have had purer motives back then and worked to help the people if the government only provided the cure to soldiers.

"Meh." She scrolled past it.

A heading of 'Limited Persistence/Area Denial' caught her eye. According to that white paper, Fade virus lingered in the wild for only seventy-two hours, after which it became inert and harmless. A link chain of internal communications over the past four years led Maya to a series of messages that made her jaw hang open wider and wider.

Once the old governments had collapsed to anarchy, Vanessa worked out an idea to pacify the unruly population and give them something worse than the government to fear. Ascendant refined the Fade virus and began to manufacture it, using the supposed bioassay testing drones to spray live agent every so often, all the while making up rumors of aliens or asteroid mining. Subsequent to each infection cycle, sales of Xenodril spiked, providing Ascendant the financial means to exert enough influence over the Authority to effectively rule the Eastern Seaboard.

Much of the inland portions of North America remained under the control of unaffiliated city states and tribes of nomads, but pockets of established civilization existed in some areas, with almost as much in southern California and Seattle as the east. Only, the Authority didn't have direct power over them. Ascendant *did* market medicine to the California-Washington-Commonwealth, but the CWC had a separate military force more closely akin to that of the prewar government... and apparently not on great terms with the Authority.

Maya blinked. *They'd love to know it's Ascendant making Fade. Uhh... that would start another war.* She bit her lip, unsure if it would be wise to tell them. War would kill a lot of innocent civilians as well. *I'll ask Mom.*

An article on 'Maximum Effective Impact' detailed the schedules for falsified reports of airborne contamination. By controlling the forecast for bacteria, they could manipulate the population into windows of not wearing breathing gear. Whenever they announced a 'three-day record' for clear air, a release of live Fade always followed. This technique resulted in a thirty-five to forty-five percent increase in infections each time. Which in turn resulted in another sales spike of Xenodril. They sometimes sent long-range drones far enough west to drop infections, and of course only Ascendant made Xeno. Thus far, it seemed the CWC had resisted any attempt by Vanessa to gain political influence, though they had caved and purchased Xenodril.

Maya clamped her hands over her mouth to keep her dinner inside. She'd known Vanessa to be cruel, but this... the idea that Vanessa had actively been killing people to make money... Ashley's face came to mind, and Maya shuddered with sorrowful rage. She tapped several of those articles and swiped them into an e-mail. The terminal stuttered and slowed, then flickered to a lockdown screen.

Oh, shit.

She grabbed the paper and ran out, stopping six steps away. After going back to lock the office door, she ran to her bedroom and took the bag with her into the closet. Remaining in the apartment seemed foolish, but her body couldn't stay awake much longer. And going outside didn't sound like any less of a crappy idea. The best thing she could do would be to act casual and play innocent if someone caught her here. She could always blame hackers. Hiding in the closet would cause suspicion.

With her alarm set for 8:00 a.m., she climbed into her old bed. Exhaustion stalked her guilt, and within minutes, she'd passed out.

THIRTY- FIVE

STAGED

aya's eyes peeled open ten seconds before the alarm buzzed. She rolled over and slapped it silent before lying still for a little while, unable to find enough energy to get up. Knowing Genna was alive, at least according to the computer, took a ten-ton weight off her heart. Today, if everything went well, she would be back home.

Excitement got her upright. She went to the kitchen and fixed herself a Hydra omelet. A moment or two after she swallowed the last forkful, the front door hissed open. She considered hiding in a closet, but discarded the idea when a flash of blue armor moved at the end of the hallway connecting to the front room.

She had to get rid of the blueberry fast, before he found anything or got suspicious. Legs crossed, one bare foot bouncing at a casual bob, she glanced up at the Authority Officer when he barged into the kitchen with a rifle pointed at her.

"Put that thing down." She scraped the meal tray with her fork and nibbled on a few scraps of stringy meat.

"This apartment was empty. Who are you and what are you doing in here?"

"Who am I?" She shifted her eyes to him without moving her head. "Are you an idiot? You *do* know who you're talking to, don't you?"

His weapon dipped a few inches. "Maya Oman was abducted two weeks ago."

"Oh?" She looked down at herself. "I don't feel kidnapped. Maybe you're hallucinating."

"I was here. Seven officers were killed, one of whom I went to the damn academy with." He shuddered with rage. "What the f—hell is going on?"

Maya uncrossed her legs and stood, took two steps closer, and leaned up on her toes. "Oh, that is sad. Sorry. The whole thing was staged."

"Staged?" He glowered at the wall. "But... Marc and Darian... they're dead."

"Do you think Vanessa cares?" Maya lowered herself flat on her heels. "Do you really believe someone could kidnap *me*?" She threw a dismissive wave at the wall. "Please. My face is everywhere in this city. They wouldn't be able to go two blocks before someone recognized me." She scoffed, twirled her hand about, palm up, fingers with a slight curl. "And, do you think Vanessa is going to mind a couple of bl—officers getting killed? I'm sorry people you knew were hurt, but I don't have any control over what my mother does."

He squinted. "That doesn't seem—"

"Plausible? Really? Do you even know what she's like? How many 'criminals' get executed for *probably* being the people that are wanted? Look at me with a straight face and tell me she'd lose a nanosecond of sleep over a couple of dead officers. Her staged kidnapping almost got *me* shot in the head, and that didn't bother her at all. I wasn't supposed to be *actually* removed from the apartment. The security detail was *supposed* to kill the terrorists who showed up. We exposed two Brigade people who'd infiltrated the Authority. The whole thing was a set up to lure them out. Considering how badly things screwed up, it's a miracle it worked."

He let his rifle fall slack at his side. "Damn."

Maya softened her tone. "Look, I'm not like her, but I'm not going to tolerate having a gun pointed at me in my own home. I'm sorry your friends were hurt, but don't make me tell Vanessa you gave me a hard time... Officer Quinones."

"So they just planted you back in here like nothing happened?" He shook his head. "Everything okay? Are you okay?"

"Yes. I'm fine. You can go." Maya fell into the chair, gaze down.

The blueberry glanced around the kitchen, seemed satisfied, and walked out. A few seconds before the door hissed closed, he muttered, "Secure."

Maya draped herself over the table and exhaled. *That was too close.* Once she caught her breath, she hurried to her bedroom to grab the bag and carried it to Vanessa's room. At the back of the woman's closet, a small door led into a sub-closet where a handful of lab coats hung on a rack in front of a metal cabinet door.

She pulled the small fridge open and grinned at glass shelves with medicine samples. She gasped at a ten-pack of Fade vaccinations, unable to help herself but read the box. The label confirmed one application was good for life.

Exposure to Fade after a vac shot worked like a re-inoculation. The people at *home* could use that, so into the bag it went. The cabinet only had three bottles of Xenodril tablets, and everything else in there consisted of either dangerous vanity meds or mildly useful things like diarrhea cures.

The pills rattled as she dropped the three bottles of Xeno into the bag. Even if they couldn't get anything out of Parkville, she'd make sure Ashley and the others at that Fade Ward got Xeno. Maya headed out to the hallway and stared at the living room for a few minutes, debating between going barefoot or wearing heels. Neither seemed like a good idea. Heels would slow her down and a girl her age in them would attract attention, increasing the chances of someone recognizing her. Until she reached the prison, that would be bad. She pulled off the sweater and ran back to the laundry machine to reclaim the black tee shirt Diego gave her. Maya Oman would never wear something like that, but at least the basic black matched her leggings. The nightdress went into the bag too. She'd still need it for sleeping.

The sweater almost went flying, but she couldn't bring herself to chuck cashmere. The bag had room.

Maya took one final look around the place and didn't feel anything but a twinge of fear at the memory of Moth threatening her with a gun. The only emotions the walls here held included that terror, loneliness, and anger at being a prisoner. She padded to the elevator and hit the button.

"Maya, you do not have permission to go outside."

Shit. The same thing it always said. She *was* really locked in. A fist pound on the button repeated the same message. Blind want for her real mother triggered a frenetic button mashing fit that accomplished nothing.

"Maya, you do not have permission to go outside. Please behave yourself."

She fumed while pacing in circles for a few minutes before getting an idea and storming over to the patio door, which opened. She pulled it aside and walked out onto warm, wet concrete. A loop of a ladder came up and over the edge on the far side of the helipad. Maya ran to it and caught herself on the bars while peering over. The thin ladder led down three stories to a sub-roof littered with boxy machines and ventilation ports. Near the base of the ladder, a plain grey door stood next to a card-reader box. No other ladder seemed to exist, meaning the only way down without a helicopter would be free-falling ninety stories. She glared at the Ascendant office tower less than two miles away, a spire of white and cyan stabbing the clouds. Maya hated every panel of glass in the place.

"No…" She sniffled. "No. Mom…"

She ran inside, bag bouncing against her back, and skidded to a halt in front of the elevator. Lying to people was easy, but to an AI? What possible excuse... She dropped the bag and hurried to Vanessa's bedroom. A quick climb and shimmy down the vents brought her once again to the office. Since no one had kicked in the door and hauled her away, the terminal lockdown had to be a local failsafe triggered by extra security on those specific files that blocked them from being added to an e-mail.

She crept up to the desk and poked the terminal, almost jumping up and down and clapping when it presented a password prompt. The recorder lay on the rug where she'd dropped it yesterday, and the spliced verbal password once again let her in to the system.

I'm an idiot. I should've done this first.

Her hands moved like an orchestral conductor from screen to screen. In the scheduling and appointment calendar, she created an entry for a public relations/goodwill photo shoot at the Arlington Rehabilitation Center where they held Genna, and set it for noon. Two seconds after she hit save, a text message popped up.

‹Nice.›

She stared at the black box with white letters.

‹It's ZI. I'm in. Still want help?›

Tears of joy gathered at the corners of her eyes. She typed 'yes,' but the letters didn't appear anywhere.

‹C U there. Saw what you did with the Xeno. I buried the prod.ctl file a little deeper and spoofed the source to a terminal in the plant. That should keep anyone from noticing.›

Maya blinked, and typed, ‹ok, thx!›

She locked the terminal and ran out, not bothering to secure the door. At the elevator, she grabbed her bag, slung it over her shoulder, and pushed the button.

"Maya, for the last time, you are not—"

"I've got a photo session today. Mother can't make it... again." She tried to sound annoyed. "I'm going down to meet the driver."

"Appointment confirmed." The elevator slid open.

She hopped in before it could change its mind and poked the button for the parking garage. The elevator felt too much like a jail cell for her liking over the next two minutes. She shivered by the time the doors opened, though that could've been from the frigid floor and overpowered air-conditioning.

The parking deck held the summer warmth and chased away the shakes.

She kept her head down and walked straight to the exit ramp. Daylight made getting spotted more likely, though she didn't look like a ragamuffin anymore and would blend in like any other Citizen kid, unless someone questioned her lack of shoes. Two cross streets later, she joined a line waiting for a NBSZ Transit bus. The post-commuter crowd was thin, and only a few people took notice of her.

"Morning," said a man.

She didn't look up. "Hi. I'm not supposed to talk to strangers."

"Fair enough." He edged away.

For about ten minutes, she stood at the curb, fidgeting with the bag strap, wobbling her knee, and trying to force time to move faster with her mind. Eventually, a white-and-cyan bus labeled 'New Baltimore Sanctuary Zone Transit' rolled up and stopped with a wash of hot air that rolled over her feet. She hopped on, hurried to a side-facing seat about halfway down, and pulled her computer out of the bag. With the screen opened all the way, it took on the shape of a tablet, and she used it to hide her face as much as open a map of the Sanc. She plotted a route to the prison complex, pulled up the bus's travel path, and superimposed them. They called it a rehabilitation center... probably the same way they called the Fade area an 'integration' ward. She frowned.

The bus drove on. Every so often, someone waved or smiled at her. Maya had to work to hide her nerves and sound disinterested with each "hello" or admonition about talking to strangers. It took twenty-eight minutes for the bus to reach the closest point on its circular route to the Arlington Rehabil—prison.

Maya hopped off on another street lined with high-rise buildings and advertising banners. At twenty after eleven, the food carts had begun to emerge from wherever they hid in anticipation of a legion of office drones seeking safe haven from the horribleness of their cafeteria food. Since anyone could eat whatever they wanted and fix anything with a pill (that had a one-in-sixty chance of killing them), unhealthy food abounded. Most of it smelled nauseating. Maya spun in place until the navigation client in the computer figured out which way she faced, then set off at a fast walk.

Two weeks ago, if anyone told her she'd have to *walk* three-point-one miles, she'd have pitched a whining, screaming fit. Compared to the eleven or so she'd managed to the Spread, the trip to the prison would be nothing. While on the warm side, the constant fresh (ish) breeze and clear sky made being outside pleasant. If not for the weight of what she planned to do on her mind, she might've thought it fun.

Perhaps looking like she knew where she was going and not seeming lost or scared kept people from bothering her. Perhaps no one gave a shit. Maya didn't care why. This designer body of hers took to physical activity far faster than she'd imagined possible. She stopped at red lights, darted across a few intersections, and followed the little arrow on her handheld computer. Around 11:48, the high-rises gave way to a one-block area where an imposing white building with narrow barred windows took up most of the space, plus its yard.

Maya leaned her head back and stared at the clouds until an onrush of nerves subsided. "Okay. It's show time."

THIRTY- SIX
THE GRAND TOUR

aya ducked into the closest alley, out of sight from the street, and stripped down to her underpants. She stuffed the t-shirt and leggings into the bag before pulling out the shiny teal dress and wriggling into it. After wiping sand and grit off her feet, she stepped into the sparkly, matching high-heeled shoes. While squatting over the bag, she rummaged a small makeup case. A dash of teal eye shadow, a tweak of indigo mascara, and a quick swipe of bright green lipstick later, she repacked everything and zipped the bag closed.

She stood for a moment fussing with her hair, pulling it as straight as she could with only her fingers for a comb. *Blueberries won't care.* With her nylon bag perched on her shoulder like a special operations commando's version of a purse, Maya strutted out into view, heading for the front gates of the prison compound. Halfway across the street, she cringed at forgetting the white elbow-length gloves and earrings that went with that dress, but she'd gone too far to go back now. And again, the blueberries wouldn't notice her fashion crime.

When she arrived at the front gate, she stopped and glanced around with a faux-irritated scowl, tapping her foot. A camera overhead swiveled toward her. Maya looked left and right at the empty road, gestured in a frustrated wave, and performed an exaggerated eye roll before storming past the gate and crossing the prison's courtyard.

She headed for the door labeled 'visitor center.' By the time she reached it, three Authority Officers in cloth jumpsuits had come outside bearing expressions of confusion and worry. Maya took deep breaths in her nose. *I can do this. I acted like a robot with that caveman pointing a giant gun at my face. I let a fu—Mom doesn't want me saying that one—damn roach crawl on my foot without freaking. I can do this.*

Maya walked up to them, keeping her fear in a tight little ball at the bottom of her gut, and glared at their nameplates. "Of *course* they're all late. Has anyone else gotten here yet?"

"Uhh," said Officer Cole. "Miss?"

"Unbel*iev*able." Maya let off a heavy sigh. "I get dragged out of bed at six thirty in the morning." She shook clenched fists on either side of her head. "Everyone's nagging the crap out of me, worried that I'm going to be late, and no one else is here? Screw this. I'm going home. One of you get me a car."

"What's going on?" asked Officer Edwards. "Miss Oman?"

"Oh, great. That figures. Let me guess, no one in marketing bothered to tell you?" She waved her arms about with emphatic gestures while continuing to rant. "There's supposed to be some kind of public relations thing here. One of the nitwits in PR came up with this *great* idea. I'm supposed to smile and pose with your staff and maybe a low-risk inmate or two. Better make sure they're trustworthy. If something happens to me, Vanessa is going to want asses."

"Maybe we could get a few of the guys to put on the orange instead," said Cole. "That way, there's no chance of anything going wrong."

"There's too many people out there going over every image to twist things out of control. They'll see an officer's face on a supposed prisoner and go crazy." Maya shook her head. "Andy said he found one woman here who's in for stealing food. Helps she's photogenic too. She looked kinda scary, but you can keep me safe."

"Who?" asked Edwards.

Maya blinked and pressed her free hand to her chest. "You're asking *me?* How should I know who you've got shut up in here? I saw a goddamned picture for three seconds. No one told me her damn name. How many dark-skinned women *do* you have on food theft charges? They said she was picked up like a week ago. All I know is she's got fat dreads with a bunch of beads and shit in them."

They muttered amongst themselves about how best to deal with this situation. It sounded too much like they wanted to verify everything first.

"Hey. Since you guys need time, and none of the idiots are here yet..." She softened her expression to a childish smile. "Can I have a tour? I've never seen the inside of a Rehabilitation Center before. You must be pretty brave to be around bad guys all the time. Maybe this ad campaign will make people sign up to be officers."

"Cole," said Edwards. "You're it."

The look on the man's face could've melted steel. He probably considered it gambling with his career, freedom, or even life to interact with the daughter of Vanessa Oman directly. He forced a pleasant smile and opened the door for her. Oh, if only she could've put that fear into Baxter when he'd hit Sarah.

Maya walked in, nose in the air, looking around as if she owned the place and everyone in it. Her heels *clicked*, echoing off the walls. "It's cleaner than I expected."

"Oh, yeah. Part of the rehabilitation process is instilling a good work ethic in the detainees. We don't have cleaning staff. The detainees do it."

Officer Cole ignored a case full of plaques and awards and headed for a hallway three-quarters white with a dark grey strip closer to the floor. The facility looked like a hospital... with bars. Motivational nonsense slogans appeared every few feet like: "This is not the destination but the start," "Your future is in your hands," and "Opportunity is everywhere." Officer Cole led her to a room at the distant end, a few feet away from an airlock-style security gate composed of thick bars. She doubted even Moth could have broken it. A tremble caused her to wobble on her raised heels. The mere sight of such a barrier made Genna seem so much farther away. Maya shivered, clueless what she'd do if the blueberries didn't go for the posing with inmates thing...

Cole pushed the door open and came close to touching her back to guide her in. He pulled his hand away from her like a hot stove and smiled. Maya stepped in, acting impressed by a plain grey-walled room covered in large monitor screens. A weary-looking man in his early thirties and a drab blue jumpsuit sat behind a complicated console. Other than a baton, he didn't appear to be armed.

The man looked over. "What the hell is this? Little young for soliciting."

"I'm in a good mood today," said Maya. "I won't tell Vanessa that you just called me a prostitute. One more like that and you'll be scraping shit out of the Fade ward toilets."

"Uhh, watch it, Paulie. This is M.O."

"No shit. What's she doing here?" He returned his attention to the console.

Images on the larger wall-mounted screens cycled among inmate cells, viewed from ceiling-mounted cameras. The rooms looked tiny, one person per holding cell. All wore bright orange smocks and plastic shoes. Some paced, some slept, a few pleasured themselves in flagrant disregard of the cameras, and three happened to be on the toilet.

"Some kind of recruiting PR campaign. Just waiting on the rest of the circus to get here. Miss Oman requested a tour."

Paulie shrugged. "Mmm."

"This is one of four control stations in the facility," said Cole. "From here, we can monitor everything that goes on in Pod C. Cameras, door security, everything. We can even flush their toilets." He chuckled.

Pod C! Mom is in C! "Wow." She went wide-eyed and leaned over the console. "That's amazing."

The screens on the desk in front of Captain Drab showed maps of this quarter of the building, overlaid with status indicators for the various locks on cell doors and mid-hallway gates. Other onscreen widgets adjusted climate control, lights, alarms, tranquilizer gas, and fire-suppression systems. She looked up with a false grin. Before she could say something vapid like 'that's so cool,' Genna appeared on one of the large monitors hanging from the wall, sitting on the side of a prison bed with her head in her hands. Though no tears showed apparent, her body language said enough.

After four seconds, the image changed to a huge man doing pushups.

"Can you go back on that screen?" Maya pointed.

Paulie tapped at the console and Genna reappeared.

Maya studied the image. The sight of her mother looking so hopeless stabbed her like a knife in the chest, but she kept her voice sounding normal. "I'm sure that's the woman I was supposed to take pictures with. Andy said she was determined no threat. She looks sad. Can I go talk to her?"

"Isn't that the one they think's with the Brigade?" Paulie tapped at one of the screens and a familiar record came up. "Huh? Food theft? Hah. Guess she's got a rich daddy or thick knee pads. I could swear she's the one Lewis said tried to shoot her."

"Do you believe anything a pilot says? Lewis didn't seem confident on the lineup." Cole shrugged. "Not my call. I am not risking my ass on cheering up some Orange who's feeling sorry for themselves. They should've thought about that before they did whatever. Paulie, watch her a sec will ya? Gotta hit the head."

Cole scooted out before the man could finish yelling, "Don't you dare."

Maya's chest tightened with panic. It could be a matter of minutes before everything fell to pieces. She had to do something *now*. Console. Screens. Fire extinguisher. Armory cabinet. Bathroom. *Whoa.* She looked at the metal door on the wall labeled 'Armory.'

"What's that do?" She pointed at a red button on the console.

"Nothing you need to worry about. Go sit down and keep quiet." Paulie didn't bother looking at her and gestured at a bench under the monitors, right in front of his desk.

She bit back the urge to make a snide remark and walked around to the seat. He seemed not to pay the least bit of attention to her. A change of light on his face and chest gave away that he'd switched screens as soon as she couldn't see anymore. *Hopefully, it's porn and he's not paying any attention to me…*

Maya edged sideways to the armory cabinet. It had a simple ring-latch that didn't seem capable of locking. Perhaps they relied on the heavy magnet on the entrance to this room instead. Then again, it would kinda suck to need a gun *now* during a prison riot and have to fumble with keys or an access code. She kept her gaze locked on Paulie, reached up, stuck one finger in, and pulled the door open.

Five handguns perched on a metal rack between two shotguns set vertical against either side. Below the pistols, several red boxes contained .40 caliber ammo. Below the ammo, five yellow and black Hornet stunners stuck out of charging sockets. After a glance back to make sure Paulie still hadn't noticed her, Maya tugged one of the stunners out and tucked it up behind her back. *I need to thank Sarah's dad.* She picked at one of the ammo boxes until it popped open and dumped fifty bullets all over the ground.

"God dammit, kid!" yelled Paulie. "Get out of that!"

She took a step back, keeping the Hornet out of sight, and did her best impression of a demanding brat. "*I* wanted a tour and *you* aren't showing me anything."

Paulie grumbled and got out of the chair. He stormed over, wagging his finger at her. "Sit your little butt on that chair and don't move."

Maya feigned a gasp of offended shock.

He took a knee and started to collect the loose bullets.

"You shouldn't yell at me," said Maya. She flicked the selector switch to touch mode.

"I don't care who you are." Paulie didn't look up. "Just a spoiled little—"

Brzzzat!

Maya held the tip of the Hornet to the side of Paulie's neck for three seconds. He thrashed about in a violent convulsion before flopping as still as a corpse, though he did continue breathing. The odor of shit reached her nostrils seconds later, making her gag and step back.

"Well." She glanced at the Hornet, wisps of smoke rising from the prongs.

"Guess this is Plan B."

THIRTY-SEVEN
MOTHER

aya dropped the Hornet and ran to the security desk. Ignoring the chair, she looked back and forth across the controls until she found a standard terminal screen. Fortunately, whatever Paulie had done to change the one monitor back to Genna's cell had taken it off random cycling and she remained visible. Her hands shook so much she had trouble typing, but after a few false starts, she keyed a line of text and hit enter.

‹Headcrash was fucked in the head.›

A chat box popped up.

Maya looked at the image of Genna and typed BSZ-99401, the number printed on her jumpsuit.

Zeroice sent back ‹searching.›

She breathed into her hands for a few seconds, trying to think of what to do next. None of the blueberries had come back yet, which likely meant they hadn't been able to confirm the photo shoot and a series of video calls would be making the rounds among a rather stunned Ascendant marketing team. They would probably all have panic attacks when they saw a calendar event created by Vanessa—not one of her assistants—that they hadn't noticed before. It might be as long as an hour before someone had the balls to ask Vanessa's executive assistant about it. Maya could not be here when that happened.

And by here, she meant in the Sanc.

She ran-wobbled on high heels back to the armory cabinet and pulled down one of the real guns, a lot heavier than she thought it would be. It had a button that looked like the one that popped the ammo out of the Hornet, and sure enough, it turned out to be the magazine release. She hit it, nodded at the loaded mag, and slid it back until it clicked.

Shit. What am I doing?

She carried the gun back to the console and clutched it like a doll while watching the text box for any sign of life. Nausea came and went, as did shivers. According to the console clock, only forty-six seconds had passed, but it felt like hours.

Text pattered into the window: ‹Got her. One sec. Dicking with the security cameras.›

Maya bit her knuckles. ‹How do I get there?›

More text: ‹Out. Turn left. Take second left. Take next right. Sixth cell on the left. Will open in one minute… starting now.›

She picked up the gun and crept to the exit. The door out of the security room buzzed at her approach. Maya pulled her shoes off before darting into the corridor. Neither loud clicking nor breaking an ankle while running appealed to her. Five feet from the door, the first heavy security barrier emitted a buzz and slid open. She slipped past as soon as the gap grew wide enough. When it closed, trapping her in a small space between barred walls, she almost fainted. Before panic could grow to that point, the inner door buzzed and rattled open.

Maya sprinted out and rounded the second left turn into an off-white corridor filled with plain metal doors bearing tiny rectangular windows at an adult's eye level. A pushcart piled high with dirty food trays sat against the wall. She dipped around it and headed for a right turn a few yards later. At the sixth door on the left, she stopped. It struck her that holding a gun in the middle of a prison would probably not rank on her list of smart accomplishments. She tucked it under her dress and held it between her thighs. Not four seconds after she smoothed the dress down to cover it, a blueberry emerged from a hallway deeper in and came walking up to her. She pivoted to face him and keep her back to the wall, knowing the gun's handle would be sticking her dress out behind her.

The officer rushed over. "What the hell are you doing—?"

"I am having a tour." She held her nose high. "Officer Cole told me to wait here because he had to piss."

"Oh." He gave her a wary look while raising one hand to hide his nametag. "Okay."

Maya exhaled once he walked away. The Xenodril tablets in her bag rattled as she drooped.

"Maya?" whispered Genna. "Is that you out there? Am I going nuts?"

"Mom." Maya put her hand on the door. "Mom... I'm here." She started to cry.

"What the devil are you doing in this place, baby?" Plastic shoes scuffed around, pacing in the cell.

Maya pawed at the door without handles. All the dread she'd felt at possibly losing her mom crashed into the joy of their almost-reunion, blooming into a furball of emotion stronger than anything she knew how to cope with. Maya couldn't force a single word out of her throat and emitted a pitiful whine, never having hated anything before as much as this inch-thick steel door. Tears grabbed her mascara and ran off with it. Indigo spots pattered on the pure white floor around her feet.

Buzz.

The cell door slid to the left, gliding into the wall. Genna fell on her knees and grabbed her by the shoulders for two seconds of eye contact before crushing her into a hug. It took all she had, but Maya fought the urge to break down sobbing.

"W-we gotta go," mumbled Maya.

"What the hell are you doing here?"

"You already said that." Maya sniffled. "I brought you something."

Genna swallowed and wiped her nose. "You look adorable."

Maya pulled her dress up.

"God damn." Genna grabbed the pistol, checked to ensure it had a round chambered, and stuffed it into the pocket on the front of her prison-orange jumpsuit.

"Try to act calm." Maya sniffled. "They think I'm here to take publicity photos with a well-behaved inmate."

She took Genna by the hand and pulled her back the way she'd come in, holding her breath until the airlock gate opened and let them out. Zeroice had to be monkeying with cameras and security doors, keeping blueberries away from them. Only the front reception area stood between them and the outside world.

Officer Cole emerged from the security room. "Command, we got a situation here. Paulie's down, there's a weapon missing, and the VIP is gone."

He turned three shades paler when he looked up and spotted them.

"I found the prisoner I'm supposed to take pictures with." Maya tried to smile, but her voice had too much cry in it.

Cole raised his left hand. His right crawled toward his sidearm. "Easy."

Genna scooped Maya up and pressed the gun into the side of her head. "Don't."

Maya hung limp, not fighting. "Please don't shoot me."

She'd directed the comment at Cole, but Genna's arm tensed.

Cole raised both hands. "Think about what you're doing, Orange. You know who that is? You pluck one hair from that head and you're ass is meat."

"Back up. Toss the gun in there." Genna nodded at the security room. "Ain't no one need to get hurt here."

Maya reached both hands up and gripped the arm across her chest. It didn't matter that Genna had a gun to her head; her *mother* held her. She lost control and sobbed out of joy. The blueberry and Genna took the outburst in two entirely different ways. Genna secreted a kiss to the back of Maya's head while Cole looked clueless.

He threw his sidearm into the security room and backed up while yelling, "Okay, okay."

They moved in a slow creep to the visitor center lobby where she had first entered. Cole kept his hands in the air as they passed the empty desk and deserted lounge chairs.

Maya sniffled and blinked. "Please do what she wants. You can catch her later, but you can't fix me if I die."

"Think about it, Orange. There's no way you're getting out of here with that kid."

"Let me go," said Maya. "Do you have any idea what that woman is gonna do to you?"

Genna pointed the gun at him. "Cuff yourself to that desk. That woman don't give a damn about this girl."

Cole's eyebrows notched up. "It *was* you on the roof. You're one of the mercs who grabbed her."

"That pilot cadet's got some imagination." Genna kept the gun on him.

"Yeah, well." Cole smiled. "Calling someone a damn murdering coward while you're trying to shoot them in the back tends to leave a mark."

"Cuff yourself or I gonna do somethin' more permanent."

"I saw the fallout report. I know what went down." He looked at Maya. "Amazing. We thought you'd been killed out in the mud pits. How did you even get back into the Sanc undetected? You've got a lousy poker face, kid." Cole flopped in the chair and pulled cuffs from his belt. "Worst case of Stockholm I've ever seen. It almost seems like you're really happier with her."

"Vanessa doesn't want me," whispered Maya. "Genna's my mom."

"Yeah." Cole locked himself to the desk. "She is a bit on the cold side."

"Just a bit," said Genna.

"You go out that door and it's a one way trip, Maya. No more power. No more servants. No more easy life. Make sure it's what you want."

"I'm sure." She tried to pull her mother's arm even tighter against her chest.

"That was fast," said Cole.

"'Cause it's real." Genna lowered the gun. "We out."

"Authority used to enforce the law. Now you only do what Vanessa wants." Maya looked down. "I don't think you're *all* bad. When are you going to stand up to her? She's killing people."

Maya held on as Genna ran, carrying her down a short corridor, the nylon bag bouncing and clattering. She rushed down a shallow staircase and out tinted glass doors—into the sights of ten blueberries with rifles trained on them. Maya whimpered when the gun jabbed her in the side of the head again.

The Authority officers aimed in silence. Genna's hard breathing puffed down the right side of Maya's neck. No one spoke or moved for almost a minute, until a shimmering cloud of light formed a few feet in front of the line of armored figures.

A hologram of Vanessa Oman materialized, in a low cut violet evening gown. The image made her look over six feet tall, but thin. The two women seemed to stare at each other for an eternity before Vanessa's purple-painted lips twisted into an amused smirk.

"Well, well. You're still alive."

"Sorry to disappoint you." Maya glared.

Vanessa sighed. "I was talking to the criminal holding you. Oh, Maya. You mistake my refusal to be manipulated with the want to harm you. I hope that someday you realize I did what I had to do in order to protect everything we have. You are too young and too naïve. You will learn how the world works eventually."

"She don't want your blood money," said Genna.

Maya glared. "If you wanted me, you'd have answered the phone when I called to say good night. You'd have talked to me. You'd have not left me alone all the time locked in that apartment. You might've even *had* me as a baby instead of ordering me like a pizza! You called me an *it!*"

Vanessa pursed her lips, foot tapping. The line of blueberries shifted, exchanging fearful looks.

"Emotions are a weakness to be exploited," said Vanessa, eyes narrowing. "There are too many people out there who present a threat."

Genna glared. "So you keep your own damn kid out of sight so ya don't bond? That ain't even human."

"No!" yelled Maya. "I'm not her kid. *You're* my mom!"

Vanessa sighed, glancing at her watch. "I don't care who you are or what you want. I don't have time to deal with yet another 'crisis.' Whatever you did before, surrender now and you won't die." She held up a silencing finger. "Before you bore me with the whole threatening nonsense, the child is easy enough to replace." The image flickered, performing a 180-degree turn in an eye blink. "Give her four seconds, then fire. I'd appreciate it if you at least tried to aim around the girl and save the cost of having another one grown."

The illusion of Vanessa Oman disappeared.

Genna let her gun arm fall limp.

Maya gulped. "I guess she doesn't want to watch this time."

"No, baby. She knows I ain't gonna risk it."

THIRTY-EIGHT
MOVING VIOLATIONS

The Authority officers exchanged bewildered glances. Vanessa's order had appeared to sow confusion among their ranks, and they hesitated. Six seconds passed with no one doing anything. Genna's body shuddered with a tremble too faint to see. One blueberry let his weapon droop an inch, evidently unwilling to fire through a little girl.

Maya squirmed around to face Genna and grabbed her in as tight a hug as her arms could manage while sobbing. "Please don't kill us. You heard Vanessa. She doesn't want me. Please just let us leave." Words failed her and she succumbed to incoherent bawling.

Genna rubbed her back, muttering comforting things. "You win. I'ma put her down and back off. No bullshit. Don't shoot."

"No!" yelled Maya. "Mom!"

"I'm sorry, baby." Genna squeezed her. "I can't let them hurt you. Better you be with that bitch and alive than dead with me."

Maya held on with everything she had as her mother tried to put her down. She wrapped her legs around Genna and clutched fistfuls of prison orange.

The whirr of a straining e-car motor accompanied the squeal of tires. Maya screamed when a few rifle shots rang out, but felt no pain. Genna lurched into a sprint amid the scratch of plasticized armor striking the ground and skittering.

Hands that had been trying to pry Maya away clamped down tight, cradling her like a football going into the end zone. She kept her eyes closed and screamed until Genna tore her loose and threw her flat on the back seat of a mid-sized car. Maya looked up at a tan roof with a faltering dome light. A bullet clanked off the car somewhere unseen. Genna draped herself between the two front seats, looming over her, aiming the handgun out the back window, but none of the blueberries fired on the car. She rocked with inertia as the vehicle took off. Two turns later, Genna startled and raised the gun.

A shot deafened her. Maya rolled onto the floor, hands clamped over her ears. Genna's next two shots sounded far away and underwater. Maya curled up with her head between her legs, adding her knees to the effort of keeping sound out of her ears. Fragments of safety glass rained on her like snow. Genna flew out of sight during a sudden deceleration, and let off a barrage of curses from the front seat.

Maya skidded ass-first toward the passenger side door and thrust her feet out to absorb the effect of a hard left turn. Bullets holed the door above her head and sprayed her in the face with upholstery foam. She screamed again, too terrified to think.

Genna reappeared and fired three more times. Seconds later, an explosion from overhead pounded the air. "Damned drones."

After thirty seconds of relative calm, Maya risked sitting up. Genna balanced on one knee between the two front seats, spinning around in a 360 while the car drove itself. The back window as well as the windscreen had been blown out, letting a stiff wind tear through the interior. Distant sirens echoed among the buildings.

Maya smiled. "Mom."

"I can't believe—"

The e-car slammed on the brakes without warning, driving Genna's back into the console for a second time. Maya rolled against the passenger seatback and bounced away to the floor. An Authority patrol car zoomed sideways past the nose and crashed into the window of a jewelry store. Their car peeled out, throwing Genna head first into the back seat.

"I'm gonna fuckin' kill someone." She reached a chicken wing arm up behind her back and rubbed. "That hurt."

"We almost got t-boned," said Maya. "Are they trying to kill us?"

"Probably not; crash foam... but I bet they past the point of givin' a crap." Genna pushed herself up. "We gotta get underground. Drones are gonna be all over our shit. Already shot one down."

She dropped the handgun on the driver seat and stripped out of the jumpsuit, revealing a plain black bra and panties. Genna wadded the incriminating day-glo orange thing up before jamming it into the glove compartment.

"What are you...?" Maya blinked. "Doing?"

"Tracker chips sewn into it everywhere. Plus it's bright goddamned orange. Doesn't go with my eyes."

Maya giggled despite tears.

"Does your mother know you're wearing that?" Genna poked her in the stomach. "You don't got anything to show off with a neckline like that."

"My *mother* is looking at me right now." Maya pulled the dress off and rolled it up.

"Cover your ears." Genna pointed the gun at the back window again.

Two shots sent another Authority car skidding into a mass of parked vehicles.

"Are there more?" yelled Maya.

"Yeah, but I can't see 'em."

Maya opened the bag and wriggled into her tee shirt and leggings before packing the expensive teal thing and the heels inside.

"Got anything my size in there?" Genna smiled.

"Vanessa didn't have anything except a Cailliermo skirt suit and a couple of Dori Kavan evening gowns. Not your size."

"Figures. She looks that cheap."

"Cheap?" Maya blinked at her. "That's a joke, right?"

Drone fan whirr tone-shifted as they shot under one. Genna leaned out the driver's side window and fired three times into the air. Maya whirled around to look back. A spray of .50 caliber ammo tore up the side of an office building in the midst of an out of control spiral that ended with the drone smashing upside down on the road and exploding in blue flames.

The car squealed, tail end swinging out as it skidded into a right turn. Buildings around them got shorter and farther apart, the area taking on the aesthetic of an industrial section. Maya clamped on to her bag to keep it from flying out the window. Maybe Zeroice wanted to bring them to the reservoir area where she'd come in. Another moment later, it swerved to the side of the street and stopped.

"Who or what is driving this thing?" asked Genna.

"Zeroice." Maya pulled herself up from the floor. "I think he wants us to get out."

"Who?"

"Alfonse?" asked Maya.

"Who the hell is that?" Genna ducked and aimed up at the sky, but didn't fire.

"Headcrash had a friend." Maya clung to her bag.

The car horn tooted once.

"He can hear us." Maya smiled. "He probably heard you say tracker, so he's going to drive it around and lead them away."

The horn tooted again.

"Right on." Genna got out. She looked down at her plastic-baggy shoes. "I feel ridiculous."

Whirring, like a swarm of a million locusts, echoed from everywhere.

Maya climbed out and pointed at an alley. "They're coming. Run!"

Genna picked her up and rushed into the shadows. Drones and Authority cars blurred past the mouth of the alley but none of them followed. The distancing rattle of a heavy machinegun preceded metallic *clanks* and squealing tires. A heavy metal crash that could've been a car or drone made Maya jump, but the shooting continued.

They kept going for a few minutes before Genna hooked a right and slowed to walk out on a congested street filled with rickety booths built in the shadow of the Sanctuary Zone's exterior wall. Maya squirmed around to look in front. This close, the gargantuan barrier made her feel insignificant and tiny. Fabric and plastic in an array of reds, greens, and white clung to pipe frames or thick ropes. The aroma of spiced rat meat mixed with the burnt-silicon smell of an electric stove pushed past its prime drifted by on a mild uptick in the breeze. Some of the stalls sold trinkets, handmade (and probably deadly) moonshine, or street food. They appeared to be a higher-class version of the unfortunates who lived in plastiboard boxes out in the Dead Space. Maybe the Authority didn't care about what went on in the outermost reaches of the Citizen's city. More likely, these people didn't have anything worth taking, and kept far enough out of everyone's way that the Authority overlooked them.

"Open the bag," said Genna.

Maya complied.

Genna stashed the pistol and closed the zipper before taking her hand again. The locals in the street market regarded them with curiosity. A few people clapped at Genna's exhibitionism, but she didn't slow down or react in the least, even to the men who offered her a couple NuCoin to take her underwear off or flash them. She followed the slight curve of the road past four streets leading back into the city. Eventually, Genna ducked into the ground floor of an abandoned building at the deepest part of a dead end crammed with pitiful shanty shelters. Maya held on, content to be carried across a wide-open room past piles of debris that used to be walls. At the back corner, they descended a flight of stairs to a basement full of tattered strips of unidentifiable material dangling from the ceiling, casting hundreds of scary shadows.

Maya shivered.

At the corner opposite the stairs, Genna twisted a water valve on an old pipe. A *click* came from the wall, and a patch of cinderblocks opened outward revealing a room about the same size as the prison cell, but it offered concealment rather than hopelessness. She set Maya down on a dingy brown cot and pulled the heavy door closed. Weak light filtered in from a street level window too small for even Maya to fit through. Genna's plastic shoes rustled in the stillness. She edged over and sat beside Maya.

Genna lay back, feet still on the floor, and covered her face in both hands. "You shoulda gone home. You be happier with all that money."

"No." Maya cuddled up to her. "Home is out there."

"You coulda got yo'self killed." Genna ran her hand down Maya's back in a repetitive, soothing motion. "Didn't anyone try to stop you?"

"Yeah, everyone. I snuck out. Sarah's going to be mad at me for scaring her."

"Try an' rest. We hide here a bit. Give shit a chance ta settle down, then we move." Genna let out a long sigh.

"Mom," whispered Maya, sniffling as tears came on. "You're alive."

Genna gave in to crying as well. "Yeah. Surprise the shit outta me too."

They wept, clinging to each other, for a while. In the subsequent silence, Maya stared past Genna's stomach, rising and falling with her breaths, at the darkness. She mulled over her anger toward Vanessa, her disgust at all the suffering the woman caused, and tasted victory in one tiny thought.

Maya snuggled tighter to Genna's side. Vanessa would never know what it felt like to have someone willing to do *anything* to help them.

PART V
UPRISING

THIRTY-NINE
A MOMENT OF REST

aya awoke to a hand under her shirt, tickling her stomach. She squirmed and made a weak groan of protest at being conscious. A 'shh' washed over her hair. Maya opened her eyes to an impenetrable black void. Only knowing she curled up at Genna's side kept her from losing control to fear. Despite the darkness, she nodded.

Seconds later, she felt stupid and whispered, "'Kay."

Genna withdrew her hand out from under Maya's shirt and patted up her front until she found her shoulder.

"It's all right," whispered Genna. "Heard some people in the basement."

Maya sat up and wiped sleep crumbs away from her eyes.

"So." Genna pulled Maya onto her lap. "You found a net pirate?"

"By accident. He helped me." She explained her odyssey of smuggling hacker drugs to get into the city.

Genna pulled her close, unable to speak for a good few minutes. "Baby... you should'a stayed safe. Damn miracle you didn't get your ass shot off."

"I'm sorry." Maya sniffled.

"Flyin' on a damn drone..." Genna sighed. "I don't wanna think how bad that coulda gone."

"I had to find you." Maya sniffled. Her voice broke down to cry-speak. "They... they were gonna kill you. That guy was on vacation or they would've..." She clung, sobbing again.

"Vacation? Hey, baby, it's all right. Shh. I'm here."

A few minutes went by before Maya collected herself enough to speak. She explained about the Authority's delay since they couldn't tell 'for sure' about

Brigade involvement. If not for that one person being away to give approval...

Genna shivered. "Well, don't do anything like that again."

"'Kay," she muttered. "Don't get arrested again."

"Heh. Ain't on my list of shit to do, but I don' want you doin' no more stupid shit on account o' me. Better you be alive and lonely than dead, somethin' happens ta me."

"Well, don't let anything happen to you."

Genna fumbled around with something. Pills rattled, and an instant later, the bag pressed into Maya's chest. "Here. Hold that. Now, spill it."

"Spill the bag?"

"No, silly girl." Genna ruffled her hair. "I mean tell me everything."

"He's in a hotel called the Emerald Oasis."

"You dodgin' my question. How did you go from safe in our building to walking into a damn Authority prison?"

"If I tell you what I did, you're going to be mad at me."

Genna leaned her to the side and planted two playful smacks on her butt. "There. Consider yourself punished ahead of time."

Maya laughed, gasped, and covered her mouth. "Sorry."

"Probably don't need ta be so quiet." She stood and set Maya down standing on cold concrete.

"Well... Barnes said it was too dangerous to try and save you."

"He was right." Genna muttered several curse words over the sound of her patting the wall. "Aha!" A jigsaw slab of cinderblock opened. Outside, the abandoned basement crawled with shadows cast in the light leaking in from a hole at the far corner ceiling, where stairs led up to the ground level. "Still can't believe those bastards found me so fast."

"Mom." Maya followed her out into the room. Paper and plastic trash crinkled underfoot. "It was Brian. He called the Authority hoping to get a reward for me. He thought I was kidnapped."

Genna stopped. "What?"

Maya took a step back. Sometimes a woman in only underwear and puffy white plastic booties could be damn intimidating.

"I'm gonna feed him his balls."

"He said he thought he was helping me. Please don't kill him. He's going to have a baby."

"Damn right he is. I'ma hit him so hard he's gonna give birth his damn self." Genna scowled and stomped forward. "I won't do nothin' Doc can't fix."

Maya clung to her bag on the way back to the street full of shanties. She muttered in a low tone, offering up every detail of everything that happened from the moment of the raid on their home. The explanation of what she did to Mason got Genna to stop and gawk.

"Well, damn." She exhaled, lips fluttering. "That man's done."

Maya smiled.

One by one, the locals stopped what they were doing to stare at them. Genna ignored a cascade of catcalls, though each one hardened her glare a little more. A few streets up, she took a left, heading deeper into the city. Not long after the buildings around them became modern and tall, three figures slipped out of the dark. Knives flashed orange, red, and green in the overhead light from innumerable advertisements.

"Nothin' to steal," said Genna, sounding too calm.

"Oh, you got all we need." A man of average height and build stepped into the light and flashed a cruel smile. "No blood. Just a bit of fun. We won't even charge ya for babysitting."

A fourth man circled closer to Maya, holding a long metal pipe. "Be a good girl and no one gets hurt."

"Stay away from me! Mom..." Maya took a step back, shaking her head.

Genna sprang at the first man to appear and grabbed his wrist with her left hand while slamming her right elbow into his jaw. As he staggered backward, she drove her fist into his sternum with a loud *thump* that blasted him off his feet. The second man rushed in behind his knife. Genna spun into a reverse sweep that ducked the blade while taking his feet out from under him and knocked him flat on his back. She pounced before he could recover his wind, grabbed his weapon hand, and drove the blade into his heart with his hand still gripping it.

Maya averted her eyes, focusing on the steel pipe coming closer. "Mom?"

The third man raised a crowbar, but Genna jumped into him with a knee to the gut before twisting his wrist outward, breaking it, and slipping behind to grab him in a headlock. She whispered at his ear before the muscles of her biceps, shoulders, and chest swelled. A loud *crack* came from his neck. He slipped down out of her arms and rolled limp on the ground.

Maya backed away from the man looming at her. She fumbled with the bag, trying to get the pistol, but Genna went for him before she could even find the zipper. He pivoted at the scuff of her plastic booties and raised his club while backpedaling. Genna shoved her right palm into his elbow, stalling his swing, at the same instant grabbing the pipe with her other hand. Between pushing the elbow back and pulling the club down, a vicious *crunch* came from his shoulder.

He lost the weapon and staggered sideways, whimpering. Maya figured out how to work the zipper and pulled the gun out from between the wadded up teal dress and her sweater. Genna swiped it before Maya could point it at anyone, and raised it at the one remaining conscious man.

"You got three seconds to take everything off."

"Aaah!" He sprinted away.

Genna aimed, hesitated a second, then lowered the gun. "Shit. Too damn loud. I hate drones."

Maya looked at the man with the knife sticking out of his chest. "Were they going to hurt me or just threaten me to make you do what they wanted?"

"No way to know, but I didn't like the way he said 'babysitting.'"

Maya shivered. "Neither did I."

Genna pulled the ubiquitous oversized grey poncho from the thug she'd left merely unconscious and pulled it on; it wound up serving as a short dress. She replaced the baggy booties with the smallest man's beat-up combat boots, after which she rifled their pockets, collecting NuCoin as well as a few sheets of pills.

"Aren't you going to take pants?" asked Maya.

"You ain't close enough ta smell them. I got *some* standards. Least we got a couple coins now."

Genna put the gun in the large front pocket on her new filter coat and pulled the hood up.

Maya wiggled her toes. "Is it enough for shoes?"

"Yeah, probably. Won't be no designer shit though."

"What?" Maya faked a look of horror. "I... I'd rather stay barefoot than suffer the embarrassment of peasant footwear."

Genna snickered and pulled her close. Soon, they emerged from the more dangerous remote alleys to a pedestrian street and blended with the crowd. Maya held Genna's hand as they walked about a mile and a half to a low-end mall quad frequented by people who lived out in the Habitation District and commuted to work. The second place they checked had some stuff in child sizes, but all the children's shoes sat in a giant canvas bin, and not in matched pairs. Maya climbed in and rooted around until she found a matched pair of black sneakers that fit with some room to spare.

She put them on and tightened the Velcro strips before climbing out of the bin to give them a test walk. Having non-high-heel shoes felt strange and awesome at the same time. Genna waited at the counter, making idle conversation with a fortyish Chinese woman wearing huge glasses. Maya walked over, smiling.

"Found something?" Genna glanced down.

"Yes. I hope they're not too expensive." Maya raised one leg to show off the sneaker.

The clerk peered over her glasses. "Nah, hard to sell. No one who shop here buy little one sizes. Live in bad area, stole for drugs money. Citizens buy very 'spensive cheap fall-apart things last not even year. Those she take, hand made in Hangzhou. Last 'til she have kids of her own."

"They won't fit me in a year." Maya blinked. "Maybe two."

"That why hard sell," said the clerk. "But they made good. You have kids, they wear them too."

Genna held up a dark grey tank top and black BDU pants for herself. "These too."

"Ten NuCoin or forty dollar."

"Why does she talk like that?" asked Maya.

The shopkeeper smiled. "It adds to the atmosphere." Wrinkles gathered at the corners of her eyes with her laughter. "Makes it frustrating for people to trick me when they think it's difficult to communicate. Sometimes, it lets me trick obnoxious people when they think I'm stupid."

"Here." Genna handed over a few of the clear plastic NuCoins.

The clerk held them up to the light, studying the chromatic silver patterns. "Ahh, excellent." She smiled and bowed. "Come back any time."

Outside, Genna stopped by a vendor stall where a giant cauldron of boiling water balanced on three sticks over a cluster of portable burners. Maya grinned from ear to ear, adoring the feel of having shoes on. Genna bought two massive dumplings from the cart vendor and handed one to Maya. They munched while continuing to walk.

"You look like a little ninja," said Genna. "Black shirt, black leggings, black shoes."

"These feel weird." Maya grinned and gestured at the pants draped over her mother's arm. "Are you gonna put those on?"

"Not yet. I need a shower. What, you've never worn sneakers?"

"No. Traction socks in the apartment or high heels outside. You're not thinking of showering at that motel are you?" Maya shivered. "You'll get scummier."

"It can't be that bad."

Maya gave her 'the look.'

About a quarter mile from the Emerald Oasis, Genna made a seemingly random turn and entered the lobby of a regular (as in not by the hour) hotel. She went straight to the stairs, bypassing the front desk. Maya followed, trying to act as though she knew what was going on and belonged there. On the fourth floor, Genna stopped at the first door on the left and knocked.

"Do you have a minute to discuss the wisdom of Jeva?" asked Genna in an overly placid tone.

"Fuck off," yelled a man inside.

Maya covered her mouth to suppress a laugh.

Genna repeated the process with similar results over the next three doors. On the fifth, no one answered. She grabbed the lock plate around the knob and wrenched it open, making Maya's eyes bug out in awe. A moment or two of fiddling with wires later, the door clicked.

"You're stealing a room?" Maya blinked.

"No. Just the shower."

Maya followed her into the bathroom.

Genna raised an eyebrow. "Do you mind?"

"Can I stay with you? I don't want to be alone." Maya looked down.

"Okay."

Maya sat on a shaggy oval rug, vaguely aware of the distortion of dark brown skin on the other side of the translucent shower curtain to her left. Genna groaned in relief and spent a few minutes standing motionless under a spray of hot water, emitting noises of contentment.

"I guess your arm is better." Maya smiled.

"Yeah." Genna stretched her head side to side. "Doesn't even hurt now."

"I promised someone I'd do them a favor."

A cloud of steam billowed out into the room as Genna pulled the shower curtain back to look at her. "Why do I get the feelin' this is going to hurt?"

"Remember that Xenodril you wanted for a ransom?" Maya opened and re-stuck the Velcro on her right sneaker.

"Yeah."

"I set one of the production lines to repackage it like A-Profen and sent it to the Parkville warehouse. The security there sucks. They couldn't seem to fix it, so Ascendant only uses the place for low-value meds now. No one cares about A-Profen since it's cheap headache pills."

Genna slipped back inside the shower and lathered up. "So what's this favor?"

Maya explained about Doctor Janus, Ashley, and the people in the Fade ward she had promised to help. At her description of five-year-old Ashley, Genna's jaw clenched tight.

"How much Xeno we talkin' about?"

"Not that much." Maya shrugged. "Six palettes."

A loud *boom* from the fiberglass bathtub startled a gasp out her. Maya jumped and whipped her head around to look—at Genna's legs sticking straight up.

"Ow."

"Are you okay?" Maya lunged to her feet and poked her head past the curtain.

Genna sat up and rubbed her hip. "I slipped. Did you say six *palettes*?"

Maya nodded.

"Holy shit." Genna wiped soap off her face. "We gotta get that out of there before someone catches it... that's like—"

"Equivalent of about sixty million dollars resale at what the bitch charges." Maya returned to her seat on the rug. "Those people need help."

Genna clambered upright. "A lot of people do. Yeah. We'll help them. Hey, lean your face in here again."

Maya did.

Genna wiped the lipstick and eye makeup off her. "You don't need that stuff on anymore. Makes you stand out."

"I got some vaccine shots too, but those are for Sarah, Emily, Pick, Anton, and Marcus... and probably Doctor Chang."

"Wow." Genna whistled. "You've been busy. Where'd you find vac shots?"

"Samples cabinet at the penthouse. I didn't expect it to have anything good, but I had to check." She smiled. "I got lucky."

Zeroice jumped out of his chair when Genna slammed the door open. Maya crept in behind her, clutching the doll by virtue of it being inside her bag. He stood and ran a hand over his hair. He had no shirt on, and wore a scrap of bright red for pants that barely covered his junk. The bit around his waist was as thin as the spaghetti straps on her nightie. Tufts of hair leaked out the sides.

He gawked at her. "Maya... wow. Holy shit. You did it."

She blinked at his miniscule pants. "I feel like a crime is happening just by being in the room with you wearing that."

His face reddened with a tint of blush. Zeroice grabbed his shirt off the back of the chair and pulled it on.

Genna looked around. "Damn. I'm glad I believed you 'bout the bathroom.

So you're Zeroice?"

"Yeah." He scratched at the back of his neck.

Maya pointed. "Go look."

"Need you to do us a few things, Zero." Genna's boots thumped on the floor as she walked across the room. She recoiled from the bathroom with an expression as though she'd seen actual zombies. "What the..."

Satisfied at being proven right, Maya folded her arms and smiled.

"Well, I already did quite a bit." Zeroice flopped on the side of the bed and tapped his chin with one finger. "But after what that kid gave up, there's still a whole lot of credit on the tab, per se, so consider me at your disposal for a while."

"What exactly did she 'give up?'" Genna glared.

"Jeva creeps. Does *everyone* think with their groin? Data, Genna... data." He looked sick. "How could you even *think* that?"

"It worked?" Maya looked up at him.

"Damn straight it worked. I'm all over that shit, but I'm taking it slow. Don't want them noticing. Lot of hard ICE in there. So what do you need?"

"Can you get me off Ascendant's radar?" Genna glanced around the room. "Ah, shit this place is foul."

"Already done. Replaced you in the records and all the video feeds with a computer-generated version that almost sorta kinda looks like you, but isn't. You won't come up on facial recognition scans anymore... unless you get caught doing something again. Only problem you might run into is if you get seen in person by one of the fine, upstanding blueberries who dealt with you at the prison."

"Those fat bastards don't go on sweeps in the Hab." Genna sighed, relieved.

"I wish I could cover the little one's tracks, but she's uhh... unique."

"That won't be a problem." Maya shook her head. "I can be replaced. Besides, they have enough roll of me to make digital composites of anything."

"Can't believe you let Head die." Zeroice shook his head. "He was strange, but kinda cool."

Maya looked sideways at Genna. "Moth killed him."

"Damn, that dude was as tweaked as Head." He squinted at Genna. "Where did you find that guy?"

Genna clapped Zeroice on the shoulder twice. "We're all a little tweaked. Second thing. Need cyber cover for an op. We're hitting an Ascendant warehouse. I also need to get a ninja pigeon to Longball."

"Right." Zeroice dragged himself upright and shambled over to his desk to plug in. "Yeah, I know about the warehouse. Helped her hide the stuff a little deeper so it wouldn't get noticed. Figured that was coming."

"What did you just say?" Maya leaned against Genna.

"I asked him to send an encoded message to Barnes. We're going to need help to move all that Xeno."

Maya furrowed her brows. "How do you get Barnes out of Longball?"

Genna grinned. "It's his old callsign. He used to run a MRLS unit. Artillery rockets from miles away."

"Oh." Maya grimaced at the way the rug squished underfoot. "Can we go? I think I'm getting sick *through* my shoes."

"Everyone's a critic," muttered Zeroice. "Place is cheap and the berries hate coming here."

"I can see why." Genna took Maya's hand and headed for the door. "We'll contact you soon."

"I shiver with anticipation." Zeroice winked.

FORTY
THE BRIGADE

A pleasant-sounding female voice filtered out of the sky, announcing that cyberterrorists responsible for causing drone malfunctions resulting in thirteen confirmed deaths had been captured. The reporter continued in a monotone, "Four men from a reclusive free-living group based in the Wildlands attacked our peaceful society as a protest of technology and civilization."

Maya looked up toward the sound, where a five-story-tall screen on the side of a gleaming silver building showed video of the drone Genna shot down. They replayed the close up of the machinegun tearing apart the windows of nearby buildings in a loop.

Genna, walking at her side, chuckled. "Ironic. The one time it actually *is* Brigade responsible, they blame some nonexistent group."

"Maybe they got tired of blaming the Brigade all the time?"

"Heh." Genna laughed. "Somehow I doubt that."

They followed the flow of the 7:00 p.m. commuter surge, indistinct among hundreds of other weary bodies. Maya's wrist hurt from how tight Genna held her, but she didn't dare complain since she had her mother back. Thinking of all the ways anything could've gone wrong over the past few days made her sick to her stomach. A four-fanned Authority drone passed twenty feet overhead in a slow glide, the sensor ball on its nose panning side to side. Maya bowed her head, and the flying gun passed above them without incident.

Whispers and grumbles emanated from the crowd. It seemed everyone resented being under the constant eye of armed drones. Maya looked up at people. No one made eye contact and no one smiled, yet they all seemed to agree on hating the drones.

If everyone here is unhappy, why does no one say anything?

She glanced up at Genna. Unlike the crowd, she kept her gaze levelled at her surroundings rather than dragging it along the ground. She had the air of a wolf on the hunt, hiding among thousands of grey sheep. Maya's heartbeat picked up. Genna's presence made her want to get up and *do* something.

Maya lifted her head, looking up at a video version of herself reminding people to update their Xenodril supply. The mantra of '*It might not be a cold, better to be safe*' in her two-years-ago voice echoed down from on high. She was everywhere; at any point in this city, a person could turn in place and find at least four—if not more—screens showing her trying to sell drugs. The recorded girl fed the Citizens whatever Vanessa wanted them to believe. Could she possibly inspire the same feelings in other people that Genna did in her? Maya let her head droop.

Yeah right. The only thing I can inspire is 'aww how cute' or 'ooh, I wanna be that thin so I'll eat this pill.'

The endless crowd shifted and swelled. Each time a drone went overhead, the same routine repeated. People got quiet, walked slower, and no one looked up. As soon as it passed, the grumbling and bitching started. They walked for at least an hour, as best Maya could tell, toward the western part of town.

Shadows in the sky traced black smudges down from the clouds, hinting at the distant towers in the Spread. She peered past the shifting bodies surrounding her at the distant gloom and lost a few minutes wondering if Pope had heard her screaming at him. She let off a startled gasp when Genna pulled her to the right.

Maya stumbled to keep up with her mother's motivated stride, wincing at the pressure around her wrist. "Ow."

Genna slowed a little and eased back on her death grip. "Sorry. Nervous in this part of town. Lot of blue here."

They headed for a steel-faced building with a sign made to look like riveted letters spelling out 'The Hangar.' A tall man with a shiny-bald head and dark glasses stood sentry at the door in a tight black tank and white/grey camouflage pants. He might've been taller than Moth even, but nowhere near as thick. He pulled his glasses to the end of his nose, giving Maya a 'seriously?' look when it became evident Genna meant to go inside.

"Gotta be eighteen." He shook his head at Genna. "I don't give a shit what kind of fake ID you try to show me for that kid, I ain't gonna believe it."

"Nice to see you too, Rodolfo. Why don't you run it by Harlowe and see what he thinks?"

"Oh, shit. I didn't recognize you without all that shit in your dreads." He looked left and right before leaning forward to whisper, "Get her in the back fast. Someone sees a kid in there, it'll cause problems."

"Love you too." Genna winked.

Air-conditioning mixed with the scent of beer and motor oil blew Maya's hair back when the door opened. Airplane parts, bombs, and missiles hung from chains on the roof, some of which appeared genuine and scavenged from wrecks while others had the obvious artificiality of plastic models. Two women and a man waited tables, dressed in blue uniforms that reminded her of history e-learns.

Maya rolled her eyes. "You'd think the branch of the military responsible for fighter planes could come up with a cooler sounding name than just 'Air Force.' How... literal."

Genna hustled her down a wood-floored passageway between a long wraparound bar and an area full of restaurant-style tables. One of the servers winked at Maya on the way by and whispered, "your daughter's so pretty." Sporting a huge grin, Genna stiff-armed the kitchen door out of their way and guided her past people in white preparing food. Another set of doors in the back led to a storeroom. She walked up to a shelf full of huge cans.

Maya glanced at chicken soup, ketchup, tomato puree, and peanut butter in giant steel cylinders she could almost hide in. After a moment of standing there doing nothing, she looked up. "Umm?"

"Give them a minute." Genna tapped her foot.

"Okay."

They waited in silence for a little while until the shelf emitted a belabored mechanical whine and rose half an inch into the air, then slid left on rails to expose a hole in the ground and a basic metal stairway. Maya went down first, still with her wrist in a death grip. She raised her arm up over her head so Genna could keep holding it.

Two green pipes as big around as Genna's thigh ran along the left wall over dusty cinderblocks painted beige. Maya jumped when loud machinery behind the stairs roared to life and moved the shelf closed over the stairway, sealing them in.

"Is it safe?" whispered Maya.

"Not the most dangerous place you've been recently." Genna smiled. "Yeah. They're good people."

They walked a short distance to a ninety-degree right corner and a longer corridor that ended with a reinforced metal door. A small view port opened, from which a man's eyes regarded them. At Genna's approach, he backed away and opened the door, letting them into an underground lounge.

Three sofas, a television, a pool table, bookshelves, and a number of chairs surrounded an octagonal table littered with rifles, gun parts, hand grenades, and ammo. Two women, one pale with snow-white hair down to her shoulders, the other Indian, reclined on the middle couch watching some old war movie. Four men sat around the octagonal table, all of whom looked their way. The guy who opened the door sealed it again and followed Genna to the group.

Maya walked up to the table's edge. A dark-skinned man with a long nose and short, dense hair did a double take at the sight of her. Next to him, a younger man with sandy brown hair covered his face and chuckled. In the middle, a silver-haired man with military bearing stared between her and Genna with an expression as if she carried a live bomb.

"I'm not one of those androids that explode." Maya tilted her head and smiled.

Wisps of smoke rose from the center man's fingers, gliding past his head. He took a drag from an actual burning cigarette butt rather than a vape machine before stuffing it into an ashtray and exhaling a cloud to the side. "Barnes said you got pinched."

Genna let go of Maya's arm and folded hers. "He's right. They let me out early on good behavior."

Everyone but the two women chuckled, though they seemed more focused on the film.

"How's that?" asked the dark-skinned guy on the left. "Never heard of anyone getting out of the roach motel."

"I almost didn't." Genna glanced at the silver-haired man. "New guy?"

"Genna, Sidiqi. Sidiqi, Genna. Now that introductions are out of the way, I need to hear something to convince me you're not on the other side of the fence."

Genna nodded at Maya. "She pulled it off."

Maya stared down at her sneakers. "I had help."

"I'm feelin' like I got a C5-E coming in with 5,000 pounds of grade A fermented horseshit, and no runway big enough for the bastard."

Genna laughed.

Maya tugged on her mother's arm. "Who's that?"

She helped herself to a chair and pulled Maya into her lap. "That is Captain Harlowe, former USAF, current big cheese in the area."

"That is who I think it is, isn't it?" Harlowe sat up straight. "This better be a good story."

"She is, and she's on our side. We have a once in a lifetime opportunity. Before she got me out of Arlington, she redirected *six palettes* of Xeno to a low-security warehouse at Parkville." Genna went back and forth over the need to locate the disguised drugs and get them out before someone noticed them as being more than headache pills.

When all eyes fell on Maya, she cleared her throat and tried to project confidence. She gave a basic retelling of her initial kidnapping, how she twisted everyone into a chaotic meltdown, and once Genna figured her out as real and didn't tell anyone, decided to trust her. She detailed the Authority raid, Sarah being knocked out by a rifle butt (and what she did to Baxter), her trip to the city, the prison break, and how they had Zeroice on standby for assistance with Authority security. "He'll be able to suppress drone activity in the entire area around Parkview while we go in as well as turn off their security systems and locks. The biggest variables are somewhere between six and ten on-site guards as well as the physical location of the palettes in the warehouse. I don't have that information."

"Whoa, hold on." Harlowe held his hand up at her for a second before pointing at Genna. "One, this kid is fucking scary. Two... she's still a kid and we are not bringing her in on an operation."

"I'm not leaving her side again," said Genna. "Not until I get her home first. We don't have time to run out to the Hab and drop her off. I ain't sayin' we bring her inside. We can plant her outside with a comm. She can be our eyes."

Harlowe scratched his chin. "Kris, Ravindra." The two women looked over the couch at him. "Need recon on the Ascendant shipping facility at Parkview. Yesterday."

They nodded and hurried out—after pausing the movie.

"How soon can we do this?" asked Genna.

"Two hours?" asked Sidiqi.

"That's pushing it, but not impossible," said the sandy-haired man.

"If we move too fast, we risk a screw up. If we wait too long, we risk them figuring it out. That's a lot of Xeno to gamble with." Harlowe gestured at the men around him. "Sid, take Jameson and Binks with you. I'll get word to Carver to bring a transport. We still have one with Ascendant markings from that mess in Jerz last month."

Genna shivered. "Did they get all the blood off it?"

Harlowe smiled. "Let's hope so."

"I hate Trenton," said Binks, wandering off. "I really fuckin' hate Trenton."

Maya pulled on Genna's arm again. "I'm hungry."

"Any chow down here?" asked Genna. "That's a damn fine idea."

Sidiqi shook his head. "Nah. Gotta go upstairs."

"Be right back." Genna stood, set her on the chair, and kissed the top of her head before walking back out the way they'd entered from.

Maya gripped the seat, trying to conceal her nervousness. She jumped when the door closed. A momentary worry that everything continued to be an elaborate plot to kidnap her into the hands of the Brigade stalled the breath in her throat. What if Genna had done her part by bringing her here and that had been her cue to go away and never come back. Maya picked at the seat. *Stop being stupid.* She closed her eyes and put herself back in that little hidden room where Genna had broken down and cried. That wasn't fake.

A few minutes went by in silence before footsteps scuffed up alongside her.

"So, you really loaded up that shipment, kid?" asked Binks, a skinny man with dark brown hair. He had an edgy twitchiness and a wiry musculature that unsettled her, though his smile seemed friendly enough.

"Yes, but I promised some of it to people who need it. Doctor Janus at—"

"What?" Harlowe leaned forward. "How do you know about her?"

"I was running away from some blueberries and hid in the Integration Ward. I didn't know Doctor Janus helped the Brigade."

"Ballsy," said Sidiqi.

"Not really. You guys do know it's not contagious after forty-eight hours." Maya stole a peek out of the corner of her eye at the door. "I've been vaccinated. There's people there who are going to die if they don't get Xenodril soon. Some are younger than I am. Ascendant doesn't care because they don't have any money."

"Hmm." Harlowe tapped his finger on a bottle opener. The wiry man handed him a glass-bottled beer from a plastiboard case on the floor. "And you want to just give it to them."

"Of course." Maya blinked. "It's my fault if they die."

Harlowe popped the cap with a *pffsh*, and flicked it onto the table. "You definitely ain't your momma's daughter."

Maya narrowed her eyes. "That bitch isn't my mother."

Harlowe raised his bottle to her. "All right then. You know how to work a PCM-6?"

"No. I'm not even sure what that is."

The sandy-haired man, Jameson, dragged his chair around next to her and spent the next few minutes teaching her how to use a small radio communicator. Once she got the basics of it, he held up a thin, black elastic strip studded with two tiny metal discs.

"This is a throat mic. It picks up your voice so you don't look like you're using a radio. Hold your hair off your neck." When she did, he leaned around behind her and pulled the mic taut to her neck before securing a fastener and running the wire down under her tee shirt. He lifted the bottom of the tee enough to discover her leggings had no pockets. "Hmm. Bink, we got any spare BDU tops?"

The wiry man jogged over to a locker cabinet and rummaged up a large long-sleeved shirt—also plain black. He threw it to Jameson who held it up for Maya to slide her arms in. The garment engulfed her to the shins.

"Perfect." Jameson turned the communicator off, slipped it into the lower front left shirt pocket, and connected the wire. "No one will notice it."

"I'm guessing I'm not going to carry a gun, right?" asked Maya.

"You *are* a genius." Harlowe smiled.

She looked back at the door when the motor noise started in the hall. "What will happen if someone grabs me?"

"Then I figure Genna's gonna be ripping someone's nuts off." Harlowe swallowed a few gulps of beer.

Maya looked down, thinking about the three men in the alley. As scary as watching her kill people had been, knowing her mother could do that if she had to made her feel safe. Those idiots never saw it coming. "Yeah."

About ten minutes later, the door flew open at the behest of a boot, and Genna walked in carrying two yellow plastic baskets. The smell of fried food and spicy sauce followed her to the table. Maya stood to let her mother sit in the chair, then hopped into her lap and shot a quizzical look at a pile of long lumpy brown things doused in orange sauce on one side and the most pathetic looking donuts she'd ever seen on the other.

"What is it?" Maya sniffed at it and grabbed her nose when spice burned up inside. "Ow."

"Chicken fingers and onion rings."

Maya teased at the choker around her neck while she ate, drinking quite a bit of water to mitigate the spicy sauce. She wouldn't hurt anyone, but she *was* going to help. Genna kept a protective arm across her back. Despite the torrent of butterflies battling for space with her lunch, she felt happy—for however long it would last.

FORTY-ONE

OVERWATCH

aya huddled between Genna and Sidiqi in the front seat of a huge box truck. Tire treads deep enough for her to use as a ladder caused a continuous vibration that permeated the seat and left her legs feeling weird. Binks sat behind them with Jameson at his left, and Carver, who looked old enough to be Genna's dad, drove. The flat-nosed truck and giant windshield made her feel as though she flew with nothing between her and the street. Whiny electric motors changed pitch each time they slowed or sped, and one of the dials kept flickering off and on.

Clicking from the back seat announced Binks checking his weapon for the fifth time since they'd met up with Carver. The older man had picked them up about six blocks from The Hangar. If anything went wrong, the Authority cameras wouldn't be able to connect the truck to the bar.

Maya slid her hand into the shirt pocket and grasped the radio. Her upcoming role was simple. Kris, the snow-blonde woman, had picked out a secure position from which Maya could do what they called 'overwatch.' She'd take up a perch on the fourth floor fire escape of an apartment building with a perfect view of the warehouse and the surrounding streets. From there, Maya only needed only to sit still, stay awake, and give them warning if anything approached. They repeatedly told her that if anything went wrong, she should climb down and walk away as calm as if she had nothing to do with the warehouse hit.

That, more than anything else, got her shivering—the idea that this operation could go so wrong.

Carver muttered about idiots when an indecisive car in front caused them to get stuck waiting for an extra cycle of a red light. His agitation spread to Sidiqi in the middle seat, who's fidgeting squished Maya. She pressed her arms out and squirmed, trying to fight for more room. Jameson slid a magazine into a compact rifle and racked it. Binks handed another one past the gap between the seats to Genna. She held it low between her knees to keep it out of sight. He passed her a magazine, and she clapped it home.

Sidiqi's rifle glided over her head. He pulled it down fast enough to make her flinch, but guided it with a dexterous touch so it didn't hit her. Binks held a magazine out. Maya reached up and grabbed it. Sidiqi tilted the rifle and pointed at the opening. She turned the mag around and placed it in the slot.

"Not bad. You got a little commando, Gen." Sidiqi patted the mag down and racked the slide.

"Safe on," said Carver.

Genna, Binks, Jameson, and Sidiqi replied "safe" one after the next.

Maya looked at the bag between her feet. She leaned down and pulled the doll out.

"Aww," said Binks. "That's adorable."

"Concealment." Maya smoothed the doll's hair. "Makes me look more normal. Not every girl plays with dolls. Mom didn't."

Genna studied her lap with sad eyes and ran her hand over Maya's hair. "Things were so different when I was your age. How the hell does a war that only lasted nine months fuck up the world for ten years?"

"Officially..." said Carver, sounding distracted. "Shit kept going on for a few years. There's still some old officers left back there with little kingdoms."

"More than ten years," said Binks. "Been almost eleven now, and it's gonna be fucked awhile more. At least they held off on using the big thermo-nukes or we'd be sittin' naked around campfires eatin' prairie dog."

"Bah, war would'a happened sooner or later. Planet wasn't big enough for all the people trying to control it." Carver battled with the gearshift, slowing as he took a rightward turn. "One minute out."

"You stay put and don't leave 'til we come out, got that?" Genna pulled Maya into her lap.

"I understand." She clicked the radio unit on and took a bud out of the breast pocket, which she stuffed in her left ear. "Comm check?"

Binks chuckled. "Good idea. Might help if we all turned on. Freq 229."

Maya pulled the radio out enough to see the LCD screen and flicked the frequency over to 229.

The truck eased to a stop alongside an older-looking apartment tower where fake brick facing had flaked off in large chunks. Similar buildings occupied the street behind them on both sides, but to the left, a wide-open area surrounded an H-shaped warehouse. Ascendant logos marked the walls as well as the security booth by the gate. Chain link surrounded the whole property, though the razor wire was missing in more places than it remained.

One man in a white uniform shirt, not even armor, sat in the booth with his feet up. Rapid flickering light of a television screen shimmered over him. He slurped coffee and seemed at total peace with the world.

A mass of folded grey cloth flew over Maya's head and hit the windshield in front of Genna. Another landed in Sidiqi's lap. Except for Carver, who already wore one, the adults put the Ascendant worker jumpsuits on over their clothes.

Genna opened the passenger door and dropped out. When her boots hit pavement, her head wound up at shoe level. Maya climbed from the seat to the floor, sat, and slid off into waiting arms. Genna carried her across a sad excuse for a strip of lawn to a metal scaffold style fire escape a few yards past the corner.

"The ladder's too high."

"I'll give you a boost."

Maya raised her hands and stared at the folded ladder. "Okay."

Genna dipped, then tossed her airborne. Maya clamped one hand on the cold metal and dangled for a few seconds, legs flailing. Genna grabbed her by the sneakers and pushed up once Maya stiffened her legs. She got her other hand around the rung and pulled herself onto the second floor platform.

"I'm okay."

"C'mon back," said Carver in the earbud.

Genna remained under her, looking up with worry all over her face.

Maya peered at her through the grating. "I'm okay, Mom."

Fear didn't stand a chance facing the guilt brought on by the memory of little Ashley's half-grey face. Maya leapt to her feet and hurried up two flights of metal stairs to the fourth floor. She crept to the corner and dangled her legs between the bars.

"Don't sit like that," said Binks. "Takes too long to get up and move if there's a problem."

"You forgot the doll." Sidiqi's voice sounded in her ear, but he waved the blonde toy at her from the truck.

Maya pulled her feet up onto the platform. "I don't need the doll. No one's gonna see me up here anyway."

Genna jogged back to the truck and pulled the door closed with a muted *whump*. They drove away, leaving Maya scowling at the slogan 'Building a better you' under the word Ascendant on the side of the box. She always thought the white/cyan pyramid logo looked stupid. She hated it more now since she pretty much despised everything even remotely connected to Vanessa.

"Hey boys and girls," said Zeroice over the earbud.

"What the hell?" asked Carver.

"Relax." Genna cleared her throat. "That's our net man."

"How'd he get on this channel?" asked Sidiqi.

"Did a frequency sweep in the area via an old cellular tower no one bothered to shut down. Those prewar radios are the only things using that range. Easy as pie to find it."

"Fuck," said Binks.

"Authority ain't even looking for it," said Genna. "Everything goes over the net now. We're off the grid."

"She's right," said Zeroice. "They don't even have the kind of equipment needed to eavesdrop on this stuff. Guess Head did you all a solid from beyond the grave. You wouldn't believe the junk he's got."

"You raided his place?" asked Genna.

Zeroice chuckled. "Nah, I moved. Beats that shitty hotel."

Maya grabbed the bars of the fire escape porch and pulled herself up on her knees. From her elevated perch, she had a wide-angle view of the warehouse and both streets. It wasn't quite seven at night yet, so no commuters clogged the streets, though this area had what passed for cheap rent inside the Sanctuary Zone. It looked every bit as crappy as the area around Block 13, but probably cost ten times more to live in.

"Nothing's out here," whispered Maya.

"Copy," said Carver.

The truck pulled up to the gate at the entrance to the warehouse. Maya listened to half the conversation in her left ear as Carver presented a falsified shipping manifest that Zeroice had sent back by way of the Brigade's two scouts. The guard didn't seem motivated enough to even look at it and buzzed them in.

A few seconds after the truck's rear end cleared the gate, Binks muttered, "We're in."

"All right, people," said Carver. "Keep the weapons out of sight. Maybe we can do this clean."

"What are we looking for again?" asked Sidiqi.

"A-Profen," whispered Maya. "Six pallets with the same lot number. Xeno bottles are squat and fat with a cap the same width as the rest. A-Profen bottles are flat on the bottom and curve to a cap half the diameter of the bottle."

"You are scary, kid," said Binks. "Can we keep her as a mascot?"

"I put the actual shipment number on the documents." Zeroice chuckled. "It should look legit."

Various grunts and mutters of agreement filtered over the earbud. Maya kept pushing it back in place as it hadn't been designed for a small ear. The truck disappeared around the right spar of the H-shaped building, sliding between two rows of parked forklifts.

She shifted her weight rearward onto the balls of her feet to spare her knees more punishment from steel grating. At a hiss, she glanced over at a medium-sized beige car gliding across wet paving.

"Car, coming from my right. Two inside. Looks like, uhh, old people," whispered Maya.

The elderly couple drove past the warehouse, past her, and off out of sight to the left.

She looked up at an Authority drone emerging from between two high-rise buildings about six blocks beyond the warehouse, coming straight at it.

"Drone incoming," whispered Maya.

"How's it look?" asked Carver.

"Um. Blue, four fans, big gun."

Binks chuckled. "Love this kid."

"Not what I mean," said Carver. "Is it tilted forward moving fast, or does it look like it's doing its normal lazy patrol thing?"

She pulled the oversized black shirt up around her neck. "Oh. It's high and slow."

"I'm on it," said Zeroice. "It won't pick up your weapons through the roof unless it comes within thirty yards. Gimmee fifteen seconds."

Maya stared at the approaching drone. The whine of its fans getting louder and louder tightened her fingers around the metal struts. It reached the far edge of the warehouse before it wobbled and performed an abrupt about-face, heading back and to the left, not quite the way it had come in from, while gaining altitude.

"It's leaving," whispered Maya.

"That was nineteen seconds," said Sidiqi.

Zeroice chuckled in her ear. "I changed its status monitors. It thinks it needs to go charge."

"Damn, this feels like real labor," said Jameson. "Any of you guys know how to work a pallet jack?"

"It ain't rocket science," said Genna. "Out of my way."

Maya leaned against the railing on her right, still squatting. She let go of the bars and clamped her hands over her knees to rest her fingers. A blue-and-white car with bar lights nosed onto the road to the left of the warehouse, turning in her direction. Maya remembered what Pope said about motion attracting attention and resisted the urge to roll flat. She kept as still as she could force herself to.

"Authority car coming. Left side. Looks quiet."

"Noted," said Carver.

She moved only her eyeballs to track it. The officer drove up to the corner where the truck had dropped her off, lingered a few seconds, and turned left, departing along the road that ran parallel to the near side of the warehouse.

"Passing left side... and gone," she whispered. "How much longer?"

"Two more palettes," said Genna. "Hang on."

Maya remained calm until a rectangular steel box atop the warehouse split open down the middle a few minutes later. Two hatch doors opened outward, releasing a three-fan Ascendant drone. Her heart raced, making her dizzy.

"Ascendant drone coming out of the roof." The want to whisper collided with the need to scream, resulting in a raised voice. "No! It's moving around where the truck is."

She jumped to her feet and clung to the railing as the drone slid forward and cleared the edge of the building. Carver muttered, sending Binks and Jameson for rifles. Genna grunted as if moving something heavy.

The drone kept going, not turning until it reached the distant edge of the warehouse property, at which point it swerved left and began what appeared to be an orbital patrol path.

"It's at the end of the parking lot, going left," she whispered.

"Timer release," said Zeroice. "I can't recall it without setting off an alarm, but I can blind it. The thing should continue going in circles for hours no matter what happens."

"Baby," whispered Genna. "Get to the ground and wait for us at the corner. I'm"—she made a straining grunt—"loading the last pallet now."

Maya ran to the fire escape stairs, clanking and clattering to the second floor platform. After a couple of bounces, the ladder extended, and she rode it more than climbed to the street level. A few feet away from the sidewalk, she jumped and trotted over to the corner.

"Street's clear," she whispered.

She shivered from nerves, paced back and forth, and leaned against a streetlamp post. Two civilian e-cars went by. One man glanced at her, though the look seemed one of curiosity. Neither vehicle slowed. Five or six blocks to her left, an Authority patrol car crossed the street, visible only for a few seconds.

Drone fan whir echoed off the walls, loud enough to be close. Maya looked straight up, expecting to see one pass over the roof of the building she'd been perched on. When a blast of wind and blinding glare hit her from the right, she screamed.

A standard blue Authority drone hovered over the intersection, about even with the middle of the second floor. It spotted two searchlights on her and aimed its .50 caliber machine gun.

Maya spun to face it, arms rigid at her sides, standing at attention with her chin up. The grid of green laser light spread over her. *Please. Nice drone. I'm not doing anything wrong. These ones aren't supposed to do this…*

She expected the usual happy chirp, but it made an angry digital squawk and erupted with a bevy of red flashing lights.

"By order of the Authority, you are to surrender. Place yourself on the ground immediately with your arms and legs apart. Any attempt to flee or sudden motion will be considered an admission of guilt and result in immediate termination."

Mom! She trembled, unable to move. When a scary clicking noise came from the long-barreled cannon slung along its underbelly, she slid her hand into the pocket with the radio and squeezed the transmit button. The throat mic wouldn't pick up the drone, but the microphone on the box itself would.

"By order of the Authority you are to surrender. Place yourself on the ground immediately with your arms and legs apart. You have four seconds or you will be shot."

Maya dropped, flat on her chest. She hoped the transmission was enough of a call for help and stretched herself out in the shape of an X. Head turned to the side, she rested her cheek on the sidewalk. "Mom, help!"

"Do not attempt to move," crackled the electronic voice overhead. "Authority officers are on their way to collect you. Any attempt to resist will result in lethal force."

Gunfire erupted inside the warehouse. Maya closed her eyes, afraid to even shake too much lest the drone kill her. Voices shouted in her earbud, though she couldn't make out what they said over the roar of fans overhead. Rippling gunfire from three or four people firing bursts at the same time preceded a labored whirring of distant drone fans and an explosive crash.

Maya flattened herself as much as she could, fingers trying to grip the ground. She risked a peek toward the warehouse, where the booth guard screamed into some kind of phone.

"G-gate g-guard's o-on the p-phone," said Maya, unsure if the throat mic would pick it up with a drone so close overhead.

"You are not authorized to move," said the drone.

She let her cheek hit the ground again. "Please don't kill me. I'm only a kid."

"You are not authorized to speak," said the drone.

Shattering glass preceded another ripple of gunfire by a split second. The drone swiveled up and to its right. Maya rolled onto her side and clamped her hands over her ears as the heavy machinegun went off, aimed in the direction of the warehouse. Huge empty shell casings rained down around her. One bounced off her knee before rolling into the street. In the instant of silence following its short burst, *clanks* and *pings* echoed overhead. The drone careened forward, both front fans sputtering, and bottomed out in the middle of the road. It slid and spun over the paving in a spray of sparks before slamming into a line of parked cars. More shots followed, sounding like toys compared to the .50 caliber cannon. Blue fire washed over the drone amid a crackling explosion similar to fireworks.

Maya shrieked when a hand grabbed her arm a moment later. She snapped her head up to find Genna, covered in blood, rifle held in one hand.

"Mom!"

"I'm okay." Genna hauled her into the air and spun to face the warehouse.

Maya twisted around, aghast at the guard station windows shot out and stained red. The man inside slumped face down on the desk. Chromatic light from whatever video he'd been watching made the parts of his shirt that remained white flicker. *They heard me.*

She didn't have time to wonder if she'd caused that man's death. Genna whisked her up in a full sprint, heading across the street. Maya averted her eyes once it became apparent they headed toward the booth. Genna reached in the shattered window and hit a switch that caused the long rolling gate to open.

The truck barreled around the corner of the warehouse, nearly tilting over from taking a turn too fast. It knocked two forklifts out of the row as it pulled a hard left to approach the exit and skidded to an almost-stop by the booth. Sidiqi shoved the passenger door open. Genna ran alongside and tossed Maya up and into his arms before she jumped in. Maya stared at the empty back seat. Carver had blood on the right side of his face, but it looked like someone else near him had a bad day.

Carver leaned on the accelerator. Electric motors whined in protest, but the truck lurched forward, bouncing over the sidewalk and onto the road. He spun the wheel, heading left, opposite the way they'd come in. Genna grabbed Maya and clung tight.

Maya stared around numb. Sidiqi bled from his left shoulder and a few shards of glass or plastic stuck in the side of his head. Crimson poured out of Carver's nose, which had turned purple from a blunt impact.

Genna buried her face in Maya's hair. "Oh, baby... I'm sorry. We should've left you at the safehouse."

"It wasn't the kid," said Carver. "They were waiting for us. Dammit. We should've known they would have noticed that much Xeno redirected. Damn nine-year-old isn't going to beat Ascendant at its own game."

"The Xeno *was* there, wasn't it?" Genna offered a mournful smile.

"Where's Binks and Jameson?" whispered Maya.

"In the back." Sidiqi sounded grim.

Maya looked down. "Are they dead?"

Carver wrung his hands on the wheel. "Not yet, but it ain't lookin' good for Binks. Took a .50 to the chest. Jay is with him in the back."

"I'm sorry." Maya sniffled. "It snuck up on me." *It didn't think I was a Citizen...*

"This is a war." Carver sighed. "We all went in knowing this could happen. He didn't hesitate. We couldn't have gotten a hold of that much Xeno without you, kid... even if they did technically let you get away with it."

The truck bounced over a rough patch in the road, causing a loud groan from the back. Carver slowed a bit since no drones or Authority cars seemed to be chasing them.

Maya thought it over. "I don't think they let me. Vanessa wouldn't gamble that much money. If they knew, they'd have swapped it back for A-Profen and let us think it's Xeno. This warehouse was repeatedly written up for bad security."

"Looks like they beefed it up some." Sidiqi chuckled. "Poor bastards. There's gonna be a couple job openings."

"Transponder," crackled Zeroice's voice from a box on the floor. "The truck doesn't have one. It took them a while to catch on, but their security thought you guys were just some crew there ta steal shit."

"Where's the Authority?" Genna glared at the side mirror. "Why aren't they all over us?"

"I expect the requisite bowing and worship at some later point," said

Zeroice over the radio. "Your panic-stricken warehouse guards were begging a couple of my AIs for help... not Authority dispatch. However, you should get that rig out of sight sooner rather than later. Oh, and that roamer that spotted Maya... had to be random. There's nothing in their system about a raid."

"Copy," said Carver.

Maya shifted around and cuddled up to Genna. "I wanna go home."

"We will." Genna rocked her a little. "We will."

Two heavy *thuds* hammered on the back wall, with the muted quality of a human fist. Sidiqi bowed his head and whispered in a language Maya didn't recognize.

"Honor and Glory, Bink." muttered Carver.

"I was right fuckin' next to him." Genna shivered. "That could'a been me. Damn, Bink. Your ass was always first through the door." She cried. "You should've ducked."

Maya felt a moment of relief that the drone decided to fire first at Binks and not Genna. Guilt squashed her happiness, and she cried along with her mother.

"'Bout six minutes," said Carver while turning right onto a road that would take them most of the way across the city heading south.

"It saw me. I killed Binks." Maya rested her head against her mother's chest and stared out the window at meaningless patches of color gliding by. Buildings, cars, people, everything blended into a milieu of sorrow.

"No, baby. No you didn't." Adrenaline shudders rattled Genna's body; she tightened her arm around Maya's back. "The Authority killed Binks."

"Binks' inability to duck killed Binks," said Sidiqi with enough of a smile for no one to take it as a serious statement.

"He got that drone's attention first." Carver sighed. "Binks would be happy it got him instead of a little girl."

"Yeah." Sidiqi tapped a fist on his knee.

Genna's hand stroked over Maya's hair in a soothing repetition. Minutes passed in somber silence before the truck came to a stop at a traffic signal. A holographic advertisement on the corner projected another dolled up version of her. The life-sized animation struck a fashion model pose with a box of Chromacin—'Let out the real you'—in her outstretched palm. Digital aftereffects caused her skin to go from pale white to as dark as Vanessa and back again. Maya stared at the window, where her reflection hovered superimposed over the illusion selling lies.

She dug her fingers into Genna's shirt. "Ascendant killed him."

FORTY-TWO

A PROMISE KEPT

Carver maneuvered the truck down a narrow alley, managing to back it up past walls lit by flashing yellow lights. Maya perked up in Genna's lap, recognizing the area in front of Integration Ward 4. She bounced with anticipation as beige-painted cinder blocks slid past them on either side. Gate signs grew larger and larger in the side mirrors. As soon as brakes hissed, Maya lunged for the door handle.

Genna didn't hold her back. Maya jumped onto the door and rode its outward swing before dropping to the ground. Some of the sick people approached the inside of the fence with suspicious stares and angry grumbles. At the sight of Maya sprinting up to them, they went quiet. A few looked surprised, their expressions giving away they hadn't expected to ever see her again.

"Is Doctor Janus here?" she asked.

Ashley squeezed out from the group and wriggled past the gap in the fence. She dragged her right leg more than walked on it, waving her left arm as if it would help pull her forward. "You came back! I didn't forget you yet. My head still works."

Maya hugged the smaller girl until the tromping of boots came up behind her.

"Who's this?" asked Genna.

Ashley lifted her head. The instant the half-grey face of a five-year-old peered up at Genna, the woman collapsed to her knees, both hands over her mouth. She reached a trembling hand out, touching one finger to the girl's cheek.

"Those bastards…" Genna pulled both girls into a crushing hug. "This ends. I'ma burn motherf—Ascendant to the god damned ground. Every last greedy one of 'em."

Ashley gave Maya a 'help me' look as the force of Genna's embrace forced yet more dark yellow snot out of her nostrils.

"Mom. You're squeezing her too hard." Maya squirmed. "She's leaking."

Doctor Janus emerged from the sea of Fade victims and opened the padlocked chain. Carver banged a fist on the truck door, which opened a few seconds later. Jameson, a bloody mess, slumped to one knee. Behind him lay the remains of Binks at the center of a massive puddle of blood. Six square palettes of plastiboard cartons sat at the front end of the trailer, all labeled as A-Profen.

"Headache pills?" asked Doctor Janus. "They're going to need something stronger than that."

"That's how we got it out." Maya smiled. "It's Xenodril, mislabeled."

At the X word, a hush fell over the crowd of sick.

"Dropping off one," said Carver. "The rest are slated to go to Miami, Richmond, Philly, Boston, and Atlanta."

"That should last awhile." Doctor Janus smiled.

Maya looked at Ashley. "How long does it take to fix them? Is she going to be okay?"

The doctor took a knee and brushed Ashley's hair away from the grey patch. "If that's really Xenodril in there, she's got a good chance. Ashley hasn't shown any signs of memory loss yet, but I can't say she'll ever regain full strength in her right leg and arm. She's quite young though, so who knows. Children are often surprisingly resilient." She examined the girl's right eye. "Too early to say if she'll see with that eye again."

Ashley looked down. "My mommy's gone to sleep. She doesn't hurt now."

Maya clamped onto her and sobbed. Genna balled her fists in her lap, barely keeping herself from screaming in a rage.

Doctor Janus picked the little redhead up once Maya quieted. "She'll be okay. Let's not make her wait any longer."

Maya sniffled and went limp in Genna's arms. "Okay."

"Is it gonna hurt?" asked Ashley.

"No. It's only a pill." The doctor motioned for some of the able-bodied sick to come forward and help unload the pallet. "You'll feel a little sleepy, but that's it."

Sidiqi backed away as a group of shrouded people approached. Without a jack, it took quite a few hands to drag a pallet to the rear end. Rather than attempt to carry the entire thing out at once, they tore the plastic wrap open and passed the medicine carton by carton in a line of handoffs. Doctor Janus carried Ashley into the compound. The girl waved at Maya with a big grin from the half of her mouth that still moved. Even her milky eye sparkled with hope. The doctor disappeared with her into the main tent.

Maya whirled and clung to Genna, drowning in guilt. The idea that she shared at least some genetic material with Vanessa Oman made her sick to her stomach. Genna comforted her for a few minutes before grumbling about being a slacker, and set her down to join the handoff train. A palette's worth of Xenodril flowed into the main medical tent along a human conveyor belt.

After the last box went inside, the Fade victims clustered around, thanking Carver, Sidiqi, and Jameson, approaching Genna and Maya last. She blubbered through apologies for what her ex-mother did to them. When all the grateful looks, head pats, and hand grasping ceased, the sick went back inside, awaiting their turn to take pills.

Maya looked up at Genna. "Are you sure no one will try to steal it?"

"I don't think they will. One, Janus is giving it away to people who need it—she ain't chargin'. Two, most people who aren't sick won't go anywhere near a Fade ward." Genna sniffled and wiped a tear. "They don't pay much attention to what happens here, expecting people to rot 'til they die. All these poor bastards have been written off. Figure they'll probably stay here acting sick for a while, enjoying the free food... and disappear one by one. Janus isn't stupid. Everyone leavin' at once would get noticed."

Two white-shrouded men approached Carver and offered to help move Binks' remains to the crematorium.

"There's a damn crematorium right here?" asked Jameson.

"Yes." Maya frowned. "That's how they are expected to leave this place."

Maya clasped her hands in front of herself, gaze downcast. She stood a few feet away from the tray that, in a few minutes, would carry Binks into fire. Carver, Genna, Sidiqi, and Jameson formed a horseshoe around him. The woman with all the extra skin sagging under her gauzy Fade shroud hovered by the door out. She coughed into her fist a few times while muttering a prayer. Three men who'd already had their first dose of Xenodril joined her, though at only an hour since taking it, none looked any different aside from a little bleariness in their expressions. All bowed their heads in reverent silence.

"Well Binks, ya never did tell anyone what your real name was." Carver chuckled. "You made the ultimate sacrifice for the mission. The Brigade will make sure your name is carried into the next century. On behalf of all of us, I bestow the Silver Star for valor in action." He choked up and made a 'your turn' wave at Sidiqi.

"My friend... You were quick with the wiseass remark and quicker getting around panties. It was an honor to fight beside you. We will meet again." Sidiqi patted Binks on the shoulder and stepped back.

Genna suppressed a cough. "I can't say I'm sorry that I never gave it up to you, Bink." Her lips curled with a wistful smile. "Suppose I was a bit of a bitch at times, but I had my own demons to work out." Her lip quivered. "I shouldn't have dragged a kid along with us on—"

"Secure that, Genna." Carver inhaled a sharp breath. "That girl is precious, both because of who she is and... well, just because. She had her ass down and compliant. The drone wouldn't have hurt her. Binks rushed to open fire knowing the risk. It ain't your fault, and it ain't Maya's fault."

"Copy that." Genna squeezed Maya's hand.

"Ya know." Jameson glanced sideways at her. "Binks was enough of a sick bastard he might appreciate a handie right now."

Genna punched him in the shoulder. "You did *not* just say that." She cracked up laughing with tears in her eyes. "You know, he might."

Nervous chuckles swept around the group.

"Later, mate," said Jameson. "We had a good run." His lip quivered; he sniffled. "Y'always said it'd be me. S'pose I am a bit too cautious after all. I..." He looked down, unable to go on.

Maya didn't say anything. A moment of silence hung heavy over the room before the once-obese woman dragged herself to a control box on the wall. She pushed a few large red buttons, causing whooshing noises to erupt from within the chamber at Binks' feet. Soon, the glow of orange flames licked at the bottom of a door blocking the conveyor from the furnace.

At the bewildered look Maya gave her, the woman let off a resigned sigh. "The man who showed me how to operate these controls went down the belt a month ago. Funny the things you learn out of necessity." She flicked a pair of switches and turned a knob. The hissing inside the oven got louder. "On account o' you, I don't need to hurry up and train someone before I'm ridin' the Devil's bobsled myself."

"I'm sorry," whispered Maya, too quiet for anyone to hear.

Genna trembled. Her reddened eyes bugged, and her head kept moving in a subtle no shake as the woman threw a lever switch. The hatch scraped upward, revealing a yawning inferno that let off a wave of intense heat. A red button started the conveyor; Binks slid forward on rattling metal wheels, vanishing into the flaming maw. The door closed behind him, muting the roar.

"Mom?" Maya wrapped her arms around Genna's waist.

She rested her hands on Maya's shoulders, speaking in a distant tone. "I was right behind him. If I'd'a taken one step more to my right, that bullet would'a got us both."

"Mom." Maya looked up and around at the other Brigade people. "There's something else. It's not aliens or asteroids. Fade should've been gone by now. It was designed to dissipate in seventy-two hours."

All eyes fell on her.

"Ascendant is making Fade. I saw files on Vanessa's terminal authorizing it. The bioassay drones aren't scanning for it. They *release* it in the upper atmosphere when Ascendant needs an uptick in Xenodril sales. They're poisoning everyone on purpose... for profit. I wanna go home and be happy, even if we don't have any money or barely any clothes and aren't sure if we'll be able to eat... but we can't let them keep doing that."

The Fade victims stared at her.

Carver walked around the end of the empty conveyor and took a knee at Maya's side. "I'm not going to ask a little girl to get her hands bloody, but you can still help." He looked over his shoulder at the anger brewing among the formerly doomed. "You can be the face of change."

"You want me to make a video. Barnes asked too."

He nodded. "We can come up with something right here in the alley."

Maya turned her gaze to the gauze-wrapped bodies. They regarded her in a way she couldn't recall ever experiencing before. Not the fearful stares of Vanessa's underlings, the put-upon annoyance of the marketing people, or the simmering resentment of a population who saw her wherever they turned. An odd thing lurked in the expressions of these weary sick—respect. Maybe she *could* inspire people the way Genna inspired her.

She looked Carver in the eye. "Okay. I will."

FORTY-THREE
BROTHER LOST

Soft *clanks* of boots and sneakers on a grated walkway echoed down a long, rounded tunnel. Maya hurried behind Genna in single file. The pipe offered only a few inches of clearance over the woman's head, smaller than the broken tubes of the Jigsaw River. A full night's rest curled up with her mother in the basement of The Hangar had washed away much of the terror of the warehouse raid. It seemed easy to think of it like a movie she'd watched rather than lived. Still, no one had spoken much last night. The men stayed up late, drinking too much and celebrating Binks' memory.

Maya had trouble falling asleep, too riddled with disgust and guilt over the idea not-Mom had poisoned all those people only to make money. The Xenodril had taken a bite out of Ashley, leaving the little girl exhausted and unable to get out of bed, though she couldn't stop smiling because she knew she'd get better. Maya had spent a little while visiting her before they'd left the Fade ward. It twisted her up inside to hear a five-year-old talk about it being *good* her mother had 'gone away,' since it meant the pain stopped.

Hours later, Maya shuffled along an underground passage, sneaking out of the Sanctuary Zone. Genna knew of several routes that allowed Brigade operatives in and out of the New Baltimore Sanctuary Zone, some pipes, some abandoned subway tunnels. They'd climbed a ladder along the outside of a spherical three-story water tank and gone down the huge pipe at the bottom. Being inside the enormous tank, staring at the drain, had scared her, even with it being empty. No wonder the Authority hadn't found it—no one in their right mind would go into a place like that. Maya shivered, terrified at the thought of being trapped inside it when someone turned on the flow. It took over a mile of walking before she'd stopped trembling at the thought a drowning torrent might come out of nowhere and sweep them down the drain.

She peered up at the blank, pale grey tube. Seams passed every few paces. Most likely, this pipe passed under the flattened devastation around the city that she had previously flown over, a two-mile-wide swath of rubble where tiny fires burned in the once-basements of tall buildings.

Genna's mood had improved after a night's rest, and she moved at a pace Maya found difficult to keep up with. She didn't complain, focusing instead on switching between fast walking or running whenever she lagged too far back.

A left turn led to a smaller pipe that forced Genna to crawl and Maya to stoop. Unlike the one with the grating to walk on, the offshoot had no lights. Before long, darkness surrounded them. She kept a hand on Genna's back. The nylon bag bumped against her legs, the rattle of pills loud in the metal tunnel.

Eventually, Genna stopped. "Here we are." The woman shifted position and pulled Maya forward. She felt around until she located Maya's arms, and guided her hands onto the rung of a thin metal ladder. "I'm gonna go up first, make sure it's clear."

"Okay," whispered Maya.

Genna climbed past her, coming dangerously close to stepping on Maya's fingers. The rustling of her pants stopped a short while later. A grunt preceded an ear-splitting squeal of metal. Blinding daylight leaked in from a crescent shape when Genna pushed up on a dome hatch with a red wheel on the bottom. She stretched up and peered out, twisting left and right. A few seconds later, she heaved the hatch up and climbed out.

Maya raced up the ladder. Soft grey silt surrounded a three-foot-tall section of pipe jutting out of the earth. Except for the crumbling fragments of concrete walls, the ground looked like something that belonged more on the Moon than in Baltimore. Genna slipped her hands under Maya's armpits and plucked her out of the pipe before setting her on her feet nearby and closing the hatch.

She kicked at the silt. It reacted like snow, only not cold.

"Ash," said Genna. "It's all ash."

The wall of the Sanctuary Zone lurked a ways off to the east. They had emerged about three quarters of the way across the debris moat surrounding the Sanc. A faint breeze carried traces of mildew, burning plastic, and a clingy chemical smell. Genna pulled her along by the arm and ducked under a large angled slab of wall propped up on a bent steel I beam. She held a finger to her lips in a shushing gesture and waited while tapping her finger on her knee to mark time.

After twenty-eight seconds, drone fans passed overhead. Genna made no attempt to move, tapping on. Maya kept quiet. Seventy seconds later, another set of drone fans passed. She continued counting, but glanced back at Maya with a meaningful stare. When the next set of fans went by at exactly seventy seconds, Genna tapped twice more and rushed forward.

Maya ran, jumping over smaller steel beams sticking out of the ash and darting around larger chunks of concrete. The farther away from the Sanctuary Zone they got, the less flat the terrain became.

"Sixty one," said Genna, before diving into a trench under another wedge of concrete wall, this one fanged with twisted rebar.

Maya slid down the incline into the dugout and Genna whisked her in, holding her tight. They lay in silence until another drone passed overhead.

"I don't wanna scare you, but these drones ain't gonna try to scan us first."

"No." Maya swallowed saliva. "That's not scary at all."

Genna marked time with her finger, gazing up at the concrete. *Tap... tap... tap...* "We're almost clear."

At the next passage of fans, which sounded farther away, Genna crawled out the other side of their cover and sprinted. Maya followed suit, grabbing the strap of her bag to keep it from flying off. Beyond twenty yards of flat ash field up ahead, the moonscape gave way to dirt by a wall of thick grass. Genna dashed over the powdery ground and leapt into the brush.

Maya crossed her arms over her face and plowed right in, not caring how many bugs waited to climb all over her. She trudged along the trail Genna left, fighting against wild blades of meadow grass that stretched over her head. A few minutes later, she stumbled clear onto a dirt road—and into a hug.

"We're far enough away now." Genna smiled at the sky. "They won't bother with us here."

Still a fair walk to the west, the hulking forms of the Spread stacks gleamed in the sunlight. It wasn't yet noon, putting the sun to their backs and painting the massive junkyard in a brilliant array of colors. Cargo containers of red, green, orange, pink, and rust-smeared white swayed in a breeze that didn't blow at ground level.

Genna headed left, due south, following an open dirt path. Maya smiled at her sneakers. Would someone try to steal her clothes like they'd done to Sarah? Possibly in the Dead Space—those people living in plastiboard boxes.

Most of the children there only had scraps of plastic or fabric tied on as skirts, a few, not even that. Would someone think it fair to steal from one child so another suffered less? Maybe Sarah had been exaggerating to scare her into staying with the group.

"Mom? Do people really steal clothes out here?"

"People out here will steal anything they can get away with. Most leave me alone because they know the look in my eye. You stare at them with that 'go ahead, give me a reason' face, and they'll back off."

"I don't think I'd scare anyone." Maya smiled. "Not 'til I'm bigger."

"Well, I suppose you better not run off alone again."

Maya looked up. "Don't get arrested again."

Genna laughed. "Yeah. I'll work on that." Her mood darkened. "Reminds me. I gotta have a talk with ol' Brian... and show you the elevator. We got a secret way out."

"I don't think he'll do it again." Maya jumped over a puddle.

"Yeah." Genna shook her head, making her long, ropey hair swish back and forth. "That's for damn sure."

Weeds parted on the right, and a familiar rifle-bearing figure in a poncho emerged.

Genna reached for her handgun.

Maya grabbed her arm. "That's Pope." She let go and looked up at him. "You came after me..."

"Yeah. When you didn't come back overnight, I uhh... got a little worried." He shook his head while chuckling. "This that momma of yours?"

Genna and Pope held eye contact for a long moment before she allowed a smile. "Yeah."

"Well, all right then." A curious mixture of disappointment and relief came over him. "S'pose I got some solar panels to tend to then."

Maya hugged him. "Thank you for your help. If you get tired of living in the tunnels, there's a lot of open apartments in our building."

"He don't look like he'd be able to make the rent," said Genna with a grin.

"Pope's a veteran too." Maya smiled. "Doesn't he get a discount?"

Genna offered a hand. "Nice meetin' ya Pope. Where'd you wind up?"

"75th Rangers."

"Aw shit!" Genna grabbed him with a huge handshake. "I was with the 494th."

"Night Terrors." He clapped her on the shoulder. "*Nunquam vidi.*"

"Damn straight. Maybe we could use some like-minded friends." Genna nodded toward the Hab.

He patted Maya on the head. "Got some stuff ta deal with... I might just take you up on that someday. Take care of yourself, Ranger, and take care of this kid. She's a handful."

"I hear that."

Maya smiled. "You too."

Pope wandered off into the tall grass.

Once the rustling of his passage faded to the low whorl of the wind, Maya looked up at Genna. "He's not married."

"Secure that shit, soldier." Genna grabbed her shoulder and pulled her along.

Maya laughed. "You were looking."

A trace of a smile played at her lips, but her mother kept a hard expression pointed at the world. Maya held her hand, eager to be home.

They walked for hours, munching on a chewy meat-like substance Genna referred to as 'jerky.' It didn't taste bad, but Maya's jaw ached after only a few pieces. The nice dirt path curved the wrong way, forcing them to divert over a short field of dead grass and onto a smashed-up paved road.

High-rise buildings, gutted and twisted by bombs, loomed ahead. The wind tore howls from the exposed frames and girders. Now and then, a *click* or a *snap* announced some piece of concrete, debris, or a random object falling to the ground. Maya gazed around at the destruction, trying to reconcile the scenery with history e-learns that had pictures and video of how everything used to be.

"How many people died?"

Genna looked down at her. "That's kind of a vague question."

"In the war." She punted a fist-sized rock to the side.

"They say between sixty and seventy percent of the Earth's population. The lucky ones went right away to the nukes, but that's only a small portion. The ground fighting that followed made death by bomb seem like a mercy. Savage. Russia and China were kicking the shit out of each other. For whatever reason, we got our teeth into North Korea and wouldn't let go. It stopped being about national identity and turned into this ugly mess. Like we had to kill all the Koreans out of some twisted sense of payback. Command structure broke down after the second wave of missile strikes. Majors and lieutenants in charge of individual units suddenly found themselves at the top of the chain. They all had different ideas of what we should be doing. My CO wanted to retake Seoul. The SOKOs had a real shitty time of it. They were on our side, but in all the chaos, they still looked Korean." Genna sighed. "Damn miracle *anyone* walked away from that."

"Are people always bad?" asked Maya.

"Maybe that's why we're still around. In the middle of it all, the enemy stopped being people and became bugs we had to step on. I'm sure the NOKOs felt the same way about us. It took a couple of weeks, but eventually there weren't enough of either side to really call a military anymore. Our officers started goin' after each other, claimin' territory. They didn't bother telling us the government was gone. When we found out, most of us grunts walked away. There was no war, no country left to fight for, nothin' but killin' for the sake of havin' nothin' better to do. Shit got tribal and ugly over there. Europe was the same way, far as I know. I'm not sure what made people settle down, but eventually, maybe five years ago, it all got quiet. Sometimes I like to think there's this collective human consciousness, and we all got the fuck tired of fighting."

Maya nodded.

The shady haze of the Baltimore Habitation District appeared in the distance hours later. By then, the sun had passed overhead, lengthening the shadows stretching away from the old buildings within the Dead Space. Genna circled farther to the west than Maya's attempted beeline trip to the glowing Citizen city. Her route avoided much of the population living in boxes, as well as the cannibalistic wanderers.

Maya told Genna about them. When she finished, Genna stopped, took a knee, and stared into her eyes with her hands on her shoulders.

"If anythin' like this ever happens again, you promise me you gonna stay where it's safe. You got so goddamned lucky..." Genna crushed her with a hug.

Maya basked in the feeling of being loved and yelped at a swat on the backside.

"That's for runnin' off alone." Genna smiled despite a few tears.

"Aww, that's damn heartwarming," said a male voice.

Maya leaned to the left to peer past Genna's arm.

Two men in shredded versions of the ubiquitous grey filter ponchos stepped out. Both had the breathing masks up over their faces; the man on the left also wore sunglasses but didn't seem to have any pants, and neither of them had shoes. Both shivered, twitched, wiped their noses, and blinked in a continuous cycle of nervous tics. The one on the right appeared to be wearing heavy purple-black eye shadow, but made from bruise rather than cosmetics.

She grimaced at their hairy chicken legs, grateful the shredded garments were long.

"We don't wanna hurt ya. Leave everything in a pile and go 'way."

Sunglasses raised a handgun at them.

"Everything?" asked Maya.

"Yah," said the other man, brandishing a machete large enough to qualify as a sword. "If you ain't born with it, drop it and get walkin'."

"It warm," said the sunglass-wearer. "We need cash more than you need them clothes."

"Boots are mine," said the sword man.

Maya held still, staring at the pistol. When Genna didn't say or do anything, she swallowed a lump of anger. Losing the vaccine shots was far worse than being left with nothing on. Clothes could be replaced. She'd happily endure walking naked the rest of the way home if she had to in order to give Sarah and the others vaccine shots, but these men would take that too. Anger left no room for fear. *If I can get close, I can grab the gun. Mom took those other guys out so fast. All she needs is a second...* "O-okay. You can have our stuff. Please don't shoot my mom." She reached up to pull the large BDU shirt off.

Genna put a hand on her shoulder and shook her head. "You're not going to shoot us." She advanced at the men in a slow walk.

Maya tugged the shirt back onto her shoulders.

"No?" The quivering pistol lifted to aim at her face. "I can still sell your shit with blood on it."

"Chill," said the sword-man. "We ain't gonna touch you... or the kid. All we want is stuff to sell. Drop the shit and get outta here."

"No." Genna took another step. "For one thing, you're not going to want to attract all the Frags within a half mile by firing that. For another, a gunshot will also draw Authority drones. They scan that ten-mil of yours, and they'll blast you into salsa."

Spittle foamed between his teeth; his quaking intensified. "B-back off. I ain't gonna warn you again."

Genna kept creeping up on them. "The third and best reason you're not going to shoot me is that there's no ammo in that thing. No magazine, and that little dot of firing pin at the end of yo' barrel tells me the chamber's empty."

Before the man could react, Genna swung her arm in a sideways motion that ripped the handgun out of his grip. Maya grinned with exhilaration. She dropped in place, squatting with her hands on the ground for balance.

"Damn bitch," the sword guy yelled.

He drew his arm back to swing. Genna hurled the pistol at his head, making him duck, and pounced. She seized his wrist, torqueing it over until he lost his grip on the blade. Mr. Sunglasses ran at her and caught a sidekick in the gut for his trouble, which knocked him over backward. He crumpled onto his ass and wheezed.

Genna swung the former swordsman around by his arm and threw him face-first into the wall of the high-rise near the alley where they'd emerged. He bounced away and stumbled in a disoriented circle. Once he recovered his balance, he lurched at Genna, throwing a poorly aimed punch. She caught his arm, flipped him to the ground on his chest, and wrenched the limb up, breaking the elbow backwards with a splintering *crunch*.

He howled.

Sunglasses raised his hands, still curled in a ball on the ground. "Stop." He gasped. "You win. I give up."

The other man rolled on his side, cradling his right arm and moaning.

Wearing a broad grin, Maya marched up to Genna's side. She shook her head at Sunglasses. "My mom was in the 494th Night Terrors. You're lucky you're alive."

Genna started to smile, but forced herself to look menacing. She pointed at them, thrust her finger out like a dagger, and turned away. Once the men could no longer see her face, she grinned.

Soon, the scuff of Maya's sneakers on the pavement overpowered the whimpers and groans from the two desperate dosers. Genna clasped her hand and led her along a series of side streets and alleys to an open lot next to a strange ornate building that looked like a poor attempt to recreate a fantasy castle. Multicolored glass chips gathered in piles underneath pointed arch-shaped window holes, where only a tangle of black metal wiring remained.

The lot held several rows of small white stones covered in ash and dust. Near the front left corner, a handful looked more recent. These appeared to be made of concrete debris from surrounding buildings rather than neat carved stone. Genna slowed to a trudge, scanning the stones. She stopped at the fifth one and took a knee.

Maya stood at her side, hands clasped the same way as at Binks' cremation. Genna traced her fingers over crude lettering chipped into the hunk: "Sam."

A few minutes of silence passed. Genna rolled back to sit on the ground and wiped tears from her face. "Guess you gotta wait a bit longer ta see me again, baby." She sniffled. "You got a little sister now."

Shards of broken glass clinging to dark wire sang disharmonic chimes in a breeze that blew over the shattered windows of the strange building. The hollow structure resonated in the wind, a giant creature drawing breath. Maya shied away, leaning closer to Genna. She stared at the gaping arches, into shadows that seemed to look back at her. It hit her that every stone here marked a spot where someone had been buried. She quivered, wondering if ghosts were real or if her mind had run away with itself.

Genna put an arm around her back and pulled her close. "Nothing to be afraid of here, baby."

Maya slipped down to kneel, touching her fingers to the stone. "Hi, Sam. I'm Maya."

Though she knew no one would blame her for Fade, making commercials for Xenodril felt the same as if she'd helped Vanessa kill him.

"They're wrong. You *did* love him." The lines she had to recite made her burst into tears. In her mind, the blond boy in the bed beside her turned into Sam.

When Maya started sobbing, Genna's outward calm broke apart. Only a trace of the sun's glow remained on the horizon by the time the tears stopped.

"Who said I didn't love my son?" Genna scowled at the fence.

Maya explained the commercial for Xenodril she'd made. Genna threw a deadly glare in the direction of the Sanctuary Zone. "I'm sorry. I didn't mean that... they made me say it. I understand why you were so angry with me at first. I deserved it."

"It's all right, baby." Genna pulled her close and kissed the top of her head. "And no, you didn't. You're just a kid doin' what you was told."

She sniffled.

"He was a lot like you. Smart. Liked to read. He had hope. Sam thought the world would rebuild itself and be better." Genna wiped her eyes again, crying despite smiling. "He used to do these drawings with green plants growin' outta buildings and happy people. He'd be thirteen now."

"I'm sorry."

Genna stood, picking Maya up. "Stop. It ain't your fault. Come on. Let's get you home."

Maya threw her arms up around Genna's neck and watched her older brother's grave recede farther and farther away. When the churchyard fence blocked her view, she leaned her head against Genna's and closed her eyes.

FORTY- FOUR
ABSOLUTION

A tiny voice echoed in the air far above. Maya looked up, squinting from the sunset glare where a band of light painted the building from the seventh floor to the tenth. At the center of a huge gash in the wall one story down from the roof, Sarah jumped up and down, hair fluttering to the side in the wind. She waved her hands back and forth over her head. Emily appeared next to her, followed by Pick and the twins.

"She's going to fall," said Maya, squirming. "They're too close to the edge."

Genna set her down, holding her hand as they crossed the walkway to the little stoop. Sarah's excited shouting echoed from the main stairwell inside the area full of mailboxes. Maya pulled Genna over to wait by the nonworking elevators.

Sarah came flying down the stairs a short while later, and raced into a hug. A minute or so later, the joyous crying wound down. "You're in so much trouble!"

Maya sniffled and squeezed her friend. "I'm sorry for scaring you."

"Everyone was bummed." Sarah laughed and cried more. "The cards—they're still set up. I didn't put 'em away 'cause I thought if I did then you wouldn't come back."

Such guilt hit Maya that she couldn't talk, and stood there sniveling.

Emily, still in her costume dress, zoomed in and grabbed on to Maya's arm. "She's back!" The seven-year-old bounced up and down, cheering. "I tol' you! I tol' you the faeries said she'd be back."

Pick ran out from the stairwell, but stopped at the front doors. He smiled and waved. "Hi."

Genna set her hands on her hips. "That was damn foolish of her to run off. She won't do it again, right?"

"No," said Maya, staring at the floor.

"But she did some incredible things." Genna gestured at the building. "Come on. I miss my damn bed."

Sarah's perma-smile emerged from the somber gloom. "You wanna finish the game?"

The twins hurried out into the hallway. They flanked the Maya-Sarah-Emily group, and added themselves to the hug. Maya kept her head down, muttering "sorry" a few more times in Sarah's general direction. Marcus attempted (poorly) to conceal that he cried.

Genna ushered them upstairs.

Maya set her heels on the sixth. "Mom. I need to talk to Doctor Chang." She pointed at the other kids. "And you all need to come."

"All right." Genna held the door as the children spilled through.

Maya hurried down the corridor to the apartment where Zoe, Emily, and Doctor Chang lived. She knocked and walked in without waiting. Zoe looked up from a chair by one of the worktables where she tinkered with the guts of a laptop computer.

"Maya!" Zoe looked to the back hallway. "Mike, get out here." She got up and ran over.

"Hi, Mrs. Chang. I'm sorry for scaring everyone."

Genna leaned on the doorjamb and folded her arms.

Zoe smiled at her. "Holy shit! We heard you got bagged."

"Almost." Genna shook her head.

Doctor Chang swept in wearing only boxers. He halted at the crowd, made a funny face, and ran to the back. The kids giggled. A moment later, he returned with pants, shirt, and a white lab coat on.

"Doctor." Maya set her nylon bag on the corner of the nearest table. "I got some medicine." She took out the box of vaccination shots and handed it to him.

"This..." He gawked.

"Is for my friends." She gestured at the kids. "And you should take one 'cause you're a doctor and it would be silly for a doctor to get sick."

"Is that a needle?" asked Emily. Her exuberance died an instant death.

"What's that?" asked Marcus.

"It's going in the ass," said Pick, preparing to drop his pants.

"No, Ruben." Doctor Chang shook his head. "This is not a tetanus vaccine.

This is…"

"A shitload of money," said Genna. "And peace of mind don't have no price tag. Is the shit still good?"

Doctor Chang opened the box and studied the plastic cartridges inside. "Seems like it."

"Is it safe to give to children?" asked Zoe.

"Yes." Maya nodded. "They gave it to me before I was even one year old."

The doctor nodded. Emily began to cry, so Zoe pulled her into her lap. The twins shifted with unease.

"This is Fade vaccine. After this shot, you can never get sick from it." Doctor Chang went over to the area with all the medical equipment and unearthed a pressure-jet injector.

Marcus and Anton rushed up, both shaking.

"Really? No Fade?" Sarah pulled a strip of her curtain-dress off her upper arm. "Please…"

Emily whined.

"Where was that shit when our parents died?" asked Anton.

Marcus gave him a shove. "Ain't her fault. She coulda got her ass killed for stealin' that. Be nice."

Maya thought of Ashley and took the girl's hand. "Em. It won't hurt. It's not technically a needle. It's only liquid pressure."

She patted Emily's hand. The girl screamed when the jet injector touched her arm—and kept screaming for several seconds after the shot finished. Seeing it done, she sniffled.

One by one, Doctor Chang swapped out cartridges and vaccinated Sarah, the twins, and Pick. He administered one to himself last.

Zoe stared at the four remaining shots.

"You can give one to Zoe too." Maya grinned. "Save the others for if anyone has babies." Maya pulled the two bottles of Xenodril out of the bag. "I got this too. You might wanna keep it hidden or locked up."

"What the hell did you do, rob an Ascendant warehouse?" asked Doctor Chang.

"Well…" Maya tapped the toe of her sneaker on the rug.

Genna looked sad for all of two seconds before a grin took over. "Actually, we did. But that little stash she got on her own. I got a carton for you as well."

Doctor Chang gave a brief lecture on the importance that none of the kids told anyone about the Fade medicine, because people might come here to steal it. "Of course, if you find someone sick, it's okay to tell them to see me. There's no reason to let anyone die. We just don't want druggies to steal it for money. This stuff is so valuable people *will* hurt you to get it, even if you are small."

All the children nodded.

Naida's voice echoed in from the windows, calling for Ruben.

Pick smirked. "I gotta go." He meandered to the door, hesitated, and ambush-hugged Maya before sprinting out.

A knock at the door preceded Brian walking in. He looked at Genna. "I can't think of anything to say." His gaze fell to the floor. "Ain't got an excuse aside from being a moron. Whatever you gotta do, do it."

"Huh?" asked Zoe.

Brian sighed. "I'm... I wanted the reward for Maya. Thought she was kidnapped. Didn't know she *wanted* to be here. It's my fault the Authority came."

Doctor Chang glared.

Marcus and Anton contributed some naughty words.

Sarah shivered and rubbed the side of her head. "Why? They gave me a concussion. They could've killed me."

"Brian didn't make you sass off ta the blueberries," muttered Marcus.

Sarah raised a fist, but grumbled and dropped it.

"I'd shoot or stab you," said Genna. "But I don't wanna waste Doc's supplies. For what you put my daughter through, I oughta feed you your balls. You know no one here will ever trust you again, right?"

He grimaced. "Ain't like I'ma make the same mistake twice. I thought... money, baby..."

"And the next time you think you got some line on an easy way, who you gonna fuck over to do it?" Genna tromped over to him.

"I didn't think I was fuckin' anyone over... thought she'd been abducted." Brian fidgeted. "Tell me you wouldn't do the same for her?"

Genna exhaled. "To save her life? I'd do anything. To *maybe* make her a little more comfortable, I ain't never sell out my people. There will be consequences, but not right now. I ain't gonna kill you. Only 'cause I don't wanna do that to Arlene an' your as-yet-to-be kid."

His lips flickered to a halfhearted smile. "She's kinda upset with me right now. I told her."

"Good." Genna pointed. "G'won back ta her. I'll find ya when the time's right."

He trudged off.

"Can I go to Sarah's for a little while?" asked Maya.

Genna looked at her bare wrist and grumbled. She found a clock on Zoe's table, and smiled. "It's almost eight. I want you home before ten."

Maya nodded. "Okay."

She ran out and chased Sarah to the stairwell with the twins close behind. Since Sarah's place didn't have a clock, ten would have to be a guess.

FORTY-FIVE

IGNITION

Maya opened her eyes and yawned. The slow up-and-down motion of Genna's breathing kept her hovering at the precipice between sleep and consciousness for a little while. She stretched, her body quivering, yawned again, and went limp. It had gotten warmer over the past three days, so she'd taken to sleeping in her underpants instead of the silk nightie. Her sneakers remained safely hidden under the bed unless she planned to leave the building. She only half worried about them being stolen; rather, she felt bad that none of the other kids had shoes.

Over the past two days, Zoe had installed a new fridge that didn't cause instant asphyxiation if the door opened. Genna had taken Maya a couple of blocks deeper into the Habitation District to buy what passed for groceries out here from an open air market where a bunch of different farmers collected to sell produce outside a store that had a random variety of boxed and canned goods.

She'd asked Genna about it, and didn't much like the answer that when given a choice between food or comfort, everyone out here opted to eat. Even someone like The Dad who had a regular (albeit weak) source of income hesitated at using money on clothing his daughter would outgrow. Before the war, huge companies existed that manufactured more stuff than anyone needed, most of it made overseas since it cost less. Now, all the manufacturing happened within the Sanctuary Zones, and as capitalism tended to do—rarity begat high prices. Citizens, able to get decent-paying work, bought whatever they wanted while everyone else had to make crappy choices.

Maya had countered that The Dad buying beer instead of clothing for his daughter constituted a crappy choice.

After a third yawn, she sat up. Today was the day. She hopped off the bed and shook Genna awake. Genna ruffled her hair, kissed her cheek, and stumbled to the bathroom while scratching her butt. Maya giggled and walked to the kitchen where she hopped on a chair, swinging her feet back and forth while waiting. Soon, Genna emerged from the back, having put on a pair of black fatigue pants. She cooked up some spray can eggs and toast, and sat at the table across from her.

"You sure you're all right with what they gonna do?" asked Genna.

"Mmm." Maya nodded with a mouthful of spongy yellow saltiness. "Yepf."

Genna reached across the table and squeezed her hand. "Things will get better. They prob'ly gonna get worse first, but we'll get there."

Maya plucked bits of egg from her stomach and legs. "I know."

They finished eating in silence, though Maya didn't let go of Genna's hand. She helped gather the plates and pots, and dried dishes while her mother washed. After, Maya scurried to the bedroom and pulled on her black tee shirt and a clean pair of leggings from the bag. She flattened herself out on the floor and stretched to grab the sneakers from their hiding place under the bed. Even though she didn't expect to leave the building, she'd need them for her 'mission.'

Genna met her in the living room, catching her by the shoulders. "Be careful. I'll be up in a bit, need to get my ass in the tub."

Maya nodded, hugged her mother, and darted out the door. She ran down the hall to 137 and knocked.

Mr. Barnes appeared in a few minutes. "Last chance, kid. You sure you want to do this?"

Maya frowned. "I'm already on the shit list. That drone was gonna kill me if I moved. Besides, Vanessa doesn't do revenge. It costs too much for no tangible benefit."

"All right then. Hang on." He walked inside, leaving the door open. He returned soon and handed her a rectangular aluminum frame an inch thick and about the size of a book. Green printed circuit boards on either side still smelled like fresh soldering. "Remember the process?"

"Yep. Unload the driver, install the card, update the driver, and open the door for Brennan back at the Hangar."

"Right." He handed her the component.

She took the card in both hands. "Thanks."

"No." He put a hand on her shoulder. "Thank you."

"How much time?"

"Two hours about."

Maya backed up. "Okay."

She ran to the end of the hall and banged on Sarah's door for a little over two minutes before an annoyed moan came from inside.

Sarah pulled the door open and stood there looking dazed, her hair wild, one eye closed, and nothing on other than the dirt up to her knees and elbows. "What? It's still early."

"Uhh, where's your dress?"

Sarah yawned. "I was asleep. You woke me up. Dad said it's not healthy to wear the same thing all the time and sleep in it too, and it was hot last night."

"You don't have a nightgown?"

"What for? There's sheets and a blanket."

A heavy snore came from the back hallway.

Maya frowned. "He needs to get you some clothes."

"He needs his b—"

"He needs to take proper care of you." Maya folded her arms. "If he won't, I will."

Sarah looked down, kicking her toes at the carpet. "Umm, with what money?"

"I..." Maya scowled, grabbing at the air in frustration. The girl had a point. "But... it's not... You have a damn curtain held on with pins. It's not even a real dress."

Sarah leaned her head back and let out a long yawn at the ceiling. She stood straight again, blinked a few times, and offered a weary smile. "No one will steal a scrap like that. Look, thanks, but I'm okay. Really... it's cool. What's up? Why'd you drag me out of bed so early?"

"Come on. I gotta show you something."

Sarah drifted back into the apartment, leaving the door half open. "Okay. Gimme a sec to get dressed."

"Sorry for waking you." Maya fidgeted with the component. "I promise it's important."

Sarah trudged down the hallway to her bedroom, yawning again. Maya kicked at the shredded carpeting for a little while, trying to formulate a way to get her friend real clothing. Eventually, Sarah returned in the only set of clothes she owned: the yellowing curtain-dress held together by safety pins. She still looked ready to close her eyes and go straight back to sleep.

"Are we going outside? You've got your sneakers on."

"Sort of." Maya winked. "It's a surprise."

She went downstairs to collect Pick, stopped by Zoe's to get Emily, and climbed up to the ninth floor to wake the twins. With her entourage complete, Maya led the way to the top of the stairs and the roof access, a heavy steel door painted pale grey. She rammed herself into the push bar, having to heave with her whole body to open it. The kids followed her outside.

"Be careful," said Sarah. "It's not safe up here. There's spots that'll fall in."

Maya examined a route from where she stood to a green metal structure about the size of a cargo van near the center with vent slats on the side and a complicated panel of dials. Whatever the machine had been in life, it no longer worked. On top of it sat the orange and white antenna Barnes had described. Made of interlocking metal bars, the transmission tower stretched about fifteen feet higher than the dead machinery. An intact black wire as thick as her wrist emerged from a hole in the roof and ran up the side to a little past the halfway part, where an open cabinet the size of a suitcase emanated faint glowing light.

The kids followed her across the roof to the enormous box. Maya used an open hatch for a ladder, stepping on internal machinery to climb to the top of the old air handler.

"Maya!" yelled Sarah. "You're going to fall. Get down."

"I'm okay. I gotta do this. Genna's too heavy." She held up the device Barnes gave her. "It's important. I'm not doing it to be reckless like Pick. I need to go up to the computer."

Sarah held a hand over her eyes to block the morning sun. "What idiot put it all the way up there?"

"Barnes said it's to keep scavvers and dosers from damaging or stealing it," said Maya.

"Yo." Anton patted the green metal side of the air handler twice. "Be careful, right?"

"Yeah, umm." Marcus fidgeted. "Don't get hurt."

Pick stuffed his finger up his nose and smirked at her.

She faced the antenna. After tucking the electronic box in the waist of her pants, she grabbed on to the metal tubes and pulled herself upward. The wind felt as though it would push her off at any second. Each time the breeze picked up, it whipped her hair into her face. Twice, she got scared enough to cling until a stronger gust subsided. Sarah kept yelling at her to come down. Emily stayed quiet. It took both twins to hold Pick back from attempting to follow her because it looked fun.

Three minutes later, Maya reached the computer box. Barnes said it had been months since they bothered using it since one of the boards had burned out. Between not having a reason to use it and no one really wanting to make the climb, it remained broken. At the bottom of the housing, a four-wheel physical code lock accepted 8157, and she pulled the outer shell open. Beneath an array of blinking lights and wiring, a horizontal rack held four components similar to the one she carried, only a bit older and more worn. The third unit from the left had black soot marks above and below it.

That's gotta be the right one.

Amid the wires, she unfolded a tiny keyboard, which doubled as a protective covering for an eight-by-eight monochrome monitor, offering her a command prompt:

RELAY- SSG9 # >

Typing with one hand (since she refused to trust stability to only her legs holding on) took her a while, but she entered the commands Barnes had shown her.

RELAY- SSG9 # > CARDMANAGER DISABLE CHASSIS[0] : SLOT[3]

After a few seconds' delay, a message popped up:

DISABLING EXPANSION CARD 4 IN CHASSIS 0:

* * STOPPING SERVICES . SUCCESS!

* * POWERING DOWN . SUCCESS!

THE EXPANSION CARD MAY NOW BE SAFELY REMOVED FROM THE CONTROL CHASSIS.

Maya braced her legs against the antenna tubes and tugged on the dead card in slot three until it came free with a jerk that nearly sent her flying off. Sarah screamed; had the girl not been struggling to hold Pick back, she probably would've come flying up the antenna. Maya tossed the dead component like a Frisbee. Eager to escape the pointy aluminum corners jabbing her in the thighs, she pulled the replacement out of her pants and removed the scrap of paper with the commands on it. She lined up the pins on the inside edge. It took a bit of fidgeting to get it slotted in the socket one-handed while clinging to a wobbly antenna twenty-some odd feet above the tenth floor roof. As soon as it stopped snagging, she slammed it home.

When nothing caught fire, she returned to the keyboard, holding the paper scrap with her left hand, which also clamped around an aluminum tube to keep her steady.

RELAY- 5509 # > PACKAGER - -
FORCE INSTALL

2001: D88: 8543: 0: 0: 842B: 370: 7
334: / AUTHLESSVIDSOURCEPACKAGE

A few seconds later, the screen showed:

CONNECTING TO REPOSITORY
001: D88: 8543: 0: 0: 842B: 370: 7334

RESOLVING DEPENDENCIES - NO
DEPENDENCIES REQUIRED.

The machine sat there doing nothing for almost a minute. Maya twitched from worry, hoping she didn't mistype anything. Wind made the scrap flutter against her hand. Terrified it would blow away to oblivion she squeezed as hard as she could. In the middle of her comparing her line to the contents of the paper, the screen flashed to life again.

DOWNLOADING PACKAGES:

(1/ 1)
AUTHLESSVIDSOURCEPACKAGE -
5.9MB/ S - 00: 00

"Whew." She slouched with relief until a gust made her cling tight to the aluminum tubing.

"Come on!" Sarah pulled herself up to stand on top of the air handler, and grabbed the antenna tower. "Get down before you fall."

"I'm almost finished," shouted Maya. "It won't be long."

The download finished in fourteen seconds and the screen scrolled with more text, each line popping up a second or three after the one before it:

PROCESSING TRANSACTION

INSTALLING:
AUTHLESSVIDSOURCEPACKAGE 1/ 1

CLEANUP:
AUTHLESSVIDSOURCEPACKAGE 1/ 1

VERIFYING:
AUTHLESSVIDSOURCEPACKAGE 1/ 1

COMPLETED!

Grinning, Maya reached up and one-finger typed the last command.

RELAY- SSG9 # >
AUTHLESSVIDSOURCESERVICE START

The system thought about her command for a few seconds before the screen displayed:

**LISTENING FOR INCOMING VIDEO
TRANSMISSIONS ON PORT 59152**

**STARTING SERVICE
AUTHLESSVIDSOURCE _ SUCCESS**!

**THE SCREEN RETURNED TO AN
INPUT PROMPT.**

RELAY- SSG9 # >

That should let Brennan in... Maya bit her lip, staring at the prompt, wondering if she'd see him type or if his connection wouldn't update the terminal. Before long, the entire cabinet lit up with a brilliant array of fiberoptics.

"Yes!" She cheered.

Maya closed the keyboard back against the screen before shutting the cabinet door, concealing the light within. Satisfied, she took a deep breath and climbed down. For no reason she could understand, working her way back to the roof scared her more than the climb up.

Sarah grabbed her as soon as she could reach, holding on as Maya climbed to stand beside her. Once they got down off the ancient machine, the older girl flung her around and shoved her against the big green box. "What are you doing? Did you bring us up here to watch you fall and die?"

"No. I had to fix the transmitter. Mr. Barnes said I was the best one to do it 'cause I don't weigh much and I know computers. Zoe would break the whole antenna."

"My mom isn't fat," said Emily.

Sarah sighed. "Please stop doing dumb things."

"This isn't dumb." Maya hugged her. "It's completely crazy."

"What did you do?" asked Anton, his eyebrows a flat line.

"You'll see." Maya waved them to follow and walked to the north edge of the roof. She felt almost as nervous as if she'd pulled a gun on a blueberry, but at one thought of Ashley, and the others in the Fade ward, she dismissed any regrets.

The wall around the perimeter came up to Maya's shoulders. She folded her arms across the top and rested her chin on them. Pick ran off and returned dragging a plastic crate to stand on so he could see over it. Sarah stood at her right, clutching the top of the wall like a nervous weasel.

"What are we waiting for?" asked Marcus.

Maya glanced at him for a second or two before she resumed staring out at the Sanctuary Zone. "The truth."

She started telling them the story of what happened after she'd run off in the middle of the night, but stopped a few minutes in when Genna arrived. Her mother walked over and stood behind her, hands on her shoulders. Maya relayed her journey to everyone, apologizing several times for making them worry. A little over an hour later, around the time she detailed her leap off the drone into the reservoir, a subdued *beep beep beep* emanated from the box on the antenna.

"It's time." Maya looked out at the city.

"Whoa, wait." Anton shook his head. "You rode a drone? For real? You can't just stop there. What was it like?"

Maya shivered. "The scariest thing I'll ever do. I'll *never* do that again."

"But what happened?" asked Marcus.

"I'll finish telling you later. This is more important." Maya pointed out over the Hab toward the Sanc. "Look."

All the kids, plus Genna, tucked up to the wall.

The change in scenery began subtle. An advertising holo-billboard across the street went dark. Then another. After a few seconds, they winked out in clusters of three or four, and distant screens, mere points of light in the Sanctuary Zone, went with them. In fifteen seconds more, the entire world in front of them had become dark of technology.

All at once, Maya's face appeared everywhere. Gone was the glammed up little girl dressed like a woman; instead, the world saw the real Maya. Dirty, hair askew, wearing a man's black BDU shirt. Thousands of Mayas covered the landscape, from forty-foot tall close-ups of her face to full-body images standing in front of a generic beige cinderblock wall.

Her voice spread like a tsunami of eerie calm over the city.

"Hello. I am Maya Oman. Or at least, I used to be. The smiling princess you see every day is an illusion. My smile was fake. I was not happy. I said things that weren't true. I have been lying to you. I said what I was told to say. Ascendant lies to you.

"Fade should have disappeared ten years ago when World War Three ended. Ascendant made Xenodril to save people hurt by old governments who wanted to kill everyone they could not control.

"Now, Ascendant makes Fade for only one reason—profit."

Maya's image faded to reveal Ashley's pleading face.

"This is Ashley. She's five. Her parents couldn't afford Xenodril. Did you know that it costs Ascendant forty-seven cents to manufacture one dose of Xenodril, but they charge two hundred dollars for it? Ashley's mom *did* love her. She didn't buy Xenodril because she couldn't *afford* it. Ashley's mother can't love her anymore because Ashley's mother died to Fade."

Maya's face reappeared on the screens.

"Ashley's mother, and thousands of other people, are dead for forty-seven cents. Ascendant wants to keep you scared. They own the Authority and they own everyone who gives in to fear. The Authority used to represent law. They used to be worth respecting. Now I have a question for the men and women of the Authority. Why do you look the other way while Ascendant turns you into thugs?"

She paused for effect.

A few of the screens fluttered out; no doubt, a war raged between the Brigade's hackers and Ascendant's network operations people.

"Are you afraid?" asked video-Maya. "The masses can only be controlled if they remain frightened. Citizens, are you listening? There are five hundred of us to every one of you. When I walked the streets of the Sanctuary Zone, I heard you. I know that even Citizens are tired of being treated like cattle. Everyone complains about the drones in quiet grumbles, yet none of you will admit it out loud. Will you let your children grow up under the constant threat of flying guns? Will you let your grandchildren inherit a world where anyone who questions Ascendant disappears?"

The camera zoomed in on Maya's face.

"I'm no longer Maya Oman. I'm just Maya. I am nine years old, and I am no longer afraid."—the video closed in until her intense gold-brown eyes filled the screen—"Are you?"

All the holograms and billboards went dark. Two seconds later, an image of the e-mail chain showing Vanessa ordering Fade production appeared. Shutdown spread like a creep, starting in the Sanctuary Zone and spreading out until it blackened all the displays in the Habitation District.

Maya gasped. *Zero got it!*

It seemed as if the entire world froze in stunned silence.

Genna squeezed her shoulders, one tear running down her cheek.

Sarah turned toward Maya, her face as pale as a dead girl's. "What did you do?"

Maya took her hand and held it tight. "I started a fire." She waited a second before smiling. "Wanna play more Magic?"

"Okay," whispered Sarah. "At least until they kill us all."

"They won't." Maya smirked. "Not worth the cost."

Genna wiped at her eyes, nodding permission since she seemed unable to speak.

Maya led the way to the stairs, eager to get off the dangerous roof. She paused by the door and glanced back over her shoulder at a faint rush in the air. The noise built and built, until the distant roar of thousands of angry people echoed in the streets.

She smiled.

Maybe humanity wasn't completely screwed.

ACKNOWLEDGMENTS

Thank you to everyone at Curiosity Quills for making *Heir Ascendant* a reality. Especially Lisa Gus for the suggestion to write the book. Originally, I conceived a short story (*Innocent Deception*) where Maya is abducted for ransom and saves herself by turning her captors against each other. The intent of the story was to create doubt as to whether Maya existed as a real person or an android.

Lisa liked the story quite a bit, and some months later asked me if I had considered writing more in the world that it established. I told her I had, and I'd been stuck trying to decide between maybe aging Maya up to a teen or switching to Genna as a primary character. Her reaction was more or less a "No! Leave Maya nine!"—so I came up with the story you just read.

So, a big thank you to Lisa, as without her suggestion, the book would not exist.

A great thanks to Olivia Swenson for her wonderful assistance editing this novel.

Many thanks to Eugene Teplitsky for the amazing cover art!

Also, thanks go to Martin Capdevielle for Linux technical details.

ABOUT THE AUTHOR

Born in a little town known as South Amboy NJ in 1973, **Matthew Cox** has been creating science fiction and fantasy worlds for most of his reasoning life. Somewhere between fifteen to eighteen of them spent developing the world in which Division Zero, Virtual Immortality, and The Awakened Series take place. He has several other projects in the works as well as a collaborative science fiction endeavor with author Tony Healey.

Matthew is an avid gamer, a recovered WoW addict, Gamemaster for two custom systems (Chronicles of Eldrinaath [Fantasy] and Divergent Fates [Sci Fi], and a fan of anime, British humour (<- deliberate), and intellectual science fiction that questions the nature of reality, life, and what happens after it.

He is also fond of cats.

THANK YOU
FOR READING

© 2017 **Matthew S. Cox**

www.matthewcoxbooks.com

Please visit http://curiosityquills.com/reader-survey to share your
reading experience with the author of this book!

Prophet of the Badlands, by Matt Cox

For most twelve year olds, being kidnapped is terrifying. For Althea, it's just Tuesday. Her power to heal the wounded and cleanse the sick makes her a hunted commodity in the Badlands. For as long as she can remember, they always come, they always take her, and she lets them. Wandering after an escape, she is found by a loving family who helps her find the courage to defend herself. Her newfound resolve is tested by an ancient evil, and a dangerous man bent on exploiting her abilities.

Prelude to Mayhem, by Edward Aubry

In the ruins of his world, Harrison Cody follows a mysterious voice on the radio as he and his pixie sidekick travel on foot across a terrifyingly random landscape. They discover Dorothy O'Neill, who has had to survive among monsters when her greatest worry used to be how to navigate high school. Together they search for what remains of Chicago, and the hope that civilization can be rebuilt.

Shadow of a Dead Star, by Michael Shean

As an agent of the Industrial Security Bureau, it is Thomas Walken's duty to keep the city of Seattle free of black-market technology. But when a trio of living sex-dolls he has recently intercepted are stolen from custody, Walken finds himself seeking a great deal more than just contraband. He will be forced to use his skills and preternatural instincts to try and keep his career, his freedom, and his life.

Cipher, by S.E. Bennett

Cipher Omega is sixteen years old, and a failed experiment. Born in the underground laboratory known as the Basement, when her home is destroyed Cipher finds herself the sole survivor of a secret society that never accepted her. As Cipher struggles to learn the rules of the new world she's now a part of, it becomes clear that everything is not as it may appear...

CPSIA information can be obtained
at www.ICGtesting.com
Printed in the USA
BVOW03s2332281117
501331BV00025B/108/P